DUDLEY PUBLIC LIBRARIES

The loan of this book may be renewed if not required by other readers, by contacting the library from which it was borrowed.

D0801057

Spanish Scandals

Spanish Scandals:
Secrets at
Sunset

LYNNE GRAHAM

JENNIE LUCAS

LAURA IDING

MILLS & BOON

First Published in Great Britain 2020
By Mills & Boon, an imprint of HarperCollins*Publishers*
1 London Bridge Street, London, SE1 9GF

SPANISH SCANDALS: SECRETS AT SUNSET © 2020
Harlequin Books S.A.

The Spanish Billionaire's Pregnant Wife © 2009 Lynne Graham
Carrying the Spaniard's Child © 2017 Jennie Lucas
Her Little Spanish Secret © 2012 Laura Iding

ISBN: 978-0-263-29830-7

MIX
Paper from
responsible sources
FSC™ C007454

This book is produced from independently certified FSC™ paper to ensure responsible forest management.

For more information visit: www.harpercollins.co.uk/green

Printed and bound in Spain
by CPI, Barcelona

THE SPANISH BILLIONAIRE'S PREGNANT WIFE

LYNNE GRAHAM

CHAPTER ONE

LEANDRO CARRERA MARQUEZ, Duque de Sandoval, awoke when his valet opened the bedroom curtains and bid his illustrious employer a cheerful good morning. His lean, darkly handsome face grim, Leandro doubted that the day ahead would be the slightest bit different from any other day in recent months. Fresh towels were laid out in the bathroom for his shower. A custom-made designer business suit and a monogrammed silk shirt and toning tie were assembled in readiness for his getting dressed.

Elegant and, as always, immaculate in appearance, Leandro finally descended the magnificent staircase of the family *castillo* with all the cool assurance and dignity of his grand forebears. He knew that he was bored and he scorned the feeling, well aware that he was bountifully blessed with health, wealth and success. The walls he passed bore the portraits of his predecessors—the very flower of proud Castilian aristocracy—ranging from the first duke, who had been a famous soldier and a contemporary of Christopher Columbus, to Leandro's father, a distinguished banker who had died when his son was barely five years old.

'Your Excellency.' Having been greeted by Basilio, his major-domo, and two maidservants at the foot of the stairs with much the same pomp and ceremony that the first duque would have received in the fifteenth century, Leandro was ushered into breakfast where the day's papers, including the leading financial publications, awaited him. There was no need for him to ask for anything. His every need and wish were carefully foreseen by his devoted staff and perfect peace reigned while he ate, for his preference for silence at the breakfast table was well known.

A phone was brought to him. His mother, the dowager Duquesa, Doña Maria, was on the line asking him to lunch with her at the town house in Seville later that day. It didn't suit him. He would have to reschedule business appointments at the bank. But Leandro, uneasily aware that he spent little time with his relations, gave reluctant assent.

As he sipped his coffee his brilliant dark eyes rested on the full-length portrait of his late wife, Aloise, on the wall at the other end of the room. He wondered if anyone else in the family even appreciated that in forty-eight hours the anniversary of Aloise's death would take place. Aloise, his childhood friend, who in dying almost a year earlier had left a gaping hole in the settled fabric of his life. He wondered if he would ever get over the guilt induced by her tragic demise and decided that it would be wise to spend that day away from home working in London. Sentimentality was not one of Leandro's failings.

He spent a very busy morning at the Carrera Bank, an institution that had been handling the same clients' fortunes for generations and where his own services as one

of the financial world's most fabulously successful investment bankers were much in demand. Strikingly intelligent
and gifted in the field of wealth preservation and asset
management, Leandro had been marked out early as a
genius at analysing world money markets. Juggling
complex figures gave him considerable pleasure and satisfaction. Numbers, unlike people, were easy to understand and deal with, he acknowledged wryly.

When he kept his luncheon appointment he was surprised to see that his mother's sister, his aunt Isabella, and
his own two sisters, Estefania and Julieta, were also
present.

'I felt that it was time to talk to you,' Doña Maria
murmured with a meaningful look at her only son over the
appetisers.

Leandro elevated a questioning ebony brow. 'About
what, precisely?'

'You've been a widower for a year now.' It was Estefania
who responded.

'Is there a point to that obvious statement?' Leandro
enquired drily.

'You've spent enough time in mourning to satisfy the
conventions. It's time to think of remarriage,' his mother
informed him.

His lean, strong face rigidly controlled, Leandro stared
steadily back at the older woman. 'I don't agree.'

Julieta, his younger sister piped up, 'Nobody is going
to replace Aloise, Leandro. We don't expect that and
neither can you—'

'But you must put the family's unbroken line of inheritance first,' Doña Maria declared with gravity. 'There is

presently no heir to the title or the estate. You are thirty-three years old. Last year when Aloise died we all learned how fragile and fickle life can be. What if something similar were to happen to you? You *must* remarry and father an heir, my son.'

Leandro compressed his handsome mouth into a blood-less line that would have encouraged less determined opponents to drop the subject. He had no need of such reminders when he had spent his life being made aware daily of his many responsibilities. Indeed he had never known an hour's freedom from the weighty burden of expectations that accompanied his privileged social status and great wealth. He had been raised in the same traditions as his ancestors to put duty and honour and family first. But an exceptional spark of rebellion was finally firing inside his lean, well built body.

'I'm aware of those facts, but I'm not ready to take another wife,' he retorted crisply.

'I thought it would be helpful if we drew up a short list of potential brides to help you,' Doña Maria contended with a wide smile that struck her angry son as bordering on manic.

'I don't think that would be helpful. Indeed I think it's a ludicrous idea,' Leandro replied coldly. 'When and *if* I remarry, I will choose my own wife.'

His aunt Isabella, however, would not be silenced. She put forward a candidate from a family as rich and prominent as their own. Leandro dealt her a look of scorn. His mother was, however, even quicker to name her own selection—a young widow with a son and, therefore, what the older woman termed a *proven* fertility record. An expression of unhidden distaste crossed Leandro's classic dark features. He knew exactly why that point was being made. Unhappily, talk of fertility records reminded him of livestock breeding. His elder sister, Estefania, was not to be outdone and, oblivious to the disbelieving glances of her relations, suggested the teenaged daughter of a personal friend as being perfect bride material. Leandro almost laughed out loud at that idea. As he was well aware, marriage could be a most challenging relationship, even for those who might seem very well matched as a couple.

'We'll hold a party and invite some suitable women,' Doña Maria announced, continuing on her theme with the stubborn insensitivity of a woman determined to have her say. 'But not the teenager, Estefania. I really don't think so young a woman would be appropriate. A Marquez bride needs to be mature, well versed in etiquette, educated and socially accomplished, as well as being from a suitable background.'

'I will not attend any such party,' Leandro declared without hesitation. 'I have no intention of remarrying at this point in time.'

Julieta gave him an apologetic look. 'But at least if you went to the party you might fall in love with someone.'

'Leandro is the Duque de Sandoval,' Doña Maria countered in a deflating tone of ice. 'Thankfully, he knows who he is and he has no nonsense of that variety in his head.'

'There will be no party,' Leandro decreed, implacable outrage igniting steadily beneath his cool façade at their comments. He could hardly credit that his own relations could be so crass or interfering. But then he was willing to admit that none of them was close. The formality and reserve that his mother had always insisted on had driven wedges of polite behaviour between them all.

'We are only thinking of you and what is best for you,' Doña Maria murmured sweetly.

Leandro studied the woman who had sent him to an English boarding school at the age of six years old and remained impervious to his tear-stained letters begging to be allowed to come home. 'I know what is best for me, Mama. A man must act for himself in such a personal matter.'

'Happy birthday, Molly! What do you think?' Jez Andrews prompted, standing back from the car with a flourish.

Wide-eyed, Molly Chapman studied her elderly car. Jez had repainted it a cerise pink colour that she loved on sight. She walked round the vehicle, stunned by a transformation that had caused all the rust, dents and scratches to disappear. 'It's amazing! You've worked a miracle, Jez.'

'That's what mates are for. Hopefully it'll pass the MOT test now without any major problems. I've replaced a lot of parts. I knew that helping you to keep your car on the road was the best present I could give you,' her friend and landlord admitted.

Molly flung her arms round him in an exuberant hug. A stocky fair-haired man of medium height, Jez was still a comfortable seven inches taller than Molly, who was tiny in stature and build, with a mop of dark curls and enormous green eyes. Her quick graceful movements crackled with the energy of a lively personality. 'I don't know how to thank you.'

Jez shrugged and backed off, embarrassed by her gratitude. 'It was no big deal,' he said awkwardly.

But Molly knew the full value of his generosity and it
touched her to the heart that he had sacrificed so much of
his free time to work on her beat-up car. But then, Jez was
her closest friend and he knew that she needed the vehicle
to get round the craft shops and fairs where she sold her
wares at weekends. Molly and Jez had been in foster care
together as children and their ties went back a long way.

'Don't forget I'm staying over at Ida's tonight,' Jez
reminded her. 'I'll see you tomorrow.'

'How is Ida?'

At the thought of the sick older woman, Jez vented a
sad sigh. 'About as well as can be expected. I mean, it's
not like she's going to get any better.'

'Any word of her getting into the hospice yet?'

'No, but she's top of the list.'

Thinking how typical it was of Jez to be helping to
nurse the woman who had fostered him for a while in his
teens, Molly went back indoors. It was almost time for her
to go to work. Jez had inherited his terraced house and
garden in Hackney from a bachelor uncle. That piece of
good fortune had enabled him to finance and set up a car
repair shop where he was currently making a comfortable
living. Jez had been quick to offer Molly a bedsit in his
home and the valuable opportunity to use the stone shed
in the back garden to house her potter's kiln.

Success, however, had so far eluded Molly. She had left
art college with such high hopes of the future, but even
though she worked every hour she could for the catering
company that employed her she still struggled to pay the

rent and keep up with her bills. Her dream was to sell enough of her ceramics, which she made in her spare time, to make it worth her while to work full-time as a potter, and she often felt like a failure in the artistic stakes because she never seemed to get any closer to achieving her goal.

Like Jez, Molly had had a chequered background, which had encompassed constant change, broken relationships and insecurity. Her mother had died when she was nine years old and her grandmother had put her up for adoption while choosing to keep Ophelia, Molly's elder teenaged sister. Molly had never quite recovered from the simple fact that her own flesh and blood had handed her over to social services simply because she, unlike her sister, was illegitimate and, even worse, the embarrassing proof of her mother's affair with a married man. The sheer hurt of that unapologetic rejection had made Molly wary of trying to seek contact with her birth relations again once she grew up. Even now, at the age of twenty-two, she tended to block out the memories of the early years of her life and scold herself for the sense of loss that those dim recollections still roused. Molly was a survivor who, while priding herself on being as tough as old boots, had a heart as soft as a marshmallow.

That evening, her employers were catering for a wedding party at a big house in St John Wood. It was an upmarket booking for a new customer and her manager, Brian, was very anxious to get everything right. Molly tied her apron on over the narrow black skirt and white blouse that she wore for work. The bride's mother, Krystal Forfar, an enervated and emaciated blonde dressed in an oyster-pink dress, was rapping out imperious instructions to Brian in a shrill voice.

Brian signalled Molly. 'My senior waitress, Molly… There'll be a bloke here tonight—'

'Mr Leandro Carrera Marquez,' the bride's mother interposed haughtily, pronouncing the foreign name in the sort of hallowed tones that most people reserved for royalty. 'He's a Spanish banker and, as my husband's employer, our most important guest. Make sure you wait on him hand and foot. Ensure his glass is never empty. I'll point him out when he arrives.'

'Fine.' Molly nodded acquiescence and sped off back to the kitchen where she was helping to unpack equipment.

'What was all that about?' Vanessa, her fellow waitress, asked.

Molly explained.

'Another toff with more money than sense, I'll bet,' the redhead opined.

'If he's a banker, it's to be hoped he has both!' Molly joked.

The bride, stunning in a sophisticated sheath of white satin, appeared with her mother to check the buffet table. Molly watched while Mrs Forfar fussed over her daughter, twitching her train into place and adjusting her tiara. Unappreciative of the proud parental attention she was receiving, the bride uttered a sharp complaint about the colour of the napkins—*so* last year and not what she had ordered. Brian surged forward to apologise and explain the substitution, while Molly wondered why she herself had failed to win her mother's love, and why the only affection she had received during the first nine years of her life had been from her sister. Had her mother been so ashamed of her illegitimacy as well?

A few minutes later, Molly was summoned to the doorway to have the Spanish banker singled out for her scrutiny. The tall dark male engaged in conversation with the bride's parents was so breathtakingly good looking that Molly felt her heart jump inside her chest as she studied him. He was downright dazzling, from the crown of his fashionably cropped black hair to the flawless planes of his classic bronzed features, and he was further blessed with the sleek, broad-shouldered, lean-hipped and long limbed muscular physique of a classical god.

'Go offer the VIP a drink,' Brian urged.

Molly snatched in a ragged breath, shaken and embarrassed by her excessively appreciative reaction to the Spaniard. It wasn't like her. She had never been into men in the same way as her peers. Her birth mother's volatile relationships with a long line of men who had treated her badly had left their mark on Molly even at a young age. She had known even then that she wanted something different for herself, something more than casual sex with men who didn't want to commit, contribute to the home or play any real part in a child's upbringing. And she didn't want to be hurt or damaged, either. With the exception of Jez, the sort of men Molly had met in the years that took her to adulthood had merely increased her wariness and distrust of the opposite sex. There had been boyfriends but nobody special; certainly nobody she had had any desire to sleep with. So it was a total shock to look across a room and see a guy who, just by being there, stole all the breath from her lungs and all the sense from her thoughts.

The closer Molly got with her tray of drinks, the taller the Spaniard seemed to get and her curious gaze rested on him, greedily noting every detail of his stylish sophisticated appearance. His suit had the classic tailoring and sheen of the most expensive design and the highest quality. He looked rich to her and more as if he *owned* a bank than worked in one.

'Sir?' Molly extended the tray and spoke to gain his attention. He gazed down at her and she discovered that he had wonderfully thick sooty eyelashes for a man and eyes the colour of hot golden honey. Meeting those glorious eyes, she felt as dizzy as if she were suddenly falling from a height.

'Thank you.' Leandro accepted a glass and drank thirstily, for his mouth was very dry. Had it not been for the fact that the Forfars were also close friends of his mother's, he would have definitely stayed at home that evening. A throat infection and a course of antibiotics were making Leandro feel under par. His conscience would have found it a challenge, however, not to show up even for the evening party when he had already successfully avoided attending the actual wedding. In the mood to be alone, he had also given his usual entourage of chauffeur and bodyguards a night off and had driven himself out.

His attention rested on the bridal couple, who were clearly engaged in a dispute, which gave the bride a shrewish look and the groom the pitiful air of a discomfited man wishing he were anywhere but where he was. Leandro knew that feeling. He didn't like weddings either. The artificial jollity left him cold and the divorce statistics made nonsense of the romantic frills and the heartfelt promises. He could not imagine *ever* wanting to marry again and cherished his freedom from that constraint.

Picking her way through the knots of chattering guests, Molly was taken aback when she caught the tall, dark handsome banker's gaze resting on her face. She went pink, wondered why he looked so forbidding and could not resist smiling in the hope of cheering him up.

The little waitress's sunny smile was as enchanting as her face, Leandro acknowledged, the dark mood that had overtaken him lightening at that fresh sight of her. Almond-shaped green eyes like a cat's sparkled above an unrepentantly upturned nose, dimples and a ripe rosy mouth with a pronounced Cupid's bow. The instant he registered that he was staring, he questioned what he was doing and directed his attention back to the drink in his hand. But, strangely, all he could still see were those bright feline eyes and that marvellously full pink mouth that contrived to combine her curious mix of girlish innocence and feline sex appeal with astonishing efficiency. He was surprised at himself and even more disturbed by the sexual heat stirring him, for he had not been with a woman since Aloise had died. Guilt had killed his libido as surely as death had claimed his wife.

'Over here, luv!' a bold voice called.

Molly hastened to serve drinks at a greater speed for the reception rooms were steadily filling up. A trio of young men who had evidently already enjoyed a few drinks made frank comments about her curvaceous figure as she served them. She gritted her teeth and ignored the over-familiar cracks, walking away as soon as she could. She went back to the bar to collect more orders.

'The VIP's got an empty glass,' Brian warned her anxiously. 'Look after him.'

Molly tried not to look at the banker this time, but her heart was thumping even as she walked across the room towards him. The sense of anticipation and the craving were too great a temptation for her and she surrendered and looked at him again: he really was *gorgeous*, his black hair gleaming below the down lighters that accentuated his superb high cheekbones and hard masculine jaw line. Her mouth ran dry, helpless longing piercing her like a cruel thorn being driven into her flesh.

The power of what she was feeling shocked her. He was a stranger and she knew nothing about him, would most assuredly have nothing whatsoever in common with him. It was a purely physical craving but almost irresistible in its pulling power. For the first time she wondered if something similar had drawn her late mother to her married father and if she herself was guilty of being meanly narrow-minded and unsympathetic in despising her parent for getting involved in an extra-marital affair.

Leandro watched her walking back to him, marvelling at how dainty she was—a pocket Venus with child-sized feet and a waist he could probably clasp his hands around. She seemed to move in time to the music. *Dios mio!* What was wrong with him? She was a waitress and not fair game; he was not the sort of low life who hit on serving staff. But his wayward gaze remained stubbornly nailed to her surprisingly voluptuous proportions, noticing the tight fit of her shirt over her round little breasts and the peach-like curve and sensual jut of her bottom below her skirt. Her curling lashes lifted, her green eyes looking up direct into his. He felt the jolt of connection like an electric shock travelling through his lean, powerful frame to set off a chain reaction in his groin. He set down his empty glass on the tray she extended and lifted another drink. For a moment it crossed his mind that his thirst might be more wisely quenched with water than alcohol, but what happened next turned his thoughts in a different direction.

Hailed by the same noisy clique of men she had served earlier, Molly walked over. They read her name off her identification badge and called her by it. One man made a crude comment about her breasts, while she went rigid as another closed an arm round her, trapping her in place.

'Let go of me!' Molly told the offender with icy contempt and annoyance. 'I'm here to serve drinks—that's *all*!'

'What a crying waste that would be, little lady,' the red-faced male imprisoning her lamented. Unconcerned by her angry reproach, he tossed a high-denomination bank note down on the tray. 'Why don't you come home with me later? Trust me, I could show you a really good time.'

'No, thanks. Get your hands off me right now,' Molly demanded.

'Have you any idea how much I earned this year?'

'I couldn't care less and I don't want the tip,' Molly told him curtly, stuffing the note back into his hand and pulling free the instant his grip loosened. How dared he speak to her as if she were a hooker for hire and try to bribe her into doing his bidding? She walked away quickly to the accompaniment of a chorus of male laughter. Brian was watching her uneasily from the doorway and she went straight over to him to warn him that he needed to keep an eye on the rowdy group before they got completely out of hand.

'I won't stand for being touched or spoken to like that. I'm entitled to make a complaint when someone does that to me,' Molly pointed out angrily.

Dismay at that threat sent the manager's brows flying up below his hair. 'Those blokes are only fooling around and trying to flirt with you. You're a pretty girl and there aren't many here. They've had too much to drink. I'm sure nothing offensive was intended.'

'I disagree. They didn't care and I found their abuse deeply offensive,' Molly countered and stalked back to the bar, furious that her complaint was not being taken seriously. She was well aware that the manager was keen to avoid any unpleasantness that might endanger the chance of new business from any of the well-heeled guests present. But for the first time ever, Molly resented her lowly station in life which evidently made Brian feel that her complaint was of less importance than the comfort of the arrogant ignorant oiks who had insulted her.

Leandro drew in a slow deep breath of restraint. He had witnessed the whole scene and had almost intervened on her behalf with the drunks. He thought her boss should have protected her from such harassment. So her name was Molly—he had overheard the men. Wasn't that a diminutive for Mary? And if it was, why the hell should it matter to him? he asked himself in exasperation. He didn't like the feeling that he was off balance. Accompanied by his hostess, Krystal, Leandro allowed himself to be introduced to some of the other guests.

Lysander Metaxis was present without his wife whom, he readily explained, was close to giving birth to their third child. If he was looking for congratulations he didn't get them. When children entered the conversation, Leandro had nothing to say and even less interest. But he did wonder if it was fair of him to suspect that the macho Greek tycoon was boasting about his virility.

There was nothing to distract Leandro from watching Molly as she approached the drunks who were signalling her for more libation. Tension was etched in her tight heart-shaped features and her reluctance to respond was clear. The heavily built blond man snaked out an arm to entrap her again and ran a coarse hand down over her shapely derrière, pausing to squeeze it. As an angry objection erupted from Molly Leandro was already striding forward.

'Take your hands off her!' Leandro commanded.

The drunk freed Molly and pushed her aside to take a swing at the Spaniard. Shaken that Leandro had come to her rescue, Molly was all too well aware of the greater danger of him being beaten up by the three drunks he had dared to confront. She sped forward to interpose herself between the men and forced her assailant to deflect his punch in an attempt to avoid hitting her. Leandro still took a blow across one temple that sent him crashing to the floor. The back of his head banged off the tiled floor and for an instant there was blackness and he knew nothing. Time seemed to move seamlessly on, however, for when his eyes opened again he was staring up into instantly recognisable vibrant green as the waitress crouched over him, her anxiety obvious. She was close enough for the lemony scent of her curling hair and creamy skin to flare his nostrils and awaken a powerful sexual response.

When Molly collided with Leandro's honey dark gaze, it was as if the whole world ground to a halt and sent her spinning off into the unknown. Heat uncoiled in a lazy entangling loop in her pelvis and cut off her ability to breathe. Her body came alive in embarrassing places and throbbed as if a switch somewhere inside her had been flipped on.

The drunks cleared off and vanished into the gathering crowd when they realised how many people were watching the scene. Krystal Forfar waved away Molly with an angry gesture. 'I think you've caused enough trouble! Mr Carrera Marquez? Shall I call a doctor?'

Molly sprang upright and watched Leandro stagger slightly as he straightened while coolly denying the idea that he might require medical attention.

'I think you should go to hospital,' Molly volunteered unasked. 'You blacked out for a moment and you could have concussion.'

'Thank you, but I have sustained no injury,' Leandro drawled with arrogant assurance, smoothing down his rumpled jacket. 'I think I would like some fresh air, though. It's a little stuffy in here.'

'What the heck happened?' Brian demanded, hustling her away for a private chat.

Molly explained while Vanessa hovered.

'The Spanish guy is a real hero—just imagine the likes of him bothering to interfere because a drunk pinches your bum!' Vanessa exclaimed. 'It's not what you expect, is it?'

His behaviour had astonished Molly as well, but it had also impressed her, because the only other man she knew who would have intervened to stop a woman being harassed in that way was Jez. Molly took a plate over to the buffet and picked out a choice selection of the food and placed it on the tray with a drink. She carried it out through the French windows onto the balcony where Leandro Carrera Marquez had gone. Lean bold profile taut, he was leaning on the parapet and looking out over the bright lights of the city.

'I wanted to thank you for telling that guy to lay off me. It was very brave,' Molly murmured in a rush as she set the tray down on the table behind him. 'I'm sorry you got thumped like that.'

'If you hadn't got in the way I would have hit him back,' Leandro traded, turning to look at her. He was still marvelling at the surge of rage that had gripped him when he'd seen the drunk touching her body. The sight of another man getting familiar with her had been deeply offensive to him.

'There were three of them and only one of you.' Molly stretched up on tiptoe to brush her fingertips very gently over the darkening bruise forming on his olive skin. 'You could have got really badly hurt and I feel guilty enough. I've brought you some food. Please eat something.'

The swell of her firm pointed breasts rubbed against his chest and her proximity gave him another opportunity to smell the already recognisable citrus-fresh scent of her hair. Raw sexual desire fired inside Leandro again with the force of a blowtorch. He studied the full soft curves of her generous pink mouth and burned to taste her. 'I'm not hungry for anything but you,' Leandro breathed thickly.

CHAPTER TWO

WHILE Molly looked up at him with vivid and curious green eyes, Leandro ditched all effort to resist temptation. He reached out and closed his arms round her to pull her into place against his lean powerful body.

Molly leant into him, her encouragement instinctive but new and strange enough to startle her. Long brown fingers meshed into her tumbling curls to tip up her face. She stretched up again and let her hands slide shyly through the silky depths of his springy hair. Her need to touch him was overpowering every inhibition. His wide, sensual mouth claimed hers with explosive passion.

Molly had never been kissed like that before, had never known such heat and urgency and excitement, and it was like being plunged into the eye of a storm. She felt dizzy and out of control. His tongue plunged between her lips and withdrew and quivering, scorching hunger pierced her like the blade of a knife. Elemental need leapt through her and screamed demands she was ill equipped to deal with. She trembled in sexual shock from the rush of sensation, her soft mouth still clinging to his as the peaks of her breasts tightened into taut, tingling buds. While her senses reeled from the touch and the taste of him her fingers closed into the edges of his jacket to hold onto him and keep herself steady.

A car alarm shrilled out somewhere in the street below and Leandro tensed and jerked his dark head up, his thoughts diving into a free fall of shock as he recognised that he was acting on impulse and without his usual intelligent restraint. Yet, letting go of her slight figure which seemed to fit so very neatly to his more solid masculine frame was one of the hardest things he had ever had to make himself do for he was painfully aroused.

'I'm sorry,' he murmured, and it was a mental challenge for him even to come up with the right phrase in English.

Molly was in a daze as well and quite unable to muster rational thought. 'Why? *Sorry?*' she queried as his lean hands closed over her narrow shoulders and set her very deliberately back from him.

Molly blinked, watching him curve a hand round the balcony's ornate ironwork balustrade until his knuckles showed white with tension below his brown skin. He had beautifully shaped hands with long, elegant fingers. The steady beat of music and the pound of feet on the dance floor travelled out from the wedding party inside the house. Her attention roved up to his strong jaw line, straight classic nose and stunning profile. She wasn't surprised that she couldn't take her eyes off him: he had the sleek, dark, sinful beauty of a fallen angel. But what had she been playing at? Letting one of the guests kiss her when she was supposed to be working? Was she crazy? Her job was all that stood between her and unemployment. She had been there once and didn't want to undergo that humiliation and stress again.

'It shouldn't have happened and normally it wouldn't have,' Leandro breathed, finally opting to acknowledge the strange restless mood that had afflicted him for the past week.

Molly recalled the fact that he had virtually pushed *her* away and a shamed flush swept across her face as high as her hairline. No, that embrace shouldn't have happened and it said nothing in her favour that he had been the first of them to register that truth and act on it. Where had her wits been? But she still felt hot and shivery and awesomely aware of him. The lure of the excitement he had generated was potent and her body was cooling into a state of taut disappointment. The hot colour in her cheeks refused to disperse.

'I'm not quite myself. Perhaps I've had too much to drink. What other explanation could there be for my behaviour?' Leandro demanded with chilling cool, noting the way her complexion had coloured and wondering what age she was, for at that moment she looked very young to him. '*Dios mio!* You are the waitress.'

In receipt of that blunt rejection of who and what she was, Molly turned very pale. She was a person, an individual, another human being before she was a waitress, she thought painfully. 'I should have realised that you'd be an out-and-out snob. Don't worry. You don't need to make excuses. I'm not naïve enough to think a kiss meant there was a relationship in the offing and you're not my type anyway!'

In a series of brisk, no-nonsense movements, Molly cleared the tray on the table and headed back indoors.

'You're gorgeous, *querida*,' Leandro heard himself murmur huskily. 'I didn't need any other excuse.'

Her colour fluctuated at that unexpected compliment as she walked away. Gorgeous? Since when had she been gorgeous? She had been called pretty once or twice when she was all done up, but there was no truth whatsoever in the label he had just given her. She was five feet one inch and she had a mane of black curls that was often impossible to control. Her skin was good and she considered herself lucky in that she could pretty much eat what she liked without gaining weight. Those were her only advantages in her own estimation.

'Were you outside with Mr Carrera Marquez?' the bride's mother demanded angrily, planting herself combatively in Molly's path. 'Why did you go out there to bother him?'

'I wasn't bothering him. I needed to thank him for intervening with those men on my behalf and I took him some food.' Molly lifted her chin at a defiant angle.

The tall blonde woman stared down at her with angry superiority. 'I've already told your manager that I won't have you working in my home again. You've got the wrong attitude,' she censured curtly. 'You had no business making a personal approach to one of our guests and spoiling my daughter's wedding.'

That unjust rebuke made Molly's eyes prickle with angry tears and she had to bite back a sharp retaliation. She had done nothing wrong. She had been insulted verbally and physically, but nobody was about to say sorry to a mere waitress. She went back into the kitchen where Brian suggested she start helping the chef to clean up. She worked steadily and fast. The evening wore on until the chatter of the guests slowly died down along with the music and people left to go home.

'Do another check out there for glasses,' Brian instructed.

Molly took out a tray and the first person she saw was the Spanish banker, leaning up against a wall at an elegant angle and talking into his mobile phone. He was ordering a taxi. She refused even to look in his direction as she hurried through to the next room to pick up a collection of abandoned glasses. The whole time she was within view, Leandro watched her small figure like a hawk.

She had said he wasn't her type but he was convinced that that had been pure bravado. Yet she was definitely not the sort of woman he had gone for in the past. Tall, elegant blondes like Aloise had always been Leandro's style. But Molly got to him on a much more basic plane. The sensual sway of her curvaceous hips would have attracted any red-blooded male's attention, Leandro told himself grimly. The wild mop of black curls anchored on top of her small head, the huge green eyes and the gloriously full inviting mouth were drop-dead sexy attributes before he even glanced below her chin. Just looking at her, he got hot and hard. Remembering the soft allure of her mouth opening for him and the eagerness of her response did nothing to improve his condition. He needed a cold shower. He needed *a woman*, he acknowledged, his wide mouth compressing into a line, for he was furious that he could have so little control over his own body.

The rooms were almost empty by the time Molly had finished helping to load the catering van. Putting on her coat, she walked back round to the front of the house on her way to where she had parked her car. It was a surprise to find the Spanish banker standing out on the pavement.

It was a freezing cold wintry night and he had no coat on over his suit. Wind was whistling down the street and he looked chilled to the marrow.

'Didn't your taxi come yet?' she asked before she could think better of taking notice of him.

'Apparently they're very busy tonight. I don't think I have ever been so cold in my life. How do you bear this climate?' Leandro enquired between gritted white teeth.

'Choice didn't come into it.' Molly thought what a miserable evening he had had and sympathy softened her stiff stance and expression. 'Look, I would offer you a lift home but I don't want to give you the wrong idea—'

'How would I get the wrong idea?' Leandro cut in, knowing it was going to be a very long time, if ever, before he went out again without his chauffeur and limousine to transport him around. It had not occurred to him until it was too late that he could not possibly drive himself home when he had had several drinks.

Molly tilted her chin, luminous green eyes proffering a challenge. 'I'm not stalking you or in any way expressing a personal interest in you,' she spelt out with scrupulous care.

Leandro studied her with sudden intense amusement because what was in his mind was the exact opposite—he was thinking that if he just let her walk away he would never see her again. *Never.* There was just one problem: Leandro was discovering that he was not prepared to accept that eventuality. 'I know you're not stalking me. I'll take a lift,' he murmured softly.

'I'll get my car.' Having crossed the road, Molly went round the corner and unlocked and climbed into her ancient Mini. She was already asking herself what had come over her, why she hadn't just walked on past and left him to freeze. She hadn't even asked where he lived and suspected that it would most probably be well out of her way.

The appearance of the vibrant pink car initially took Leandro aback. It was as quirky and full of personality as he suspected its owner was. He attempted to get in, realised that he had to shift the seat back to accommodate his long legs and did so before folding his lean, powerful length into the tight space. 'You like pink,' he remarked.

'It's an easy colour to spot in a car park. Where do you live?'

His address was as exclusive and expensive as she believed he was, but it was comparatively close to the part of town they were in. 'How did you get to the exhibition tonight?' she prompted.

'By car, but I've drunk too much to drive,' Leandro stated.

'Is that why you said you weren't yourself earlier?' Molly queried, shooting him a curious look as she stopped at a set of traffic lights. He turned his handsome dark head to look at her and she marvelled at the hot gold colour his dark brooding eyes acquired in stronger light.

'No. Today was the anniversary of my wife's death a year ago. I've been unsettled all week,' Leandro imparted, and immediately wondered why he was admitting something so personal to her, since it was not at all like him.

For a split second, Molly froze, and then her natural warmth and sympathy took charge of her response. She reached across and squeezed his hand. 'I'm so sorry,' she said sincerely. 'Was she ill?'

Startled by that affectionate gesture of support, Leandro had stiffened. 'No, she crashed her car. My fault. We had an…exchange of words before she went out,' he said tautly.

An exchange of words? Did he mean they'd had a row? 'Of course it wasn't your fault,' Molly told him with firm conviction. 'You shouldn't be blaming yourself. Unless you were physically behind the wheel, it was a tragic accident and it's not healthy to think of it any other way.'

Her outspoken candour and practicality were a refreshing change when compared to the majority of people, who carefully avoided making any reference to the thorny subject of Aloise's sudden death. Perhaps it was true that it was easier to talk to strangers, Leandro mused reflectively, for he was unable to recall any other occasion when he had spontaneously abandoned his reserve to confide in anyone else.

He was a widower, Molly thought ruefully. She didn't know how she felt about that, only that it was an unexpected fact. 'You feel guilty about kissing me as well, don't you?' she guessed.

His classic bronzed profile went rigid at that reminder. She had hit a bullseye. Suddenly her candour was unwelcome and gauche in the extreme. 'I don't think we need to discuss that,' he drawled in a tone of finality.

Molly changed gear and her knuckles accidentally skimmed a length of lean muscular thigh as she did so. 'Sorry,' she muttered uncomfortably. 'There isn't much space in this car.'

The atmosphere was tense.

'How long have you worked as a waitress?' Leandro

asked, gracefully negotiating a passage through the awkward silence that had fallen.

'I started out as a part-timer when I was at art college. My earnings helped to keep my student loans under control,' Molly told him. 'I'm a potter when I can afford to be, but waitressing is what it takes to pay my bills.'

Silence fell again. She parked near the strikingly modern apartment building he pointed out. He thanked her and tried to get out but the door wouldn't open. The faulty handle, which she had thought was fixed, was acting up again. With a muffled apology, Molly got out and hurried round the bonnet to open the passenger door from the outside.

Leandro climbed out and straightened, relieved to be escaping the cramped restrictions of the car interior. Molly, he noticed, barely reached the middle of his chest. There was something intensely feminine about her slight build and diminutive stature. He had a sudden explosively sexual image of lifting her up against him and only with the greatest difficulty did he manage to shut it out. Even so, his body reacted with instant enthusiasm. He wanted to pull her into his arms, seal her lush body to his and make love to her. He was stunned by the amount of restraint it took to keep his hands off her and furious that he couldn't keep his libido under better control.

With a swift goodbye, Molly hurried back round the car and jumped in. She watched him stride across the road and enter the well-lit foyer of the block. She got a last glimpse of his lean, darkly handsome face as he exchanged a greeting with the porter on the desk before turning away and moving out of view. She felt horribly let down, shockingly disappointed that he was gone.

Shaking her head at her own foolishness, she was clasping her seat belt, when she noticed something lying on the floor. Undoing the belt she bent down and stretched out a hand to scoop up the item. It was a man's wallet and it could only belong to the man who had just vacated her car. With an impatient groan, she undid her belt and climbed out again.

The porter had no problem in identifying whom she was talking about and he offered to deliver the wallet. But Molly preferred to return the item in person. The porter tried to phone Leandro's apartment but when there was no answer he advised Molly to go on up to the top floor in the lift. While it whirred upwards, she asked herself what she was playing at. Here she was literally chasing after him. Perhaps she should have let the porter return the wallet. Had she secretly wanted an excuse to see Leandro again? Her face was burning with colour at that suspicion when the lift doors whirred back with an electronic clunk. She stepped out into a snazzy semi-circular hall. The Spaniard was standing in front of the only door going through his pockets. He wheeled round at the sound of the lift. His winged ebony brows lifted in surprise at the sight of her.

'Is this what you're looking for?' Molly held out the wallet. 'I found it lying on the floor of my car.'

'Exactly what I'm looking for.' He flipped open the wallet to extract a card and opened the door straightaway. 'Thank you…no, don't leave.' He strode back to her to prevent her from walking back into the lift. 'Join me for a drink.'

'No, I can't. That's not why I came up here,' Molly protested, her discomfiture unhidden.

'But it should have been, *querida*.' Intent dark golden eyes glittered down into hers. 'Why are we both trying to walk away from this?'

And Molly didn't need to ask him what 'this' encompassed because she already knew. From the minute she saw him her every thought had contained him and even then it had required effort not to just stand still and stare at him while she memorised every tiny facet of his appearance for future recall and enjoyment. The thought that she might never see him again upset her even though she didn't know him. She was as drawn to him as an iron filing to a magnet and her brain had nothing to do with the terrifyingly powerful hold of that attraction.

'Because it's crazy!' Molly exclaimed jerkily, backing away a step as if she was trying to steel herself back into departure mode again.

Leandro closed a lean hand round her narrow-boned wrist and urged her into his apartment. 'I don't want to stand out here talking. Our every move is being recorded by security cameras,' he explained.

He flipped on lights to reveal a large hall with a marble floor and a fashionable glass table bearing a bronze sculpture. It looked like a picture out of a glossy interior design magazine and it unnerved her. 'Look at the way you live!' Molly shifted an uneasy hand in a demonstrative gesture. 'You're a banker. I'm a waitress. We might as well be aliens from different planets.'

'Maybe that novelty is part of the attraction and why not?' Leandro fielded, moving slowly forward to close both hands round her fragile wrists to maintain a physical connection with her. 'I don't want you to leave…'

The pads of his thumbs rubbed gently at the delicate blue-veined skin of her inner wrist. She looked up at him and knew it to be a fatal act, for when she met those stunning dark eyes she could hardly think straight, never mind breathe. Although she didn't want to leave, she almost never took risks of any kind. Life had taught her that the costs of being anything other than sensible and cautious were likely to be high and painful.

'Feeling like this terrifies me,' she confessed in a whisper.

'You make me feel more alive than I have felt in more years than I care to recall, *querida*.' His brooding gaze was welded to her while he momentarily fought to comprehend the intensity of his desire for her. 'That's not scary, that's cause for celebration.'

It shook her that he was describing exactly what she was feeling as well. Somehow it seemed to make her reaction to him more acceptable and she shut out the misgivings striving to be heard in the back of her mind. Even as she looked back at him sensual energy was leaping and dancing through her small, taut frame, tightening the tender peaks of her breasts into taut buds and spilling heat between her thighs in a storm of powerful physical responses that turned her bones to water and her brain to mush. With a stifled imprecation, Leandro bent down and drove her pink lips apart in a demanding kiss.

Molly gasped. His urgency was exactly what her trembling, eager body craved. She felt him peel off her coat. She was locked to the muscular strength of his lithe powerful physique, her breasts crushed against his hard chest, her lips parting in welcome to the erotic plunge of his tongue in her mouth.

In receipt of her response, Leandro shuddered, sinking his hands to her hips in the fitted skirt and hauling her bodily up against him. She locked her hands round his neck and kissed him back with breathless fervour.

'Do you want a drink?' he asked her.

'Not if it means you'll stop kissing me,' Molly told him, small fingers delving into his luxuriant black hair to hold him to her. She had the same sense of wonder she experienced when she created a new design on her potter's wheel, that same heady glorious conviction that what she was doing was eerily exactly right.

'I *can't* stop,' Leandro groaned, trailing his lips down her slender neck in a series of darting, rousing kisses that made her squirm and whimper as he discovered newly erogenous zones of skin. Her unconcealed enthusiasm only added to his pleasure in her. His tongue flicked the sensitive roof of her mouth and she shivered violently. 'Stay with me tonight,' he urged.

At first surprise and dismay gripped her and then her agile brain pulled free of sensual lockdown for long enough to reason that invitation out. They weren't teenagers kissing on a doorstep. She might be a good deal less experienced than many a teenager, but she was a grown woman and he was very definitely an adult male. What happened next was entirely her decision. She thought about letting go of him, saying goodnight, probably never seeing him again. Her skin chilled and her insides turned hollow and cold at that threat. Her arms tightened round him. She wanted to lock him up and keep the key to his captivity safely attached to a chain round her throat. She had never felt that way before about a man and she wasn't at all sure she liked it.

'But I'm a waitress,' she reminded him shakily.

'It doesn't matter. It truly doesn't matter, *mi muñeca*,' Leandro asserted in a driven undertone. 'What matters is who you are when you're with me.'

She looked up and was ensnared by a smile that made her heart pound and rocked her world like an earthquake. Suddenly being sensible and careful had zero attraction. He made her want to be daring and the sort of female who inspired men to acts of madness. 'I'll stay—'

His arms tightened round her and the hungry ravishment of his mouth on hers left her in no doubt of his reaction to her agreement. She felt the rigid heat of his erection against her and she trembled, both intimidated and excited by the effect she had on him. He was so much a man, so male in comparison to the youths she was accustomed to. He carried her out of the hall into a room lit by moonlight. He sank down on the wide bed and lowered her to her feet between his spread thighs.

'Now you're at my level it will be much easier to kiss you,' he pointed out thickly, reaching up to unclip her hair and using his hands to brush the lush mane of blue-black curls back from her brow and guide the tumbling mass down over her slight shoulders. 'You have the most beautiful hair.'

'Far too much of it and it's horribly curly,' she told him helplessly.

'Not for me, *querida*.' Leandro ran slow possessive hands over her, his thumbs brushing the protuberant nipples that were visible through her thin cotton blouse, his palms smoothing over the full curve of her hips below her tiny waist. 'You also have the most wonderful shape.'

The hungry heat burning through Molly was reaching a boiling point of impatience. She leant forward and brushed her soft pink lips over his in an experimental fashion while she yanked his silk tie loose, slipped the knot and cast it aside. Her breath fanned a smooth bronzed cheekbone as she gazed into eyes that were dark as ebony in the moonlight and unfathomable. 'I hope you're not going to be a mistake,' she muttered anxiously, conscious that she was taking a chance on him by throwing caution to the four winds.

Having shed his jacket, Leandro hauled her back to him and kissed her with passionate, probing force until she was breathless. 'Nothing that feels this good could possibly be a mistake,' he declared.

She wondered if he would feel the same way in the morning, wondered how she would feel as well, but while his skilful hands were moving over her, sending her every pulse and skin cell crazy with wild hunger, she found it impossible to second guess the future. He unzipped her skirt and pushed it down, lifting her out of it and just as quickly unbuttoning her shirt and extracting her from it. The ease with which he undressed her suggested a level of sophistication that made her nervous. Her breasts spilled from the cups of her bra and he moulded the soft, pouting mounds with a masculine growl of appreciation. His fingers teased her swollen pink nipples and he cradled her across his thighs to let his sensual mouth and tongue play with the delicate straining buds.

So much unfamiliar sensation engulfed Molly that a stifled sob of response was dredged from her. The power of what she was feeling was overwhelming. Her skin was damp with perspiration, her heart thumping like a road drill while an ache of longing close to actual pain throbbed between her slender legs. She was desperate to touch him as well, but he didn't give her the chance. He laid her down on the bed and got up again to undress.

CHAPTER THREE

DRY-MOUTHED, Molly watched as Leandro stripped. She had sketched nude models in life class at college, so the masculine anatomy was far from being a complete mystery to her. But she had never seen a male body that could aspire to the sheer magnificence of Leandro's sleek bronzed physique. He was superbly built from his muscular chest to his hard flat stomach and long, powerful thighs.

He was also fiercely erect. Her rapt gaze widened slightly and red stained her cheeks, for there was a good deal more of him in that department than she had expected, a discovery that sent a mortifying stab of virginal uncertainty through her slight frame. For the first time she wished she were a little more practised. Unconcerned by his nakedness and silvered by moonlight, he strolled fluidly back to the bed to join her. Her palms smoothed over his strong pectoral muscles. He felt like warm, hair-roughened bronze, the pelt of black curls on his chest arrowing down into an intriguing line over his belly.

'Show me that you want me,' Leandro growled.

Emboldened by that request, she dipped her hands to

touch him with greater intimacy. She traced and stroked the iron-hard length of his sex, fascinated by his alien masculinity and encouraged by his low-pitched sounds of pleasure.

But it wasn't long before he made her desist and gathered her into his arms again. 'I can't take much of that, *querida*,' he confessed, plunging his mouth down on a succulent nipple as lush as pink velvet, dividing his attention between it and its equally responsive twin while his fingers finally delved into the hot, moist, tender core of her.

In the first moments of that erotic exploration, Molly thought she would not be able to bear anything at all. Her body instantly felt like a fire raging out of her control. Ripples of lascivious wanton pleasure enveloped her from the first expert invasion of his fingers. He found the tiny bud that controlled her response and lingered there with devastating effect. Her breath rasped raw in her throat and she whimpered beneath that sensual torment of sensation. She couldn't speak for excitement. Her body twisted and jerked like a puppet in the hold of a tyrannical master. There was a tight, tormenting ball of need swelling in her loins and pushing her to an agonising pitch of hunger.

'I can't wait any longer,' Leandro confessed, coming over her and pinning her hands to the bed beneath his while he slid between her thighs. His brilliant eyes smouldered pure gold as he stared down at her. He had never wanted anything or anybody as much as he wanted her at that moment. He had never known such a high of sexual intensity. With her raven hair spread across his pillows, her crystalline green eyes shimmering and her voluptuous mouth swollen from the onslaught of his, he thought she was irresistible.

Molly cried out as he drove into her resisting flesh with one urgent thrust. His power was too potent to be denied and he forged a bold passage into her honeyed depths, stretching and filling her to capacity.

'I hurt you!' Leandro exclaimed and stilled.

'No, it doesn't matter!' Molly protested, for she was embarrassed and the discomfort was already ebbing as her receptive body slowly adjusted to him. He felt amazing inside her and a rising tide of heat consumed her again. 'Don't stop.'

Leandro was astonished by what her behaviour in combination with her body was telling him. His ebony brows drew together in a questioning frown. '*Dios mio!* Are you a virgin?'

'*Was*,' Molly countered awkwardly, keen not to discuss the matter just at that moment.

His lean, darkly handsome face was taut. 'You should have warned me, *mi gatita.*'

'It felt too private to mention,' Molly admitted uncomfortably.

Leandro dealt her an incredulous look and then he flung back his proud dark head and laughed with rich appreciation. 'You make me smile.' He dropped a teasing kiss on her bemused brow and shifted his lean hips, reacquainting her with his presence until she gasped in shaken response.

The hot, hungry heat burned inside her again, her body eagerly quickening to the sexual dominance of his. He sank deep into her and withdrew again and repeated that torturous cycle again and again until she was shaking and arching beneath him, almost driven out of her mind by the urgent desire he had ignited. Nothing mattered but the satisfaction she was reaching for and the delirious excitement of the pace he set. Tiny feverish tremors passed through her. She moved against him, caught up in the intensity of her hunger. When she reached orgasm, it was as if the whole world stopped and flung her sky-high. Waves of exquisite pleasure gripped her and she writhed under him in an ecstasy of abandon. In the throes of the same satisfaction, he shuddered and drove deep and she lifted her hips to receive him and held him close in the aftermath.

Afterwards she was in a state of sleepy wonderment at what she had just learned about her own body's amazing capacity for enjoyment. She wanted to stay awake because she had never before felt so close to another human being and she loved that sense of intimacy, but she had also never felt so tired in her life. He kissed her and he muttered some Spanish stuff.

'I don't speak the lingo,' she mumbled sleepily.

'I'm too tired to speak English.'

'So shut up and go to sleep,' Molly countered, snuggling up to him and closing a possessive arm round him.

In the moonlight, Leandro elevated an ebony brow and turned her over so that she was lying on her side. A mark at the base of her spine caught his attention. A scar? His finger traced the tattoo of hot-pink lips. He pushed back the sheet and saw another illustration on her ankle. It was of a tiny trail of silvery blue stars. He smiled, covered her up again and tugged her back against him. She was totally different from any other woman he had ever met or bedded. Definitely not Duquesa material—but the perfect candidate for the role of mistress.

Why not? In bed she was pure enticement and as hot for him as he was for her. He had a very healthy sex drive and too many years had passed since he was able to give his libido a free rein. The idea of having relaxation time with a warm, willing woman like Molly at the end of a long stressful day at the bank was immensely appealing. He enjoyed the fact that she talked to him on a level as if he were an ordinary person. She was comfortable and confident within herself. He couldn't ever remember a woman telling him to shut up before—even as a joke. She was novel, she was fresh and he was bored and determined to break free of the web of duty and responsibility that entrapped him. Just for once, Leandro mused, he was going to do exactly what he wanted to do and to hell with the consequences!

Wakening, Molly lifted her lashes and registered that she was lying in a strange bed in an equally strange room. It was still dark but the dawn was lighting up the distant horizon. The décor had a cool art deco style and the room was really large. Only someone very rich could afford that amount of space and that kind of furniture in a city as expensive as London. The events of the previous night flooded back to her and she went rigid. She had slept with Leandro and she couldn't even pronounce, never mind spell, his surname. As she sneaked a leg towards the edge of the bed to get up a long masculine arm closed round her and drew her back.

'Don't even think about leaving, *querida*,' Leandro husked, his breath stirring her hair. 'It's only seven.'

'This is really embarrassing,' Molly mumbled. 'I don't even have a toothbrush with me.'

Leandro worked hard at not laughing at that inept admission. 'I have a spare. I'll order breakfast. I have something I would very much like to discuss with you.'

All Molly wanted just then was a magic wand to wave that would whisk her from being naked in his bed back to the sanctuary of her own bedroom. Her clothes were scattered on the polished wood floor. I'm a slut, she thought wretchedly, a total slut.

Leandro was talking on the bedside phone in Spanish at a great rate. He sounded like someone accustomed to rapping out instructions. But what did she know about him? He was amazingly good-looking? Chivalrous towards humble waitresses? Fantastic in bed? Averse to the cold? A widower? Well, these days that last fact did tell her something about his character, she reasoned. He had been prepared to commit to a future with someone and had got married at a reasonably early age, which was unusual.

'I'll use the bathroom next door,' he told her lazily.

To his list of attributes, Molly added a plus for tact. Without turning her head, however, she waited until she heard the door snap shut on his departure before she scrambled out of bed, gathered up the clothes she had been wearing the night before and raced into the en-suite bathroom clutching them.

Her curls looked as though she had stuck a finger in an electric socket. She groaned out loud and rifled the drawers of the vanity unit for the toothbrush she had been promised. The corner shower was digitally operated so she couldn't work out how to use it and made do with washing at the sink as best she could. As she dressed she was conscious that her body ached even worse than it had after the charity mini-marathon she had done with Jez the previous year.

She had a dim erotic memory of wakening during the night and making love with Leandro again. She had made the approach, which had resulted in his long, achingly slow and spellbinding seduction that had made her cry out his name at the top of her voice. She cringed at the recollection of her audacity while she fiddled with her hair, struggling to tame her wild curls into some semblance of order without the aid of her usual weapons. Only when she no longer had any excuse to linger did she emerge from the bedroom. She only knew one thing: had she had the chance to go back to the previous night she would still have chosen to stay with him and experience what had followed.

The dining room enjoyed a stunning view of the Thames. A waiter was there presiding over a trolley stacked with a wide selection of food and Molly was astonished by the concept of anyone buying in breakfast for two complete with service. But her wide eyes still swivelled straight across to Leandro, who was poised by the window. He commanded the scene, sheathed in a superbly tailored black pinstripe suit that was the very epitome of banking chic. He looked sinfully beautiful but cool and remote. Her tummy gave an uneasy lurch as if she were under threat. She didn't know how to behave or what to say to him.

With an authoritative nod, Leandro told the waiter he could leave because they would serve themselves. Her face flushed as she carefully avoided a direct meeting with his thickly lashed dark eyes, Molly wiped damp palms down the sides of her fitted black skirt. It was obvious to her that ordering people around came very naturally indeed to Leandro. She had never been more conscious of her lowly status than when she was standing there still garbed in her work clothes while he summarily dismissed the waiter from his duties.

Conscious her tummy was rumbling, she lifted a small box of cereal and put it in a bowl before taking a seat. The apartment was even more opulent than she had initially appreciated and she felt more like a fish out of water than ever.

'Last night…' Leandro hesitated, searching for the right words with which to outline his offer as he helped himself to fresh fruit. 'It was fantastic.'

'Hmm.' Molly nodded, her mouth too full to speak and even if it hadn't been she had no idea what she might have replied to that surprisingly intimate comment. Clothed and in daylight, Leandro was horrendously intimidating. She could barely credit that she had spent the night in his arms.

Leandro breathed in deep. 'In fact it was so incredible that I want to hang onto you, *querida*.'

Molly almost choked on her cereal. 'Hang *onto* me?' she parroted without comprehension.

'I lead a very busy existence in which I rarely have time to lighten up, which is one very good reason why I would like you to become a part of my life. I like your cheerful attitude and I need to relax more,' Leandro imparted levelly. 'We both have something that the other needs. It would be an exchange of mutual benefit. You would enjoy the financial security to indulge your ambition to be an artisan potter and I would be happy to make that possible.'

Her smooth brow had indented and her almond-shaped eyes were bright with bewilderment. 'What on earth are you trying to say?'

'That I would be prepared to buy you somewhere suitable to live and money need no longer be a source of concern for you,' Leandro spelt out softly. 'No more wai-tressing—I would cover all your expenses. It would be my pleasure to do so.'

Molly studied him fixedly, her heartbeat thumping so fast and loud that it felt as if it were trapped in her tight throat. 'Why would you offer to buy me somewhere to live? Why would you want to pay my bills? Exactly what kind of a relationship are you offering me?'

'I want you to be my mistress and stay in my life, *querida*. In the background of my life rather than the fore-front of it, it is true,' Leandro conceded, belatedly won-dering whether she was capable of being discreet. 'But you would still be important to me.'

As he quantified his objective, Molly had turned pale and then suddenly colour ran up like a banner beneath her creamy skin and burnished it to hot pink. Anger strongly laced with outrage left her light-headed and threatened to erupt from her like a volcano. Her jewelled eyes fiery with disbelief, she rammed her hands down flat on the table top and pushed herself upright. 'You arrogant, condescending rat!' she launched at him furiously. 'Your *mistress*? What was last night supposed to be? A trial run for the position? You have no business even suggesting such a thing to me!'

'You don't need to use abuse to make your point,' Leandro censured with freezing cool. 'In my world such arrange-ments between men and women are common and accepted.'

'Not in mine!' Molly gasped, stricken by the awareness that if he had just asked to see her again she would have snatched at the opportunity. Instead he had put an offensive commercial price on any future relationship and made it very clear that she wasn't good enough to occupy any more equal or public role in his life. That clear fact hurt like a knife twisting inside her, echoing as it did the painful rejections she had had to deal with throughout her life. *Not good enough.* Sometimes it seemed to Molly that she was never good enough for anything she really wanted.

Leandro, his lean, strong face impassive, continued to study her with a detachment that chilled Molly to the marrow. 'You can't be that naive.'

Leandro had never been with a woman who didn't want to profit from being with him in some way. Even as a teenager he had been the target of elaborate female stratagems designed to attract his interest and entrap him. Fabulous wealth was a very powerful draw. He had learned young that sex was invariably offered in the expectation that the act of sharing his bed would be rewarded with frequent bouts of financial generosity. And then there were the women who didn't primarily want his money, but who had their social ambitions squarely set on marrying him and using his ancient name and aristocratic lineage to gain an entry to the most exclusive and privileged stratum of Spanish society.

'Listen to me—I don't need anyone but myself to make my dreams come true,' Molly told him half an octave higher. 'I certainly don't need any man to keep me and I *never* will! I manage fine on my own—'

'You're capable of being more than a waitress,' Leandro contended grimly.

'And a great deal more than being your mistress too!' Molly launched back at him in heated challenge. 'However low I may sink in life, you can be sure that I'll never be desperate enough to surrender my self-respect and sell myself to you for sex!'

'Shorn of melodrama, was that a no?' Leandro surveyed her with level dark as midnight eyes, his lean, powerful face tight with reserve and cool. Displeasure radiated from him like a force field but his self-control, unlike hers, was absolute.

'Yes, that was a *no*, and now I think it's time I cleared off and went home.' Her voice sounded choky and tears were stinging the backs of her eyes. 'How could you belittle me with a sleazy offer like that? I'm not interested in being some dirty little secret in your life!'

'It wouldn't be like that between us. I only want to keep you close—'

'But only in the most demeaning way!' Molly cut in with biting scorn. 'Not as an equal. You wear your belief in your superiority like a medal, don't you? But I'm not some little toy you can buy to entertain yourself in your free time and where do you get off suggesting that I am?'

Affronted by her sustained verbal attack, Leandro unfolded from his seat to his full imposing height and viewed her with sardonic eyes. 'You were happy enough to be with me last night. Did I treat you like a toy?'

Molly's cheeks burned hotter than fire, as she suspected that she had been more guilty of treating him like the ultimate adult woman's plaything the night before, for she had fully satisfied all her curiosity. 'Last night was last night. I didn't know what was on your mind then. I liked you until we had this conversation—'

A black brow quirked. 'Did you? I would have said that you wanted me the same way I wanted—and *still* want—you. Can you really switch off like that?'

Taut as a bow string, she stared back at him, knowing that it would not be so easy to switch off her responses or forget that overwhelming passion that had proved so very addictive. His stunning eyes rested on her, cool and unreadable. 'Yes,' she lied curtly. 'Yes, I can. I'm not a forgiving person, either!'

Molly stalked out to the hall where she had seen her coat lying across a chair. She had only snatched it up when it was removed from her grasp and politely extended for her to slip into by Leandro.

'You really put the "o" into offensive with your offers, but, hey, you've got exquisite manners!' Molly sniped as she dug her arms into the sleeves and spun back round to face him.

Leandro nudged her coat out of his path and slid a business card into the front pocket of her white blouse. 'My private phone number. For the moment when you come to appreciate what you're passing up.'

'That moment will never come—I'm making a lucky escape from a guy who belongs in the Dark Ages and still thinks it's all right to treat women like sex objects!' she hissed back.

Leandro curved lean fingers to her cheekbones to hold her steady and plundered her soft pink lips in a smoulderingly sexual kiss that lit a fire in her pelvis and made her tremble. 'You'll come running back—you won't be able to help yourself, *mi gatita*,' he forecast huskily. 'I won't let you go. That's a promise.'

He didn't have her phone number, he didn't even know where she lived, so Molly wasn't too concerned by that macho assurance, which set her teeth on edge. She walked into the lift with an oddly bereft feeling dogging her mood. She refused to acknowledge it and her thoughts were soon turned to much more practical matters when she discovered that her car had acquired a parking ticket since she had left it the evening before. Such penalties were incredibly expensive and she was, as always, broke. With a grimace of annoyance, she drove off.

Leandro called his security team to ensure that she was followed. There was no way he was letting her go again. The more she fought, the more he wanted her for he now recognised her absolute uniqueness. She wasn't after his money or his social pedigree, but she did *want* him very much. Purely as a man. He had no doubt whatsoever on that score. Indeed a hard slanting smile of amused satisfaction banished the grim cast of his handsome mouth. He remembered her in his bed last night. She had carefully nudged him awake, her Cupid's-bow mouth soft and coaxing and pure dynamite on his shoulder and his chest before travelling to more sensitive places as she became ever more enterprising. He recalled her helpless giggles when she got it wrong and the white hot glory of pleasure engulfing him when he showed her how to get it right. No way was he letting her walk away from him now. In the most basic terms and on a level that appealed to his every atavistic masculine fibre, she was *his* discovery and *his* creation.

It was only when she was gone and he was striding out to his limousine to head for the bank that Leandro stilled and realised in shock that the night before he had been guilty of a glaring oversight. He had not used condoms with her and, bearing in mind her lack of experience, it was unlikely that she was taking any contraceptive precautions on her own behalf. He swore soft and low in Spanish, stunned by his omission. Although, given the five childless years of his marriage, it was a challenge for him to believe that there could be a genuine risk of her falling pregnant by him…

CHAPTER FOUR

IN THE act of trying to listen to a long involved speech from one of the bank's most senior directors, Leandro drifted into an erotic daydream.

As the self-justifying speech went on and endlessly on Leandro added elaborate layer on layer to the fantasy. He pictured Molly spreadeagled naked in the golden glow of the hot Spanish sunshine, her lush white breasts crowned by straining pink peaks that glistened damply with the champagne he was licking from her voluptuous curves. He was remembering the tantalising glide of her hair across his stomach and the velvet soft glory of her mouth…

'Mr Carrera Marquez?'

Leandro pulled instantaneously free of the seductive images that had captured an imagination he had not known he possessed. Even though his body was hot and heavy with discomfort and sexual need was a tormenting pulse-beat through his big powerful frame, he snapped straight back into cut-throat business mode.

'My opinion? In a nutshell? Get tough. Don't accept excuses for poor performance. Sack the management team. They've had their chance and blown it. Give that opportunity to hungrier employees,' Leandro advised without hesitation, and he brought the meeting to a close with the cool, economic efficiency that had made him a living legend in financial circles.

Closely followed by his phalanx of aides, his handsome dark head held high, Leandro strode down the corridor. He was incensed by the erotic recollections that had recently dared to cloud his concentration at inappropriate moments during his working day. But had sex ever been that good for him before? That wild? That hot? If it had been, he couldn't recall it. Possibly he had waited too long to ease the natural needs of his body and now all the pent-up hunger of a year's celibacy was tormenting him for release.

To that end, he finally made use of one of the many phone numbers he had had pressed on him since Aloise's death. He dined out with a beautiful blonde divorcee who had thrown herself at him previously with an enthusiasm that any sex-starved male should have revelled in. Unhappily, Leandro discovered that his seething libido was stubbornly impervious to the blonde's attractions. He still wanted Molly and it seemed that no other woman would do.

But why make a production out of that fact? Leandro asked himself with the equivalent of a mental shrug. He had had a lot of women in his life before he married and now that settled phase was well and truly over. Life was short. Sex was just sex and he was young and healthy. He worked hard, why shouldn't he play hard as well? There was nothing wrong with the pursuit of pleasure. Furthermore he had the perfect excuse for seeking out Molly again: he had to check that their night together had had no lasting repercussions.

* * *

Molly vented her exasperation with a groan of frustration when she removed her pots from the electric kiln in the shed. Several pieces had stuck to the trivet because she had been too liberal with the glaze. Under pressure from her, those items cracked. More unnecessary breakages! In recent days she had made more than her fair share of costly mistakes while she'd worked.

But then her emotions were eating her up because she was still so angry with herself for sleeping with Leandro, Molly acknowledged ruefully. Meeting Leandro and falling victim to his charms had forced her to accept that she had more in common with her birth mother, Cathy, than she had ever wanted to know. Cathy had been very prone to following casual impulses with men she'd never taken the time to get to know and she had called those urges, 'love', and their fulfilment, 'spontaneity'.

In comparison, Molly was less kind with her labels and over the past week and a half she had at various times called herself terminally stupid, reckless and naive. Leandro's attitude to her the morning after had been the ultimate put-down and had set the seal on her humiliation. She had given her body to a guy who wanted a tame woman to lock in a custom-built cage for his sexual gratification. He had neither respected nor appreciated her. How much lower could she have sunk?

She was in the kitchen making coffee when the front doorbell went in two shrill bursts. With a perfunctory brush down of the clay-stained overall she wore, she went to answer it.

A shock of recognition jolted her when she saw the tall, dark, well-dressed Spaniard on the doorstep. She was stunned into silence, her tongue clinging to the roof of her dry mouth. Bathed in spring sunshine, luxuriant ebony hair ruffled by the breeze, lean, bronzed classic features set in serious lines, he was devastatingly handsome.

'May I come in?' Leandro studied her intently. She had turned pale, her shock at his appearance palpable. Emerald eyes bright as jewels glanced evasively off his, her wealth of black curls tumbling down past slight shoulders now rigid with tension. She was wearing a shapeless garment liberally daubed with clay.

'Why? What do you want?'

Leandro quirked a brow at her intonation. She was a rough diamond in the manners department. 'To see you—what else?'

Molly let him in only because she didn't want to start an argument with him on the doorstep. He had no right to come to her home, a voice screamed inside her head. She felt cornered and her brain cells felt as though they had been frozen into inactivity. When she caught a glimpse of the vast car sitting out on the street, her jaw simply dropped. 'Does that limousine belong to you?'

'Sì…yes.' Leandro settled the ice bucket he was carrying into her hands, startling her. 'I thought we could share a drink.'

Dumbfounded by the gesture and clutching the bucket awkwardly, Molly stared fixedly down at the bottle protruding from the ice. It was very expensive bubbly, the very best: Bollinger Blanc de Noir. 'It's the middle of the day,' she muttered helplessly.

'So?' Brilliant dark eyes with a mesmeric glimmer of gold nailed hers head-on when she was least prepared for the collision. Her tummy flipped, butterflies fluttered and dangerous warmth surged between her thighs. For a terrifying moment she was out of control of her body and the surge of memories that she had worked so hard to suppress engulfed her in a relentless tide. But now here he was in the flesh and suddenly she was remembering his weight on her, the raw burn of his sexual possession and the wild, hot excitement of it. 'Join me for lunch, *querida*.'

'No, I'm firing stuff…in the kiln,' Molly extended unevenly. Prompted by a defiant streak of vanity, she set down the ice bucket and began to remove her overall.

Leandro thrust the front door uneasily shut behind him. His lacklustre surroundings had already shot him out of his comfort zone. 'So this is where you live,' he remarked, a lean shapely hand encompassing the dreary hallway, which was no more than a narrow passage to provide access to the rooms. Like the ugly urban street outside and the tired furnishings, it spoke of a poverty he seldom saw and had certainly never experienced.

'How on earth did you find out where I lived?' Molly questioned tautly, pushing open the door of her bedroom and going in, only because she felt trapped standing so close to a male as tall and well built as Leandro in a confined area. The lounge was Jez's private space and always messily awash with dismantled car parts, motocross magazines and beer cans.

Leandro immediately saw her personality in the vibrant splashes of colour in the room. A multicoloured earthenware parrot plaque adorned the wall next to an oriental screen. The bed was draped with a vivid blue embroidered silk shawl. The floorboards had been painted white. An onion-shaped vase with a distinctive iridescent glaze drew his attention and he lifted it. 'Yours?' he asked.

Her smile, for she was pleased that he had guessed that the piece was hers, lit her heart-shaped face with a glow of warmth that ensured she retained his attention.

Leandro relived the sensation of that lush ripe mouth pleasuring him and almost grabbed her into his arms there and then. Breathing in deep, hanging onto control of his rebellious body by a hair's breadth, he watched her step out of her flat shoes and into a pair of peep-toe polka-dot high heels that only accentuated the eccentricity of her attire. His devouring gaze zeroed in on the star tattoo etched above one fragile ankle. She wore a short black floral print dress belted to her tiny waist and black leggings that stretched only to mid-calf. Yet even though his tastes had never run to the Bohemian and he was a very conventional guy, he thought she looked incredibly sexy.

'You didn't tell me how you found out where I lived,' Molly reminded him.

'No, I didn't, did I?' Leandro fielded, his attention torn between the charms of her voluptuous mouth and the shadowy cleft visible between her high breasts when he gazed down at her. 'I had you followed home that morning—'

'You did…*what*?' Molly gasped in shock.

His level dark gaze had an unrepentant gleam. 'I told you that I wasn't prepared to lose you again, *gatita*.'

'But *followed*? By whom?'

'My security team.'

'Just how rich are you?' Molly whispered, her incredulity unhidden.

'I'll never go hungry,' Leandro quipped. 'And when I find you living like this, it only makes me more determined than ever to look after you.'

Molly lifted her chin, feline green eyes flashing an acid shade of warning in his direction as she squared up to him. 'Only children need looking after—'

'Or very beautiful women,' Leandro, who had never suffered from a lack of assurance, ignored her aggressive stance and closed his hands to her shoulders to draw her closer.

'I didn't want to see you again. I made that quite clear,' Molly told him bluntly.

Leandro backed her up against the wall and pinned her there, his hands closing over hers to imprison her. Ensnared by scorching dark golden eyes, Molly could barely get breath into her straining lungs. Her awareness of the raw masculinity of his lean powerful body soared sky-high. Her nipples pinched tight beneath her clothes, erotic heat tingling low in her pelvis. '*Dios mio!*' he growled in urgent contradiction. 'You little liar. You did want to see me again and right now, you're burning up for me.'

Molly's knees were wobbling, but she continued to fight. 'You have quite an opinion of yourself—'

'Why not?' His brilliant eyes burned with unholy amusement as he bent down to her level to murmur huskily, his breath stirring the curls at her temples, 'Didn't you give me good cause that night?'

A hot, mortifying wave of guilty pink washed Molly's delicate features. 'I don't want to talk about that—'

'Talking in the bedroom is a heavily overrated pursuit, *querida*.' With a hungry groan of impatience, Leandro hauled her up to him and crushed her soft, pouting lips with ravenous urgency beneath his. As he banded both arms about her slight body to hold her to him she wrapped her arms round his neck, her breath rasping in her throat and her heart pounding inside her chest. She had forgotten how incredible he tasted and the sheer extent of the primal rush of excitement he could induce just by plunging his tongue into her mouth. He did it again and again too, racking her with desire and enforcing his sensual dominance.

There was no thought of denial in Molly's head. His deep drugging kisses and the lancing invasion of his tongue destroyed her defences and brought her treacherous body stingingly back to life. She wanted more. She told herself that in a couple of minutes she would push him away, tell him to leave, spell out the news that he had picked on the wrong woman. Just another minute, she bargained helplessly with herself while his skilful hands shaped the tender thrust of her breasts and sent a piercing arrow of longing zinging from her sensitised nipples to the damp core at the heart of her.

She writhed under him, frustrated by the barrier of their clothes. Her hunger for him was like a leaping flame tormenting her from inside her own skin. And evidently fully aware of the unbearable ache that was building up inside her, he cupped her mound beneath the leggings, making her gasp and moan and part her slender thighs in encouragement. The power of her own wanton response shattered her.

'You want me very much, *gatita*,' Leandro husked thickly, his hot appreciative gaze pinned to her. 'And you make me want as I didn't know I could want all the time.'

All the time, three crucial little words that jolted Molly, for she was facing the same challenge. She couldn't get him out of her head, day or night. It was as if she had caught a virus for which there was no cure. He pressed his mouth to the unbelievably tender skin below her ear and used the graze of his teeth to make her gasp and quiver, while he fought through layers of clinging fabric to touch her where she most craved his touch. Her spine arched, her body jackknifing, a cry of helpless pleasure escaping her when he found the hot, moist cleft that revealed her response. She was desperate for his caresses, her breath sobbing in her throat while she twisted and turned beneath the sensuous stroke of his fingers. The excitement built so fast she couldn't catch up with it. Instead she was wholly at the mercy of exquisite sensation while the knot of need tightening low in her stomach coiled ever tighter.

'Stop fighting it,' Leandro urged rawly, devouring the expressions on her passion-glazed features and the thrashing abandonment of her excitement.

She couldn't find a voice to answer him with. Control was long gone. He pushed a single finger into her tight entrance and suddenly she lost it completely, flying into the sun with an ecstatic cry while ripples of ever-spreading wondrous pleasure spread out from her pelvis to engulf her entire trembling body. A split second later she went into shock at what she had allowed to happen.

'Before I bury myself in your beautiful body, there's a

conversation we really must have, *querida*,' Leandro purred. 'I'll get the champagne.'

With frantic hands, Molly put her clothing back in order while her treacherous body continued to sing and tingle with sensual euphoria. She was convinced she would never look Leandro in the face again. She had intended to throw him out and instead she had allowed him to give her a mind-blowing orgasm. There was no explaining that, no going back from that point to a claim of coolness. He had made a bonfire of her nonsensical rejection and trampled her pride in the ashes.

'Glasses?' Leandro prompted silkily when he reappeared to set the ice bucket down on the dresser.

Shame engulfing her in a tidal wave, Molly slid off the bed in an eel-like motion. 'I realise that I'm giving you very mixed messages, but I really don't want to go to bed with you again,' she proclaimed in a tight defensive tone.

Leandro dealt her an amused appraisal, knowing that he would cherish the past few minutes for a very long time. She was blushing like a schoolgirl, her lack of sophistication never more obvious to him or more appealing. 'I'm not fixated on beds, *querida*. The way I'm feeling right now, anywhere will do, any *way*,' he savoured softly, heightening her colour with his intimate tone. 'Glasses?'

'I don't have any.' Molly backed away from the bed much as if it was the scene of the crime. 'What was the conversation you said we had to have?'

Leandro tensed at that timely reminder and then breathed in deep. 'On the night that we met I didn't use condoms when we made love. Are you using any contraception?'

Molly stared at him, alarm bells jangling noisily inside her head in tune with startled shock waves of dismay and anger. 'No,' she admitted tightly. 'But I assumed that *you* did.'

'I'm afraid not, but I think it's unlikely that you will conceive,' Leandro admitted in a calm, dismissive tone of finality that only inflamed her temper more. 'I assume you have no idea one way or the other as yet?'

'You assume right and I'm glad to know that you're not losing any sleep over the risks you took with *my* body and *my* future!' Molly slung at him in furious attack. 'But the risk of falling pregnant is not just something that I can shrug off and hope for the best about. How could you be so careless?'

His lean, strong face was unreadable, his brilliant dark eyes semi-screened by his luxuriant black fringe of lashes. 'It took two of us to be careless,' he reminded her drily.

Molly threw her head back abruptly as though he had slapped her. 'You're a lot more experienced than I am. I was in an unfamiliar situation and I just didn't think of that angle—what's your excuse?'

Leandro shot her a sardonic appraisal. 'I don't make excuses. I made an oversight for which I apologise. If there's a problem, we'll face it together and I will give you my full support, but I seriously doubt that that necessity will arise.'

Molly wondered angrily why he was so infuriatingly confident that there would not be consequences. Did he lead a charmed life in which nothing ever went badly wrong for him? He had made love to her three times. Didn't he appreciate that she was young and fertile?

'I do not want to be pregnant!' she told him vehemently. 'In fact the very idea of it terrifies me—'

'This is my problem as well,' Leandro cut in forcefully.

'But I can't dismiss it as easily as you appear to. Maybe
because I know that the world is not a forgiving place for
a child who is born against other people's wishes, a child
whose very existence may cause offence—'

His ebony brows had pleated in a bemused frown as she
became increasingly emotional. '*Qué demonios*? What
are you trying to say to me?'

'I'm illegitimate and the result of my mother's affair
with someone else's husband,' Molly spelt out grittily, her
slim hands tightening into taut fists of constraint by her
sides. 'My mother died when I was nine and my grandmother took charge of my older half-sister and me. My
sister was born within a marriage. My grandmother
handed me over to social services for adoption because,
as far as she was concerned, I was an embarrassment who
should never have been born.'

Leandro was more unsettled than he was prepared to
admit by that sad little tale. He knew that births had been
concealed and most probably worse had happened in his
own family's history over the centuries. He also knew that
even in today's more liberal society, respectability and
other people's opinions still remained his mother's most
pressing concern. She kept his younger sister, Julieta, on
a tight social leash, fearful that too much freedom would
lead to embarrassing media headlines.

'I'm sorry that you had that experience—'

'Talk's cheap!' Molly sizzled back at him. 'But I don't
want any child of mine to suffer that kind of rejection.'

'There won't be a child. Let's tackle trouble if it comes, not look for it in advance,' Leandro advised drily.

'But what are you going to do if I *am* pregnant?' Molly spun away, her voice shrill with her angry distress, for she knew that the fragile foundations of her security would be utterly destroyed by the advent of single parenthood. She worked unsocial hours in a casual job without prospects. There was no room for childcare in her tight budget, no supportive family circle to help out and she knew all too well how hard it was to raise children alone, for hadn't her birth mother failed dismally at the same task?

'We'll tackle that when and if it happens. Are you always such a pessimist?' Leandro enquired with silken derision, exasperated by her angry attack over the risk of something that he was convinced was unlikely to happen. 'Such a tragedy-queen?'

A furious flush lit Molly's cheeks at that crack and she stepped forward. 'How dare you?' she snapped. 'This is my life we're talking about in the balance, not yours. So I want to know where I stand. Why shouldn't I? I'm pretty sure that the best you'll offer me in a tight corner will be the cash for a termination!'

His lean, darkly handsome face clenched with distaste. A storm of outrage roared through Leandro. 'How dare you make such an assumption?' he demanded in a seething undertone. 'That is not how I would behave.'

'Well, whatever!' Molly shot back at him, her furious distress undiminished by that assurance. 'Let's hope we never have to explore that predicament.'

Leandro had had more than enough drama for one morning and he refused to be the ongoing target of her resentment and disdain. His lean, strong face was etched into forbidding lines and his stunning eyes were hot with indignation. 'When are you planning to take responsibility for your own behaviour? And stop trying to blame me for it?'

Mortified colour washed Molly's face, for he hit right home with that rejoinder. 'Right now, all I want is for you to leave—'

'Don't worry,' Leandro derided. 'I have no desire to stay.'

Just at that moment the bedroom door opened and framed Jez's broad, solid frame. He stared at her and Leandro with frowning blue eyes. 'Why are you shouting, Molly? What's going on in here?'

'Leandro was just about to leave,' Molly snapped.

'I'm Jez Andrews, Molly's friend,' Jez addressed Leandro while at the same time taking up a protective stance beside Molly. 'I think you should do as she asks and go now.'

Leandro was taken aback by the sudden appearance of another male and aggressive instincts threatened his rigid self-discipline. He was quick to recognise the possessive light in the younger man's expression. Annoyance and suspicion slivered through Leandro, for it was not only obvious that Molly and Jez lived below the same roof but also that they were on familiar terms with each other.

'You know how to get in touch with me if you need to,' Leandro drawled in a tone of pure ice.

Molly was frozen where she stood until she heard the slam of the front door. Then she crumpled and tears rained down her face. Even while she fought to get a grip on herself, all the pent-up emotions of recent days were taking their toll and overflowing. Unused to her crying, Jez wrapped his arms round her in an awkward hug.

'Who on earth was that bloke?' Jez demanded when she had calmed down a little. 'And what's he got to do with you?'

After that, the whole story came tumbling out because Molly was so unnerved by the fear that she might fall pregnant she just had to get her feelings off her chest there and then. Before her reddened eyes, Jez's expression grew more and more censorious. Although he said nothing and uttered no criticism, his surprise at her behaviour spoke volumes and pierced her pride. He was, however, a good deal more vocal when it came to Leandro.

'A girl like you doesn't belong in a limo.' Jez saw her wince and hastened to add, 'A bloke with that kind of money could only be messing around with you because he's bored with his own kind.'

Jez had a shrewd streak about people that Molly respected. 'Imagine asking me to be his mistress, though!' she framed with a humourless laugh. 'Do I look the ornamental type?'

'I wish I'd thumped him,' Jez growled, unamused. 'You can do a hell of a lot better than him—'

'Not if I fall pregnant,' Molly interposed with a shiver of fear. 'If I end up with a baby my whole life and my prospects go right down the tubes. I'll never stop struggling to survive.'

'Let's hope for the best,' Jez advised stonily, his face tightening while he considered that possibility. 'You know, I always used to think that eventually you and I might get together.'

Molly settled dismayed eyes on him, for it had never occurred to her that he might look on her as anything other than an honorary sister. 'But we're *friends*—'

'Yes, well.' Jez shrugged defensively. 'Why shouldn't friendship be the first step in something more? We get on well. We know each other right through. There'd be no nasty surprises. It would have made a lot of sense.'

'Don't say any more,' Molly urged unhappily, for she had never once considered Jez in that light. 'All you're doing is reminding me that getting involved with Leandro was like giving way to a sudden attack of madness.'

'No point beating yourself up about it,' the heavily built blond man pointed out in a tone of practicality. 'That won't change anything.'

Molly attended two craft fairs that weekend and the sale of several pieces of pottery lifted her spirits. As the following week wore on her mood steadily declined when her menstrual cycle failed to deliver the reassurance she sought. She was working long hours and her usual energy seemed strangely absent. She began feeling incredibly tired at about the same time as she started feeling nauseous and off her food. Anxiety took her over then, because she feared the worst and the shadows below her eyes deepened while she lay awake at night fretting. She was planning to go out and buy a pregnancy test when Jez persuaded her to go to the doctor instead to get a more reliable diagnosis.

The doctor was very thorough and he assured her that there was no doubt that she was carrying her first child. Although Molly had believed she was prepared for that possibility, she was devastated when her biggest fear was confirmed. Jez phoned her from his workshop to ask the result and she gave it in a deadened voice, staring at her reflection in the hall mirror while she tried and failed to imagine her slender body swollen with pregnancy.

A baby, a real living, breathing, crying baby, would be looking to her for total support in less than nine months' time. A termination wasn't an option for her. Her own mother had given her the chance of life in equally unpromising circumstances and Cathy had done her best, even if her best hadn't been that great. Could she herself do any less for her own child? She dug out Leandro's business card and decided to send him a text message, because she really couldn't face speaking to him just at that moment and when they had parted on such bad terms.

'I need to see you URGENTLY.'

In the conference room of the Carrera bank where he was involved in a meeting, Leandro read the message and appreciated the appeal of the block capitals. He was convinced that she had discovered that she was not pregnant and now wanted to tell him that she was sorry for making such a fuss. He walked into his office to phone her.

'Join me for dinner tonight,' he suggested. 'I'll send a car to pick you up at eight.'

Molly winced at the prospect of breaking her news over a dining table and then scolded herself for caring about such a triviality. He was as much to blame as she was for the development, so why was she getting all worked up at the prospect of telling him?

When Jez came home from work, he joined her in the kitchen. 'How do you feel?' he enquired awkwardly.

'Like I want to kick myself for being so stupid,' she told him truthfully.

'Have you told *him* yet?'

'I'm telling Leandro tonight—not that I expect that will make much difference to my plans—'

'You already have plans?' Jez queried.

'Just getting on with life as best I can,' Molly muttered dully.

Jez reached for her hand where it was clenched on the edge of the sink. 'But you don't have to do it alone…'

Molly looked up him uncertainly. 'What do you mean?'

Jez breathed in slow and deep. 'I've thought hard about this since we had our conversation, so take a minute and think about it before you say no. I'm willing to marry you and bring up the kid as my own—'

Molly was astonished by that suggestion. 'Jez, for goodness sake, I wouldn't let you sacrifice yourself like that—'

'I want to help, Molly. Together we could make a good team,' the blond man reasoned earnestly. 'I'm not expecting you to love me but, in time, I'm sure we'd become closer.'

Tears were clogging Molly's throat and she was too choked up to speak. His generosity was almost too much for her to bear. She grasped both his hands in hers and squeezed them to express her feelings. But for the first time she didn't feel she could say anything she liked to Jez because she now knew that he thought of her as more than a friend and cherished hopes that she could not fulfil. She loved and trusted him, but she wasn't attracted to him and felt that anything other than platonic friendship would be doomed by that fact.

'You're too kind for your own good,' she told him chokily and she went off to get dressed, feeling more than ever as though her security was breaking up beneath her feet. How could she possibly remain living in Jez's home now? It wouldn't be fair to him if she stayed on. He was too involved in her life and it wasn't healthy. He was less likely to make the effort to meet someone else while she was still around, she acknowledged unhappily.

Dead on the hour of eight, a uniformed chauffeur rang the bell to tell her that the limousine was waiting for her…

CHAPTER FIVE

LEANDRO watched Molly cross the restaurant. Male heads turned and followed her progress. Her dress was unremarkable, fitted enough to hug her rounded breasts and just short enough to reveal shapely knees and accentuate the high heels she favoured to combat her diminutive height. But the men didn't stop looking and neither did he. Maybe it was that eye-catching waterfall of jet-black curls, the enormous emerald green eyes and that full quivering pink mouth that he only had to look at to get hard and ready. A woman hadn't affected him that way since the teenage years when fantasy had driven his hormones and that simple fact still annoyed the hell out of him.

'This is a really fashionable place,' Molly remarked unevenly, striving not to stare at him and allow his magnetic attraction to influence her. But he looked drop dead gorgeous in a light grey suit and sky blue silk tie and her heartbeat quickened to a trot and her pulses quickened even before she sat down at the quiet corner table.

'I often eat here in the evening. It's quicker than ordering food in,' Leandro responded. 'You look beautiful, *querida*.'

Stiff as an iron bar trying to bend, Molly rearranged the salt and pepper and shook her head in immediate disagreement. 'No, I don't. I assumed you'd want to eat somewhere quieter, the sort of place we could talk.'

Talk? Leandro did not like the ominous sound of that word. His needs and wishes were the height of masculine simplicity: he wanted to feast his eyes on her and take her home with him at the end of the meal. Her cloaked appraisal, however, set his even white teeth on edge and made him commence their meal with a leading question. 'Isn't it time you told me about Jez?'

Alerted by the tough edge to his tone, Molly lifted her head from the menu she was studying. 'Why do you think that?'

His dark eyes were hard as granite. 'You're obviously on very familiar terms with him. How does he fit into your life?'

'He's my best friend,' Molly confided. 'He owns the house so he's also my landlord.'

Leandro had never had much faith in platonic male and female friendships and his conviction that Jez had a more personal interest in Molly was not dispelled by that explanation. 'He behaved more like a man guarding his turf and warning off the competition—like a boyfriend.'

Uneasy colour warmed her cheeks. It bothered her that Leandro had only had to meet Jez once to immediately question the calibre of their friendship. Was that a tribute to Leandro's shrewd grasp of human nature? Or a sign that he was the jealous type? 'Jez is very fond of me,' she said defensively, 'but there's never been anything else between us. We've known each other since we were in foster care together as kids.'

'I thought you were adopted,' Leandro countered.

'Not for very long. I was older—there weren't many takers. An older couple who already had a son took me because they wanted a daughter. My adoptive father died of a heart attack six months after I moved in,' Molly explained ruefully. 'My adoptive mother got very depressed and decided she had enough to handle without taking on an extra child. I was back in foster care by the end of the year.'

Leandro could only think of his own privileged childhood. He had been encouraged to believe that, as heir to a massive estate and centuries of proud heritage, he was the most important little person in the household. Long, lonely stretches at boarding school had contrasted with an excess of luxury and attention during the holidays.

'That must have been hard on you,' he remarked.

Molly lifted and dropped a thin shoulder. 'I survived. I'm quite a strong character, Leandro. I don't think you see that in me.'

Leandro measured the resolute angle of her pointed chin and the light of challenge in her clear gaze and vented a sardonic laugh of disagreement. He wondered how he had contrived to stumble on one of the very few young women in Europe who wouldn't snatch at the opportunity to have a billionaire make all her material dreams come true. 'Don't I?' he traded drily. 'I find you very argumentative.'

At that inopportune moment the waiter appeared to pour the wine. Annoyed by Leandro's censure, Molly put a hand over her glass and requested a soda and lime instead. When they were alone again, she snapped, 'I am *not* argumentative!'

'I don't stage rows in public places,' Leandro delivered with contemptuous cool. 'Raise your voice again and I walk out of here.'

'I really could throw something at you at this moment,' Molly confided in a shaken undertone; she was taken aback by the sizzling strength of her annoyance.

'Don't try that either,' Leandro warned her with a freezing glance that chilled her fury with the efficiency of a bucket of ice.

'In my experience, most men walk the other way when things get difficult,' Molly rejoined with a scornful shift of her dark head.

'I'm incredibly tough.' His strong jaw line hardened while his brilliant dark golden eyes lit on her like burning flames. 'Your problem is that you want me but you can't handle it, *gatita*.'

'That is absolutely not true!' Molly protested, staring back at him in as frozen a manner as she could contrive while desperate to get the dialogue back on track.

'The truth can hurt,' Leandro drawled smooth as silk, thick black lashes low over his acute gaze.

Molly shifted like a butterfly stabbed by a display pin. 'Haven't you already guessed why I contacted you?' she pressed, the tip of her tongue stealing out to moisten her plump lower lip.

That little play with her tongue sent an erotic thrill arrowing straight to Leandro's groin. 'You were keen to reassure me that you're fine and we have nothing to worry about?' he suggested.

Molly tensed at that unfortunate misinterpretation. 'No, I'm not fine in the way that you mean.'

The waiter reappeared to take their order while Leandro wondered what on earth she was talking about because he could not believe that she might be pregnant.

'Meaning?' he prompted.

Molly could not comprehend why he was being so obtuse. 'Isn't it obvious? I saw a doctor today, Leandro. I'm going to have a baby!'

Leandro studied her in brooding silence, transfixed by that staggering claim. He had almost but not quite come to terms with the suspicion that he was infertile and would never father a child. He had planned to go for tests some time and find out for sure. Molly's announcement hit him like a bolt from the blue and stunned him. His lean, darkly handsome face clenched and he paled as he studied her, marvelling at her words while wondering what she could possibly hope to gain from a lie.

'All right, so you're shocked. Well, so was I, but there's no doubt and no mistake. I am very definitely pregnant,' Molly spelt out, enunciating each word of that affirmation with care.

Leandro veiled his stunned eyes. Was it possible that he could father a child? It was true that Aloise had failed to conceive, but his late wife had also refused to pursue the matter with her gynaecologist. Could one random night turn his world upside down? Could Molly's tiny frame be carrying his baby? For a split second, a primitive leap of satisfaction and relief lanced through him that he was not, after all, unable to ensure the continuation of the family name. Squashing that leap of satisfaction, he surveyed her with impenetrable dark eyes, fierce tension thrumming through his big, powerful body. If she did prove to be pregnant, he would have to marry her for the baby's sake. He could see no other solution to the situation. Unfortunately, Leandro was in no hurry to marry again. One taste of freedom, he reflected grimly, and then it was gone. It was a shame that he hadn't made the most of his liberty while he still had it.

'Say something,' Molly urged unhappily.

'This is not the place to discuss such a private matter. We'll talk at my apartment after we've eaten.'

For the first time Molly fully appreciated how skilled Leandro was at controlling his emotions and concealing his reactions. No expression that she could interpret crossed his lean, bronzed features. That comprehensive reserve and self-discipline unnerved Molly, who wore her feelings on the surface and rarely hesitated to express them.

The fish course that Leandro had selected arrived at the table. Molly caught the aroma from the dish and it curdled her stomach and made her stiffen in dismay. 'Certain smells make me feel sick,' she confided.

And that was the last conversation they had for some time, for Molly fought the nausea until she could bear it no longer and then abandoned the table to flee to the cloakroom. Leandro took the hint and had the fish removed. The minutes ticked past. Eventually he asked one of the serving staff to check that Molly was all right. Soon afterwards she reappeared, looking pale as a wraith with shadows lying like faint purple bruises below her eyes.

'Sorry, I'm really not hungry now,' she muttered, pushing her plate away untouched.

Leandro suggested that they leave. She protested that

he hadn't eaten. He said he wasn't hungry either and it was true. His appetite had vanished. He felt like the condemned man at his last supper and even that final meal had been denied him. But he knew what his duty was, and with a supportive arm banded to her slight figure, he escorted her out of the restaurant. Outside, he stilled in surprise when several cameras went off and Molly shrank in dismay against him. His security team had been caught unawares and had neglected to warn him because it was a long time since Leandro had done anything to attract the attention of the paparazzi. He was annoyed by that renewed interest at the optimum wrong moment in his life. It was certainly not the instant he would have chosen to introduce Molly to the public eye.

'I want you to see a doctor,' Leandro announced in the limo.

'It's just morning sickness—'

'It's half past nine in the evening,' he objected.

'Well, apparently it works like that with some people. It doesn't mean anything's wrong. I just have to put up with it,' she replied.

Leandro studied her slender figure. There wasn't much of her to study and concern assailed him, for she didn't seem strong enough to survive missing many meals. His innate sense of practicality was already processing the concept of making a second marriage and doing so at speed. What choice did he have? He owed a duty of care towards Molly and their unborn child. He owed it to his family name. But that didn't mean that he had to *like* the prospect of surrendering his freedom again. Even so, if he came out of it with the next generation in the family secured, perhaps it would be worth the sacrifice, he reasoned grimly.

Nervous as a cat, Molly watched Leandro restively pace the floor in the elegant main reception room of his apartment. The lights of the city illuminated the darkness beyond the floor-deep windows. He might not have said one word out of place, but even he could not hide his tension. She found it hard to look away from him. It seemed juvenile to her to still be thinking of how gorgeous he was, but she couldn't help it. His chiselled masculine features and his spectacular heavily lashed dark eyes grabbed her attention with embarrassing ease. Encountering her anxious gaze, he strode forward.

'Once you've had the pregnancy confirmed, we'll get married as soon as it can be arranged.'

Molly blinked in astonishment. 'You can't be serious. You hardly know me—'

'You're carrying my baby and it's expected. That's all I need to know for the moment. If the baby is a boy, he will be my heir and the next Duke of Sandoval—'

Her bright eyes widened in amazement. 'There's a title in your family?'

Leandro nodded.

'So who's the current duke?'

'I am, but I only use the title at home.'

Molly had suddenly become as stiff as if she had had a poker strapped to her spine. 'You're a duke…and you're asking me to marry you?'

'I'm not giving you a choice on this. You cannot bring up any child of mine alone,' Leandro breathed tautly. 'I want my child to grow up in my home with his family and to speak my language. We can only achieve that end by becoming man and wife.'

'But you're still getting over your last wife,' Molly mumbled. But as soon as she had spoken and noticed his face shadow she wished she had kept that thought to herself.

'I'm not an emotional man, *querida*. Nor do I make tasteless comparisons. I find you extremely attractive and see no reason why we shouldn't have a successful marriage.'

Unnerved by his dispassionate outlook, Molly shook her head slowly. 'I want to be loved by the man I marry.'

Leandro released his breath in a slow hiss of frustration. 'I can't give you love,' he responded without hesitation.

He was a duke, a *real* Spanish duke, and Molly was horrified by that revelation, for she could not imagine how someone as ordinary as she believed herself to be could possibly become the wife of a man of such wealth and high status. 'I respect your sense of commitment towards the baby,' she told him tensely.

'And to you, *querida*,' Leandro added, reaching down to close her hands into his and urge her up out of her seat.

Her mouth ran dry as he drew her close. 'Only a couple of weeks ago the only thing you thought I was good enough for was being your mistress. If I couldn't even make it into the girlfriend category, how can you sincerely say that you want to marry me?'

Leandro was already picturing her in his gilded four-poster bed at the *castillo*, a seductive image that acted as an opportune sweetener to his reluctance to remarry. He stared down at her with hot dark golden eyes that made her feel overheated and dizzy. 'My libido isn't fussy about labels. I want you, regardless of who you are.'

Molly trembled in contact with his muscular, powerfully aroused body. He desired her and she could feel the unashamed evidence of his desire. But was a hunger that left her boneless sufficient to base a marriage on?

'It would be diplomatic to forget that I once invited you to be my mistress. If you're having my baby, that is no longer feasible,' Leandro completed.

'You're determined that the baby should have your name?'

'Do you want your child to be illegitimate?'

Molly lost colour and dropped her expressive eyes. 'No, I don't, but I don't want to make a hasty marriage that I live to regret either.'

Leandro surveyed her with considerable coolness, for he had expected—not unnaturally in his own opinion—a much more enthusiastic response to his proposal. Few women in her position would have hesitated. What was her problem? What was holding her back? The blond guy with the oil stains on his hands?

'There will be no possibility of a divorce,' Leandro added.

Molly was impressed rather than put off by that statement, for she didn't want to trust her future to a man likely to give up on his marital vows at the first hurdle. She didn't want empty promises from him either. But though he couldn't offer her love he could give her other things. Marriage to Leandro would bring financial security and every material advantage her child could ever want. Even more crucially, it would also give her child a father, indeed a normal two parent family. Possibly, she reflected uncertainly, she should be thinking about what such a marriage would do for their child, rather than what it would do for her on a more personal basis.

'Molly...what's your answer?' Leandro pressed.

Molly was all flustered. 'I need time to think—'

'But we haven't got time. What do you have to think about?' Leandro demanded imperiously.

'That you even ask that question reveals the depth of your arrogance,' Molly murmured tautly.

Dark eyes cold as ice, his fabulous bone structure hardened. 'I won't accept a negative response, *querida*. If you won't marry me, I'll be forced to fight you in court for custody of our child.'

The speed with which he resorted to that threat shocked Molly. Aware that he was watching her every move like a hawk, she backed away from him. 'Are you trying to intimidate me?'

'No. I'm telling you the truth. I'm telling you what will happen if you don't marry me. Do you expect me to lie?' Leandro raked back at her drily. 'You need all the facts before you can make a sensible decision.'

'You would actually try to take my baby away from me?' Molly was appalled by that threat that sunk like a deep chill into her bones.

Leandro closed a confident hand round her wrist to prevent her from retreating further. 'I think you're too sensible to go to the wall on this. I believe you'll reach the right decision for all of us.'

But his ruthlessness shook her rigid. She was as unprepared for it as she had been for the mistress proposition he had put to her two weeks earlier. Suddenly she was appreciating how misleading his cool façade and exquisite manners were. Below the skin, Leandro was every bit as aggressive, dominant and cruel in his instincts as a street fighter protecting his territory.

'I'd like to go home now,' she told him flatly.

'In the morning we'll have your pregnancy confirmed and you'll give me an answer. But first,' Leandro breathed, pulling her to him.

Molly meant to resist and imitate a wax dummy in his arms but the hot hard hunger of his sensual mouth and the erotic plunge of his tongue sent wanton excitement roaring through her in a relentless tidal wave. She clutched at his jacket to steady herself. She was out of breath and her knees were wobbling and a forbidden ache of emptiness was stirring between her slender thighs.

'You don't want to go home, *querida*,' Leandro murmured silkily.

Molly wanted to either slap him or scream at him, but knew that either response would merely make her look childish and out of control. He watched her with smouldering dark eyes and, although every treacherous fibre of her being urged her to fling herself back into his arms, she withstood the temptation. Unfortunately the thought of another night in bed with him banished all coherent thought and conscience and made her hate herself. Winning that mental battle with herself still felt like losing because he was right on one score: she didn't want to leave him.

Jez intercepted her in the hall when she walked through the front door. *'Well?'*

'Leandro asked me to marry him.'

Jez was visibly taken aback.

Molly registered that she was secretly pleased that Leandro had contrived to confound her friend's expectations. 'I said I'd give him my answer tomorrow.'

Jez grimaced. 'You're infatuated with him. You're hardly going to say no.'

Molly flung her head high. 'He's the father of my baby. Shouldn't I at least give him a chance?'

She couldn't get to sleep that night. Was she infatuated with Leandro Carrera Marquez? She supposed she was, because from the hour of their meeting she hadn't been able to get him out of her head for longer than five minutes. Lying there, she relived the fiery heat of his mouth on hers and discovered that it only made her long for a more intimate connection. Ashamed of her craving for his touch, she buried her face in the pillow. He had threatened her with a custody battle. He had made it very clear that he wanted the child she carried, whether it was born in or out of marriage, and shouldn't she respect him for that? She did not want to raise her child alone. She could not offer her baby the security, comfort or advantages that marriage to Leandro would bring. How could she possibly say no to him?

And yet to marry a man she hardly knew and move to another country, another culture, when she did not even speak the language would also be a great challenge. It certainly wouldn't be the easy option, she recognized heavily. In addition, she would be a second wife and she wasn't entirely sure that she fancied that role, of filling a position previously held by a predecessor. He had said comparisons were tasteless, but did that simply mean that she could not compare on any level to his first bride? Or was she being paranoid? Paranoid, Molly decided for herself. In truth she didn't want Leandro to have *ever* been with another woman, much less have cared enough to marry one.

He picked her up shortly after ten the following morning and accompanied her to an appointment with a gynaecologist in Harley Street. A pregnancy test confirmed what she already knew. She was scolded for being so thin, which annoyed her intensely since that was her natural state of being and she ate like a horse as a rule.

'You're not supposed to argue with your consultant,' Leandro censured when she climbed back into his limousine.

Molly tossed her head, black curls rippling across her shoulders 'Well, you did say how argumentative I was,' she reminded him flippantly. 'I'm small and skinny. I was *born* small and skinny, get used to it!'

'Will I be getting the opportunity…to get used to you being small and skinny?' Leandro enquired lazily, brilliant dark eyes nailed to her cross face. In a short-sleeved colourful blouse and a denim skirt, she looked barely old enough to be out of her teens and struck him as being almost as volatile.

Molly turned her head, emerald green eyes very bright and challenging. 'You didn't give me much choice when you threatened to go to court for a custody battle—'

'So, that's a *yes*?'

Still playing it cool and unconcerned, Molly shrugged agreement.

'I'm not very fond of weddings,' Leandro admitted with a crashing lack of tact. 'I'd like a discreet church ceremony to be held here with only witnesses present before we fly straight out to Spain.'

Molly was not impressed. He didn't seem to care about what she might want. So he had been married before and all that bridal hoopla was a bore to him, but she was hoping to only marry once and she would have preferred a proper wedding. Impervious to her lack of enthusiasm, he took her to an exclusive jeweler to choose wedding rings. Lunch at an exclusive hotel followed. But by then her silence was really getting on his nerves. 'What's wrong with you?' he asked icily.

'You're so bossy, it's intolerable. I don't know whether I'm back at school or in prison because you never stop telling me what to do and how things will be,' she complained.

'You should speak up,' declared the man who had already called her argumentative. 'I have a naturally authoritative streak.'

'I'm naturally defiant.'

Leandro dealt her a measuring look. 'Then we will clash.'

But over the following ten days there was little chance of the prospective bride and groom clashing because Leandro returned to Spain on business and occasional phone calls were their only means of communication. Generally, an aide passed on Leandro's instructions during his absence. She signed a pre-nuptial agreement, gave up her job and began packing up her life in London. Leandro sent her a credit card and told her go shopping for an outfit for the wedding and also clothes to wear in a warmer climate. She went to Harrods and bought herself a wedding dress with his money. He had suggested something, 'elegant and sober', but she ignored his advice completely and fell for a white lace corset top teamed with a gloriously full skirt and towering high-heeled shoes.

When she got home that day she found an intriguing letter in her post. From a leading City lawyers' office, it invited her to attend an appointment to discuss a confidential matter. Curious about why such mystery should be necessary, she rang to make enquiries but could gain no further information on the phone.

'Do you think it might be someone in your birth family trying to get in touch with you?' Jez enquired. 'Or an inheritance from them?'

'I doubt it. There was only my sister and my grandmother left, and she handed me over to social services,' she reminded him ruefully.

But curiosity and her undeniable hope that against all odds her relatives *were* attempting to reconnect with her ensured that Molly attended the appointment. She was shown into a smart office and greeted by Elena Carson, a svelte lawyer in her thirties, who invited her to take a seat.

'I understand you're soon to be married, Miss Chapman.'

'Yes.' Molly frowned, immediately wondering how the other woman had come by that information and why it was even being mentioned.

'I must ask you to be patient while I explain why you've been invited to come here today,' the brunette advanced smoothly. 'My client wishes to remain anonymous and has engaged me to approach you with a generous financial offer.'

'A *financial* offer?' Molly questioned in bewilderment. Disappointment settled over her like a fog that blocked the sunlight. Self-evidently, the appointment had nothing to do with her blood relatives and she felt foolish for ever having cherished the hope that it had.

'My client wants to stop your marriage taking place,' Elena Carson explained.

Struggling to focus on that startling admission, Molly gave the brunette a stunned appraisal. '*Stop* my marriage?'

'My client is aware that it would be a very advantageous marriage from your point of view and is willing to give you a large sum of money to compensate you for changing your mind,' the lawyer delivered calmly.

In shock, Molly parted dry lips and slowly folded them shut again. Someone wanted to pay her not to marry Leandro? Who? A member of his family? Another woman with designs on him?

'I'm not interested in changing my mind,' she replied without hesitation. 'Have you thought about how hard it might be to fit into a titled Spanish family, who can trace their ancestors back to the fifteenth century? Have you thought about how difficult it might be to live up to your future husband's high standards?'

Molly was steadily reddening with anger. 'I don't want to listen to any more of this nonsense. If Leandro was a king, I would feel equal to the challenge, because he is the father of my baby and I assume that he knew exactly what he was doing when he asked me to be his wife!' she heard herself proclaim heatedly, only to inwardly squirm a second later at what she had given away with that outburst.

The other woman, however, did not bat an eyelash. 'My client wants to act in everyone's best interests and recognises that you would be making a considerable sacrifice in choosing not to go ahead with the marriage—'

'Oh, does he…or is it, does she?' Molly interrupted furiously as she shot to her feet.

'And on that basis is prepared to offer you two million pounds towards making a new life for yourself somewhere else and never contacting Mr Carrera Marquez again,' the older woman stated with complete cool.

'As I'm not marrying Leandro for his money, you can't use money as a bribe to persuade me not to marry him!' Molly proclaimed with angry pride.

'That was not my client's intent, Miss Chapman. My client is aware that you are expecting a child and wishes to ensure that both you and your child will enjoy a secure future. You should consider the offer. It has been suggested that if you sign or have already signed a pre-nuptial agreement with your fiancé, you might well receive a great deal less money in any divorce settlement.'

Having signed such an agreement a couple of days previously, Molly was well aware of that fact. In short, any act of adultery, desertion or what was hazily termed 'unreasonable behaviour' during the course of their marriage would result in her instant impoverishment. But Molly was desperate to know who was prepared to offer such a vast amount of money to prevent her from marrying Leandro in the first place. The solicitor, however, refused to divulge that information. It outraged Molly to be kept in the dark when it was obvious that what she considered to be her own private business was clearly very far from being private. How many people had Leandro told about her pregnancy? And if she informed him about the offer that had been made to her, would he know who was behind it?

With only forty-eight hours to go before the wedding, Molly barely slept that night while she agonised over whether or not to tell Leandro. What if it was someone in his own family who was trying to buy her off and persuade her to disappear? With the kind of money involved she could only think that the culprit was most likely to be a close relative of his. Leandro would be outraged. Did she really want to risk causing that amount of trouble and strife within the family circle before she even arrived in Spain? Would it not be wiser to keep quiet for the moment and give people the chance to at least get to know her first...?

CHAPTER SIX

MOLLY examined her reflection in the wardrobe mirror from every angle.

Certainly Leandro would not be able to accuse her of looking insufficiently bridal. She had purchased every frivolous piece of finery possible for the occasion, right down to the filmy underwear and the lace garter adorned with a blue ribbon. Her dress was a fairy-tale dream of fluid organza styled over matt satin. The glass beading and metallic embroidery on the basque bodice and full skirt caught and reflected the light. Diamanté butterfly combs confined her mane of curls to the back of her head and, keen not to overdo the frills, she had added nothing else.

'Are you ready?' Jez asked. 'The limo driver is panicking. But, you know, it's not too late to change your mind.'

'I know what I'm doing,' Molly told her oldest friend. 'I want my baby to have what I never had—a *proper* home and a family.'

'Let's hope Leandro is up to the challenge,' the blond man responded drily.

'I don't think he'd be so keen to marry me if he wasn't,' Molly answered, striving to look more positive than she actually felt. The offer of a bribe not to marry Leandro had seriously dented her confidence. Was it possible that she was unsuitable as a wife for him?

Jez had agreed to act as a witness at the ceremony. Molly was glad to have her friend's support as the limo ferried them through the traffic to the church. The photographer Molly had engaged for the occasion snapped her on the church steps with her bouquet of pink rose buds and her lucky horseshoe favour and told her that she had a lovely smile. Her heartbeat was pounding frantically fast at the base of throat when she walked down the aisle with a hand braced on Jez's arm. Leandro, accompanied only by one other man, awaited her at the altar. Sheathed in a charcoal-grey pinstripe suit, which he'd teamed with an immaculate white shirt, he looked breathtakingly handsome.

Leandro, still recovering from the unexpected ordeal of having to pose or the photographer who had intercepted him outside, surveyed Molly, who looked every inch the blushing bride. Her green eyes were luminous pools in her delicate face, her pink mouth as lush as the roses she carried and as full of sensual appeal as the creamy swell of her rounded breasts above the neckline of her romantic dress. As she knelt down by his side it was a challenge for him to take his eyes from her and the tightness at his groin merely intensified.

Molly spoke her vows in a clear voice that betrayed nothing of the nervous butterflies in her tummy. She was fiercely aware of Leandro's proximity. She allowed her gaze to linger on his hard, bronzed profile and felt her pulses leap when he turned lustrous dark eyes on her as they exchanged rings. He was her husband now, she thought with a rush of disbelief at the concept when the ceremony ended. He introduced her to his lawyer, who had acted as his witness, and it took her aback that he had not asked a friend to perform the office as she had.

Both witnesses declined the invitation to join them for lunch. Jez gave her an emotional hug as he knew they were flying straight out to Spain after their meal.

'I can't believe we're married,' Molly told Leandro chattily over the lunch, which was served in a hotel suite. Having been too nauseous to eat earlier in the day, she now made up for it with a healthy appetite.

In comparison, Leandro had felt married from the instant he'd walked into the church. He was already fighting off an oppressive sense of confinement, which had not been helped by his mother's hysterical last-minute phone call pleading with him to change his mind while assuring him that he would live to regret making the biggest mistake of his life. Perhaps he had been too optimistic in expecting his family to see the sound good sense of his decision. After all, a pregnant bride met two of their expectations at once. He remained uneasily conscious, however, that when he looked at Molly her radiance and glorious curves grabbed him first and made her fertility status the very last thing on his mind.

'I suppose I'd better get changed,' she said, rising from the table.

'No…keep the dress on, *querida*.'

Molly's brows pleated. 'For the flight?'

'Why not?' Dark golden eyes hot with hunger, Leandro closed a hand over hers to pull her close and savour the fresh lemony scent that he had come to associate with her presence. 'I want to take it off you. You can change before we land.'

Colour turned her cheeks poppy-red. His sensual appraisal sent raw sexual awareness shooting through her in a responsive wave. Her nipples swelled and damp heat stirred between her thighs. He had taught her to want him and, although it annoyed her a great deal, she couldn't yet keep a lid on her desire for his touch.

'What was your last wedding like?' Molly asked on the way to the airport, while gritting her teeth and refusing to look at him. The question had been hovering at the back of her mind all day and she had kicked it off her tongue a dozen times before finally sacrificing her pride and voicing it.

Leandro froze as if she had turned a gun on him. 'I don't think we should discuss that.'

Offended by his reticence, Molly sent him a glimmering look of suspicion. 'Why not?'

Leandro breathed in deep. 'It was different—a big society wedding.'

And that was it, one sentence and he fell silent. Nevertheless, he had said enough to satisfy her curiosity. Molly wished she hadn't asked, for she was making all the tasteless comparisons he would have condemned. He had pushed out the boat without complaint for his first marriage, which really told her all she needed to know about how he viewed his second excursion into matrimony. But, then, hadn't he already displayed his indifference to her feelings most effectively? He hadn't once smiled or paid her a single compliment on the day when all women expected to feel special.

A lot of people turned to stare at her in her wedding dress at the airport. Molly ignored them, but she could feel how much Leandro disliked the scrutiny. His lean, dark features settled into grim lines and his silences got more extended. It didn't help when his security team weren't quick enough to prevent a photographer from stepping into their path and taking a flash photo of them.

'You should have let me get changed,' Molly told Leandro while he bit back a curse after having been snapped by a paparazzo.

'I thought you were enjoying the attention, *querida*,' Leandro drawled with silken derision. 'You did dress to attract it and hire a photographer to record the occasion.'

Molly breathed in so deep and long to control her temper that she was vaguely surprised that she didn't burst with the effort of holding her ire in. She did not require his dislike of public attention to warn her that the VIP lounge was not the place to start an argument with a guy who wouldn't go down without a very aggressive fight. Biding her time, she clenched her small white teeth together until they had boarded his private jet. Even while she was appreciating the sheer luxurious comfort of the cabin, she was already wondering how sound-proofed it would be as she didn't fancy their row providing entertainment for the air crew.

Layers of white organza foaming all around her, she settled into a leather seat and did up the belt.

'Possibly asking you to keep the dress on wasn't a good idea,' Leandro conceded soon after take-off.

'Oh, well, at least you didn't ask me to put a paper bag over my head and pretend I didn't know you back at the airport!' Molly snapped back.

An imperious ebony brow climbed. 'What is the meaning of that strange comment?'

'That when you criticise me for hiring a photographer, you expose just how unreal your expectations are!' Molly extended, jerking open her seat belt to plunge upright again. 'This is supposed to be my wedding day. Unlike you, I haven't been there and done it before and I would have enjoyed a more memorable occasion. Of course, what I might want doesn't matter in the least to you…you're not just naturally authoritative, Leandro—you're well on the way to being a domineering tyrant!'

'You're hysterical,' Leandro informed her coldly.

'No, I'm not. If I was hysterical I would be throwing things and screaming. As it is, I'm just furious with you. Of course I wanted photos of my wedding! Some pretence that this was a normal marriage may come in useful in the future. Or would you be happy to tell our child that we have no photos because it was a shotgun wedding and you didn't see the need to dignify or celebrate the occasion in the usual way?'

Simmering dark golden eyes lit on her with punitive force. 'If you had wanted a photographer you should have mentioned it to me—'

'When? You were abroad and I wasn't allowed to have anything to do with the arrangements,' she reminded him.

'I assumed you'd be relieved to have everything taken care of for you,' Leandro retorted with cool assurance.

'What was wrong with asking me how I felt about it? But then you don't ask me anything, do you?' Molly sniped. 'You don't care how I feel, so why would you bother?'

'If I didn't care about you, you wouldn't have that ring

on your finger,' Leandro shot back at her with deflating conviction.

'No, if you cared you wouldn't have threatened me to ensure you *got* that ring on my finger!' Molly traded without skipping a beat. 'That was the act of a very ruthless guy, who doesn't care what he has to do to get what he wants.'

Smouldering dark golden eyes collided with hers in direct challenge. 'I regard it as a necessary act, driven by my understandable concern for your welfare—an action which ensured that I am now in the perfect position to look after you and my unborn child. Right now, I see that role as my primary purpose in life.'

Her cheeks hectically flushed and her eyes bright with indignation, Molly wanted to jump up and down with thwarted rage. He wasn't yielding a shamefaced inch to her perfectly reasonable complaints. Even worse, he was justifying his behaviour without a blush. How was she supposed to argue with a guy who wouldn't roll over and play dead for even twenty seconds? Worse still, a guy who clearly genuinely thought she couldn't cope without him.

'You don't know *how* to have a relationship, do you?' Molly accused next, one hand fiercely gripping the back of a seat to stay steady as air turbulence buffeted the plane. 'Instead of trying to win my trust and appreciation, you used threats. Maybe aggression works well in business, but you can't forge healthy relationships with human beings that way.'

Watching her sway, Leandro strode forward and swept her right off her feet and up into his arms. He supposed she would see that as aggressive as well, but if she didn't have enough sense to sit down or at least remove her ridiculously high and unstable shoes, he had no plans to wait until she fell and hurt herself.

'Put me down, Leandro!' Molly shouted at him, all fear of being overheard by the air crew overpowered by that very unwelcome demonstration of superior strength.

Leandro elbowed open the door of the sleeping compartment and lowered her with exaggerated gentleness down onto the bed. He sank down on its edge and flipped off her high heels with confident hands. 'You're my wife now. Of course I care about you. We will be celebrating our marriage with a very large and stylish party at my home tomorrow evening, *gatita*.'

Tumbled back against the pillows, her black curls rumpled, Molly opened her green eyes very wide at that announcement. Her wounded feelings were instantly soothed by the idea that he was willing to show her off as a wife at a big party. Such an act would, in some measure, make up for the disappointing wedding he had subjected her to. 'You should have told me that sooner.'

'I don't like parties much more than I like weddings,' Leandro confided.

Locked in connection with his heavily lashed dark eyes, Molly was finding it a challenge to breathe. He had a lot of faults, but he was gorgeous to look at, she conceded abstractedly, the hum of his magnetic attraction pulsing through her like a wake-up call and stealing what remained of her annoyance. Her fingers closed over the tip of his silk tie to tug him down to her. 'You're a lost cause. You don't tell your wife something like that on your wedding day,' she sighed.

'Was it that bad?' he queried in sincere surprise.

'Yes, but you're going to make it better,' Molly muttered, one slender hand curving over a hard, muscular thigh.

Leandro was enthralled by the covetous look in her expressive eyes, the hunger she just couldn't hide. It set alight a desire that only ever ignited in her radius. He pressed her back against the pillows and captured her pouting pink lips with the intoxicating urgency of his, parting them with a stroke of his wicked tongue and delving deep with a provocation that made her gasp beneath the onslaught and shiver.

Molly surfaced to the discovery that her corset top and bra were being deftly unhooked. She felt limp on the outside and hot as hell on the inside. The little responsive quivers still lingering in intimate places swiftly expanded into wholehearted pleasure when he cupped the warm weight of her bare breasts and his thumbs rubbed the protruding pink points of her nipples. The stiff, swollen peaks were tormentingly sensitive and the feel of his mouth on the throbbing crests soon wrenched a moan from her throat while her hips writhed in helpless reaction.

'I love your breasts, *querida*,' Leandro husked, lingering over the creamy swells to ensure that he wrung the utmost enjoyment from her responsive body.

She was twisting under him when he dragged his appreciative mouth from a lush wet bud and dispensed with her flowing skirt. He sprang off the bed to remove his jacket and tie. As he peeled off his shirt Leandro feasted his masculine gaze appreciatively on his bride's bewitching appearance in delicate white panties and lace stockings. All of a sudden he was willing to concede that marriage could have definite compensations.

'You look fantastically sexy,' he told her in a roughened undertone. 'I can't take my eyes off you.'

Molly was suffering from a similar problem. The golden-skinned physique he was revealing as he stripped was drop-dead gorgeous, from his well-defined pec and ab muscles to his narrow hips and long, strong thighs. Her admiring appraisal sank to the potent erection visible below his clinging boxers. A tight feeling knotted deep in her pelvis and a surge of answering heat washed up through her. Embarrassed by her susceptibility to his spectacular dark good looks, she focused on her bare toes instead. The strength of her passion for him shocked her.

When he came down on the bed beside her she closed her arms round him, loving the scent of his skin and the warm, hair-roughened feel of him against her own softer skin. She wasn't going to fall in love with him, though, she warned herself. She was darned if she would give him more than he was prepared to offer her. He extracted her from her remaining garments and slowly worked his erotic way down over her squirming body, giving her pleasure with his every caress. The tense sensation at the swollen heart of her was like a sweet pain that kept on twisting tighter and tighter while her squirming hips dug into the mattress beneath her, blindly seeking the satisfaction he withheld.

His hair brushed her stomach, his tongue dipping to swirl round the shallow indentation of her navel before progressing to a more intimate destination between her slender thighs. She went rigid with surprise, but he was persuasive and her body was too hot for her to resist. The wild, fierce longing inside her had neither conscience nor shame. Wherever he touched she burned, her heart thumping frantically fast in receipt of the exquisite delight of his exploration. She didn't recognise herself in that storm of excitement that drove her out of control and left her helpless in the spellbinding hold of his caresses. A single forefinger probed her tight delicate entrance and she cried out and bucked, feverishly ready for him.

'*Dios mio, querida*… I can't wait,' Leandro confessed in a throaty growl of impatience.

Her excitement was at an unbearable height when he pulled her to him and began to push into her wet, silky depths. The pleasure was so intense for her that she cried out. He stole the sound with his mouth. And then he was moving, driving his thick, virile shaft into her, satisfying the hollow ache that had tormented her with the energising force and rhythm of his masculine need. She rocked up to receive him and he pushed a hand below her bottom to hold her there while he ground into her with ravenous hunger.

'Nothing has *ever* felt this good,' Leandro groaned with earthy satisfaction, scorching golden eyes welded to her as he took and gave pleasure, a faint sheen of sweat dampening his lean, bronzed face.

The waves of excitement came closer and closer together until her awareness exploded into a world of searing light and ecstatic sensation. Her whole body clenched in the melting throes of her climax and he shuddered over her and thrust deeper still so that the rapturous tremors quivering through her went on and on and left her drowning in hot, sweet pleasure.

'Hmm.' Leandro growled, rolling back on the pillows

and lifting her over him. 'In bed you're absolute perfection,' he confided in a tone thick with male satisfaction.

Her arms easing round him while she revelled in the kisses he was stringing across her brow, Molly wondered how she really felt about that particular compliment. She supposed sex was the true single source of her attraction and, whether she liked it or not, a very important component in the future success of their marriage. She supposed it was unrealistic and greedy for her to want more than that from a guy who she felt was rather out of her league when it came to looks and success.

'I'd like to stay here for hours, but it won't be long until we land. A helicopter will fly us to the castle, where I know my family will be waiting to meet you,' Leandro advanced without any audible enthusiasm.

Molly's head shot up, tousled black curls almost standing on end. 'What castle?' she gasped.

'My home.'

'You live in a…*castle*?' Molly prompted in a panic. 'And I'm going to meet your family *immediately*?'

Leandro watched in astonishment as his bride leapt free of him and off the bed. 'What's wrong?'

'Look at me!' she launched at him in dismay as she caught her reflection in a mirrored wardrobe. 'I'm a mess and what am I going to wear?'

'Your cases are here—'

'But I don't know what to wear in a castle.' Molly studied him with fierce resentment, because she hated the feeling that she was out of her depth and the casually proffered news that he lived in a castle had driven that fact home hard enough to hurt.

Still stark naked, she threw herself at one of the cases and tried to haul it off the floor.

'What are you doing?' Leandro sprang up to snatch the suitcase off her and lift it on to the bed. 'Don't try to lift anything that heavy.'

On her knees on the carpet, she was fumbling for her keys in the little Dorothy bag she had carried to the church. Leandro draped his shirt over her shoulders, where it hung like a tent round her tiny frame.

'What am I going to wear?' she gasped strickenly, rooting with desperate hands through a pile of casual garments in bright colours. 'I don't have anything fancy.'

'I sent you shopping,' Leandro reminded her, as if he could not credit the idea that a woman might not take the fullest possible advantage of such an opportunity.

'But I didn't buy much because I'm pregnant,' she told him in frustration. 'In a few weeks nothing normal-sized will fit me and I'll have to buy maternity stuff, so I decided not to waste money.'

'It doesn't matter what you wear,' Leandro said in an attempt to calm her down.

Molly selected a cerise and black polka dot summer dress. 'Would this do?'

'Whatever you wear will be fine. You're my wife and you don't have anyone to impress within our home.'

Molly was touched by that assurance, but he had been born to life in a castle and she was apprehensive about meeting his family and did not want to make a bad first impression. 'It's not that simple.'

Leandro closed firm hands over her restless ones to force her to look up at him. 'It *is*.'

When she redid her make-up, she thought that her flattened, somewhat messy curls and swollen mouth were dead giveaways to the fact that she might just have got out of bed with her husband. Her dress was very casual and in no way impressive. Before they boarded the helicopter she studied Leandro in the act of turning his handsome face up in welcome to the heat of the Spanish sunshine. Well-cut black silk hair in faultless order, he looked infuriatingly immaculate in appearance.

And even though she had told herself that she was prepared for a castle, she was certainly not in any way prepared for the vast building that filled her view as the helicopter swooped in low to land. Leandro's castle was the genuine article, complete with turrets, towers and medieval walls. It sat on a hill surrounded by extensive landscaped gardens and overlooked a fertile valley covered with woods and olive groves.

'No wonder you think the sun rises and sets on you,' Molly breathed, no longer marvelling at the level of his self-assurance. 'Who on earth are all those people waiting at the entrance?'

'Our staff. Our marriage is a major event for the household and everyone will want to welcome you to your new home and wish you well.'

Molly was convinced that she could only be a disappointment. Conscious of the barrage of curious eyes nailed to her, she curled herself in by Leandro's side. 'They're all staring,' she hissed behind teeth arranged into a fixed smile.

'Probably because they think I robbed the cradle for you,' Leandro breathed wryly.

But that was the least of the hurdles Molly was about to face. A few steps in through the very grand entrance hall hung with giant paintings and life-size pieces of marble sculpture, she was greeted by Leandro's mother, a tall, older woman with silvering dark hair and cold eyes. Wearing a formal suit, she was accompanied by two younger women, dressed rather like her clones. Introductions were performed and the atmosphere grew no warmer. Doña Maria and her daughters, Estefania and Julieta, simply stared woodenly at Molly while she struggled to voice friendly words of greeting and behave as though she hadn't noticed that anything was lacking in her welcome. Goodness, she certainly hoped they were not all going to be sharing the same roof.

Leandro was astonished when he strode into the crowded salon where a formal reception appeared to be in full swing. He saw faces he hadn't seen in ten or twenty years. His mother had assembled every relation they possessed right down to distant cousins to provide an intimidating line up for his bride.

'Is this the party you mentioned?' Molly whispered, feeling horrendously underdressed when she compared the other women's elegant formal wear and glittering jewellery to her own casual appearance.

'No, this is only the extended family circle. I'm sorry. I had no idea this was planned.'

Viewing the packed room, Molly swallowed hard, but tilted her chin. She had to ask, she simply *had* to. 'Does your mother live with you?'

'No, she bases herself in Seville these days and makes occasional visits.' Leandro rested an arm at her spine and guided her round to perform introductions. Many of the guests spoke English, but few had a strong enough grasp of the language for a relaxing conversation. Molly realised that if she intended to fit in, she needed to acquire a working knowledge of Spanish as quickly as possible.

'I have to learn Spanish fast,' she informed Leandro in a lull between the excruciatingly polite conversations. 'Obviously you're not always going to be around to act as my interpreter. Do you know anyone who would be willing to teach me?'

'I'll organise it. Learning even a little Spanish would make it easier for you to settle in.' Leandro looked down at her and smiled in appreciation. As his lean, darkly handsome face shed all cool and reserve she was spell-bound by the change in him and her luminous green eyes locked to him.

His sister Julieta came up and said something to him. 'A phone call,' he told Molly. 'I'll try not to be long, *querida.*'

'*Dios mio!*' the pretty brunette murmured, treating Molly's absorbed face to an assessing appraisal and then laughing. 'The way you look at Leandro! You're actually in love with my brother.'

Hot colour drenched Molly's cheeks and she was about to argue with that statement when it occurred to her that, as Leandro's bride, it might be wiser for her to keep quiet on that score. Was there some particular way she looked at him? Embarrassment claimed her.

Away from her intimidating mother, Julieta was a different girl. She lifted two glasses from a passing tray and offered one to Molly with a friendly smile.

'I can't drink,' Molly responded with an apologetic grimace.

'Sorry…I forgot you were preggers,' the attractive brunette confided in perfect colloquial English. 'We're all still in shock about that. It took you five minutes to achieve what Aloise couldn't manage in five *years*!'

That one illuminating sentence satisfied Molly's curiosity on several scores. Her husband's first marriage had lasted five years and his wife, Aloise, had failed to conceive. Did that history explain why Leandro had been so convinced that Molly wouldn't fall pregnant? She rather thought it did.

'Come and meet Fernando,' Julieta urged, tugging at her elbow. 'He's younger and more fun.'

Fernando Santos was the estate manager and a handsome athletic young man in his late twenties. Julieta got very giggly and juvenile with him and the couple exchanged jokes, until Doña Maria sternly beckoned her daughter back to her side from the other side of the room.

'Are you the person I should ask if there is a vacant shed I could use to house a pottery kiln?' Molly enquired hopefully, glancing in Leandro's direction and wondering why her husband was staring fixedly at her just at that moment.

'Yes, Your Excellency. There may well be a suitable building in the old farmyard,' Fernando replied. 'We had to build new sheds for the agricultural machinery and several are now vacant.'

'Call me Molly,' Molly suggested. A sunny smile of satisfaction wreathed her animated features at the knowledge that there was no longer a day job preventing her from fulfilling her artistic ambitions and doing what she really wanted to do with her time.

Brown eyes resting admiringly on her vivacious face, Fernando gave her an apologetic look. 'That would cause offence to your new family. You're the duke's wife and the traditional formalities are carefully upheld on the estate.'

'It's going to take some getting used to,' Molly sighed.

'But I can speak for the whole staff when I tell you that we are all pleased that His Excellency has remarried,' the young Spaniard told her warmly.

Leandro joined them at that point and Fernando became conspicuously less chatty. Leandro seemed very cool and distant. Following a conversation about the olive groves, carried out in English apparently for her benefit, Leandro walked her out onto the spacious landing. Molly glanced up at him and then stiffened, forewarned by the black ice chill of his dark gaze and the forbidding tension of his lean, powerful face that something was wrong.

'Keep your distance from Fernando Santos,' Leandro breathed with cutting cool. 'Although he is an exemplary employee, he has a sleazy reputation with women and it will do you no good to be seen to enjoy his company to such an extent.'

Thoroughly taken aback by that unexpected rebuke, Molly said, 'What on earth are you trying to suggest?'

'That you don't flirt with him and do maintain a formal distance with him when you meet.'

Furious resentment snaked through Molly's tense figure. 'I wasn't flirting. For goodness' sake, we were only talking for a few minutes,' she protested in a vehement undertone. 'I didn't have you picked as the jealous type, but thanks for the warning!'

Equally taken aback by that wrathful retaliation, Leandro froze. Aggrieved gold flashed into his intent gaze. 'I have never been jealous in my life,' he asserted with freezing dignity. 'But your behaviour was attracting attention—'

'On my *wedding* day? When I'm carrying your child? Is it everyone round here who's crazy or just you?' Molly raised a disbelieving brow and stalked away from him in high dudgeon.

A shudder of steely self-restraint raked through Leandro's big, powerful frame. She was a tiny figure in a bright dress that clung to her firm, rounded curves at breast and hip and skimmed slender thighs that led down into flawless legs. His teeth gritted. He resisted the urge to drag her back and make her listen to him. She liked male company and men liked her. He knew how close she was to Jez Andrews. Her best friend was a man, not a woman, and he was not comfortable with that fact. Another man might easily misinterpret her easy smiles and friendliness as an invitation. She also seemed blissfully unaware of how very sexy she was even in that polka-dot dress, which looked as though it would be more at home on a beach…

CHAPTER SEVEN

THE following morning, Molly knocked on the communicating door in her bedroom and waited, shifting off one foot onto the other. When there was no answer she opened it and she saw yet another terrifyingly imposing bedroom containing huge ornate furniture that looked as if it had been designed a good few centuries ago. It seemed all the more intimidating when set against its backdrop of gilded paneled walls. She breathed in deep. Maybe she should have been prepared for Leandro's absence, she told herself ruefully.

After all, she had slept alone. Alone on her wedding night. While it was true that they had consummated their marriage on board his jet, she had not expected to be left by herself. But then she had not expected separate bedroom suites either, had she? Last night she had drifted off to sleep while she waited for him in solitary splendour. A maid had awoken her with breakfast in bed. It was only while she was getting dressed and chose to investigate further that the truth finally sank in on her: the dressing-room closets contained only her clothes and a door in her vast bedroom connected with his.

A knock sounded on her bedroom door and Julieta walked in. 'Oh, good, you're up. Leandro has asked me to take you shopping for a dress for the party tonight—'

'Where is he?' Molly asked.

His sister looked surprised by the question. 'At the bank, of course.'

Married one day, back to work the next, Molly reflected. Her soft mouth tightened because she refused to give way to the feeling that he had abandoned her. After all, she wasn't a child and she might be in a strange environment, but she would soon get used to it. She would manage fine without him. By the looks of it, she didn't have much choice.

Julieta chattered all the way downstairs about where they were going to go shopping, while Molly scanned her lavish surroundings with all the apprehension of an ordinary person suddenly waking up to find themselves lost in a royal palace. But the instant her insecurity was ready to rise, she crushed it flat and refused to acknowledge those feelings. Leandro's castle was where she was going to bring her baby up and the last thing her child needed was a mother who lacked self-esteem. As they reached the foot of the stairs a middle-aged manservant addressed both women in Spanish.

'Basilio says that my mother would like a word with you before we go out,' Julieta translated, showing Molly into an elegant sitting room where Doña Maria awaited her.

'Molly…' The tall older woman greeted her with an acerbic smile. 'Leandro asked me to have a word with you about the household arrangements. He doesn't think you'll be up to taking charge immediately, so I agreed to continue the job until you feel able.'

Faced with that vote of no confidence from her bridegroom while at the same time wondering exactly what came under the heading of household arrangements, Molly felt cornered and cut off at the knees. 'Right,' she said uncertainly.

'Dealing with the staff and the catering for a house as large as this one is a complex task,' Doña Maria pointed out. 'Aloise had the benefit of growing up in a similar home and knew exactly what was required. Basilio is also an excellent major-domo. He has to be. Leandro expects the *castillo* to run like clockwork.'

With a bright smile that refused to betray an ounce of nervous tension, Molly lifted her chin. 'I'm sure I'll rise to the challenge. My experience in catering will help.'

'I'm impressed by your confidence.'

Fed up with the woman's subtle put-downs, Molly lifted her head high to say, 'I can understand that your son's sudden marriage has come as a shock to you and I have no wish to fall out with you. But this is my home now and I intend to adjust to the way of life here because I want our child to be happy—'

'But you will never be the wife whom Leandro needs! Aloise was the love of his life and irreplaceable. You will never belong here as she did. You can only be an embarrassment to my son. *A waitress!*' the dowager duchesa exclaimed with a contemptuous sound of disgust. 'I *know* that you threw yourself at Leandro from the first moment you saw him—'

'Where on earth did you get that idea from?' Molly cut

in, anger betraying her determination to stay firmly in control whatever the provocation.

'Krystal Forfar is one of my oldest friends. She witnessed your first meeting with Leandro and saw you for what you are—a scheming, gold-digging little tramp!'

Cut to the bone by the older woman's abuse, Molly was rigid. 'I gather you're the anonymous party behind the financial offer that was made to me.'

'I don't know what you're talking about,' Doña Maria proclaimed, her stare unflinching.

But Molly was convinced she had found the culprit and saw no point in further dispute. Having decided to reject her son's bride sight unseen, Doña Maria was all the more bitter for being forced to accept her as a daughter-in-law.

'I would advise you not to make false allegations against me,' the older woman continued. 'Leandro would never forgive you.'

Ten minutes later, comfortably enclosed in a chauffeur-driven limousine with Julieta, Molly was considering the likely outcome of tackling Leandro about her mother-in-law. Of course, how could she prove anything? She had no documentary evidence to show and no witnesses of what had been said to her. And did she really need to run to Leandro to tell tales barely thirty-six hours into their marriage? Surely she could cope better than that? *The love of his life*, however, had a fine ring to it and she knew it would be a long time, if ever, before she forgot that description of Aloise.

'Was your mother very fond of Aloise?' Molly asked Leandro's sister.

The pretty brunette flushed and failed to meet her eyes.

'Mama knew Aloise when she was a child. We all did. She lived only a few miles away and our families were close. Her death shattered us all. The accident was very sudden and truly tragic. Aloise had so much to live for. Everyone admired her.'

By the sound of it, Leandro had selected the perfect wife. A childhood friend and neighbour, popular with his family and with whom he had shared a great deal more than he could ever share with Molly. She was also willing to bet that he had taken the love of his life away on a honeymoon.

The dress was a vibrant emerald green that gave her skin a glow of creamy perfection and highlighted her bright eyes. The glistening fabric shaped her body from bust to hip and flared out into a short skirt.

'You will turn every head in the room, *gatita*,' Leandro forecast from behind her.

Surprise made Molly jump and she spun round from her inspection of the mirror. 'I didn't know you were back.'

'I'm sorry I missed dinner. Work had piled up while I was in London. I won't be long. All I have to do is shower and change.' Brilliant dark golden eyes rested on her and her tummy flipped a somersault and her mouth ran dry. Sleek and dark in an elegant business suit with his black hair slightly ruffled and a blue-black shadow of stubble defining his hard, handsome jaw line, he looked utterly spectacular to her appreciative gaze. 'But I thought you might want to wear these this evening…'

He extended a jewellery case.

Molly lifted the lid to reveal a magnificent necklace

composed of perfectly matched large lustrous pearls and matching drop earrings. 'These are amazing.'

'There's a tremendous collection of jewellery in the safe, all of which is now yours to wear.'

Molly lifted out the pearl necklace. He helped her attach the diamond-studded clasp, his fingertips brushing the nape of her neck. She put on the earrings. Worn together, the set looked incredibly opulent. 'How old are the pieces?'

'Turn of the last century, given on the occasion of my great-grandfather's birth…

'And this is from me…' Leandro extended a much smaller box.

Her heart beating very fast, Molly opened it and studied the glittering diamond ring with stunned eyes. 'It's gorgeous.'

Leandro extracted the ring and reached for her hand to slide the ring onto the same finger as her wedding band. 'We missed out on the usual steps, *querida*.'

'I love it.' And when she collided with his shimmering dark eyes she suspected that some day she might well start loving him too, for sometimes he could do or say something that cut right to the heart of her concerns and touched her deep. The night they had met he had told her that she made him feel more alive than he had felt in years and he had called that a cause for celebration. In the same way the giving of the equivalent of an engagement ring and the recognition that their relationship had skipped several important stages made her eyes prickle with stinging tears of appreciation. 'I really love it…'

'I'd better get in that shower.' Leandro strode back to

the door between their bedrooms and a moment later he was gone.

She admired her new collection of jewellery and enjoyed the fact that he obviously wanted her to be able to hold her own amongst the other women at the party.

'So how long have the separate bedrooms for husband and wife been operating?' Molly enquired when they were descending the magnificent staircase together.

Leandro dealt her a look of surprise. 'Centuries.'

Molly leant closer and whispered huskily, 'Time for a change.'

The familiar citrus-fresh scent of her hair flared his nostrils and heated his appreciative dark gaze. 'You could be right, *querida*.'

'Is that you actually admitting that you might be wrong about something?'

'No, that's you misinterpreting me,' Leandro quipped without skipping a beat.

Knots of guests in elegant dinner jackets and exquisite gowns and glittering jewellery drifted into the beautifully decorated ballroom to greet them. As the evening wore on Molly's head swam with the sheer number of different names and faces she tried to match. She met Leandro's neighbours, friends and loads of other bankers. It was a warm evening and the crush of people and the noise of the music and the chattering voices combined in a suffocating wave that made her feel slightly nauseous and dizzy. She drifted over to the doors that stood open onto the terrace to allow fresh air to filter in. Just as she was hanging back from joining Leandro, who was patently talking business with a group of like-minded serious men, Julieta approached her. Looping her arm round Molly's to draw her into a girlie aside, Julieta whispered, 'Can I trust you with a secret?'

'If you want to,' Molly responded a little uncertainly.

'I've been seeing Fernando Santos for weeks,' Leandro's youngest sister confided in an explosive rush. 'I'm crazy about him!'

'My goodness…' Molly was taken aback by that confession and not quite sure she wanted the responsibility of it. It had not taken her long to work out that, while Julieta was warm-hearted and likeable, she was also impulsive and immature for a girl of twenty-one.

Julieta gave her a warning look. 'If the truth were to come out, my family would break us up and Fernando would lose his job, so please don't tell anyone.'

Molly nodded and hoped that Leandro was wrong in his conviction that the handsome estate manager was a womaniser. More streetwise than the Spanish girl had ever had to be, Molly paid more heed to Fernando when he came over to speak to her. He startled her by bowing over her hand and kissing it. That gesture along with his ready smile and conversation showed him to be a man who was very much at home in female company and prided himself on the fact.

'I've identified a couple of buildings that might be suitable for your purpose, Your Excellency. Would you prefer me to discuss this with your husband?' he asked.

'No, I'll deal with it. My husband is a busy man,' Molly countered.

'I'll let you know, then, when the sheds are ready for inspection,' Fernando told her, tensing as Julieta sent him a flirtatious smile and then looking away with an unease that did not bode well for the relationship. Perhaps he should have thought of the risks before getting involved, Molly thought, all her concern reserved for Julieta, whom she could see was in deep enough to get badly hurt. Perspiration beading her short upper lip, Molly suddenly sucked in a deep breath, striving to counter the sickening light-headed sensation overcoming her.

'Are you feeling all right?' Fernando asked Molly abruptly. 'You've turned very pale.'

'I'm fine,' Molly lied, hurriedly turning away to find somewhere to sit down. But that quick movement was too much and a wave of dizziness drenched her in a cold sweat of discomfort. With a gasp, she swayed and began to fall. A split second before she hit the floor with a crash, someone grabbed her.

When she recovered consciousness, she was in another room and Leandro was standing over her where she lay on a sofa and studying her with stark concern etched in his lean bronzed features. A middle-aged stranger was taking her pulse and viewing her with a frown while Leandro introduced him as the family doctor, Edmundo Mendoza.

'You should be taking more rest at this time, Your Excellency,' he censured.

'I just felt dizzy. It was so warm and airless.'

'You're not used to the climate yet and in a few short weeks it will be much warmer,' Dr Mendoza warned her. 'Give yourself time to acclimatise.'

'I should have ensured that you sat down,' Leandro groaned.

'I was just a little faint,' Molly said dismissively.

'But suppose that faint had occurred on the stairs,' the doctor urged, clearly a man who liked to visualise worst-case scenarios.

'You should rest now. Our guests will understand,' Leandro declared.

'I don't need to be treated like an invalid,' Molly muttered while she wondered if absolutely everybody present was already aware that she was a pregnant bride. She cringed at the idea.

Leandro, all macho-managing-male at that instant, scooped her up off the sofa. 'What were you talking about with Santos? At first I thought he had said something to upset you when you turned away from him. I was coming to join you and just got there in time to catch you before you hit the floor—'

Surprised that Leandro had been watching her that closely, Molly explained her need for a place to house a kiln.

'Why on earth didn't you ask me to deal with that?' he demanded.

'I didn't want to bother you and…I like doing things for myself,' Molly admitted.

'Possibly I'm going out on a limb here,' Leandro breathed tautly, 'but right now when you're pregnant doesn't seem the wisest time to be messing around with kilns and clay—'

'Don't be silly!' Molly snapped, furious at that suggestion. 'It's not heavy work—'

'I'm not artistic, but neither am I stupid.' Leandro's expressive mouth compressed. 'Loading and unloading a kiln must be arduous—however, if you were prepared to have one of the estate workers helping you with the more demanding tasks, I would have no objection.'

'Okay,' Molly conceded to that arrangement with reluctance as he laid her down on the bed and took off her shoes for her. 'But I need my own corner to work in. Will your family mind me being a potter?'

Leandro paused at the door. 'It's none of their business.'

Some of Molly's tension ebbed at that reassuringly independent response. 'Your mother and eldest sister don't like me.'

'Give them the time to get to know you,' Leandro advised. 'You don't have much experience of how families operate, do you?'

Molly stiffened defensively. 'I lived in a family for the first nine years of my life—before my mother died and my grandmother gave me up for adoption,' she explained when he frowned in surprise. 'There was me, my mother and my older sister…except my sister was more like my mother because she's the only person I can remember looking after me when I was very young—'

'I forgot that you had a sister. Where is she now?'

'I don't know. I sort of closed the door on that bit of my life and I'm not sure I would want to open it again,' she confided, thinking of the hurt she still felt at that rejection and the wrenching sense of loss she had suffered for years afterwards.

'I'll call your maid to help you get ready for bed,' Leandro murmured.

'You're sleeping here tonight,' Molly reminded him and then flushed to the roots of her hair at her nerve in making that reminder.

Leandro had come to a sudden halt. He looked back at her with brilliant dark heavily lashed eyes that made her heart thump and a slow, sensual smile curved his handsome mouth. Her desire for him never failed to excite him. He would be responsible, though, he told himself equally forcefully; he would check that angle out with the doctor first. He needed to take better care of her. It galled him that she should have gone to Fernando Santos for help sooner than ask her husband for it.

Molly dozed off soon after she got into bed and wakened only when Leandro came into the room. 'It's all right—I'm awake,' she announced when she registered that he was trying to move around quietly.

Leandro studied her in the lamplight. Her black curls fell in a dense cloud round her narrow shoulders, framing her piquant face and vivid green eyes. His desire was instantaneous and just an upgrade of the simmering need that had purred in the background of his awareness all day. No matter where he was or what he was doing, he stayed hot and hungry for her.

Molly watched him undress. Indeed she luxuriated in that intimacy and hoped that the separate-bedroom concept of living would now die a natural death, for it would not be easy for them to enjoy private moments as a couple in a household so filled with other people. Yet more than anything else they needed that time and privacy. *The love of his life*; oh, how those words were set to haunt her and disrupt her peace! But when she saw Leandro in all his naked bronzed magnificence, her thoughts became far more primitive. He had a professional athlete's hard, sculpted contours of power and rippling muscle. The bold jut of his erect sex induced a melting liquid sensation low in her pelvis.

'You want me, *querida*,' Leandro husked, settling hot golden eyes of appreciation on her and coming down on the bed beside her.

'Yes…' Her soft pink lips parted on a whisper of sound because her heart was thumping like an express train at full tilt and she could hardly breathe for anticipation.

He took her hand and encouraged her to touch him and the hammer of her heartbeat only got louder when she stroked his rigid shaft. Moist heat blossomed in answer between her thighs. He drove her lips apart with hungry urgency and she fell back against the pillows while he extracted her from her nightdress. The plunge of his tongue made her shiver convulsively. He explored the soft, firm swell of her breasts and tugged on the tender pink crests until she was moaning and shifting her hips up to him.

Molly could feel herself going out of control very fast. It was as if all the nervous constraints of the day were suddenly being torn from her and every craving were being channelled into one piercing need. She wanted him, she really, *really* wanted him with an intensity she couldn't hide. His exploration of the slick pink cleft at the heart of her drove her insane with delight.

'You feel like hot silk, *gatita*,' Leandro growled, tipping her leg back to rise over her, impatient to ease the painful ache of his arousal.

He sank into her willing body and she loosed a wanton moan of pleasure. Her excitement climbed with every powerful thrust. The raw pulse of hunger throbbing through her responsive flesh, she arched up to take him deeper. A wild cry of satisfaction escaped her as orgasm took her to the dizzy heights of intolerable pleasure and dropped her back down to mortal earth again.

'Did I live up to your expectations, *querida*?' Leandro asked teasingly, skimming long brown fingers through her mane of hair where it lay across the pillows, his attention welded to her hectically flushed smiling face. 'You surpassed them,' Molly whispered truthfully, her arms wrapping round his lean. strong frame.

Dimly she grasped that at such moments Leandro felt very much as if he was hers and she felt infinitely more close to him. Sex as a substitute for love, well, why not? she asked herself irritably. It was surely a lot safer than signing up for the kind of love slavery that had wrecked her natural mother, Cathy's ability to be content. She could be happy. She *would* be happy. A man who had married her for the sake of their child took marriage seriously and would make every effort to help her adjust to her new life.

But when Molly wakened the next day in an empty bed and fled at speed across the bedroom to check the room next door, she was no longer quite so confident. Leandro had already left. Yet it was the weekend. Couldn't he have taken time off to be with her for even one day? Or was she expecting too much? What was he telling her about his priorities? And her level of importance in his life…?

CHAPTER EIGHT

MOLLY glanced out the open doors of her studio when she heard a car enter the courtyard. It was Julieta, who came home from Seville on Fridays to see Fernando, who lived on the estate. She always parked her car in the courtyard well away from his house in the hope of defeating the gossips. Molly looked away again, minding her own business, but wishing she didn't know as much as she did about the relationship. Common sense told her that Leandro would be outraged that his sister was involved in so blatant an affair with his employee.

Preferring not to dwell on a situation that was outside her control, Molly studied the shelves of gleaming pottery against the opposite wall with a warm sense of accomplishment. She had been experimenting with a new glaze and a wood-fired kiln and was delighted with the results. In the months that had elapsed since her marriage, she had worked hard. Fernando Santos had given her very useful assistance when she had decided to set up a small pottery in the old farmyard. Her kiln was housed next door in a fire-proofed shed and organising a proper studio had been the natural next step. She gazed out the glass doors at the orchards and the blue, blue sky above. She had a wonderful working environment and plenty of free time to devote to her potter's art. So why wasn't she happy?

She could see her reflection in the glass doors and even the large heavy-duty apron she wore could not conceal her new fecund shape. Her boyish slenderness had vanished as her pregnancy advanced. She was six months along now and her pregnant tummy was a firm and protuberant little mound and even her breasts had expanded enough to make her feel top-heavy. She had worried that as her waist ebbed Leandro would find her less attractive. But that had proved a needless concern. Leandro had embraced every change in her body with masculine enthusiasm.

Yes, indeed, Molly reflected wryly. In fact in the sex department her every want was more than satisfied. No complaints there. Leandro slept with her every night and he was a very lusty guy. But somewhere along the line, maybe when she woke up alone or spent yet another solitary evening while he worked late or travelled abroad, the sizzling passion that she shared with her husband had begun to remind her more of what they *didn't* have than what they did. She had wardrobes full of designer clothes and a fantastic collection of jewellery. When he remembered her existence Leandro bought her beautiful gifts like the platinum watch on her wrist or the array of perfumes from which she now had to choose.

Unhappily, she was convinced that, while Leandro was rarely out of her thoughts, Leandro himself didn't remember his wife's existence very often. It would never occur to him to phone her when he was away from her. He would never confide his deepest thoughts in her, nor would he even answer her curious questions about Aloise. Indeed he had labelled her curiosity about his first wife 'unhealthy' and had ensured that she was very reluctant to raise the topic again.

'I think you should tell Leandro to take a running jump and come home to London,' Jez had told Molly on the phone the night before. 'You're bored, you're lonely and you're in a foreign country. By the sounds of it, you see so little of your healthy duke that you might as well move back here. He could visit the kid when he comes over on business. At least you'd have a life in London.'

'I've never been a quitter. I don't want a divorce and a broken home for my child,' she argued vehemently. 'Marriage is for the long haul.'

'Your long haul, not his. You seem to be the one making all the sacrifices,' her best friend opined.

And wasn't that the truth? Molly thought ruefully. Marriage appeared to have made very little impression on either Leandro's schedule or his attitude to her. Leandro was strong, arrogant and reserved. She loved his strength, but hated being kept at arm's length. He shut her out and she desperately wanted to be let in so that she could get close to him somewhere other than in the bedroom. She had nobody but Julieta to talk to, and during the week Leandro's sister lived in Seville where she was studying fashion design. While Molly's regular Spanish lessons with a local teacher had led to a steady improvement in her grasp of the language, it was still an uphill challenge for her to have a decent chat with anyone. At least, however, she could now make herself understood with the castle staff. For the first couple of months, while she was unable to express the most basic requests, she had felt very inadequate and isolated.

Furthermore, her mother-in-law, far from basing herself as promised in Seville, remained firmly in residence below the same roof. Doña Maria froze Molly out in company and made little acid comments and digs under cover of polite conversation. That was one reason why Molly spent the greater part of her day in her studio, which Leandro had yet to even visit. He had promised to come but never quite made it. In much the same way he had not found the time to take any interest in the nursery being decorated for their unborn child.

A knock on the door shot Molly back to the present and she spun round to see Julieta, gorgeous in white shorts and T-shirt, smiling hopefully across the studio at her.

'It's my birthday tomorrow,' Julieta reminded her. 'Will you come up to town and go clubbing with me and my friends in the evening? You can stay the night at my place.'

It was on the tip of Molly's tongue to say no because she knew that Leandro would not approve. But then when did Leandro ever take her out anywhere? She was married to a workaholic too busy to waste his precious time entertaining his wife. Sudden defiance blazed through Molly. Since when had she been the sort of girl who sat home and did as she was told? On that thought, she accepted the invitation and Julieta was ecstatic at the prospect of introducing Molly to all her friends, for the two women had formed an increasingly close friendship, united by the truth that neither of them was capable of winning Doña Maria's approval. Nothing poor Julieta wore or indeed did got her critical mother's vote of confidence.

Late afternoon, Molly drove back to the *castillo* in one of the estate Land Rovers that she had acquired for her own use. Basilio knew her routine and he was stationed at the side door in the garden she always used to avoid her mother-in-law, who sat in the grand salon off the hall at that time of day. He swept open the door and bowed low with a throbbing air of exaggerated respect that very nearly provoked Molly into giggles.

'*Muchas gracias, Basilio,*' she said punctiliously, touched by his unfailing efforts to give her the aristocratic airs she so conspicuously lacked.

She grabbed a magazine from the pile in her bedroom and went off to luxuriate in a long bath. Anticipation at the prospect of soon enjoying lively company had brightened her eyes. She was already planning to get her hair and nails done for her night out on the town the following day. She wondered what she would wear, reflecting that pregnant clubbers weren't exactly cool or fashionable, and mentally flipped through her extensive wardrobe for an outfit that would magically conceal her rotund contours. So Leandro wouldn't like it. Well, Leandro would have to roll with the punches.

In the act of flipping through the glossy fashion magazine for something to catch her interest, Molly froze at the fleeting glimpse of a woman's face. Sitting up in an abrupt movement, displaced water swilling noisily all around her, Molly flipped back frantically through the issue to find the relevant page while struggling to keep it dry at the same time.

Her heart skipped a beat when she finally relocated the photograph of a very beautiful blonde woman standing in a walled garden full of colourful flowers. It was her sister, Ophelia, she was sure it was! Barely able to breathe for excitement, Molly settled back to read the article. Ophelia was married now—well why not? Her sister was seven years older and a mother as well, Molly registered in growing astonishment. My goodness, Ophelia had already had three kids by a Greek business-man called Lysander Metaxis! Now why did that surname ring a familiar bell with her? Ophelia, who now evidently ran a plant nursery, had opened her home and garden in aid of a children's charity. Molly turned a page and stared fixedly at the picture of Madrigal Court. Her recognition of the lovely old Tudor house sent a cold shiver down her spine, rousing as it did unhappy memories.

She still remembered the initial excitement of first seeing that huge ancient house from her grandmother's car the day after her mother's funeral. She had been so hope-lessly impressed that someone she was related to could possibly have enough money to live in a mansion. But her grandmother, Gladys, who could have given Doña Maria frostbite with her nasty tongue, had soon turned Molly's youthful excitement into a sick sense of apprehension. As soon as Gladys had returned from enrolling Ophelia in her new school, she had sat Molly down and told her that she couldn't possibly give her a permanent home.

'Your sister is sixteen. You're too young a child for me to take on,' her grandmother had told her.

Molly had fearfully sworn that she would be no trouble and that she would help out round the house and not get in the way, and the older woman had had to admit the true reasons why she wasn't prepared to raise her younger granddaughter.

'Your father was a foreigner and he already had a wife when he got your mother pregnant with you. He was a loathsome man who jilted your mother at the altar long before you were born, but he still wouldn't let her alone to get on with her life!' Gladys Stewart had delivered with seething bitterness. 'It's a shameful disgrace for a woman to give birth to a child when she's not married, Molly, and that's why you can't live here with me. It'll be much better for all of us if you're adopted.'

Until today, she had never seen the big sister she adored, Molly recalled painfully. If a heart could be broken, hers had been smashed, as Ophelia had been the only stable loving influence in Molly's world since she was born. Her eyes wet from those recollections, Molly read on, eagerly sucking up every tiny personal detail about her sister's life. She hauled herself out of the bath and dried herself at frantic speed. She was going to get in touch with Ophelia. Why not? There was no mention of her grandmother in the article. She was only risking rejection and couldn't imagine the sister she remembered being that cruel. She was longing for another woman she could talk to, because it was impossible to admit the extent of her unhappiness to Julieta, and Jez was a man and didn't understand, for he simply urged her to walk out on her husband. As if that would be the easiest thing in the world to do!

Before she could lose her nerve, Molly flung on some clothes and went on the Internet in search of contact details for Ophelia. Madrigal Court had its own website and she sent an email to her sister, couched as casually as she could manage it, asking after the family parrot, Haddock, and including her mobile phone number. After all, Ophelia might not want to talk to her.

At that same moment, Leandro was in his office at the bank in Seville and sustaining a very taxing visit from an elderly uncle who professed to be very much shocked and disturbed by recent outrageous gossip on the estate relating to a family member's behaviour with an unnamed man. By the time all the complex and deeply apologetic and defensive outpourings had been waded through, Leandro was not a great deal wiser to the facts than he had been at the outset. His uncle, an old bachelor, had a highly refined sense of delicacy and honour that prevented him from being a good teller of tales, for he steadfastly refused to name the source of the gossip, the content of it or to identify the parties involved.

'Of course, some people will say that artists are like that—all passion and no common sense,' Esteban framed tight-mouthed with disapproval. 'But it is your duty to put an end to such activities and protect the family name. I am very sorry that I have had to bring this scandalous matter to your attention.'

Right up until the old man mentioned the word 'artist' and linked it with that other revealing word 'passion', Leandro had been inclined to take a humorous view of what Esteban might regard as a scandalous matter—too short a skirt? A little flirtation? A woman seen unchaperoned in male company after seven o'clock at night? But when it came to his wife's reputation, Leandro's sense of humour died. He was no more liberated than his seventeenth-century forebears who had locked up their wives and fought duels to the death over them. The only artist in his family, as far as he was concerned, was Molly.

'Fernando Santos?' he breathed between compressed lips as he shot to his feet.

Startled by that brusqueness with which that word erupted from the head of the family, Esteban nodded in grave and grudging confirmation.

To fill her time that evening, Molly was tidying up her studio. When a car drew up outside she looked out in surprise at the sight of Leandro springing out of the vehicle. He was a sleek, dark and gorgeous image in his well-cut business suit and she ate him up shamelessly with her eyes. Familiarity did not breed contempt in her experience. She might share a bed with him every night, but she remained awesomely aware of his magnificence.

Her ready smile glowed into being. 'I thought you were never going to come down and see this place,' she confided helplessly.

The faintest rise of dark colour scored the slashing cheekbones that gave Leandro's handsome face such strong lines. He glanced across the yard at the building housing the estate office and marvelled that it had not previously occurred to him that his wife was likely to become friendly with a man she was working virtually next door to several days a week.

'You've managed an impressive transformation in here,' Leandro conceded, quietly noting the scrupulous organisation and order that distinguished the studio. Molly might rush at the business of life like a tiny, intense and energetic tornado, but she did not wreak havoc on her surroundings.

'I couldn't have done it without Fernando's help. He's been invaluable. He introduced me to one of his friends who's a painter. He was able to advise me on where to buy the kiln and my supplies,' she told him.

His lean, powerful face taut and his sense of guilt growing, for he had offered her no support, Leandro picked up a bowl with a smooth, swirling mother-of-pearl finish and examined it. 'This is very attractive, *mi cielo*. I should have done more to help and I'm relieved that Santos has made himself useful. Do you see much of him?'

Sensing his edgy mood, Molly was becoming tense. 'I see him most days—I mean, his office is only across the yard.'

Luxuriant black lashes low over his stunning dark golden eyes, Leandro held her questioning appraisal levelly. 'You need to be more careful in your dealings with him—'

'What the heck is that supposed to mean?' Molly launched at him in immediate angry interruption. 'What are you trying to imply?'

Her husband looked grim. 'I'm not implying anything. I trust you. I don't think you're foolish enough to get involved with another man, but I do think you're likely to be careless of appearances. In a rural area like this where people have old-fashioned ideas about the sexes that can cause problems.'

'I haven't done anything that anyone could take amiss!' Molly exclaimed.

'I'm afraid that you must have done because one of my relatives came to tell me about it today—'

Molly took a furious step forward. 'To talk about me? And tell you exactly *what*?'

'No specifics, just a lot of suggestive mumbling and raised brows and dark hints,' Leandro volunteered in a wry tone, reaching out for her small slender hands and enclosing them deftly in his. 'I would not discuss you with anyone. I'm just warning you to watch your step for your own sake. This isn't like London. You are a person of importance here and your every move will be noted. Our neighbours and employees do talk about us and I don't want my wife to become the focus of damaging gossip.'

'I haven't done anything that anyone could talk about—unless it was your mother. I imagine Doña Maria could come up with a pretty good story to drop me in it if she wanted to!' Molly condemned bitterly, yanking her hands free of his in a pointed gesture of condemnation.

His surprise at that response patent, Leandro frowned down at her. 'This has nothing to do with my mother—'

'You're accusing me of getting too friendly with Fernando and it's absolutely not true.'

'I've nothing more to say on this issue and I'm not going to be drawn into an argument about it.' Leandro surveyed her with forbidding cool. 'I didn't intend to upset you.'

'Of course, I'm upset. You approach me with no names, no facts and tell me to watch my every move like I'm some silly airhead of a schoolgirl likely to cause you embarrassment! Well, I may not be from a fancy aristocratic background like yours, but I do know how to behave,' she proclaimed fiercely.

'Is Santos making a nuisance of himself?' Leandro shot at her suddenly. 'Is that the problem?'

'No, *you're* the problem, Leandro!' Molly was trembling with furious resentment. It was humiliating that he should feel the need to warn her about her conduct with an employee. She shook her keys noisily and waited at the exit until he had walked past her. She then locked up the studio and stalked back towards her own vehicle.

'Leave it here. I'll take you back. I don't want you to drive in a temper,' Leandro breathed in a raw undertone, angry that she had reacted so badly to what he viewed as a mild and reasonable admonition. He was already wondering if there was more substance to the gossip than the narrow-minded rumours without foundation that he had assumed.

'I'll do whatever the hell I like!' Molly raked at him, wondering why he was so possessive of her. Evidently he didn't appreciate just how powerful a hold he had on her.

'No. You won't, *querida*,' Leandro asserted as he bent and lifted her off her startled feet to stash her bodily into the passenger seat of his car.

Molly was so taken aback by that very physical intervention that they were halfway back to the castle before she mastered her fizzing rage with him to the point where she could speak. By then she had also remembered Aloise's accident and the row that had evidently preceded that tragedy. Her tummy lurched as she understood why he had been so determined not to let her get behind the wheel in such a mood. He wouldn't talk about his precious Aloise but Molly felt positively haunted by her predecessor. She knew so many facts about Leandro's first wife but virtually nothing of a personal nature. All she had was the gorgeous blonde in the portrait in the dining room to go on for an image and the scarcely heartening knowledge that Aloise had been a successful barrister, renowned for her charity work and her talents as a hostess—an impossible act to follow as far as Molly was concerned.

'There are times when you make me so angry I could go into orbit without an engine. I can't stand being bossed around,' Molly admitted shakily. 'And I sincerely hate you when you talk down to me like I'm stupid!'

'I don't do that. You're a very passionate personality—'

'And I'm proud of it,' Molly muttered without apology.

'I'm getting used to it,' Leandro confessed, studying her delicate profile with an instinctive sense of fascination. He could feel the powerful emotion she was struggling to contain. It was that same vital life force matched with sensuality that powered their astonishingly good sex life. He rationed the time he spent with her, though. It was better that way, he told himself grimly. Everything in moderation, nothing to excess. It was the rational line to follow. He remembered how he had felt when he saw Santos responding to her sex appeal. He hadn't liked his reaction. As long as he stayed in control he need never feel that way again.

Before she went to bed, Molly logged on and checked her email box and then scolded herself for expecting a reply from Ophelia so quickly. Most probably an employee would see her email first and pass it on and it might well be some time before her sister even laid eyes on it. Maybe she had made a mistake getting in touch, she thought anxiously. Fear of rejection had kept her from travelling the road to a reunion for years, but the need to reach out to Ophelia had overwhelmed her at a vulnerable moment. All her optimistic dreams about what she might make of her marriage were slowly crumbling into dust around her.

In the spacious bedroom of her town apartment the following evening, Julieta put down her mobile phone and turned stricken eyes on to Molly, who was outlining her mouth with pillar-box-red lipstick and trying not to yawn because it was already hours after her usual bedtime. 'That was my mother…'

'I thought it might be.' Molly sighed sympathetically. 'Before I managed to get in the car to come here she told me that I was dressed like a slut and that no decent woman would go out to a nightclub without her husband.'

The leggy brunette by her side slowly shook her head in disbelief. 'I've never heard Mama in such a rage.'

'Blame me. I didn't pay any heed to her.'

'But she has no right to speak to you like that. Leandro would never stand for it. Why don't you tell him how she treats you?'

Molly shrugged. 'I don't want to get in a row with someone who's always going to be in our lives. I hoped she'd get fed up and move out.'

'It was selfish of me to invite you tonight. I don't want to cause trouble between you and Leandro. I had no idea that there were rumours that *you* were getting too friendly with Fernando!'

Molly raised a brow as she realised that her mother-in-law must already have got a hold of that tasty titbit. 'It's only silly tittle-tattle—'

'Or someone who's seen *me* at Fernando's house or in his car and made the mistake of assuming that it was you!'

Julieta was unable to hide her horror at the idea that her secret relationship might be on the brink of exposure. 'Fernando is looking for another job, but he won't get one if he can't get a good reference from my brother.'

Molly tried to conceal her relief at the prospect of Fernando moving on to employment elsewhere. Angry as she was with Leandro, she felt guilty for keeping quiet about Julieta's affair and would be glad when the liaison was no longer being conducted on her doorstep. The evening before, Leandro had worked late in his study and had slept in his own room. Molly had had to fight off a powerful urge to go and join him there. Sex made her feel important and close to him, but those comforting feelings invariably evaporated in the harsh light of day. Yet, how could he be so possessive of her and not feel something for her? Were his strictures about Fernando just the male territorial instinct operating and nothing deeper?

Her mobile phone rang while she was at a fashionable tapas bar with Julieta and her friends. It was Leandro. 'Why didn't you tell me you were going out?'

'I didn't think you'd notice I was missing,' Molly heard herself reply while she smoothed down the skirt of her little black dress, which did a marvellous job of skimming her pregnant tummy.

'If you tell me where you are, I'll come and join you.'

Molly was aware that Fernando would be showing up at some stage of the evening and she knew she couldn't possibly let Leandro meet up with his sister's friends. 'No, thanks.'

'You're my wife,' Leandro growled.

'I know. Sometimes—like now—the wedding ring

feels like a choke chain,' Molly told him in an undertone of helpless complaint. 'I had a lot more fun when I was single. Look, I'll see you tomorrow.'

'Tomorrow? Where are you spending the night?' Leandro raked down the line, all pretence of cool suddenly ditched.

Molly smiled wickedly, enjoying the sensation of having surprised him. 'With your sister, of course. Please don't spoil her birthday.'

But mysteriously her bubble of enjoyment began to ebb at that point. Perhaps it was the challenge of being the only sober person in the party. Perhaps it was because, although she adored being out in company, it was already well after midnight and she was getting sleepier by the minute. Their destination was an exclusive hip club popular with the celebrity set and Fernando met up with them before they went in. A camera flash alerted Molly to the presence of the paparazzi and she was relieved to escape into the luxurious interior and sit down to watch the extravagant and entertaining floorshow.

Time began to telescope after that. She marvelled at the irony that she sat in the *castillo* most days and nights missing Leandro and that now when she'd finally got out, she was still missing him. She watched Fernando Santos conduct a very sly flirtation with one of Julieta's friends and decided that she didn't like him at all. Julieta was obviously in love, but Molly suspected that Fernando might only be with his employer's sister because she was an heiress. The music and the chatter coalesced into a droning barrage of sound and Molly's drowsiness began to gain ground on her. She fought her exhaustion because she could see that Julieta was having a great time and she was determined not to be a party-pooper. She must have dozed off at some stage, because when she stirred again she found herself outside in the night air and she only fully woke up inside the car. There were loud voices all around her and when she opened her eyes she was almost blinded by camera flashes.

'What happened…where are we going?' Molly pulled herself up into a sitting position and addressed Julieta, who was wrapped round Fernando like a vine.

'Home. Go back to sleep,' Julieta advised, not unkindly.

Woolly-minded and with a body that felt heavy and clumsy, Molly stripped where she stood in Julieta's guest room and slept almost the same minute that her head hit the pillow. The next morning, the buzz of her mobile phone startled her and she fumbled in her bag and dug it out. Whoops, she thought in consternation even before she answered it, because there were ten missed calls listed on it. 'Molly?' a female voice exclaimed. 'Is that Molly?'

'Yes, who is this?' But Molly's heart was thumping with excitement because, although she couldn't quite believe it, she was convinced she already knew who that voice belonged to.

'Ophelia…don't you remember my voice?' her sister cried, audibly anxious. 'I wish you weren't in Spain. I want to see you right now, put my arms round you and hug you!'

And Molly burst into floods of tears and that was that. She had found her sister. Within the space of a minute the two women were catching up and soon Molly, who had never been a fan of polite pretences, found herself admitting that Leandro had only married her because she had fallen pregnant.

'You don't sound very happy,' Ophelia remarked worriedly.

'I'm not,' Molly said ruefully, but didn't add that, despite this fact, she still could not imagine living without a regular fix of her workaholic husband, because that sounded very wet and wimpy.

She was stunned when Ophelia told her that they had an older half-brother of Russian extraction called Nikolai Arlov. It was wonderful for her to learn that both her siblings had been trying really hard to trace her for several years. Ophelia was eager to satisfy Molly's curiosity about Nikolai, her children and her husband, Lysander Metaxis. Her thoughts buzzing at the dizzy awareness that she did have a family of her own, after all, Molly was able to laugh out loud with pleasure when she discovered that Haddock the parrot was still alive.

Wrapped in a colourful silk wrap, Julieta put her head round the door to tell Molly that the limo had arrived to take her home and to ask her if she wanted any breakfast before she left. Molly shook her head and asked her sister if she could call her back later. Awash with wondering thoughts about seeing Ophelia again and getting to know her brother and both their families, she dressed in the combat trousers and T-shirt she had packed. By then she had also discovered that most of the missed calls on her phone were from Leandro. Guilt engulfed her and she felt remarkably like a misbehaving teenager who had broken her curfew, and who now had to go home to face the music.

She was dismayed to find a clutch of paparazzi outside

the apartment block, apparently awaiting her appearance. Questions were shouted at her in Spanish and she hurried into the limo, grateful for the presence of Leandro's security men who prevented the photographers from filming her.

She entered the castle, which was unusually silent. Basilio greeted her oozing an attitude of funereal calm and gloom. She was surprised when Leandro strode out of his study, for she was aware that he had a business trip to Geneva that day. 'I assumed you would have already left.'

'I waited to show you the morning paper.' Molly followed him into his study and glanced down enquiringly at the publication lying open on his desk. Horror seized her by the throat and she went rigid when she studied the photos on the page. One depicted a bleary-eyed and tousled woman being helped across a pavement and the second the same woman lying flat and apparently unconscious on the rear seat of a limo. That woman was her and her first foolish thought was that she had never seen more unflattering pictures. Her skirt had ridden up over her thighs and her pregnant tummy rose above them like a mountain.

'How could you get in such a condition?' Leandro raked at her furiously. 'Didn't you consider the health of the child you carry?'

'I was just very tired…I swear I wasn't drinking alcohol!' Molly protested shakily. 'The photos are very misleading—'

'You mean you weren't in a nightclub until four this morning with our estate manager? And you didn't require him to practically carry you out of it again?'

Molly swallowed hard, belatedly taking in the reality

that Fernando Santos was the individual urging her shambling and sleepy self towards the car. 'I was one of a large party of people which included him.'

Her husband's strong bone structure was bone-white with tension below his bronzed skin. 'He spent the night at my sister's apartment with you. He was seen leaving early this morning!'

Molly didn't quite know what to say to that without dropping Julieta straight into a mire from which there would be no clean return. How could Leandro think that she would sleep with another man? Why did he believe she could be so untrustworthy and disloyal? She was carrying his baby. Didn't he have any respect for her at all?

'I'm not having an affair with Fernando. He's really not my type—although I have to confess that, right now, when you're standing over me like a hanging judge, you're not my type either,' Molly confided tartly. 'I'm very sorry if the photos cause you embarrassment, but I wasn't in any way under the influence of either drugs or alcohol. I was simply very, very sleepy and I have nothing else to apologise for.'

Brilliant dark eyes cut into hers like abrasive diamond cutters. 'I don't believe you. I want the truth…'

'I've told you the truth.' Molly was torn between feeling hugely intimidated and hugely resentful that he could have so little faith in her that he instantly dismissed her explanation. 'I went out with Julieta to celebrate her birthday.'

'Then why wouldn't you tell me where you were so that I could join you?'

Molly shuffled her feet, knowing that there was no acceptable answer to that and wishing she didn't feel obligated to cover up for Julieta's private life. It was not a friendship she wanted to put at risk. 'I just wanted a night off from being your wife. Is that a crime?'

His classic features hardened at that facetious response. 'How long have you been seeing Santos?'

'Maybe you'd like me to be an unfaithful wife and then you would have grounds for divorcing me. Is that what this is about? You've realised that you made a mistake marrying me and you want an escape route?' Molly slung at him accusingly.

'You're talking nonsense,' Leandro drawled icily.

'No, I'm not. I want an escape route!' Molly threw at him in a rage. 'I want my life back, so why shouldn't you? You're an absentee husband and I'm lonely. I want a man who's interested me and who I can share stuff with. But you're so busy making money and putting everything else ahead of me, you don't have time for me or the baby that's coming. Why shouldn't I want more than your precious money, your title and social position? None of those things are important to me!'

'You've said enough,' Leandro intoned with ferocious bite, mentally stacking up those far-reaching accusations as a clumsy attempt to deflect him from her inexcusable behaviour. 'I still have a flight to Geneva to catch. I'll see you tomorrow.'

'You said you couldn't give me love—but what *have* you given me?' Molly whispered chokily.

Leandro ground his even white teeth together. He refused to listen to her. He didn't want her to start crying. He was so angry with her that he didn't trust himself to speak. As long as she continued to deny everything, there was nothing to discuss and no way forward. He would get the truth out of Julieta, and if Molly had betrayed his trust he would have no choice but to divorce her. But having reached that pinnacle of masculine decisiveness, Leandro discovered that that obvious solution had zero appeal for him. He pictured Molly in Santos's arms and he felt as if someone were trying to rip his guts out with a machete. The black rage tamped down inside him surged higher and the fierce struggle it took to stay in control angered him even more.

Molly couldn't believe that Leandro was still planning to fly off to Geneva just as if nothing had happened. His rock-hard self-discipline and devotion to banking business when their marriage was in crisis struck her as yet more proof of his lack of caring. Her mobile phone rang just as she reached the sanctuary of her bedroom. The instant she heard her sister's voice, her control over her tumultuous emotions dissolved. Suddenly she was in floods of tears and struggling to find the right words to answer Ophelia's concerned questions. Unfortunately there was no pleasant way to explain that Leandro was convinced that she had been carrying on an affair with one of his employees. Her sister was very shocked by that admission and then she explained that she was with their brother, Nikolai, who also wanted to speak to her. Somewhere just out of Molly's hearing at the other end of the line she could hear an urgent discussion taking place between her newly discovered siblings.

'Do you really want to stay with this bozo in Spain?' a very forceful masculine voice enquired a little while later. 'I can pick you up in a few hours and fly you back to England.'

Molly was shaken by the idea of leaving Spain within

hours, but it was a remarkably tempting offer when she was in dire need of comfort and support. 'Could you...I mean, would you?'

'I'm very impatient to meet my baby sister,' Nikolai confessed bluntly.

'I'm not a baby—'

'You are on my terms,' he countered with uncompromising bluntness.

Feverish indecision assailed Molly. She desperately wanted to be with her sister and meet her brother. Leandro had devastated her to the extent that she could barely think straight. He had accused her of infidelity and paid no heed to her denials. He had shown no sign of even being prepared to listen to her perfectly reasonable complaints. Was she really planning to sit and wait for him to return from Geneva for more of the same? He didn't love her. Nothing was likely to change that. She was never going to compare to Aloise and the fact that she was expecting his baby in another few months currently seemed to be a matter of near indifference to him. Perhaps he had decided that marrying her had been a mistake. That could explain why he had made little effort to make their marriage a success.

Molly squared her slight shoulders and breathed in deep. 'I'll come back home with you.'

Nikolai promised to call her when his jet landed in Spain. Ophelia was so excited when she came back on the phone that Molly could only follow about one word in three, but her sister's enthusiasm melted the cold knot of fear and uncertainty forming inside her.

She sat down at the elegant ladies desk by the window

and pulled out the fancy stationery she had never used to write Leandro a note. Tears were streaming down her tight face while she studied the blank sheet of paper in anguish. What she was feeling was forcing her to acknowledge that she cared a great deal more about Leandro than he cared about her. But she didn't want to be the sort of sad woman who settled for the crumbs from the table because she lacked the pride to believe that she deserved the whole loaf. If she was unhappy, her child would be unhappy as well. Her dream of creating a happy home and family for the three of them was exactly that: just a dream and not an achievable goal with Leandro in a leading role.

She was packing when she made a curious discovery while she was searching for a missing shoe at the back of a closet. Her fingers encountered a surprising lump below the carpet on the floor of the cupboard and she pushed it back and drew out what had lain concealed underneath. To her astonishment she realised that she was holding several packets of birth control pills. Now, who on earth would have hidden a secret stash of contraceptives there? And her imagination could only come up with one likely contender—Aloise, whose evident inability to fall pregnant might seemingly have been a deliberate choice. So the perfect wife had not been quite so perfect, after all. Molly shrugged and put the pills back where she had found them.

She left all her jewellery behind and even removed her rings to leave them lying on the dressing table. After a light lunch served in her room, she went for a nap from which she was wakened by Nikolai's call. Having dressed again, she rang for a member of staff to carry down her cases. Basilio was at the foot of the staircase, wringing his hands. She thought painfully of how much Leandro would loathe the attention that the breakdown of their marriage would create. Her baby kicked and she tensed, wondering guiltily if her child could somehow feel her emotional turmoil.

Doña Maria appeared in the doorway of the salon. The older woman looked incredibly smug, but Molly couldn't have cared less, for she could already hear the noisy approach of a helicopter flying in low. That was the exact moment that what she was doing really sank in on her, not the best time for her to realise that she had fallen in love with Leandro when she was in the midst of wondering how he had survived his cold and severe mother's upbringing. But she didn't need to wonder, did she? Leandro had developed self-reliance and rigid self-discipline at a very early age while learning to hide and suppress his emotions.

Someone rapped noisily on the front door. Basilio opened it. Molly saw a very tall and powerfully built man with dark hair striding towards the entrance while bodyguards fanned out around him. In the background sat a helicopter with Arlov Industries written across the tail.

'Molly?' he queried with a wide measuring appraisal, and then he flung back his handsome head and laughed, impervious to Doña Maria's goggling stare at him, his men and his helicopter. 'I don't believe it—you're even smaller than Ophelia!'

He snapped his fingers and one of his bodyguards hurried forward to lift her luggage. She walked out into the sunshine and part of her screamed to stay. Her nerves were stretched tight as piano wires.

'You're not sure about doing this, are you?' her companion divined with disturbing ease.

'I don't think I've any other option right now.'

Nikolai Arlov paused in his stride and rested his shrewd gaze on her troubled face. 'As a husband, I should warn you that your Spanish duke won't forgive this move in a hurry.'

Molly shrugged a feisty shoulder while she thought of all the evenings that had stretched into eternity as she had spent them alone. 'I'll survive,' she replied with determination.

'So, is this an I'm-leaving-you-for-ever or I-want-you-to-sit-up-and-take-notice walkout?' Nikolai enquired lazily.

Molly registered that her big brother knew a lot about women. 'The jury's still out on that one.'

'Because he went to Geneva? But that was work,' Nikolai pointed out, as if putting business first was a perfectly understandable act.

Sudden tears burned at the backs of her eyes. Too much was happening all at once. Her chin tilting, she blinked rapidly. She had got by before Leandro and she would get by after him just as well. But she still had to learn how to *want* to do that, she acknowledged heavily. The helicopter took off and she watched the *castillo* ebbing from view and wondered just when she would see Leandro again and whether or not lawyers would be present at the occasion.

CHAPTER NINE

LEANDRO studied his bruised knuckles with little sense of satisfaction. He had visited Santos on the way to the airport and had found the estate manager in the act of loading up his car, apparently already aware that his secret was out. A hopeless opponent, Santos had mumbled apologies and ducked a fight. How could Molly have been attracted to a man with all the backbone of a worm?

Flying out to Geneva, regardless of events, had proved a mistake. His concentration had evaporated as increasingly nightmarish images of Molly in another man's bed had interrupted his usual rational thinking processes. He had cut his meetings short to fly home. Once there, he had enjoyed an exchange of opinions with his mother that had led to her fuming departure within the space of an hour. Only then had he had the privacy to walk up to Molly's abandoned bedroom.

Her exit note was a tangled tale of the new and lately rediscovered family relationships that had led to her flight in Nikolai Arlov's helicopter. Nikolai Arlov, Leandro reflected heavily. Her brother was a Russian billionaire. But the emptiness of the room had affected Leandro much more than the revelations on paper. Her rings lay on the dressing table in rejection of their marriage. He could picture her yanking them off, green eyes blazing with anger and defiance. He could still see the indent of her tiny body on the bedspread where she had lain down. The imagery paralysed him and his fists clenched in a bitter battle with the churning emotions he had refused to acknowledge throughout the day.

He was envisaging a world without Molly and it would be a world shorn of colour or warmth. Every morning she got up to have breakfast with him and chattered tirelessly through the meal he had once enjoyed in the strictest silence with his newspapers. Now he would have the peace back and the *castillo* would echo around him again. He would no longer have her to come home to, a beacon at the end of a long working day spent in meetings or travelling. But that was as it should be, wasn't it? What odds when she had been unfaithful and only a divorce could settle their differences? But he was not capable of such cool logic. He could not get beyond one basic fact: her bed was empty and she was gone.

Someone knocked on the door and he swung round to refuse that invasion of his privacy. But it was Julieta, his younger sister, who stood flushed and tear-stained in the doorway.

'I don't want to talk to anyone right now,' Leandro breathed not quite steadily.

'Even if I'm here to tell you that I'm the one who was having the affair with Fernando?' Julieta sobbed.

There were three women in the swimming pool.

Molly lay back on her floating couch and sipped at her

strawberry smoothie while twitching her toes to the beat of the dance track playing in the unashamedly luxurious pool house at Nikolai's London home.

'You're looking better,' Abbey, her brother's red-headed, beautiful and equally pregnant wife, pronounced with approval as she awkwardly got down to towel dry her son. Danilo was a wriggling, laughing toddler with a good deal of his father's forceful personality.

'You were as pale as a waif when you arrived,' Ophelia opined. 'Now you're eating proper meals and much more relaxed.'

Molly smiled, more than satisfied with the family circle she had found and got to know over the past week. She had spent the first few days with Ophelia and Lysander at Madrigal Court, where she had also got to know her niece and nephews, the youngest of whom was only four months old. Nikolai had insisted that DNA testing should be carried out so that no one could ever question her identity, and the tests had also revealed a connection that Molly had never suspected before.

Her father, it seemed, had definitely been the Greek tycoon, Aristide Metaxis, the man who had not only jilted her unfortunate mother at the altar, but who had also become Cathy's long-term lover in later years. Molly did, in fact, have a vague memory of a male visitor, who had often given her sweets. It had fascinated her that Aristide's adoptive son, Lysander, who was Ophelia's husband, should also be her adoptive half-brother. What was more, that particular relationship would have lasting effects on her life, for, apparently, Aristide had discreetly left money in trust for an unnamed child and his lawyers were convinced that that child was Molly and that he had been well aware at the time of his death that he had a daughter.

Abbey answered the house phone by her side and then gave Molly a speculative smile. 'Your husband is here to see you.'

Molly began paddling like mad for the side of the pool with Ophelia, an unflappable blonde, following suit at a leisurely crawl. She climbed out and caught the towel that Abbey tossed to her, wrapping it round her to warm suddenly chilled skin. A whole week had elapsed since she'd left Spain. Leandro had taken his time to come looking for her. Cramming her bare feet into flip-flops, she headed into the lift to go upstairs.

Her heart was thundering in her eardrums as she padded into the opulent drawing room and she was as out of breath as though she had been running. Leandro was a very tall, still figure by the front windows. He swung round, brilliant dark eyes zeroing in on her small figure. Her casual appearance startled him. With her black curls anchored on top of her head with a clip and a bright tangerine bikini top showing above the edges of the black and yellow towel she wore, Molly took him very much by surprise.

Superbly well dressed in a black pinstripe designer suit that was tailored to enhance every muscular angle of his lean, powerful body, Leandro had a pure physical impact that engulfed Molly like a wave breaking over her head that left her struggling for breath. A masculine dream of black hair, golden skin and lustrous dark heavily lashed eyes, he looked stunning to a woman whose senses had been starved of his presence. This, after all, was the guy she woke up searching for in her bed at night. Her breasts swelled and her body tingled back to life at the mere sight of him.

'Your brother refused to tell me where you were,' Leandro growled soft and low, but with all the warning threat of a tiger flexing his claws.

Molly tensed. 'Honestly? I had no idea—'

'I first made contact with him by phone when he was flying you back to London on the day you left a week ago.' Leandro volunteered that information grimly. 'He said you didn't want to speak to me.'

Molly went pink, furious that Nikolai had chosen to make such decisions on her behalf and resenting his interference in her marriage. 'He shouldn't have done that, but he was probably trying to protect me.'

'I owe you a sincere apology for my misconceptions about your relationship with Fernando Santos,' Leandro delivered gravely, his striking dark golden eyes welded to hers. 'Julieta told me the truth.'

'Oh…' Off-balanced by his immediate apology, Molly couldn't concentrate. 'I haven't spoken to her since I left. Is she all right?'

'She was very upset about what happened between us and she's broken up with Santos, after finding out that she wasn't the only woman in his life. I think that in the circumstances you should have told me the truth.'

Molly drew herself up to her full insignificant height and breathed in deep. 'You wouldn't have believed me! From the first moment you saw Fernando talking to me, you were suspicious of us—'

'*Dios mio*, I was jealous,' Leandro admitted between

gritted teeth. 'I immediately saw his eagerness to impress you, his admiration for you.'

'For me, and I don't know how many other women. Fernando is a self-satisfied flirt,' Molly cut in, ever so slightly mollified by that unexpected confession of jealousy. 'I thought you didn't get jealous.'

His incredible cheekbones tensed. 'I believed that was the truth when I said it to you. I didn't recognise what a hold jealousy had got on my mind, so that I misinterpreted everything that happened to fit my deepest…er…fears.' His accented drawl dropped in level as he fitted in that last revealing word, low and quick. 'Of course you were correct when you said that I should have trusted you. But you're a very beautiful, sensual young woman and why should other men not be knocked out by you as I was?'

Her towel was slipping, revealing an eye-catching depth of cleavage. Conscious of his gaze dropping to the cups struggling to restrain her bountiful breasts, Molly reddened and hoisted her towel. Even so, her treacherous body was already reacting to that interest with a hot pulse low in her pelvis.

'How could you just walk out on our marriage?' Leandro demanded.

'Easily. I was the only person making an effort in our relationship. You were never there and you made me live with your mother, who absolutely hated me!'

'I wasn't aware how deep her dislike of you was until she voiced certain opinions to me after you had gone. She's returned to her home in Seville and is now aware that she is not welcome at the *castillo* unless she can treat you with the respect that is your right as my wife. Why did I have to wait for my mother to lose her temper to find out how she was treating you? Why didn't you just tell me?'

It was a fair question, Molly acknowledged. 'I didn't know whose side you would take and I didn't want to put you in that position. I honestly did believe that sooner or later Doña Maria would get tired of needling me and just accept me.'

'But you deserved better than that in your own home. Naturally I would have taken your side. I have no illusions about what my mother can be like—'

'I think she was behind the financial offer that was made to me before I married you,' Molly said abruptly.

'What financial offer?'

Molly gave him the details. He was staggered, genuinely staggered, when she shared the content of that meeting. He asked her to name the legal firm concerned and a flash of recognition lit his hard gaze. 'That firm did work for the estate at one time. It is very likely that my mother was behind that offer. I had no idea that she would go to such extremes or even that she would dare to interfere in my life to that extent—'

'She doesn't think I'm good enough for you.'

His anger was palpable and his strong jaw line clenched. '*Dios mio*, you turned down two million pounds to marry me?'

'Yeah…I'd have been wiser grabbing the cash and running for the hills, wouldn't I?' she quipped in a wry allusion to the current state of their relationship.

Leandro took a sudden step forward, his spectacular dark golden gaze narrowed and intent. 'I am very grateful that you didn't and that you went through with our marriage. I only wish I had done more with the opportunity.'

'No, I don't think you do,' Molly contradicted with a rueful grimace. 'You didn't want any more than a shallow show of a marriage for the baby's sake, but, unfortunately, I'm not as detached as you are. I couldn't live like that for the rest of my days.'

'Why didn't you speak to me sooner about how you felt?' Leandro prompted grimly. 'Didn't it occur to you that the day I believed you had spent the night with a lover was not the right moment to tackle me about my deficiencies as a husband?'

'No. As I hadn't been with a lover, that angle didn't occur to me,' Molly conceded.

'I had spent the whole night worrying about you. Again, it's all my own fault,' he framed in a harsh undertone. 'Your brother, Nikolai, left me in no doubt of that. Had you had bodyguards the paparazzi would never have got near you and I would have known where you were that night.'

'I don't need bodyguards. Nikolai is extremely security conscious.'

Leandro reached for her hands, which she was unconsciously wringing, and closed them firmly into his. Determined dark golden eyes locked with her anxious gaze. 'I am not detached from you, nor do I wish to be. I want you back, *mi corazón*. I would have told you that a week ago, had your brother been willing to tell me where you were.'

Molly tensed, hope and doubt warring inside her in a death-defying tussle of seething conflict. 'I'm sure you mean well, but marriage for me has to be about more than you doing the right thing for the woman carrying your child. I would never try to shut you out of our baby's life.'

His grip on her hands was almost painfully tight. 'How do I convince you that it will be different? This is not about doing the right thing. I'm asking you to give me the chance to *prove* how much I value your presence in my life.'

Tears were burning her eyes. This was the guy she loved, the guy she missed every hour of the day, and once again he was offering her what she craved, only this time around she was less naive. 'But the point is that you didn't value me when I was there. You didn't even come home for dinner at night. You didn't phone me. You didn't look for me or show the smallest sign that you missed me when you were away from me.'

Leandro was pale as death beneath his bronzed complexion and his handsome bone structure was rigid with ferocious tension. 'I have never found it easy to show my feelings. I would not allow myself to need you too much. I saw that as a weakness and I do not like to be in anything other than full control.'

'Whereas I let everything show, and say and do what I feel like. We're a very bad match, Leandro. I was lonely and unhappy with you and I don't want to go back to that,' she confided jerkily, fighting off temptation with all her strength because she refused to end up back where she had started. 'Now that the break has been made, it should get easier for us both.'

'I don't like my life without you in it!' Leandro launched at her rawly in the roughest tone she had ever heard from him.

'I think you should go,' Molly pronounced tightly.

'I can't walk away from you and my child!' he bit out in a driven undertone.

'You have to, if that's what she wants,' another male voice interposed from the doorway.

Molly turned her head to see her adoptive half-brothers poised just inside the room, neither of them looking particularly welcoming. 'Nikolai—stay out of this, *please*!'

Fierce aggression powered through Leandro's powerful frame when he recognised the level of family opposition in the two men's faces. 'Are you with Nikolai on this, Lysander?' he asked grimly.

'No, I don't believe in interfering in other people's marriages,' the tall handsome Greek breathed with measured calm. 'But if you cause my sister any more grief, I'll rip you apart!'

The Russian tycoon studied Leandro with cold hostility. 'Molly has us now. She doesn't need anyone else.'

'Let's allow Molly to make that decision,' Leandro countered, striding to the door and looking back at Molly to say, 'You know where I'm staying.'

Molly swallowed the lump in her throat and nodded. Every fibre of her being urged her to chase after him and stop him from leaving her. It took every ounce of her self-discipline to let him go without a murmur. She told herself that she had made the wisest decision. She didn't want to be the second-best wife of a man who didn't love her. She didn't want to spend her life saving face by hiding her love for him. She wanted to be brave and independent: she had to learn how to get by without him.

Nikolai patted her taut shoulder as the front door closed on Leandro's departure. 'You made the right decision.'

'Only if it's what Molly really wants,' Lysander interposed seriously, shooting her pale face an unconvinced appraisal.

'Molly and I both grew up without a silver spoon in our mouths.' Nikolai intoned that reminder flatly. 'What do you think she has in common with a duke who went to a British public school?'

'He's really not a snob,' Molly mumbled helplessly in Leandro's favour.

'They will soon have a child in common.' Lysander dealt his brother-in-law an impatient glance. 'And that child is a good enough reason for Molly to take her time over deciding whether or not she wants a divorce.'

Divorce! That very word struck horror into Molly's bones. Divorce would be so final. She would never see Leandro again unless he came to visit their child and she did not think she could bear the prospect of that. That conviction grew on her while she played with her brothers' children that evening. Surely when she loved Leandro so much it made sense to give their marriage one more chance? Soon after reaching that conclusion, she told Abbey that she was going over to Leandro's apartment to see him.

One of Nikolai's security team tagged her all the way to the door and it was a relief to step inside. Leandro focused on her with frowning force, her appearance clearly coming as a surprise to him. The smell of whiskey clinging to him took her by surprise for Leandro rarely drank. In addition, he was not his usual perfectly groomed self. His tie was missing, his jacket crumpled and he badly needed a shave.

'Molly?' he queried, as if he couldn't quite accept the evidence of his own eyes.

Molly leant back against the door and walked past him into the airy lounge where a half-empty whisky bottle and a single glass sat beside an untouched meal. 'I have a proposition to put to you,' she stated.

Leandro gave her an enquiring look, which would have been more impressive had his eyes been in focus and had he contrived to walk in a straight line. In actuality he managed neither, for her abstemious husband was anything but sober. 'Go ahead.'

'A make-or-break holiday of at least three weeks for just the two of us, to see if we can make something of this marriage,' Molly murmured, wondering why he was drinking alone and worrying about it.

'I can do that!' Leandro declared instantly.

'Leandro…in Spain you couldn't do one night at home with me, so don't underestimate what you'd be signing up for,' she sighed.

His lean, strong features set into purposeful strong lines. 'I'll try anything that means I don't lose you and the baby, *mi preciosa*.'

Her eyes shone with tears, for she realised that he had done some serious thinking and was finally recognising what the breakdown of their marriage would ultimately cost him. Naturally he didn't want to lose the chance to bring up the child he had married her to support. 'And no more secrets. I know you're not the sort of guy who's in touch with his feelings, but you still have them…don't you?'

Leandro studied her, poised there in a bright red raincoat with her dark curly head tilted to one side like a little inquisitive bird, and snatched in a ragged breath. '*Sí*.'

'So that's the deal: long holiday, no secrets, major effort on all fronts from you,' Molly proffered anxiously.

'Do you want to go now?' Leandro enquired hopefully.

'No, I think you should sleep off the whisky first,' Molly said wryly. 'What about tomorrow afternoon? Could you hire a villa somewhere?'

'It's done. It will be the holiday of a lifetime,' Leandro swore…

CHAPTER TEN

THE Casa Limone sat in a breathtaking Tuscan landscape of woods and hills. A Renaissance jewel with ancient walls and a tower, the former farmhouse enjoyed a contrastingly cool and contemporary interior. Surrounded by olive groves, vines and rolling fields speckled with glorious wild flowers, the house lay at the foot of a long lane in a sunlit glade of perfect peace and seclusion.

Molly was surprised when Leandro admitted that it was only one of the houses he had bought as an investment over the years and put in the charge of a rental agency. He had never mentioned his extensive property portfolio to her before. A tense expression suddenly gripped her small face as she stepped out of the four-wheel drive they had picked up at the airport. 'Did you ever bring *her* here? Aloise, I mean?' she clarified, hating herself for asking, but, all the same, desperately needing to know.

'No.' As if realising that that one defensive word was insufficient, Leandro added, 'She preferred the city.'

'Oh…' Registering that she had got a whole sentence dug out of him on that controversial issue, Molly didn't waste time about going in for the kill. 'Was it really a perfect marriage?'

The silence seemed to thunder in her sensitive ears.

'No,' Leandro breathed curtly. 'We were both miserable.'

And with that stunning response he might as well have gagged Molly. She was so shocked that she could think of nothing else to say. Her gaze locked to his tight profile and the moment was lost as he lifted their cases to take them indoors. In a handful of words, he had blown away her conviction that their relationship came a poor second to his first marital excursion. Suddenly she was on unfamiliar ground and wondering how to be subtle and tactful, rather than shamelessly eager to hear every wretched detail that had contributed to that mutual misery.

Yet how could she have been so blind to the obvious? Was it surprising that the guy who didn't like weddings had good reason for his prejudice? People were more likely to talk about happy memories, but Leandro never voluntarily mentioned Aloise's name and only now was she realising what had lain hidden behind that silence.

'What were Nikolai's last words to you today?' Leandro asked, startling her out of her reverie.

'Abbey wished us well!' Molly ducked the issue to tell him brightly. 'Nikolai just hasn't had the chance to get to know you yet and you met under the wrong circumstances.'

'But what did he say?' Leandro persisted.

'That if I can't be myself with you, it'll never work,' she divulged in an apprehensive rush.

A grim smile shadowed his wide sensual mouth. 'He's shrewd.'

'But so are you.' And gorgeous and clever and the man I love, Molly added inside her head.

'I thought I was until you took off your wedding ring,' Leandro confided in a dark, deep, abrasive drawl that shimmied down her spine like a burst of electrical energy on a still day.

Molly focused on his lean darkly handsome features, her heart buzzing like a battery-driven toy inside her chest. She had feared that she might never be so close to him again. The future had become a terrifying destination that she was afraid to face. She had lost faith in her own judgement, had questioned what she had done and the impossibility of undoing it. The pain of leaving him, of being without him, had coloured everything she thought and experienced. Just at that instant, the pure relief of being with him again made her knees turn weak.

Leandro's attention dropped to the lush pink contours of her mouth. 'Do you want your rings back?'

Molly froze, evasive eyes reflecting her insecurity. 'Let's see how things go.'

Brilliant dark eyes challenged her. 'Am I on trial?'

Molly moved her hands in a soothing motion and tried to explain what she felt. 'I suppose we both are. I don't want us to break up after our child's got used to us being together, so if we can't work things out it would be better if we separated before the birth.'

Leandro was spooked by her earnest tone, the clear fact that she had considered such matters in depth. He leant forward, splaying his hands to the painted wall on either side of her, imprisoning her there. Dark golden eyes fired down into hers. 'I will fight long and hard to keep you—'

'But it's not a failure to lose this battle,' Molly whispered urgently. 'It would just mean that we're not suited but that we did our best. I don't want you to stay with me only because of the baby.'

A rather ragged laugh escaped Leandro. 'That's not why I'm here. I'm here because I want *you, tesora mia*...' a lean brown forefinger shifted to probe the peachy softness of her full lips, lingering when they parted '...and I've spent a week living with the idea that I might never be able to be with you again...'

'Me too,' Molly confided, shaken that on one score at least they could think the exact same thoughts.

'And now that's all I can think about,' he confessed in a driven undertone. 'But that's not what you want from me at this moment.'

'No?'

Black lashes semi-screened his gaze. 'Of course, it isn't,' he told her with assurance. 'You want to talk and sit down to a romantic meal and then maybe go for a walk.'

She could tell this programme of civilised restraint had as much appeal for him at that instant as having his teeth pulled without an anaesthetic and she almost laughed out loud. Evidently he had thought a great deal about what she might expect from him and if he was getting it wrong, it was only because he had yet to grasp what she most wanted from him.

'Maybe tomorrow we could do that. Right now I want your time and your attention—which is all I ever wanted. There isn't some magical success-guaranteed blueprint of an itinerary to follow, even though I can see you wish there was.' She lifted her hands and began to unbutton his shirt. 'Whatever both of us want is perfect. We only have ourselves to please.'

He laced a possessive hand into her tumbling mane of curls, his other hand closing to her hip to tilt her against him. His mouth came down on hers with a raw, hot hunger that made no attempt to deny its urgency. The erotic plunge of his tongue provoked a surge of moisture between her thighs and she shivered convulsively in spite of the heat. She broke the kiss to finish unbuttoning the shirt and finally spread her hands across his bronzed hair-roughened torso, letting her fingers stroke and explore down to the intriguing silky furrow that disappeared below his belt while remaining awesomely aware of the revealing bulge beneath his chinos. Trembling, mortified by her own eagerness, she drew back from him, closed one hand over his and began to move towards the stairs.

'You want me too,' Leandro said thickly, his satisfaction unhidden.

'Shut up, or you'll get ravished on the stairs,' Molly warned him.

In response to that threat, Leandro pulled her slight, swollen body to him and kissed her with a passion that blew her away. He removed her dress in a shaded room where muslin panels swished across the chestnut-wood floor in the faint cooling breeze coming in through the open windows. Birds were singing in the woods behind the house. A swelling sense of happiness blossomed inside her, as if only now was she finally able to believe that she was back with Leandro.

She slid onto cool linen sheets and felt him hard, hot and rampant against her thigh and gloried in the differences between them. He stroked the full, firm globes of her breasts, lingering with tender care on the swollen pink buds of her nipples. She was all restive energy and craving, controlled by the pulsing ache in her pelvis. Everything was happening just a moment later than she needed it to happen.

'Leandro, please...' she framed, her voice tight with stress and longing.

'Trust me,' he breathed huskily. 'It'll be better this way.'

Her hips shifted up to him. She was way past caring about the exact shades of satisfaction; she was more than willing to settle for the most basic kind of all. Even before he touched the most receptive spot on her entire body she was burning up, liquid with desire and unbearably sensitive. The sound of her moans made him crush her reddened lips below his again. Her impatience tormented her, her need more fundamental than any she had ever known before.

Leandro turned her gently on her side, eased her back against him and entered her with a sweet, piercing depth that made her cry out in surprise and pleasure. And as he had promised it only got better. His slow, insistent rhythm was indescribably sensual and extremely controlled. Her excitement climbed to torturous heights as waves of pleasure began to pulse through her. She reached a shattering climax and tears wet her eyes at the wonderful intensity of her release. But nothing could have been more precious to her than the moment when Leandro vented an ecstatic groan and spilled inside her. He closed his arms tightly round her and pressed his mouth to her shoulder, muttering incomprehensible words of Spanish.

Right then at that pinnacle of happiness she recognised how fierce and elemental their hunger to make love again had been. They had needed to rediscover and share that intimacy after their separation, brief though it had been.

His fingers flexed against the swell of her stomach as the baby kicked and he lifted his tousled dark head. 'Is that our child moving?'

Molly confirmed that it was. He kept his hand in place before finally turning her round to face him and holding her close. 'I've signed you up with a local gynaecologist for the duration of our stay.'

'That wasn't necessary.' But Molly was secretly impressed that he had thought to take that precaution.

'I felt that it was, *tesora mia*,' Leandro intoned. 'Just in case we need to consult a doctor while you're here. I'm coming with you the next time you have a scan.'

'Only if you want to.'

His ebony brows pleated. 'I always wanted to, but I thought you might find my presence an intrusion at such appointments. You never showed any sign of wanting me to accompany you.'

It dawned on her that he had felt excluded and doubtful in a situation that was new and unfamiliar to him. She shifted closer and touched her mouth softly to his. 'I assumed you'd know that I wanted you there for support, but I didn't say anything about it because I didn't want you to feel obligated to go. I knew how busy you were.'

'A man who is too busy for his family doesn't deserve one, *querida*. My father died when I was five and I barely remember him. I was in boarding school a year later.'

Molly frowned. 'That's much too young to be sent away from home.'

'I think so, too. In fact, I don't believe I would send my child away to board. There is no harm in breaking with tradition for a new generation.'

The following morning they visited a charming gynaecologist, whose name had been recommended to Leandro. Molly had a scan there and then at the private clinic and was amused and touched by Leandro's fascination with their unborn son and the keen questions he asked. It occurred to her that her fear of being snubbed had ensured that she made no attempt to share any aspect of her pregnancy with him. She was warmed by the concern he couldn't hide when the doctor advised that their child be delivered by Caesarean section because the baby was big and she was small.

'Are you sure babies like bright colours that much?' Leandro studied the vibrant cot quilt and blinked quite deliberately.

'According to all the research…yes,' Molly declared.

'Colour is not my thing, *mi corazón*,' Leandro admitted evenly as they walked back towards the car in the enveloping warmth of late afternoon. He ushered her into a seat in the shade at a pavement café. 'Sit down. You're tired.'

Molly gave him a sleepy smile. If truth be known, she was tired of being pregnant, weary of hauling a larger, heavier body everywhere she went and sick of being clumsy and prone to tripping over her own feet. Yet a glorious sense of contentment washed over her as Leandro hailed the waiter and in fluent Italian ordered her favourite ice cream, a glass of wine for him and a long cold drink for her. They had sat on that particular terrace enjoying the view of the vineyards in the valley below many times, for the picturesque little hill town lay within a short drive of the house.

Their four-week sojourn in Tuscany had taught Molly that she could always relax when Leandro was around. He was great at looking after her and amazingly good at foreseeing her every need. She noticed a couple of women watching him with appreciation from a nearby table. They fancied the socks off him just as she did. She was always worrying that she betrayed her love when she looked at him. She worked hard at keeping things light and cool. He had been so upfront right from the start when he had admitted that he couldn't give her love. She was determined not to make him uncomfortable and risk destroying what they did have, purely because she couldn't settle for what she had got.

And she *had* settled for what she had with him; it was official. Last night she had put her rings back on and she had noticed that every so often he rested his attention on her hand, as if he liked to see them there on her finger.

Over the past month she had gradually let go of all her fears and allowed herself to be content. The shadow of Aloise had evaporated and Molly no longer tormented herself with futile comparisons. Even if Aloise had been the love of Leandro's life, their marriage had not worked out and Molly could no longer feel unequal or envious. She was still curious, still planning on telling Leandro about the contraceptive pills she had found, but she was too happy to want to risk spoiling the ambience they had achieved.

They had had a wonderful honeymoon six months after their wedding. She had strolled along the city ramparts at Lucca, wandered through the medieval streets of Florence and Siena, occasionally pausing to explore ancient buildings and admire spectacular art at a leisurely pace. A hundred special memories had ensured she would never forget their time at Casa Limone. The scent of new-mown grass would forever remind her of making love in the lemon orchard beside the house and lying drowsing in the languorous aftermath in Leandro's arms until it was almost dinner time. In the same way the taste of glorious chocolate would always remind her of being pregnant. She lusted after that wonderful taste-bud-melting flavour almost as much and as continuously as she lusted after Leandro, who didn't know what a full night's uninterrupted sleep was. He had confessed that he felt badly misled by the book he had read that suggested that a woman's interest in sex would wane as her pregnancy advanced.

Propping her chin on the heel of her hand, Molly surveyed her vibrantly handsome husband with dreamy appreciation. He was gorgeous and she felt that wanting to touch him pretty frequently was normal because sometimes she just couldn't believe her good luck in having him and needed to satisfy herself that he really was hers in every way that mattered.

'Are you thinking about our flight back to Spain tomorrow? Your family will be staying with us this weekend,' Leandro reminded her.

Molly smiled, recognising his concern that she might be less than eager to return to the *castillo*, but that wasn't the case. On the contrary, she was looking forward to the prospect. She was confident that everything would be different this time around. After all, Doña Maria was no longer in residence and Molly's marital home would finally be her own. To give him his due, Leandro had been appalled when he had realised that Molly had been prevented from having any input into the household arrangements and his mother had lied when she had announced that that had been his idea.

'I can't wait to see Ophelia again,' she admitted.

'But the two of you are always talking on the phone,' Leandro pointed out with a shake of his dark head.

'You'll be going back to work the day after tomorrow,' Molly said ruefully, knowing that that was normal life but dreading it all the same, for she had adored having him around all the time.

Dark golden eyes level, Leandro brushed the back of her hand in a perceptive gesture. 'I won't work the hours I used to. I won't be travelling for a while either and I'll phone you at least twice a day.'

'The sun is gleaming over your halo,' Molly teased.

'It's very important to me that you be happy.'

As she was convinced that he would have taken his first marriage equally seriously, she could not help wondering what had gone so badly wrong. That evening they dined out at a little restaurant they had visited before. On the drive home, she said softly, 'Tell me about Aloise…'

'She was all things to all people. Her family idolised her. Her colleagues admired her. I regarded her as a very close friend. Our families began pushing us together when we were in our mid-twenties. I'd enjoyed my freedom up until that point and I assumed she had as well. We could have said no, but our marriage seemed to make sense. I thought we wanted the same things out of life and you know I'm not the romantic type,' Leandro told her confidently in spite of the fact that he had lit pink candles round the hot tub and scattered rose petals on the water for her.

'So you saw your marriage as a practical arrangement?'

'I thought Aloise had the same view. She wasn't any more in love than I was, but she was very feminine and, naturally, I found her attractive After the wedding, our friendship just seemed to die. I didn't know what was wrong and she insisted that there *was* nothing wrong,' he breathed in a driven undertone.

They walked into the villa. Molly put on lights. 'What happened the day of the accident?'

Leandro dealt her a cloaked look. 'What I tell you must remain private for the sake of her family. She didn't want them to find out.' The silence hummed and his hand clenched taut as he made an awkward movement with it. 'I demanded to know why she was treating me like an enemy. So, she finally told me the truth and I lost my temper with her…'

'How?' she whispered, her attention welded to his haunted expression in the lamplight.

'I accused her of deceiving me and ruining both our lives because she wanted us to go on living a lie and… *Dios mio*, I wanted out!'

Molly was frowning. 'I don't understand. What was the truth?'

Leandro vented a harsh, unamused laugh. 'That she was gay. The moment she admitted it, I couldn't comprehend how I hadn't realised it for myself. She felt trapped in our life. Our marriage was a disaster, but she was willing to sacrifice both of us to keep her secret. At the moment she most needed my understanding and friendship, I turned on her and that's why she ran out, got in her car and ended up crashing it and killing herself.'

Molly was very much shocked and she reached out to grip his hands with hers. 'You must have been shattered and very bitter to find out after so many troubled years together. Of course you felt she had deceived you. It wasn't your fault she crashed, or your fault that your marriage didn't work. How could it have done? She was upset, Leandro. She must have been very unhappy. You both were. Let it go at that. Don't blame yourself for an accident.'

Leandro loosed his hands and bent down to lift her off her feet. 'You're always so considerate of how I feel and I honestly didn't know I had so many feelings until I met you, *mi corazón*. Uppermost was the pure erotic pleasure of a woman who wanted me just for myself,' he confessed huskily. 'Was it any wonder that I couldn't keep my hands off you?'

Molly blinked, still coming to terms with what he had shared with her about Aloise. He carried her upstairs and settled her on the big divan. 'I'm not any stronger. You're incredibly addictive,' she told him. 'I was a clean-living girl until you came along!'

Leandro gave her a rakish grin that tilted her heart on its axis. 'It meant a lot to me that I was your first lover. I think I fell in love with you the very first night we met, but I had no idea what had happened to me. Although I wasn't in love with her, Aloise hurt me,' he admitted gruffly. 'I tried so hard with her and got nowhere. I wanted to keep a distance with you, not get too involved, too close…'

Molly was transfixed by what he had said. 'You fell in love with me?'

'*Dios mio*…like a brick being chucked off the roof of a skyscraper. I'd never been in love before. In lust, *sì*. In love, never! But I couldn't tell the difference. The whole time I was in conflict with myself. I asked you to be my mistress.'

'And that hurt me.'

He crouched down in front of her, grasped her hands and kissed them in fervent apology. Her eyes shiny with love, her fingers smoothed his handsome dark head.

'It served you right that I was pregnant,' she told him. 'Why were you so careful to tell me that you couldn't give me love when you proposed?'

'I didn't know I had it to give. Love has never been my style. I was jealous of Jez for a long time.'

'Jez?' Molly yelped in disbelief.

'You and he had close ties that I found threatening,' Leandro admitted.

Molly rather liked the knowledge that Leandro wasn't as sure of himself as he always seemed. She leant forward and kissed him with loving brevity.

'Meeting you has been a humbling experience for me.' Springing upright, Leandro raised her and wrapped his arms round her in a possessive hold. 'I did everything wrong. I didn't give you the wedding or the honeymoon you should have had.'

'You were the bridegroom from hell,' his beloved

confided without hesitation. 'But really great in bed after banking hours.'

'I love coming home to you—'

'But you were late back every night!' Molly complained, unable to let that claim go past unchallenged.

'I forced myself to play it cool, so that I didn't feel out of control,' he breathed. 'I *hate* feeling out of control.'

'I like it when you're out of control,' Molly whispered, ready to take shameless liberties with her exploring hands and then suddenly freezing in dismay. 'Oh, gosh, I still haven't told you about the birth control pills I found in the wardrobe!'

Leandro was astonished, but quickly realised they could only have belonged to Aloise. 'So, she didn't want children with me.'

'If she felt trapped in her life, a child would only have trapped her more,' Molly suggested.

'What does it matter now?' Leandro tugged her down onto his hard thighs and linked his hands round the swell of her belly with an air of proud satisfaction. 'It's all so long ago and you and I belong together. The minute I saw you I was drawn to you.'

Molly thought of all the years of feeling that she was not good enough for the people and the things she wanted and needed out of life. Her new-found siblings and Leandro had between them washed away all those wretched insecurities. Bubbling over with happiness at the new knowledge that she was loved, she realised that she owed him the same honesty.

'I only realised that I loved you the day I left the castle. Leaving broke my heart,' she confided.

'It took me far too long to realise what I was doing to

you. When you walked out, I felt gutted,' Leandro admitted grimly. 'But it certainly did wake me up, *mi vida*. I had no idea you loved me.'

'Madly, passionately and for ever,' Molly swore with fervour and he surrendered to the glow of warmth in her eyes and kissed her with a passion that stole the breath from her lungs.

Eighteen months later, Molly walked down to the beach with Ophelia and her three children. The Greek island of Kastros, which belonged to her brother—Ophelia's husband—Lysander, was an oasis of perfect peace.

The latest addition to the family circle, little Felipe, slumbered in his all-terrain buggy. Black lashes as long as fly swats brushed his olive-skinned cheeks. With his black curls and green eyes, Molly and Leandro's firstborn was a handsome combination of his parental genes. A livewire toddler, usually he rarely slept during the hours of daylight. But they had had a barbecue on the beach the night before, which had kept him awake long past his usual bedtime and he was now making up for that.

Molly had given birth by Caesarean and made a speedy recovery. Felipe's birth had to some extent mended fences within Leandro's family. Thanks to Molly's intervention, Doña Maria had been allowed to attend her grandson's christening and had managed to be scrupulously polite to her daughter-in-law throughout the event. Her elder daughter, Estefania, was already a regular visitor at the *castillo*, having chosen to take her brother's side rather than her mother's when the family ructions were still at their height. Molly was under no illusions about the precise depth of her mother-in-law's warmth in her vicinity, but she preferred to tolerate occasional visits for the sake of peace and unity.

Julieta remained a close friend. The younger woman had long since got over her failed relationship with Fernando Santos and was currently dating a wealthy entrepreneur who seemed to think the sun rose and shone on her, and who had already gained Leandro's seal of approval.

Molly flew over to London regularly to meet up with her siblings and often made time to see Jez Andrews as well. Jez now had a girlfriend as committed to following the sport of motocross as he was and Molly fully expected to hear that Tamara would be moving in with him soon.

Molly's life in Spain had become frantically busy, which she loved. She had decided that the farmyard where her studio was would make a great craft village where local artists could work, exhibit and sell their wares. Financed by Leandro and by Nikolai, who had insisted on taking a financial stake in the concern as well, the concept had taken off like a rocket and had had the added benefit of providing a welcome local tourist attraction.

Once Molly had discovered just how much time and effort it took to run the *castillo*, she had hired an administrative assistant to take charge of the accounts. She had also given Basilio more power and used the older man's domestic expertise to ditch outdated working practices. Now Basilio was a much happier man. The household had come to run like clockwork and, furthermore, costs had been reduced, which had shocked and hugely impressed Leandro. The fact that his wife now spoke fluent Spanish had assisted her endeavours and she was very popular with the estate staff, who appreciated her practical, hard-working approach.

'There they are now…we should chuck rocks at them!' Ophelia pronounced with spirit as a Metaxis helicopter flew in and vanished from view to land behind her stunning contemporary Greek home. 'Lysander said he'd be back for lunch and it's almost dinner time.'

'Nikolai sent me a text saying that they had been delayed. Sorry, I forgot to tell you.' In the act of chasing after her three-year-old son, Danilo, and his toddler brother as they splashed through the surf, Abbey paused to speak in a tone of apology.

'Well, Nikolai wins in the communication stakes,' Molly acknowledged.

'Bet you anything he's put his name down on the waiting list for yet another wildly exotic car,' Nikolai's wife, the gorgeous red-headed Abbey forecast with a world-weary groan. 'We have garages full of cars. He doesn't even have time to drive them.'

'He just likes collecting them.' Molly lifted Felipe out of the buggy when he woke up with a cross little sob.

She began walking back up towards the stunning contemporary house above the beach just as the three men cleared the boundaries of the terraced gardens and began to stride down the hill to join their wives. Her heart leapt at the sight of Leandro's lean, darkly handsome face. Sometimes she loved him so much it hurt. And this was very definitely one of those times, when he was fresh back from the motor show that he had visited with Nikolai and Lysander. Unlike the other two men, Leandro couldn't have cared less about luxury cars. But in the interests of

bonding with her brothers, he had made the effort to accompany them and fit in. These days the guys got on as
well as their wives did, although being men there was a
good deal more competitiveness and joshing in their
dealings.

Felipe was opening his arms in greeting even as Leandro
swept his son out of his wife's arms and high into the air. The
little boy's shout of excitement delighted Molly. She loved
the fact that Leandro was a real hands-on father. Tucking his
son below his arm, he curved an arm round Molly.

'I missed you last night, *preciosa mia*,' he husked.

'Me too,' Molly whispered. 'We had a barbecue down
here for the kids.'

Dark golden eyes nailed to her animated face, Leandro
drew her close. Her lips tingled, heat rising in her cheeks.

'When are you two going to stop acting like honey-
mooners?' Nikolai quipped as he strode past them.

'Never,' Leandro breathed soft and low, unconcealed
appreciation in his gaze as he continued to study his wife
and wondered if she would like the very talkative parrot
he had acquired for her in London. Ophelia had offered
Haddock to Molly, but she hadn't liked to accept the parrot
when Ophelia's children were so attached to the old bird.

Confidence and happiness were winging through Molly
in a glorious wave. Later, when they were alone, she would
tell Leandro that their second child was on the way and
she knew he would be as overjoyed at that news as she was.

Felipe demanded to get down and examine the sandcas-
tle being built by Poppy and her siblings. Molly looked at
Nikolai, who was embracing Abbey while his sons clung
to his trouser legs. Lysander was presenting Ophelia with

a set of car keys and teasing her wickedly about some vehicle of his that she had crashed. Molly smiled again, loving the fact that she had a wonderful husband and such a loving and close family to share everything with…

CARRYING THE SPANIARD'S CHILD

JENNIE LUCAS

To my husband, my own fairy-tale hero.

CHAPTER ONE

BELLE LANGTRY HAD hated Santiago Velazquez from the moment she'd laid eyes on him.

Well, not the *exact* moment, of course. She was only human. When they'd first met at their friends' wedding last September—Belle had been the maid of honor, Santiago the best man—she'd been dazzled by his dark gorgeousness, his height, his broad shoulders and muscular body. She'd looked up at his dark soulful eyes and thought, *Wow. Dreams really do come true.*

Then Santiago had turned to the groom and suggested out loud that Darius could still "make a run for it" and abandon his bride at the altar. And he'd said it right in front of Letty!

The bride and groom had awkwardly laughed it off, but from that moment, Belle had hated Santiago with a passion. Every word he said was more cynical and infuriating than the last. Within ten minutes, the two of them were arguing; by the end of the wedding, Belle wished he would do the world a favor and die. Being the forthright woman she was, she couldn't resist telling him so. He'd responded with sarcasm. And that had been their relationship for the last four months.

So of course, Belle thought bitterly, he would be the one to find her now, pacing the dark, snowy garden behind Letty and Darius's coastal estate. Crying.

Shivering in her thin black dress, she'd been looking

toward the wild Atlantic Ocean in the darkness. The rhythmic roar of the waves matched the thrumming of her heart.

All day, Belle had held her friend's adorable newborn as Letty wept through her father's funeral. By the end of the evening reception, the pain in Belle's heart as she held the sweetly sleeping baby had overwhelmed her. Gently giving the baby back to Letty, she'd mumbled an excuse and fled into the dark snow-covered garden.

Outside, an icy wind blew, freezing the tears against Belle's chapped skin as she stared out into the darkness, heartsick with grief.

She would never have a child of her own.

Never, the ocean sighed back to her. *Never, never.*

"Belle?" a rough voice called. "Are you out here?"

Santiago! She sucked in her breath. The last man she'd ever want to see her like this!

She could only imagine the arrogant sneer on the Spaniard's face if he found her crying over her inability to have a child. Ducking behind a frost-covered tree, she held her breath, praying he wouldn't see her.

"Belle, stop trying to hide," he said, sounding amused. "Your dress is black, and you're standing in the snow."

Gritting her teeth, she stepped out from behind the tree and lied, "I wasn't hiding."

"What are you doing out here, then?"

"I just needed some fresh air," she said desperately, wishing he'd leave her alone.

A beam of light from a second-floor window of the manor house illuminated the hard lines of Santiago's powerful body in the black suit and well-cut cashmere coat. As their eyes met, electricity coursed through her.

Santiago Velazquez was too handsome, she thought with an unwilling shiver. Too sexy. Too powerful. Too rich.

He was also a selfish, cynical playboy, whose only loyalty was to his own vast fortune. He probably had vaults big enough to swim in, she thought, and pictured him doing a backstroke through hundred-dollar bills. In the meantime he mocked the idea of kindness and respect. She'd heard he treated his one-night stands like unpaid employees. Belle's expression hardened. Folding her arms, she waited as he strode through the snow toward her.

He stopped a few feet away. "You don't have a coat."

"I'm not cold."

"I can hear your teeth chattering. Are you trying to freeze to death?"

"Why do you care?"

"Me? I don't," he said mildly. "If you want to freeze to death, it's fine with me. But it does seem selfish to force Letty to plan yet another funeral. So tedious, funerals. And weddings. And christenings. All of it."

"Any human interaction that involves emotion must be tedious to you," Belle said.

He was nearly a foot taller than her own petite height. His shoulders were broad and he wore arrogance like a cloak that shadowed him in the snow. She'd heard women call him Ángel, and she could well understand the nickname. He had a face like an angel—a dark angel, she thought irritably, if heaven needed a bouncer to keep lesser people out and boss everyone around. Santiago might be rich and handsome but he was also the most cynical, callous, despicable man on earth. He was everything she hated most.

"Wait." His black eyes narrowed as he stared down at her in the faint crystalline moonlight frosting the clouds. "Are you crying, Belle?"

She blinked hard and fast to hide the evidence. "No."

"You are." His cruel, sensual lips curved mockingly. "I know you have a pathetically soft heart, but this is pushing the limits even for you. You barely knew Letty's father, and yet here I find you mourning him after the funeral, alone in the snow like a tragic Victorian madwoman."

Normally that would have gotten a rise out of her. But not today. Belle's heart was too sad. And she knew if she showed the slightest emotion he'd only mock her more. Wishing desperately that Santiago hadn't been the one to find her, she said, "What do you want?"

"Darius and Letty have gone to bed. Letty wanted to come out and look for you but the baby needed her. I'm supposed to show you to your guest room and turn on the house alarm once you're brought in safe and sound."

His husky, Spanish-accented voice seemed to be laughing at her. She hated how, even disliking him as much as she did, he made her body shiver with awareness.

"I changed my mind about staying here tonight." The last thing she wanted was to spend the night tossing and turning in a guest room, with no company but her own agonizing thoughts. "I just want to go home."

"To Brooklyn?" Santiago looked at her incredulously. "It's too late. Everyone wanting to get back to the city left hours ago. The ice storm just closed the expressway. It might not reopen for hours."

"Why are you even still here? Don't you have a helicopter and a couple of planes? It can't be because you actually care about Letty and Darius."

"The guest rooms here are nice and I'm tired. Two days ago I was in Sydney. Before that, Tokyo." He yawned. "Tomorrow I leave for London."

"Poor you," said Belle, who had always dreamed of traveling but never managed to save the money, even for an economy ticket.

His sensual lips curved upward. "I appreciate your sympathy. So if you don't mind wrapping up your self-indulgent little *Wuthering Heights* routine I'd like to show you to your room so I can go to mine."

"If you want to go, go." She turned away so he couldn't see her exhausted, tearstained expression. "Tell Letty I'd already left. I'll get a train back to the city."

"Are you serious?" He looked down at her skeptically. "How will you reach the station? I doubt trains are even running—"

"Then I'll walk!" Her voice was suddenly shrill. "I'm not sleeping here!"

Santiago paused.

"Belle," he said, in a voice more gentle than she'd ever heard from him before. "What's wrong?"

Reaching out, he put his hand on her shoulder, then lifted it to her cheek. It was the first time he had ever touched her, and even in the dark and cold the touch of his hand spun through her like a fire. Her lips parted.

"If something was wrong, why would I tell you?"

His smile increased. "Because you hate me."

"And?"

"So whatever it is, you can tell me. Because you don't give a damn what I think."

"True," she said wryly. It was tempting. She pressed her lips together. "But you might tell the world."

"Do I ever share secrets?"

"No," she was forced to admit. "But you do say mean and insulting things. You are heartless and rude and…"

"Only to people's faces. Never behind their backs." His voice was low. "Tell me, Belle."

Clouds covered the moon, and they were briefly flooded in darkness. She suddenly was desperate to share her grief with someone, anyone. And it was true she couldn't have a lower opinion of him. He probably couldn't think less of her, either.

That thought was oddly comforting. She didn't have to pretend with Santiago. She didn't have to be positive and hopeful at all times, the cheerleader who tried to please everyone, no matter what. Belle had learned at a young age never to let any negative feelings show. If you were honest about your feelings, it only made people dislike you. It only made people leave, even and especially the ones you loved.

So Santiago was the only one she *could* tell. The only one she could be truly herself with. Because, heck, if he permanently left her life, she'd throw a party.

She took a deep breath. "It's the baby."

"Little Howie?"

"Yes."

"I had a hard time with him, too. Babies." He rolled his eyes. "All those diapers, all that crying. But what can you do? Some people still seem to want them."

"I do." The moon broke through the clouds, and Belle looked up at him with tears shimmering in the moonlight. "I want a baby."

He stared down at her, then snorted. "Of course you do. Romantic idiot like you. You want love, flowers, the whole package." He shrugged. "So why cry over it? If you are foolish enough to want a family, go get one. Settle down, buy a house, get married. No one is stopping you."

"I...I can't get pregnant," she whispered. "Ever. It's impossible."

"How do you know?"

"Because..." Belle looked down at the tracks in the snow. The moonlight caused strange shadows, mingling her footsteps and his. "I just know. It's medically impossible."

She braced herself for his inevitable questions. Medically impossible how? What happened? When and why?

But he surprised her.

Reaching out, he just pulled her into his arms, beneath his black cashmere coat. She felt the sudden comfort of his warmth, his strength, as he caressed her long dark hair. "Everything will be all right."

She looked up at him, her heart in her throat. She was aware of the heat of his body against hers.

"You must think I'm a horrible person," she said, pulling away. "A horrible friend for envying Letty, when she just lost her father. I spent all day holding her sweet baby and envying her. I'm the worst friend in the world."

"Stop." Cupping her face, he looked down at her fiercely. "You know I think you're a fool…existing in a pink cloud of candy-coated dreams. Someday you will lose those rose-colored glasses and learn the truth about the heartless world…"

She whispered brokenly. "I—"

He put his finger on her lips. "But even I can see you're a good friend."

His finger felt warm against her tingling lips. She had the sudden shocking desire to kiss it, to wrap her lips around his finger and suck it gently. She'd never had such a shocking thought before—she, an inexperienced virgin! But as little as she liked him, something about the wickedly sexy Spaniard attracted —and scared—her.

Trembling, she twisted her head away. She remembered all those women he'd famously seduced, those women she'd scorned as fools for being willing notches on his bedpost. And for the first time, she sympathized with them, as she herself fully felt the potent force of his charm.

"You're lucky, actually." Santiago gave her a crooked half grin. "Babies? Marriage? Who would want to be stuck with such a thankless responsibility as a family?" He shook his head. "No good would have come of it. It's a prison sentence. Now you can have something better."

She stared at him. "Better than a family?"

He nodded.

"Freedom," he said quietly.

"But I don't want freedom." Her voice was small. "I want to be loved."

"We all want things we can't have," he said roughly.

"How would you know? You've never wanted anything, not without taking it."

"You're wrong. There has been something I've wanted. For four months. Someone. But I can't have her."

Four months. Suddenly, Belle's heart was beating wildly in her chest. He couldn't mean…couldn't possibly mean…

Could Santiago Velazquez, the famous New York billionaire, a man who had supermodels for the asking, really want *Belle*—a plump, ordinary waitress from small-town Texas?

Their eyes held in the moonlight. Sparks ran through her body, from her earlobes to her hair to her breasts to the soles of her feet.

"I want her. I can't have her," he said in a low voice. "Not even if she were standing in front of me now."

"Why not?" she breathed.

"Ah." His lips twisted. "She wants love. I see it in her face. I hear it in her voice. She craves love like the air she breathes. If I took her, if I made her mine, she would turn all her romantic longings on me. And be destroyed by it." He looked down at her, his eyes dark and deep. "Because as much as I want her body, I do not want her heart."

Behind the soft silver halo on his black hair, she could dimly see the shadow of the manor house, and hear the ocean waves pounding on the unseen shore.

Then Belle's eyes suddenly narrowed.

He was playing with her, she realized. *Toying* with her. Like a sharp-clawed cat with a mouse. "Stop it."

"What?"

She lifted her chin. "Are you bored, Santiago? Do you want some company in your bed and I'm the only one around?" She glared at him. "Other women might fall for your world-weary playboy act. But I don't believe a word of it. If you really wanted me, you wouldn't let anything stand in the way, not my feelings and certainly not the risk of hurting me. You would seduce me without conscience. That's what a playboy does. So obviously, you don't want me. You're just bored."

"You're wrong, Belle." Roughly, he pulled her against his body, beneath his expensive black cashmere coat. She felt his warmth as his dark eyes searched hers hungrily. "I've wanted you since Darius and Letty's wedding. Since the first time you told me to go to hell." His sensual lips curved as he cupped her cheek and looked down at her intently. "But whatever you think of me, I'm not in the business of purposefully making naïve young women love me."

Her whole body was tingling with energy, with fear, with a feeling that could only be desire. She fought it desperately.

"You think I'd immediately fall in love with you?"

"Yes."

She gave an incredulous snort. "You have no problems with your ego, do you?"

His dark gaze seared her. "Tell me I'm wrong."

"You're wrong." She gave a careless shrug. "I do want love, it's true. If I met a man I could respect and admire, I might easily fall in love. But that's not you, Santiago." She looked at him evenly. "No matter how rich or sexy you might be. So if you want me, too bad. I don't want you."

His expression changed. His eyes glittered in the moonlight.

"You don't?" Reaching out, he ran his thumb lightly against her trembling bottom lip and whispered, "Are you sure?"

"Yes," she breathed, unable to pull away, or to look from his dark gaze.

He ran his hand down her arm, looking down at her as

if she were the most beautiful, desirable creature on earth. "And if I took you to my bed, you wouldn't fall in love?"

"Not even remotely. I think you're a total bastard."

But even as she spoke, Belle couldn't stop herself from shivering. She knew he felt it. The corners of his lips twisted upward in grim masculine satisfaction.

Softly, he ran his hand down through her hair. Her body's shivering intensified. As she breathed in his scent of sandalwood and firelight, she felt the strength and power of his body against hers, beneath his long black coat.

"Then there's no reason to hold back. Forget love." He gently lifted her chin. "Forget regret, forget pain, forget everything fate has denied you. For one night, take pleasure in what you can have, right here and now."

"You mean, take pleasure in you?"

She'd tried to say the words sarcastically, but the way her heart was hammering in her chest, her tone came out wrong. Instead of sarcastic, she sounded breathless. Yearning.

"For one night, let me give you joy. Without strings. Without consequences. Stop thinking so much about the future," he said in a low voice, his hand cupping her cheek. "For one night, you can know what it feels like to be truly, recklessly alive."

His black eyes seared hers, and the cold January night sizzled like west Texas in July as an arc of electricity passed between them.

Give herself to him for one night, without consequences? Without strings?

Belle stared up at him, shocked.

She'd never slept with anyone. She'd never even gotten close. She was, in fact, a twenty-eight-year-old virgin, an old maid who'd spent her whole life taking care of others, while failing to achieve a single dream for herself.

No. Her answer was no. Of course it was.

Wasn't it?

He didn't give her a chance to answer. Lowering his head, he kissed her cheek, his lips lingering against her skin, moving slowly. Sensuously. She held her breath, and as he drew back, she stared at him with big eyes, her whole body clamoring and clanging like an orchestra.

"All right," she heard herself say, then gasped at her own recklessness. She opened her mouth to take it back. Then stopped.

For one night, you can know what it feels like to be truly, recklessly alive.

When was the last time she'd felt that way?

Had she ever?

Or had she always been a good girl, trying so hard to please others, to follow the rules, to plan out her life?

What had being good ever done for her—except leave her heartsick and alone?

Santiago's dark eyes gleamed as he saw her hesitate. He didn't wait. Wrapping his large hands on her jawline and then sliding them to tangle in her hair, he slowly drew his mouth to hers. She felt the warmth of his breath, sweet like Scotch, against the tender flesh of her skin.

His sensual mouth lowered on hers, hot and demanding, pushing her lips apart. She felt the delicious sweep of his tongue, and the cold winter air between them heated to a thousand degrees.

She'd never been kissed like this before. Never. The tepid caresses she'd endured seven years ago were nothing compared to this ruthlessly demanding embrace, this—dark fire.

She was lost in his arms, in the hot demand of his mouth, of his hands everywhere. Desire swept through her, a tidal wave of need that drowned all thought and reason. She forgot to think, forgot her own name.

She'd never known it could be like this...

She responded uncertainly at first, then soon gripped his shoulders, clutching him to her.

All her hatred for Santiago, all her earlier misery, transformed to heat as he kissed her in the dark winter night on the edge of the sea, invisible waves crashing noisily against the shore.

She didn't know how long they clung to each other in the cold night, seconds or hours, but when he finally drew away, she knew she'd never be the same. Their breath mingled in the dappled moonlight.

They stared at each other for a split second as scattered snowflakes started to fall.

Wordlessly, he took her hand and pulled her toward the house. She heard the crunch of frozen snow beneath her scuffed black flats, felt the warmth of his hand over hers.

They entered the nineteenth-century mansion, with its dark oak paneling and antique furniture. Inside, it was dark and quiet; it seemed everyone, including the household staff, had gone to bed. Santiago closed the tall, heavy door behind them and punched a code into the security system.

They rushed up the back stairs, hardly able to stop kissing long enough to stumble to the second floor.

Belle shivered. She couldn't be doing this. Impulsively offering her virginity to a man she didn't even like, let alone love?

But as he pulled her into a guest bedroom at the far end of the hall, she couldn't even catch her breath. His long black coat fell to the floor, and he pulled her into his arms. Cupping her face in his hands, he ran his thumbs along her swollen lower lip.

"You're so beautiful," he whispered, running his hands through her long brown hair tangled with ice and snowflakes. "Beautiful, and *mine*…"

Lowering his mouth to hers, he kissed her hungrily. Heat flooded through Belle, making her breasts heavy, swirling low and deep in her core. His hands stroked her deliciously, mesmerizing her with sensation, and by the time she realized he was unzipping her black dress, it was already falling to the floor.

An hour ago, she'd hated him; now she was half-naked in his bedroom.

Setting her back onto his bed, he pulled off his suit jacket, vest and tie. He never took his eyes off her as he unbuttoned his black shirt. His bare chest was chiseled and muscular, curving in the light and shadow. Falling beside her on the bed, he pulled her against him with a growl, kissing her with a hot embrace. He nibbled down her throat, and she tilted her head against the pillow, closing her eyes. He cupped each breast over her white cotton bra and reached beneath the fabric to stroke and thrum the aching nipples beneath.

Unhooking her bra, he tossed it to the floor and lowered his head to suckle one breast, then the other. The sensation was so sharp and wild and new that she gasped, gripping his shoulders tightly.

Moving up, he covered her gasping lips with his own, plundering her mouth before he slowly kissed down her body to her flat, naked belly. His tongue flicked her belly button. Then he kept going down further still.

His hands gripped her hips. He nuzzled between her legs, and she felt the warmth of his breath between her thighs. He held her firmly, gently pressing her legs apart, kissing each of her thighs before he pulled her panties off. Pushing her thighs apart, he teased her with his warm breath, then, with agonizing slowness, he lowered his mouth and tasted her.

The pleasure was so unexpected and explosive that her fingernails dug into his shoulders as his tongue slid against her, hot and wet.

Holding her hips, he worked her with his tongue until

she gripped the blanket beneath her, holding her breath until she started to see stars. He licked her softly one moment, then the next plunged his tongue inside her. She heard a voice cry out, and realized the voice was hers.

He swirled his tongue against her, increasing his rhythm and pressure until her back started arching from the bed. He pushed a single thick finger inside her, then two, stretching her wide. She gasped as the pleasure built almost too high to bear. Higher—higher—then—

Soaring to the sky, she exploded into a million pieces, falling to the earth in gently chiming shards. It was like nothing she'd ever experienced. It was pure joy.

Lifting up from her, he ripped off the last of his clothes. Positioning himself between her legs, he gripped her naked hips. As she was still gasping with pleasure, he pushed his huge, thick shaft inside her.

He'd dreamed of this.

For four months, Santiago had dreamed of seducing the sinfully beautiful woman who'd made it such a point to scorn him. He'd dreamed of having her deliciously full curves in his arms, her body naked beneath his. He'd dreamed of kissing her full pink lips and seeing her lovely face darken with ecstasy. He'd dreamed of taking her, filling her, satiating himself with her.

But now, as he finally pushed inside her, he felt a barrier he had not expected. He froze. He'd never once dreamed of this.

"You're a virgin?" he breathed in shock.

Slowly, she opened her eyes. "Not anymore."

He set his jaw. "Did I hurt you?"

"No," she said in a small voice.

Something in her expression made him tremble. Something in her voice spoke directly to his soul. He felt a strange emotion in his heart: tenderness. He bit out, "You're lying."

"Yes." Her soft, slender arms reached up around his shoulders and pulled him down, down, down against her, tempting him to his own ecstasy and ruin. "But don't stop," she whispered. "Please, Santiago…"

Hearing his name on her lips, he sucked in his breath. How could even a romantic, idealistic woman like Belle Langtry be an untouched innocent, in this modern world? *A virgin.* Santiago was the only man who'd ever touched her, this infuriating, exhilarating, magnificent woman.

His soul felt the danger of getting close to any woman so innocent and bright. It made him want to flee.

But his body, held still deep inside her, felt the opposite as he looked down at her beautiful face, glowing with wanton desire. He shuddered. Ravaging hunger built inside him, thrilling his nerves, coursing down his limbs and centering at his hard core barreled deep inside her.

He lowered his head to hers. His kiss was gentle at first, then deepened, turning to pure light. His hands roamed slowly down her naked body, cupping and caressing her breasts.

She had the most perfect body, curvy and ripe. Any man would die to have a fiery goddess like this in his bed. And that this goddess was also a *virgin*…

He shuddered a little, and without realizing it, pushed deeper inside her. The soft whisper of a moan escaped her as he lowered his lips to suckle her breasts. Her breath changed to a gasp of ecstasy.

Gripping her hips, he very slowly started to ride her, even as he kissed her lips and caressed her breasts. He sucked her earlobe and slowly licked and nibbled down her neck. He felt her body lift beneath his as new pleasure rose in her, and she began to kiss him back hungrily.

He started to lose the last shreds of his self-control. She

was wet, so wet, and somehow her tight sheath accepted all of him. His thrusts became deeper as he wondered if the size of him would be too much for her. But it wasn't. He felt her tighten around him, gripping her fingernails into his shoulders. But that small pain only added to his building pleasure. When he heard her low gasp rise to a scream of joy he could no longer hold back. His eyes closed in pure ecstasy, his head tossing back as he filled her deeply, until his own roar exploded in the deep dark silence of the bedroom. Flying in a whirlwind, he experienced pure sexual joy such as he'd never known before as he spilled himself into her.

He fell back to the bed against her, eyes closed, cradling her body against his own. For ten seconds, as he held her, he felt a deep peace, a sense of home, sweeter than he'd ever known.

Then his eyes flew open. He was filled with regret so great it tasted like ash in his mouth.

"You were right," Belle sighed, a hopeful smile on her lovely heart-shaped face. "I feel recklessly alive. That was like nothing I ever dreamed. Pure magic." She pressed back against his naked chest, pulling his arms more tightly around her, as she said dreamily, "Deep down, maybe you're not all bad. I might even like you a little."

Santiago looked down at her grimly in the moonlight from the bedroom window. He'd just known ecstasy that he'd never experienced before.

With a virgin.

A *romantic*.

Sleeping with Belle had done strange things to him. His body had never known such deep pleasure. And his soul…

She yawned. "I just hope no one heard us."

"They didn't," he said harshly. "Letty and Darius are in the other wing, and this house is made of stone." Stone like his heart, he reminded himself.

"Good. I'd never live it down if Letty knew, after everything I've said about you."

"What did you say to her?"

"I said you were a selfish bastard without a heart."

His shoulders tightened. "I'm not offended. It's true."

"You're funny." She looked up at him sleepily. "You know, no matter what you think, love and marriage aren't always a prison sentence. Look at Letty and Darius."

"They *look* happy," he said grudgingly, then added, "Looks can be deceiving."

Her forehead furrowed. "Don't you believe in anyone? Anything?"

"I believe in myself."

"You're a terrible cynic."

"I see the world as it is, rather than as I wish it could be." Eternal love? A happy family? At thirty-five, Santiago had seen enough of the world to know those kind of miracles were few and far between. Tragedy was the normal state of the world. "Do you already regret sleeping with me?"

Shaking her head, she smiled up at him, looking kittenish and shy and so damned beautiful that his heart caught in his throat. "You feel so good to me. I'm glad you're here." She yawned, closing her eyes, cuddling against him. "I couldn't bear to be alone tonight. You saved me…"

Pressing against his chest, she fell asleep in seconds.

Santiago yearned to sleep, as well. His body wanted to stay like this, with her, cuddled in this warm bed, taking solace in each other against the cold January night and all the other cold nights to come.

Warning lights were flashing everywhere.

He looked down at her, sweetly sleeping in his arms, so soft and beautiful, so opinionated and dreamy and kind. So optimistic.

You saved me.

Santiago felt bone-weary. Carefully, he disentangled

himself from her. Rising from the bed, he walked naked to his coat crumpled on the floor. Pulling his phone from his pocket, he dialed the number of his pilot.

The man struggled not to sound groggy. It was eleven o'clock on a cold winter's night. "Sir?"

"Come get me," he replied. "I'm at Fairholme."

Without waiting for a reply, Santiago hung up. He looked back at Belle one last time, sleeping in his bed, so beautiful in the moonlight. Like an innocent young woman from another time. He couldn't remember ever being that innocent, not with the upbringing he'd had.

Whatever Belle might say, she would want to love him. She would try, like a moth immolating herself against an unfeeling flame.

Of course she would. He was her first.

His jaw tightened. He never would have seduced her if he'd known. He had a rule. No virgins. No innocent hearts. He never brought anyone to his bed who might actually care.

And he'd just seduced an innocent virgin. The friend of Darius's wife.

He felt a low self-hatred. After Nadia, he'd vowed never to get involved with anyone again. Why risk your capital on an investment that was a guaranteed loss? Might as well flush your money—or your soul—straight down the drain.

He thought again of *Wuthering Heights*. He'd never read the book, but he knew it ended badly. It was romance, wasn't it? That always ended badly. Especially in real life.

Santiago silently dressed, then picked up his overnight bag. But he hesitated at the door, still hearing the wistful echo of her voice.

Don't you believe in anyone? Anything?

He'd lied to her. He'd told her he believed in himself. But the real answer was no.

Belle would wake up alone in bed and find him gone.

No note would be needed. She'd get the message. He really was the heartless bastard he claimed to be.

As if there was ever any doubt, he jeered at himself. Regret and self-loathing filled him as he turned down the hall.

He wished he'd never touched her.

CHAPTER TWO

SHIVERING IN THE warm July twilight, Belle stood on the sidewalk of Santiago's elegant residential street on Manhattan's Upper East Side. She watched well-dressed guests step out of glossy chauffeured cars, climbing up the steps and ringing at his door, to be greeted by his butler.

A butler, she thought bitterly. Who had a butler in this day and age?

Santiago Velazquez—that was who.

But the butler wasn't the problem. Belle watched a crowd of beautiful young socialites, giggling and preening, hurry up the steps of his brownstone in six-inch heels and designer cocktail dresses.

She looked down at her own loose, oversized T-shirt, stretchy knit shorts and flip-flops. She wasn't wearing makeup. Her brown hair was pulled back into a messy ponytail. She'd fit in at his fancy party like a dog driving a car.

She didn't belong here. And she didn't want to see Santiago again—*ever*—after the cold way he'd treated her after they'd slept together in January. Losing her virginity in a one-night stand with the heartless, cynical playboy was a mistake she would regret the rest of her life.

But she couldn't leave New York. Not without telling him she was pregnant.

Pregnant. Every time she thought of it, she caught her breath. It was a miracle. She didn't have any other word to describe it, when seven years ago she'd been told very firmly by a doctor that it could never happen. Pregnant.

A dazed smile traced Belle's lips as she rested her hands gently over the wide curve of her belly now. Somehow, in that disastrous night when Santiago had seduced her, this one amazing, impossible thing had happened. She'd gotten her heart's deepest desire: a baby of her own.

There was just one bad thing about it.

Her smile faded. Of all the men on earth to be her unborn baby's father…

She'd tried to tell him; she'd left multiple messages asking him to call her back. He hadn't. She'd been almost glad. It gave her a good excuse to do what she wanted to do—leave New York without telling him he was going to be a father.

But her friend Letty had convinced her to make one last try. "Secrets always come out," she'd pleaded. "Don't make my mistake."

So, against her better judgment, here Belle was, stopping at his luxury brownstone on her way out of town. The last place she wanted to be.

Just thinking of facing Santiago for the first time since he'd snuck out of her bed in the middle of the night, she wanted to turn and run for her pickup truck parked two blocks away, then head south on the turnpike, stomp on the gas and not look back until she reached Texas.

But she'd already made the decision to try one last time to give him the life-changing news that he was going to be a father. Belle always tried to do the right thing, even if it hurt. She wasn't going to turn coward now. Not over *him*.

Tightening her hands into fists, Belle waited until the last limousine departed, then crossed the street in the fading twilight. Her body shook as she walked up the stone steps and knocked on the big oak door.

The butler took one look at her, then started to close the

door as he said scornfully, "Staff and delivery entrance at the back."

Belle blocked the door with her foot. "Excuse me. I need to see Santiago. Please."

The butler looked astonished at her familiar use of his employer's first name, as if a talking rat had just squeaked a request to see the mayor of New York. "Who are you?"

"Tell him Belle Langtry urgently needs to see him." She raised her chin, struggling to hide her pounding heart. "It's an emergency."

With a scowl, the butler opened the door just enough for her to get through. The soles of Belle's flip-flops slapped against the marble floor of the mansion's elegant foyer. She had one brief glimpse of the beautiful, wealthy society crowd in the ballroom, sipping champagne as waiters passed through with silver trays. Then she sucked in her breath as she saw the party's host, head and shoulders above the crowd. With his height and dark good looks, Santiago Velazquez towered over his guests in every way.

The butler pointed down an opposite hallway haughtily. "Wait in there."

Through the door, Belle found a home office with leather-bound books and a big dark wood desk. Knees weak, she sank into the expensive swivel chair. Her cheeks still burned from seeing Santiago from a distance. Thinking of seeing him face to face, she was terrified.

The night he'd taken her virginity, passion and emotion had been like a whirlwind, flinging her up into the sky, to the stars, scattering pieces of her soul like diamonds across the night. It had been so sensual, so spectacular. More than she'd even dreamed it could be.

Right until the moment he'd abandoned her, and she'd had to go down to breakfast alone. She'd had to hide her hurt and bewilderment, and smile at Letty and Darius and their baby, pretending nothing had happened, that nothing was wrong. That was how cold-hearted Santiago was. He'd only promised one night, true. But he hadn't even been able to stick *that* out.

Leaving Fairholme, she'd returned to her tiny apartment in Brooklyn, which she shared with two rude, parent-funded roommates who'd mocked her dreams, her Texas accent—which was barely noticeable!—and her job as a waitress. Normally she would have let their taunts roll off her like water off a duck's back, but after her night with Santiago, she'd felt restless, irritable and hopeless, as she continued to be rejected at auditions, with a day job that barely paid the bills.

A month later, when she'd discovered she was pregnant, everything had changed. Her baby deserved better than this apartment shared with strangers, an insecure future and unpaid bills. Her baby deserved better than a father who couldn't be bothered to return phone calls. It was a bitter thought.

Belle had come to New York with such high hopes. After nearly a decade spent raising her two younger brothers, she'd finally left her small town at twenty-seven, determined to make her dreams come true.

Instead, she'd made a mess of everything.

She'd dreamed of making her fortune? She now had ten dollars less in her wallet than when she'd left Texas eighteen months ago.

She'd dreamed of seeing her name in lights? She'd been rejected from every talent agency in New York.

But worst of all… Belle swallowed hard… She'd dreamed that she would finally find love, real love, the kind that would last forever. Instead, she'd allowed herself to get knocked up by a man she hated.

Belle had had enough of New York. She was going home. Her two suitcases were already packed in her truck, ready to go. There was only one thing left on her to-do list.

Tell Santiago Velazquez he was going to be a father.

But now, she suddenly wasn't sure she could do it. Even seeing him in the ballroom, from a distance, had knocked her for a loop. Maybe this was a mistake. Maybe she shouldn't stay...

Santiago pushed through the door. When he saw her sitting in his chair, his glare was like a blast of heat, his tall, powerful body barely contained by the well-cut suit. "What the hell are you doing here?"

After all these months, this was how he greeted her? She stiffened in the chair, folding her arms over her belly. "Good to see you, too."

Closing the door behind him, Santiago pierced her with his hard, black eyes and said dangerously, "I asked you a question. What are you doing here, Belle? I think I made it very clear that I never wanted to see you again."

"You did."

Santiago moved closer in the shadows of the study. "Why did you trick my butler into letting you in, telling him there was an emergency?"

"It wasn't a trick. It's true."

"An emergency. Really." His lips twisted scornfully. "Let me guess. After all these months, you're realized you can't live without me, and you're here to declare eternal love."

She flinched at the cold derision in his voice.

"God help any woman who truly loved you." She took a deep breath, then glared back at him. "Don't worry. I hate you plenty. More than ever."

A strange expression flashed across his features, then he gave her a cold smile. "Fantastic. So why did you interrupt my party?"

He was glaring at her with such hatred. How could she possibly tell him she was pregnant with his baby? "I came to tell you...I'm leaving New York..."

"That's your emergency?" He gave an incredulous laugh. "One more thing to celebrate today, on top of closing a business deal."

Her hackles rose. "Let me finish!"

"So do it, then." He folded his arms, looking down at her as if he were king of the mountain and she was just a peasant in the dirt. "And let me get back to my guests."

She took a deep breath.

"I'm pregnant."

Her small voice reverberated in the silence of the study. His black eyes widened in almost comical shock.

"What?"

Slowly, she rose from the chair, dropping her arms to her sides so he could see her baby bump beneath her pregnancy-swollen breasts and oversized T-shirt. For a moment, he didn't speak, and she held her breath, afraid to meet his gaze. Some stupid part of her still hoped against hope that he would surprise her. That he would suddenly change back to that warm, irresistible man she'd seen so briefly that cold January night. That he'd gather her into his arms and kiss her joyfully at the news.

Those hopes were quickly dashed.

"*Pregnant*?"

She risked a look at him. His jaw was hard, his eyes dark with rage.

"Yes," she choked out.

She never expected what he did next.

Pulling her close, he put his large, broad hands over her cotton T-shirt, to feel the unmistakable swell of her pregnant belly.

He dropped his hands as if he'd been burned. "You said it was medically impossible."

"I thought it was…"

"You said you could never get pregnant!"

"It's a…a miracle."

"Miracle!" He snorted, then narrowed his eyes. He slowly looked her over. "And here I thought you didn't have what it took to be on Broadway. No gold digger ever lied to my face so convincingly. I actually thought you were some angelic little innocent. Quite the little actress after all."

That low, husky, Spanish-accented voice cut right through her heart, and she staggered back. "You think I got pregnant on purpose?"

He gave a low laugh. "You really had me going with the way you defended true love. Letting me find you alone, sobbing in the garden over the fact that you could never, ever have a baby. I'm impressed. I had no idea you were such an accomplished liar."

"I didn't lie!"

"Cut the act, and get to the part where you give me a price."

"Price?" she said, bewildered.

"There's only one reason you would deliberately trick me into not using a condom when you fluttered your eyes and lured me into bed—"

Her voice came out an enraged squeak. "I never did that!"

"And that's money. But I'll admit," he said carelessly, looking her over, "you earned it. No woman has ever tricked me so thoroughly. Except—" His expression changed, then he set his jaw. "How much do you want?"

"I don't want money." The room was spinning around her. "I just thought you had the right to know!"

"*Perfecto*," he said coolly. Going to the door, he opened it. "You told me. Now get the hell out."

Belle stared at him in shock, astounded that any man could react to news of his unborn son or daughter so coldly, refusing to even show interest, much less take responsibility! "That's it? That's all you have to say?"

"What did you expect?" he drawled. "That I'd fall to one knee and beg you to marry me? Sorry to disappoint you."

Belle stared up at him, incredulous. She'd waited for twenty-eight years, dreaming of Prince Charming, dreaming of true love—and *this* was the man she'd slept with!

Anger rose like bile in her throat. "Wow. You figured me out. Yes, I'm desperate to marry you, Santiago. Who wouldn't want to be the bride of the nastiest, most cold-hearted man on earth? And raise a baby with you?" She gave a harsh laugh. "What an amazing father you would make!"

His expression hardened. "Belle—"

"You call me a liar. A gold digger. When you know I was a virgin the night you seduced me!" She lifted her chin, trembling with emotion. "Was this what you meant when you called me naïve? Did you decide you wanted to be the one to show me the truth about the heartless world?"

"Look—"

"I never should have come here." Tears were burning the backs of her eyes. But she'd let him see her cry once, that dark January night, and he'd lured her into destruction with his sweet kisses and honeyed words. She'd die before she let him ever see her weak again. "Forget about the baby. Forget I even exist." Stopping at the door, she looked back at him one last time. "I wish any man but you could have been the father of my baby," she choked out. "It's a mistake I'll regret the rest of my life."

Turning, she left, rushing past the snooty butler and beautiful, rich guests who looked like they'd never had a single problem in their glamorous lives. She went outside, nearly tripping down the steps into the cooling night air. She ran halfway down the block in her flip-flops before she realized Santiago wasn't following her.

Good. She didn't care. When she reached her old 1978 Chevy pickup, she started up the engine with a roar. Her hands didn't stop shaking until she was past the Lincoln Tunnel.

From the first day they'd met, she'd known Santiago was dark-hearted poison. How could she have been so stupid to let him seduce her?

For one night, let me give you joy. Without strings. Without consequences.

Belle choked out a sob as she gripped the steering wheel, driving south on the Jersey Turnpike. She was thrilled about the baby, but what she would have given to have any other man as the father!

For the last few months, when Santiago hadn't returned her phone messages, she'd told herself that she and the baby would be better off without him. But part of her had secretly hoped for another miracle—that if she told Santiago she was pregnant, he'd want to be a father. A husband. That they could all love each other, and be happy.

So stupid.

She wiped her eyes. Instead Santiago had not only cavalierly abandoned his unborn baby, he'd insulted Belle and thrown her out of his house for daring to tell him she was pregnant!

The truly shocking thing was that she was even surprised. He'd made his feelings clear from the beginning. He thought babies were a thankless responsibility and love was for suckers.

Belle cried until her eyes burned, then at midnight, pulled over to a roadside motel to sleep fitfully till dawn.

The next day, the hypnotic road started to calm her. She started feeling like she'd dodged a bullet. She didn't need a cold, heartless man wrecking her peace of mind and breaking their child's heart. Better that Santiago abandon them now rather than later.

By the third day, as the mile markers passed and she left the green rolling hills of east Texas behind, she started to recognize the familiar landscape of home, and her heart grew lighter. There was something soothing about the wide horizons stretching out forever, with nothing but sagebrush and the merciless summer sun in the unrelenting blue sky.

Feeling a sweet flutter inside her, Belle put a hand to her belly. "So be it," she whispered aloud. This baby would be hers alone. She would spend the rest of her life appreciating this miracle, devoting herself to her child.

It was still morning, but already growing hot. The air conditioning in her pickup didn't work, but both windows were rolled down, so it was all right. Though she was lucky it wasn't raining because one of them wouldn't roll back up.

As she drew in to the edges of her small town, she took a deep breath. *Home.* Though it wasn't the same, without her younger brothers. Ray now lived in Atlanta and twenty-one-year-old Joe in Denver. But at least here, the world made sense.

But as she pulled into the dirt driveway, she abruptly slammed on the brake.

A big black helicopter was parked in the sagebrush prairie, tucked behind her house.

She sucked in her breath. A helicopter? Then she saw the two hulking bodyguards prowling nearby. That could only mean...

With an intake of breath, she looked straight at the old wooden house with the peeling paint. Her heart stopped.

Standing on the wooden porch, with arms grimly folded, was Santiago.

What was he doing here?

Fear pounded through her as she turned off the engine of her truck.

With a deep breath, Belle got out of her old pickup, tossing her long brown ponytail, slamming the door with a rusty squeak.

"What are you doing in Texas?" She lifted her chin to

hide the tremble in her voice. "Let me guess. Did you think up some new ways to insult me?"

He came down the rickety wooden steps toward her, his black eyes glittering. "Three nights ago, you showed up at my house with a very shocking accusation."

"You mean I accused you of getting me pregnant?" Waving her arm, she said furiously, "Such a horrible accusation! No wonder you wanted me to get the hell out!"

Standing on the last step above her, he ground his teeth. "I was calling your bluff. It was a negotiation. I expected you to swiftly return with a demand for a specific sum of money."

Calling her announcement of pregnancy a negotiation! He was just the worst! A lump rose in her throat. Blinking fast, she turned toward his entourage and helicopter in the field. She said evenly, "How did you find my address?"

"Easy."

"You must have been waiting for hours."

"Twenty minutes."

"Twenty! How?" She gasped. "There was no way you could know when I'd get here. Even I didn't know exactly!"

He gave a grim smile. "That was more difficult."

"Were you tracking my truck? Spying on me?"

"Stop changing the subject," he said coldly. He stepped closer on the packed dirt driveway, towering a foot over her. His black eyes traced the length of her body, from her oversized T-shirt to her shorts to her flip-flops, and a flash of heat coursed through her. "You were telling the truth? The baby is mine?"

"Of course the baby's yours!"

"How can I trust a proven liar?"

"When did I lie?" she said indignantly.

"'I can't get pregnant, ever,'" he mimicked. *"'It's impossible.'"*

"You are such a jerk." Belle shivered, sweating beneath the hot Texas sun.

His voice had been low, controlled, but she felt his cold fury. He was all gorgeous on the outside, she thought, like melted chocolate with his soulful Spanish eyes and black hair and hard-muscled body. Too bad his soul was even harder than his body. He had a soul like flint. Like ice.

Just when she'd been counting her blessings that he was out of their lives, here he was, pushing back in. For what purpose?

"You made your choice," she whispered. "You abandoned us. This baby is mine now. Mine alone."

He lifted a dark eyebrow. "That's not how paternity works."

"It is if I say it is."

"Then why tell me you were pregnant at all?"

"Because three days ago I was foolish enough to hope you could change. Now I know it would be better for my baby to have no father at all than a man like you." She lifted her chin. "Now get off my land."

Growing dangerously still, Santiago stared at her, jaw tight. Without a word, he turned to stare across the stark horizon against the wide blue sky. Against her will, her eyes traced the golden glow of the sun gleaming against his olive-colored skin, the chiseled cheekbones, the dark scruff on his jaw.

"Let me tell you what's going to happen, Belle." When he looked back at her, his voice was low and deep, almost a purr. "Today, you're going to get a paternity test."

"What? Forget it!"

"And if it's proven that the baby's mine," his black eyes glittered, "you're going to marry me."

Was he crazy or was she?

"*Marry* you?" Belle gasped. "Are you out of your mind? I hate you!"

"You should be pleased. Your plan worked. Admit you purposefully got pregnant with my child to trap me into marriage. Have that much respect for me, at least."

"I won't, because it's not true!"

"I'll admit I made a mistake, trusting you. I should have known better. I should have known your innocence was a lie. I shall pay for that." He moved closer with a gleam in his dark eyes. "But so will you."

A shiver went through her.

"I would never marry someone I hate," she whispered.

"You're acting like you have a choice. You don't." He gave a cold smile. "You'll do what I say. And if the baby is mine…then so are you."

CHAPTER THREE

SANTIAGO VELAZQUEZ HAD learned the hard way that there were two types of people in the world: delusional dreamers who hid from the harsh truth of the world, and those clear-eyed few who could face it, and fight for what they wanted.

Belle Langtry was a dreamer. He'd known that the day they'd met, at their friends' wedding last September, when she'd chirped annoyingly about the bridal couple's "eternal love" in face of their obvious misery. Belle's rose-colored glasses were so thick she was blind.

But then, you'd have to be blind to see anything hopeful about love or marriage. Love was a lie, and any marriage based on it would be a disaster from start to finish. It could only end in tears. He should know. His mother had been married five times, to every man in Spain except Santiago's actual father.

But for some reason, when he'd met Belle, so feisty and sure of her own illusions, he hadn't been irritated. He'd been charmed. Petite, curvaceous, dark-haired, with deep sultry eyes and a body clearly made for sin, she'd gotten under his skin from the beginning. And not just because of her beauty.

Belle hated him, and wasn't afraid to show it. With one glaringly big exception, Santiago couldn't remember any woman scorning him so thoroughly. Not since he'd grown into his full height at twenty, and especially not since he'd made his fortune. Women were always hoping to get into his bed, his wallet, or usually both. He hadn't realized just how boring it had all become until that exact moment that Belle Langtry had insulted him to his face.

She was different from the others. She drew him like a flame in the darkness. Her tart tongue, her apparent innocence, her brazen honesty, had made him lower his defenses. Their single night together had been transcendent and joyful and raw. It had almost made him question his cynical view of the world.

Then, three nights ago, he'd discovered how wrong he'd been about her.

Belle Langtry wasn't different. She wasn't innocent. She'd only pretended to wear rose-colored glasses to hide the fact that she was a cold-eyed liar, just like everyone else, plotting for her personal gain. She wasn't like his mother had been, pathetically desperate for love, deceiving herself to the end of her self-destructive life. No. Belle was like Nadia. A mercenary gold digger who would say or do anything, her eyes always on the glittering prize.

At Fairholme, in the snowy garden that cold January night, when Belle had wept in Santiago's arms as if her heart was breaking, she'd been *lying*.

When he'd softly stroked her long dark hair in the moonlight and whispered that everything would be all right, and Belle had looked up, her big dark eyes anguished beneath trembling lashes, she'd been *lying*.

When she'd told him she could never, ever get pregnant, and lowering his head, he'd kissed her beneath the moonlight scattered with snowflakes, as he tried to distract her from her grief, she'd been *lying*.

Santiago had known Belle was an actress. He'd just had no idea how good. He hadn't been fooled in such a way in a long time.

After she'd invaded his cocktail party and dropped the bomb of her pregnancy news, he'd paced and snarled at his guests, wondering what he'd do when Belle finally returned to make her financial demands. If she was truly pregnant with his child, she had leverage. Because as much as Santiago despised the idea of love and marriage, he would never abandon a child the way he himself had once been doubly abandoned.

What would Belle ask for? he'd wondered. Marriage? A trust fund in the baby's name? Or would she eliminate the middleman and simply ask for a billion-dollar check, written out directly to her?

He'd waited that night, nerves thrumming, but she'd never returned to his town house. The next morning, he'd discovered she'd left New York, just as she'd claimed she intended.

Now, after three days, he knew everything about Belle, except for her medical records, which he expected to have later today. His investigator had easily found her home address in Texas. The GPS of her phone had been tracked through means he didn't care to know, and someone had watched for her highly visible blue 1978 Chevy at the gas station two hours to the east, the only gas station for miles in this empty Texas prairie. He'd simply taken the helicopter here from his large ranch in south Texas.

But he could hardly be expected to reveal his strategies to an enemy. Which was what Belle now was.

From the day they'd met, she'd acted like she hated him. But he'd never hated her.

Until now.

Santiago stared down at her beneath the unrelenting furnace of the sun blasting heat from the Texas sky. He felt a prickling of sweat on his forehead. Wearing a vest, tie and long-sleeved shirt along with tailored wool trousers, he found the temperature brutal. And it wasn't even noon.

Santiago set his jaw. He wouldn't allow Belle to control the situation. Or his baby. He didn't know her goal, but the way she was playing the game—like a professional poker player without a heart—the amount she wanted must be astronomical. And why would it ever stop, when she'd have the leverage to control him for the rest of her life? She could try to control custody, or make their child hate him through her lies. She could leave Santiago like a fish gasping on a hook.

Belle had deliberately misled him, saying she couldn't get pregnant. Later, she'd ambushed him with her news and then fled New York, just to show him she meant business. She'd done all this for a reason. To get the upper hand.

But he wouldn't let her use their innocent baby as a pawn. He couldn't be forced or tricked into abandoning a child. Not after what he'd endured himself as a boy. Belle didn't know who she was dealing with. Santiago would scorch the earth to win this war.

His eyes narrowed. She thought she could defeat him? He'd fought his way from an orphanage in Madrid, stowing away at eighteen on a ship to New York City with the equivalent of five hundred dollars in his pocket. Now, he was a billionaire, the majority owner of an international conglomerate that sold everything from running shoes to snack foods on six continents. You didn't do that by being weak, or letting anyone else win.

Belle was in his world now. His world. His rules.

"I'll never marry you," she ground out, her brown eyes shooting sparks. "I'll never belong to you."

"You already do, Belle," he said flatly. "You just don't know it yet." Turning, he made a quick gesture to his helicopter pilot, who started the engine.

She gave an incredulous laugh over the rising noise of the helicopter. "You're crazy!"

Santiago looked down at her. Even now, despising Belle as his enemy, he felt more drawn than ever. She wasn't conventionally beautiful, perhaps, but somehow she was more seductive than any woman he'd ever known. His eyes unwillingly traced the curve of her cheek. The slope of her graceful neck. The fullness of her pregnancy-swollen breasts.

Belle was right, he thought grimly. He was crazy. Because even knowing her for a lying, almost sociopathic gold digger, he wanted her in his bed more than ever.

"I'd be crazy to abandon my child to you," he said evenly. He looked over his shoulder at the wooden house in the barren sagebrush field, with only a few wan, spindly trees overlooking a dry creek bed. "Or to this."

Following his gaze, she looked outraged. "You're judging me because I don't live in a palace?"

"I'm judging what you've done to escape it," he said grimly. He knew all about how she'd been raised here, and only left a year and a half before. He wondered if her dream of Broadway stardom had always been a cover story, and she'd planned to hook a rich man from the beginning. Maybe even her friendship with Letty had been contrived, to better throw Belle in the path of wealthy targets.

The only thing good about this isolated, bare land was the view of the endless blue sky. The sky above the dry grass prairie was starkly dramatic. You could see forever. The freedom. The unending loneliness.

But there were all kinds of loneliness. You could be lonely surrounded by others, as he'd learned as a child.

His own son or daughter would never know that kind of loneliness. He or she would never feel unwanted, or alone. He would see to that.

He turned away. "Let's go."

"Where?"

"Paternity test."

"Forget it—"

He whirled on her with narrowed eyes. "You hate me," he growled. "Fine. I feel the same for you. But does not our child, at least, deserve to know the truth about his parents?"

She glared at him, her eyes glittering with dislike. Then her expression faltered. He'd found the one argument that could sway her.

"Fine," she bit out.

"You'll take the test?"

"For my baby's sake. Not yours."

He exhaled. He hadn't realized he'd been holding his breath, wondering if he'd have to physically force her into the helicopter—a very unpleasant thought, especially with a woman who was likely pregnant with his child. He was relieved she wasn't being so unreasonable.

Then he realized Belle must have decided to change her strategy. She was just shifting her ground, like a boxer. Santiago's lips pressed together in a thin line. He glanced at his bodyguards, hovering nearby. "Get her things."

As his men reached into her pickup, Santiago took her arm, leading her forward. Within seconds, she was sitting comfortably beside him on a leather seat inside the luxury helicopter.

"I'll take the test, but I'm never going to marry you," she said over the sound of the propellers.

He narrowed his eyes coldly. "We both know this is exactly what you wanted to happen. So stop the act. In your heart, I know you are rejoicing."

"I'm not!"

"Your joy will not last long." He drew closer, his face inches from hers. "You will find that being my wife is different than you imagined. You won't own me, Belle. I will own you."

Her brown eyes got big, and he felt a current of electricity course through his body. Against his will, his gaze fell to her lips. So delicious. So sensual and red. Heat surged through his veins.

He'd always despised the idea of marriage, but for the first time, he saw the benefits. As much as he hated her, it had only lifted his desire to a fever. And he knew, by the nervous flicker of her tongue against her lips even now, that Belle felt the same.

Once wed, she would be in his bed, at his command, for as long as he desired. Because one thing, at least, hadn't been a lie between them.

So why wait?

For all these months, since the explosive night he'd taken her virginity, he'd denied himself the pleasure of her. Both for his own sake and, he'd once believed, for hers.

No longer.

Tonight, he thought hungrily. He would have her in his bed tonight.

But first things first.

Putting on a headset, Santiago spoke to the pilot over the rising noise of the blades whipping the sky. "Let's go."

Sitting in the helicopter, Belle looked through the window across the wide plains of Texas. Far below, she saw wild horses running across the prairie, feral and free, a hundred miles away from any human civilization.

She envied them right now.

"Those are mine." Santiago's voice came through her headset. Sitting on the white leather seat beside her, he nodded toward the horses with satisfaction. "We're on the north edge of my property."

So even the wild horses weren't free, she thought glumly. It was the first time they'd spoken in the noisy helicopter since they'd left the world-class medical clinic in Houston.

"You want to own everything, don't you?"

"I do own everything." Santiago's dark eyes gleamed at her. "My ranch is nearly half a million acres."

"Half a—" She sucked in her breath, then said slowly, "Wait. Did you buy the Alford Ranch?"

He raised a sardonic eyebrow. "You've heard of it?"

"Of course I've heard of it," she snapped. "It's famous. There was a scandal a few years ago when it was sold to some foreigner—you?"

He shrugged. "All of this land was once owned by Spaniards, so some people might say that the Alfords were the foreigners. I was merely reacquiring it."

She looked at him skeptically. "Spaniards owned this?"

"Most of South Texas was once claimed by the Spanish Empire, in the time of the conquistadors."

"How do you know that?"

He gave a grim smile. "My father's family is very proud of their history. When I was a boy, and still cared, I read about my ancestors. The family line goes back six hundred years."

"The Velazquez family can be traced six hundred years?" she blurted out. She barely knew the full names of her own great-grandparents.

"Velazquez is my mother's name. My father is a Zoya. The eighth Duque de Sangovia."

His voice was so flat she wasn't sure she'd heard him right. "Your father is a duke? An actual duke?"

He shrugged. "So?"

"What's he like?" she breathed. She'd never met royalty before, or aristocracy. The closest she'd come was knowing a kid called Earl back in middle school.

"I wouldn't know," he said shortly. "We've never met. Look." Changing the subject, Santiago pointed out the window. "There's the house."

Belle looked, and gasped.

The horizon was wide and flat, stretching in every direction, but after miles of dry, sparse sagebrush, the landscape had turned green. Between tree-covered rivers, she saw outbuildings and barns and pens. And at the most beautiful spot, she was astonished to see a blue lake, sparkling in the late afternoon sun. Next to it, atop a small hill surrounded by trees, was a sprawling single-story ranch house that made the place in the old TV show *Dallas* look like a fishing shack.

"It's beautiful," she said in awe. "The land is so green!"

"Five different rivers cross the property."

Past one of the pens she saw a private hangar, with a helipad and airplane runway stretching out to the horizon beyond. "All this is yours?"

"All mine."

His black eyes gleamed down at her, and she heard the echo of his arrogant words earlier. *If the baby is mine, then so are you.* She shivered.

The baby was his. He now had undeniable proof. When they'd gone to the cutting-edge medical clinic in Houston, she'd gotten the impression Santiago must be a very important financial donor, the way the entire staff had waited on him hand and foot. They'd taken the noninvasive blood test, drawing blood from each of them, then the highly trained lab technicians had promised to rush the results.

"But while you wait—" the female OB/GYN had smiled between them "—would you like to have an ultrasound, and find out if you're having a boy or girl?"

Belle had started to refuse. She'd already decided she wanted to be surprised at the birth. But looking at Santiago's face—his dark eyes so bright, almost boyishly eager as he looked at her—she couldn't refuse. If Santiago truly wanted to be what she herself had never had…a loving father…then she was going to do everything she could to encourage the bond between father and child.

"All right," she'd said quietly, and got up on the hospital bed. A few minutes later, as the doctor ran the wand over the sticky goo on her belly, they were staring at the image on the ultrasound screen. A *whoosh-whoosh* sound filled the room.

"What's that?" Santiago asked in alarm, sitting beside her on the bed.

Belle blinked at him in surprise. She suddenly realized that unlike her, he was hearing that sound for the very first time. Smiling, she told him, "It's the baby's heartbeat."

"Heartbeat?" he breathed. The expression on his darkly handsome face, normally hard and cynical, changed so much he looked like a different man.

"It's nice and strong. Your baby looks healthy," the doctor murmured. She pointed at the ultrasound screen. "Here you can see the head, arms…legs…and…" She turned to them with a smile. "Congratulations. You're having a little girl."

"A girl!" Belle gasped.

"A girl?" Reaching out, Santiago suddenly gripped Belle's hand tightly in his own. "When will she be born?"

"Her growth is on track for her due date in late September," the doctor replied.

"September," he murmured, looking dazed. "Just two months from now…"

Belle saw an expression on his face she'd never seen before. Bewilderment. Emotion. Tenderness.

So he wasn't a total bastard after all, she thought. There was one thing that could reach past his layers of cynicism and darkness. Their baby.

Grateful tears had risen unbidden to her eyes, and she'd gripped his hand back tightly. Their daughter would have a father. A father who loved her.

Now, as the helicopter landed at his Texas ranch, Santiago held out his hand to help her out onto the tarmac. He caught her when her knees unexpectedly started to buckle.

"Are you all right?" he asked, his eyes full of concern.

She gave him a weak smile. "It's been a crazy week."

He laughed. "That's one way of describing it."

She'd never seen him laugh like that, with his whole body, almost a guffaw. It made him more human, and somehow even more handsome, more impossibly desirable. In that instant, as she looked up at his dark, merry eyes, her heart twisted in her chest. She turned away, afraid of what he might see in her face.

"So, what happens now?" she said, relieved her voice held steady.

"Now?" he said. "We start planning the wedding."

She stopped abruptly on the tarmac. "I'm not going to marry you. We can share custody."

His eyes narrowed. "The decision has been made."

"By you. Not by me. And if you think you can bully me into marriage, on this ranch or anywhere else, you've got another think coming." She lifted her chin. "My family might not have an aristocratic history that goes back to infinity, but there are a few things we do have."

"Enlighten me."

"Stubbornness. Pure cussedness. And I'm not going to marry a man I don't love, a man who doesn't love me. I would rather scrub your floors with my tongue!"

Amusement flashed across his handsome face. "That can be arranged. Although," he murmured in her ear, "I can think of better uses for your tongue."

An unwilling fire went through Belle's body. Before she could formulate a response, he took her hand, pulling her toward the sprawling single-story ranch house surrounded by green trees.

Inside the main house, it was light and airy, with large windows and hardwood floors. A smiling housekeeper came forward. "Welcome back to the ranch, Mr. Velazquez." She turned her rosy round face in Belle's direction. "Welcome, miss. I hope you had a nice journey."

Nice didn't quite cover it, but luckily Santiago answered

for her. "It's been a long day, Mrs. Carlson. Could you please serve refreshments in the morning room?"

"Of course, Mr. Velazquez."

He led Belle down the hall, into a large room with a glossy wooden floor and a wall of windows. Comfortable furniture faced the view of green trees and a river turned gold beneath dappled sunlight. She breathed, "It's so beautiful."

"Sit down," he said. He seemed suddenly on edge.

Her knees felt weak anyway, so she let herself fall back onto the soft, plush, white cotton sofa. A moment later, the housekeeper appeared with a tray, which she set down on the table.

"Thank you."

"Of course, sir."

After the housekeeper departed, Santiago handed Belle what looked like a cocktail from the tray. At her dubious look, he explained, "Sweet tea."

Oh, her favorite. She practically snatched it from him. Drinking deeply, she sighed in pleasure at the ice-cold, sweetened, nonalcoholic beverage. Wiping her mouth, she sank back happily into the cushions of the sofa. "There are a few things about you that aren't horrible."

"Like sweet tea?"

"You're not totally a monster."

"You're welcome."

Gulping down the rest of the drink, she held the empty glass out hopefully.

His lips quirked as he turned back to the tray. Refilling her glass with the ceramic pitcher, he poured one for himself. "By the way, if you're formulating a plot to run away, you should know the nearest highway is thirty miles."

"I'm not planning to run away."

He straightened. "You're not?"

"Why would I? You're my baby's father. We have to figure it out. For her sake."

He stared at her. His handsome face seemed tense. He held out a plate. "Cookie?"

"Thank you." Chocolate chip, warm from the oven. As she bit into it, the butter and sugar and chocolate were like a burst on her tongue. She sighed with pleasure, then, feeling his gaze on her, looked up, pretending to scowl. "If you're trying to ply me with delicious food and drink to convince me to marry you, it won't work. However," she added hopefully, "you're free to keep trying."

But he just looked at her, his handsome face strained. He started to say something, then abruptly changed his mind. "Excuse me, I have to go."

"Go? Go where?"

"I'll have Mrs. Carlson show you the bedroom. As you said," he gave a smile that didn't reach his eyes, "it's been a crazy week. Rest, if you like. I'll see you for dinner. Eight o'clock."

He left without another word.

Now what was that all about? Although she wasn't going to complain, since at least he'd left the tray. Taking another cookie from the plate, Belle looked out at the leafy green trees moving softly in an unseen breeze, dappled with golden afternoon light. He'd gone to all that trouble to drag her to his ranch, and now, instead of threatening her into marriage or trying to boss her around, he'd just fed her sweet tea and home-baked cookies, then left her to relax?

But then, people had continually surprised her in life, starting with her own family. Belle couldn't remember her father, who'd died when she was a baby. She'd grown up in that house on the edge of the sagebrush prairie with a stepfather, two younger half brothers and her sad-eyed mother, who tried unsuccessfully to shield her children from both her sorrow and her terminal illness. Belle's stepfather, a wiry, laconic welder, never showed much interest in any of the children. He worked long hours then spent his evenings smoking cigarettes, drinking his nightly six-pack and yelling at his wife.

But when Belle was twelve, her mother died, and everything changed. Her stepfather started yelling at her instead, threatening to kick her out of the house, "Because you're none of mine."

So she'd anxiously tried to earn her keep by taking care of the young boys, by cooking and cleaning. By always being cheerful and smiling. By making sure she was never any trouble to anyone.

A week after Belle graduated from high school, her stepfather died suddenly of a brain aneurysm. Ray was thirteen, Joe just eleven. There were no other relatives, no life insurance and almost no savings. Rather than let her little brothers be turned over to foster care, Belle gave up a college scholarship to stay in Bluebell and work as a waitress to support them, raising them until they were grown.

It hadn't been easy. As teenagers, her orphaned brothers had gotten into fights at school, and Ray had briefly gotten into drugs. Those years had been filled with slammed doors, yells of "I hate you!" and her homemade dinners thrown to the floor.

Barely more than a teenager herself, Belle had struggled to get through it. Heartsick, exhausted and alone, she'd dreamed about falling in love with a man who was handsome and kind. A man who would take care of her.

Then, at twenty-one, she had. And it had nearly destroyed her.

"Miss Langtry?" The plump, gray-haired housekeeper appeared in the doorway with her ever-present smile. "If you're done, I can show you to your room."

Glancing at the empty tray, Belle said dryly, "I guess I'm done."

Pushing herself up from the sofa—a simple act that was getting harder by the day as her belly expanded—she followed the housekeeper down the hall of the ranch house. They turned down another hallway, then Mrs. Carlson pushed open a door. "Here's your bedroom, miss."

The room was enormous, with a tall ceiling, a walk-in closet and an en suite bathroom. This, too, had a wall of windows overlooking the river. But that wasn't the bedroom's most notable characteristic.

Belle stared at the enormous bed.

"Is something wrong, Miss Langtry?"

"Um..." Looking around the enormous bedroom, Belle managed, "This is a really nice guest room."

Her worst fears were realized when the older woman replied with a laugh, "Guest room? I know they say everything's bigger in Texas, but honey, that would be crazy. This bedroom suite is bigger than most houses. It's the master bedroom."

Belle gulped. But before she could think of a good reply to explain there was *no way* she was going to be sleeping with the master in this bedroom, the housekeeper continued to the bathroom, proudly showing off the marble tub, sparkling silver fixtures and fresh flowers, with a skylight overhead. Now this, Belle could appreciate.

"You'll find everything you could need or want... Mr. Velazquez said you were weary and dusty after traveling. We have everything you need for a nice, long bath."

She showed Belle all the perfumes, French soaps, creams, shampoos so expensive that she'd only read about them in celebrity magazines. Belle had always thought rich people must be fools for spending fifty dollars on shampoo when the cheap generic brand got your hair just as clean. But as she sniffed the expensive shampoo tentatively, it did smell nice.

"Mr. Velazquez trusts you'll be comfortable while he

conducts some business this afternoon." She opened a door. Belle followed her into a huge closet, with a chandelier and a white sofa.

The housekeeper indicated a red dress hanging alone in the closet. "He requests that you wear this tonight. Dinner will be served on the terrace at eight."

Looking at the dress, Belle breathed, "It's beautiful."

"There are shoes to match, two-inch heels so you won't be uncomfortable or off balance." She smiled in the direction of Belle's belly. "And also new lingerie." She opened one of the drawers. "Silk. Here. Next to your other things."

Lingerie? Belle blushed, suddenly unable to meet the other woman's eyes. Looking around the huge closet, she saw a few scant clothes that had already been unpacked from her suitcase. But other than that and the red dress, the enormous walk-in closet's racks and shelves were empty. "Where are Santiago's clothes?"

"Mr. Velazquez's clothes are in the master closet."

"Isn't this the master closet?"

"Oh, no." Her friendly, chubby face widened in a broad smile. "This closet is designated just for the mistress of the house, that is, if there ever should be one." Leaning forward, she confided, "You're the first woman he's ever brought to the ranch."

"I am?"

"Goodness. Getting late." Mrs. Carlson looked at her watch. "Everything you'll need is here. We arranged toiletries, lotions, lipsticks, everything we could think of that you might want. My grandson is in a school play down at Alford Elementary tonight. The rest of the staff will be gone by eight."

"You all don't live here?"

"Oh, goodness, no. There are staff cottages on the other side of the lake. You and Mr. Velazquez can be completely alone." Was it her imagination, or did the housekeeper wink? "Good night, miss."

Belle stared indignantly after her. Why had she winked? What did she think would happen if she and Santiago were alone?

Nothing, she thought firmly, and locked the bedroom door to prove it. She glanced at the enormous bed. As comfortable as it looked, she would never share it with Santiago. But since he wasn't here right now…

She climbed onto the soft, comfortable bed as days of worry and weariness caught up with her. Her head hit the pillow and she closed her eyes just for a moment.

When she woke, she realized by the fading sunlight that she'd accidentally slept for hours.

Rising from the bed, Belle saw the red dress hanging in the walk-in closet across the bedroom. Going to it, she let her fingertips stroke the soft fabric. She saw the designer tag and gulped. She didn't know fashion, but even she had heard of that famous designer. And the shoes!

But it would be bad manners not to wear it. Especially since it was the most beautiful thing she'd ever seen in real life, much less worn on her body.

Taking the dress and silk lingerie, she went to the enormous en suite bathroom and took a shower. As she stepped naked beneath the hot, steaming water, with six different spigots coming at her from all sides, she sighed in pleasure as the dust and heartbreak of the last three days were swept away. She tried the shampoo. Maybe the fifty dollars was worth it, she thought in a blissful haze. Though even a bargain shampoo would have been great in a shower like this.

Wrapping herself in a towel, she brushed out her long, wet hair. Opening a drawer, she found boxes of brand-new makeup, the high-end kind from department stores with the nice packaging, all lined up for her use, next to a variety of brand-new perfumes and pricey scented lotions.

She tried it all, then put on the silk bra and panties. She almost moaned. So sensual. So soft.

Finally, she pulled on the red knit dress, which fit perfectly over her swollen breasts and baby bump. The soft fabric felt like heaven against her perfumed skin. Even her hands, which for the last year and a half had always been red and chapped from working as a waitress at the diner, felt soft, from all the lotions. She looked in the bathroom mirror.

Her hair now gleamed, tumbling down her shoulders, dark against her creamy caramel skin. Her cheeks were flushed pink from the heat of the shower. Her lips were ruby red to match the dress. Her brown eyes gleamed in the shadows beneath dark kohl and mascara.

Even to her own eyes, she looked...different.

Was it this place? The dress? The extravagant shampoo?

Or was it being around Santiago, being pregnant with his child, being the first woman he'd ever brought to this famous ranch, spread across five counties of south Texas?

"Most of South Texas was once claimed by the Spanish Empire, in the time of the conquistadors...my father is a Zoya. The eighth Duque de Sangovia."

Santiago, the son of a duke? That surprised her. He didn't seem like a man who'd been born with a silver spoon in his mouth. Oh, he was arrogant enough. But he seemed too rough, like a man who'd had to fight so hard for everything that he no longer gave a damn about the judgment of lesser mortals.

"Your father is a duke? An actual duke?... What's he like?"

"I wouldn't know. We've never met."

That was one thing Santiago and Belle had in common, then. All she had of her father was an old picture of him, beaming into the camera as he held her as a swaddled baby, sleeping in his arms.

If Santiago had never even met his father, that explained a lot. But why did they have different last names? If his father was still alive, why had the two men never met?

Then she was distracted by a more urgent question. Biting her lip, Belle looked down at her belly, prominent in the red dress. She looked at the dress, at the luxurious toiletries, the costly, well-made shoes.

Why was Santiago suddenly being so kind to her?

She couldn't trust it, that was for sure. She'd learned that from their night together. He could be warm and tender when he wanted her, then ruthlessly toss her out of his life like garbage.

There could be only one reason. He'd realized he couldn't bully her into marriage, so he was going to try to seduce her into it.

She wouldn't let him.

She *wouldn't*.

Belle was willing to share custody of their baby. But she wouldn't share her life, her heart and certainly not her body. She would never be Santiago Velazquez's plaything again, and definitely not his wife.

Now she just had to convince him of that, so he'd let her go home.

At five minutes past eight, as Belle walked through the enormous, sprawling ranch house, down the darkened hallways, she felt strangely nervous of how he'd react.

Opening the sliding doors, she went outside onto the terrace that stretched out toward the lake. Fairy lights hung from a large pergola, covered with flowers of pink bougainvillea. The lights twinkled against the twilight as soft music came from invisible speakers.

And she saw him.

Santiago stood at the terrace railing, looking out pensively toward dark water painted red by sunset. Then he turned, devastatingly handsome, tall and broad-shouldered in his tuxedo. And he smiled.

"Welcome," he said in his low, husky voice. Their eyes locked, and held.

And Belle suddenly knew the real reason for her fear. Her heart had known it all along, and so had her body. Her brain had refused to accept it. Now she saw the truth. She hadn't been afraid of Santiago's reaction.

She was afraid of her own. Because when she'd given him her body all those months ago, she'd unwillingly given him part of her heart. And now, as he smiled at her, his eyes twinkling beneath the lights, she caught her breath.

"You're beautiful." Coming closer, he held out a champagne glass. His dark eyes caressed her as he whispered, "Brighter than the stars."

As she took the champagne glass, their fingers brushed. She saw the intention in his eyes, and it rocked her to her core.

Santiago intended to conquer her, just as he'd conquered the world. He intended to win her, as he'd won his billion-dollar fortune. He intended to rule her, as he ruled this isolated Texas ranch, big enough to be its own kingdom.

He intended to possess her as his wife. And he would not be denied.

CHAPTER FOUR

HE'D BEEN WRONG about her. All wrong.

When he'd left New York in pursuit of Belle, he'd been certain she was a gold digger, a cunning, cold-hearted actress, who'd ruthlessly lied in order to conceive his child for her own selfish financial gain.

But that afternoon, at the medical center in Houston, he'd learned otherwise.

Standing in the hallway outside the examination room as he waited for Belle, he'd stared at the doctor in disbelief. "Is this a joke?"

She'd smiled. "I never joke about medical matters."

"What do you mean, she was telling the truth?"

"Miss Langtry had good reason to think she could never conceive a child," the doctor had said. "I just received her medical records from the hospital in Bluebell. Seven years ago, she had a procedure to make pregnancy impossible. Bilateral tubal ligation." She hesitated. "I shouldn't be discussing this with you, but..."

But she was, and they both knew why. Santiago spent many millions of dollars each year supporting her clinic, so uninsured patients could get world-class care without worrying about payment. He still remembered his first winter in New York, at eighteen, when he'd been sick for months but hadn't gone to a doctor because he'd feared the cost.

Now, he said incredulously, "Belle deliberately had surgery to make sure she'd never get pregnant? Why?"

"You'd have to ask her."

"But she was only twenty-one—and a virgin! What crackpot doctor would perform such a procedure?"

"Interestingly, that doctor retired a month later. It turned out he'd been suffering from the early stages of dementia."

"So if she had that surgery seven years ago, how can she be pregnant?" Santiago said.

The doctor hesitated. "Miss Langtry is young…"

"So?"

"There is a risk of healing after that type of procedure. It's rare, but it does happen. The body finds a way. It's even more likely when the patient is young."

Santiago glared at her. "She honestly believed she couldn't get pregnant."

"Yes. Either the procedure wasn't done correctly, or her body healed over the last seven years."

It had been like a punch in the gut.

Everything Santiago had believed about Belle was wrong. She wasn't a greedy climber. She was innocent. She'd been telling the truth all along.

After they left the medical center, as their helicopter flew south from Houston, Belle had refused to meet his gaze, but he hadn't been able to look away from her. Her beautiful face, her lush body, pregnant with his child. Remembering their night together, he'd felt aware of her every movement. He'd thought of nothing but how she'd felt in his arms that night. How she'd gasped with ecstasy. How afterward, she'd cuddled against him so sweetly.

"You feel so good to me," she'd whispered. *"I'm glad you're here. I couldn't bear to be alone tonight. You saved me…"*

Santiago had left her that night because he'd known his life would change, with her in it. And he hadn't wanted it to change.

But his life had changed without his consent. In spite of incredible odds, she was pregnant.

Now there was someone else to think about. His child. Having his paternity confirmed, seeing his daughter pictured on the ultrasound screen in Houston, the idea of a baby had felt truly real to him for the first time. A daughter. An innocent child. She hadn't asked to be conceived, but now it was possible, through no fault of her own, she could be born without a name. Without a father's protection or love.

He couldn't let that happen.

He couldn't let his child be split between parents, and have the same childhood he'd endured, ignored and rejected by his biological father, watching his mother so desperate to be loved that she married man after man, each less worthy than the last.

No. His daughter's life would be different.

She would have a stable home. Married parents. Financial security. His daughter would have a happy childhood, filled with love.

When they'd arrived at the ranch that afternoon, Santiago had already made up his mind. He'd taken Belle straight to the morning room, intending to force an engagement ring on her hand, to blackmail or threaten her into it, if he had to. But something stopped him.

The thought of their daughter.

After the way he'd treated Belle from the moment they'd slept together that cold winter's night, she'd had good reason to despise him. He'd abandoned her. Ignored her phone messages. Treated her badly when she'd actually come to his house to tell him about the baby.

Standing in the morning room, he'd known he could force Belle to marry him, if he chose.

He suddenly didn't want to.

He didn't want to be her enemy. For their daughter's

sake, they needed a better foundation for their marriage, for a happy home, than resentment and hatred.

So Santiago had abruptly changed tactics.

Instead of giving Belle his ultimatum in the morning room, he'd given her time to rest, to regroup, to be refreshed. And he'd taken time to plan his own strategy. He'd organized this dinner with the help of his staff. The dress had already been purchased in nearby Alford, by Mrs. Carlson, but he'd still lacked one thing: a show-stopping engagement ring.

Fortunately, he'd thought with grim amusement, he happened to have one, gathering dust these past years in his safe. The diamond ring was tucked in his tuxedo pocket now, glinting, sparkling, obscene.

He'd tried to give this ring to a different woman, long ago; one he'd loved so much he'd built his billion-dollar fortune in the attempt to win her. Santiago still felt acid in his gut at the memory of the day he'd proposed to Nadia with this very ring, as promised so many years before, only to discover she hadn't waited for him. And the man she'd chosen—

Santiago's shoulders went tight. In the past. All in the past. Starting today, he would treat Belle, the mother of his unborn child, with respect and care. Once he did, she would see reason. She would not refuse his marriage proposal.

The sun was falling into the lake, a red ball of fire burning through the low haze of twilight, when Santiago heard Belle come out through the sliding doors onto the terrace. Turning from the railing, he looked at her.

And was dazzled.

He'd never seen such rampant beauty, all lush curves in that red dress, her dark hair tumbling over her shoulders, her lips invitingly red, black eyelashes trembling over big brown eyes.

"You're beautiful," he breathed, holding out a champagne glass. "Brighter than the stars."

She took the glass. From this close, her skin looked delectably soft. He wanted to kiss her. He wanted to pick her up like a caveman and carry her to bed, to rip off the red dress that clung to every curve, and make love to her until he felt her quiver and shake, until he heard her cry out with pleasure.

She looked up at him, her eyes regretful. "I can't drink champagne."

"It's sparkling juice."

"Juice?" Taking the glass, she gave him a nervous smile. "I can't imagine you drinking anything except black coffee and maybe Scotch."

"We're celebrating."

"We are?"

"And if you can't drink champagne, neither will I."

Her forehead furrowed in the twilight, beneath the fairy lights of the pergola.

"I think I know why you're being so nice to me," she said slowly.

"Because I know I was wrong," he said quietly. "And I'm sorry."

She could have no idea, he thought, how long it had been since he'd said those last two words to anyone. Years? Decades?

"Sorry?" She frowned. "About what?"

"You truly thought you couldn't get pregnant."

Her expression changed. "Why do you believe me now?"

"Dr. Hill told me about your medical procedure."

"She shouldn't have." She stiffened. "That's my private business."

"Not anymore. Anything that relates to you or the baby is my business now." Moving closer, his body thrummed with awareness as his gaze fell to her red lips, then further down still. Her thick dark hair fell in waves over her bare clavicle, over her shoulders, almost to her full breasts straining the red knit fabric of her dress. His body suddenly raged to pull her into his arms, tip her back against the table and ravage her right here and now. He took a deep breath to control himself.

"Won't you join me?"

Turning toward a large stone table nearby, he showed her the dishes, interspersed with big vases of flowers.

"What is it?" she said doubtfully.

"Dinner." He lifted a silver lid off the largest platter. Frowning, she peeked over his shoulder. When she saw the food, she burst into a full-bodied, incredulous laugh that he felt down to his toes.

"Blueberries? Licorice whips? I thought you'd try to serve me something nasty, like caviar!"

"I have only your favorites." He lifted another silver lid, and grinned as he heard her gasp.

"Ham and pineapple pizza!" she exclaimed. "Are you kidding me?"

"With the ranch and hot sauce you like, for dipping," he said smugly. "And for dessert…" He opened a third silver lid to reveal strawberry shortcake, thick sweet cakes covered with plump, juicy strawberries and thick dollops of whipped cream. Now, she looked at him almost in awe.

"How did you know?" she breathed.

"Magic."

"No, seriously."

"I called Letty and asked her what you liked best." He lifted an eyebrow. "She didn't sound particularly shocked to hear from me, by the way."

Her cheeks colored. "She's the only one I told about you. I knew she wouldn't tell anyone you were my baby's father.

Not after what she went through with Darius." Tentatively, she touched the crust. "The pizza is still hot!"

"I told you." He waved a hand airily. "Magic."

She looked at him skeptically.

He rolled his eyes. "There's a hot plate beneath the tray. If you make me explain, it takes the magic away. All that's left is cheap tricks." He started to add, *just like romance*, but stopped himself, since he didn't think it would help his cause. Pulling out a chair, he gave her a sensual smile. "Have a seat."

As they ate together, enjoying fruit, pizza, sparkling water and finally dessert, the sun gradually disappeared beneath the horizon, turning the sky a soft pink against the black lake.

He enjoyed watching her eat. He took pleasure in her appetite. As she started her third piece of strawberry short-cake, he leaned forward and brushed his fingertips against the corner of her mouth.

"Missed some whipped cream," he said, and then licked it off his fingertips. Belle's eyes went wide, and he heard her intake of breath. He almost kissed her then. Instead, he leaned back in his chair to look at her.

"So why did you do it, Belle?" he asked quietly. "Why did you deliberately have surgery at twenty-one, to prevent pregnancy? Knowing you as I do, it doesn't make sense."

For a moment he thought she might not answer. Then she set down her spoon.

"My dad died when I was a baby," she said haltingly. "My mother remarried a few years later, and had my broth-ers…"

"I know."

Belle looked surprised. "You know?" She glanced down as his hand enfolded her own, then said with a tinge of bitterness, "Of course you know. Your private investiga-tor told you, right?" She gave a humorless laugh. "So you know my mother died when I was twelve and my stepfather six years later. I couldn't let my brothers be sent to foster care. So I gave up my dream of college and stayed home to raise them."

Santiago tried to think of a time he'd made a sacrifice that big for anyone. He couldn't.

"It wasn't easy," she continued in a low voice. "They were angry teenagers. Sometimes I wasn't sure I could make it. Then I met Justin." She blinked fast. "He was so strong and sure. He said he loved me. Even when I told him I was old-fashioned and wished to wait until marriage to have sex, he still wanted me..."

Santiago gave an incredulous laugh. "No sex until marriage?"

"I know." She smiled wistfully. "Crazy, right? But he'd just gotten divorced. His wife'd had an awful miscarriage that broke them up. Justin was ten years older than me, but he said that didn't matter. He was even willing to help me raise my brothers, who desperately needed a male role model."

"Did they?" he said evenly, remembering all the times his own mother had married so-called "male role models" who hadn't been worth much and hadn't lasted more than a year.

"It seemed like the perfect solution for everyone to be happy. There was just one catch." Her voice was small. "Justin couldn't go through losing a baby again. So he only agreed to marry me if I...he and I...made sure to never have a baby of our own. Ever." She looked down at her lap. "So a few weeks before our wedding, I did it. It seemed like the only way to make everyone happy."

"What about you? Did it make you happy?"

A strangled laugh escaped her lips, and she looked away. "Not exactly."

The final light of the setting sun streaked across her pale, troubled face. He said grimly, "What happened?"

"He left me. Right before our wedding." She gave him a small smile. "He'd had a hard time waiting for sex and ran into his ex-wife at a bar. One thing led to another, and she became pregnant. After that, he wanted to give their relationship another try. He told me he'd never stopped loving her."

He gave a low, heartfelt curse in Spanish.

"It's all right," she said quietly. "They're happy now. They're married, living in El Paso. Last I heard, they have a big rambling house and five children."

Santiago fell silent, his jaw tight.

"I know what you're thinking." She looked up, her eyes suddenly shining with unshed tears. "Go ahead. Tell me how stupid I was, to sacrifice my own dreams for the sake of love."

Rising moonlight frosted the dark lake, and he heard the plaintive call of unseen birds. He looked at her beauty, at the way her dark eyelashes trembled against her cheeks.

Rising to his feet, he took her hand. "Dance with me."

"No, I…"

"Why?" He gave her a wicked smile. "Are you afraid?"

"Of course not. I'm just not a good dancer, I…"

But he didn't listen to her excuses. Gently, he pulled her from the chair, into his arms. He felt her body tremble against his. The fairy lights twinkled above the terrace, as they looked out at the moon-swept lake. They were alone.

"I'll lead," he murmured, and he twirled her slowly around the flagstone terrace. He watched her sway, light as air. Saw the beauty of her. The kindness. The way she'd sacrificed for her younger brothers. The way she'd sacrificed for the man she'd once thought she would marry.

Damn, he thought. What a mother she will make.

What a *wife*.

He whirled her close, then caught her tight in his arms. Her eyes widened, and she sucked in her breath as she saw his intention.

Slowly, never taking his eyes from hers, he lowered his mouth to hers.

She didn't fight him, but closed her eyes, letting him hold her close. He closed his eyes and kissed her, really kissed her.

Lightning shattered through his body, through his soul, in the embrace. He felt her tremble, pressing her body against his.

Then she ripped away, her eyes tortured.

"Why are you doing this?" she choked out.

"Doing what?"

"*Romancing* me," she said bitterly, "like the night you seduced me. I'm not going to fall for it again, so you can break my heart!" She pressed her palm against his chest, pushing him away. "Just tell me what you want from me."

The stars above them sparkled in the wide, velvety black sky as he looked down at her. It was too soon. He had barely started to seduce her as he wished. But she wanted him to speak plainly, so he would. He had that much respect for her.

"Very well," he said quietly. Reaching into his tuxedo jacket pocket, he lowered himself to one knee, holding up the huge diamond ring. It glittered brighter and bigger than the full moon shining across the endless Texas sky. "I want you to marry me, Belle."

She gaped at him, looking from the ring to his face and back again.

"I know I've treated you badly," he said. "But I'll never make that mistake again. I'll never lie to you, Belle. We'll be more than lovers. We'll be partners. Parents. I know you want love, and I regret I cannot give you that. But I offer you something better."

"Better than love?" she whispered. He nodded.

"My loyalty. You never betrayed me. I will never betray you. I've made very few promises in life, but I'm making one to you now. If you marry me, I'll make sure you're never alone again. Our marriage will be for life."

"For life?" She looked stricken. She said hoarsely, "I might consider a temporary marriage…to give our baby a name…"

"No." His expression hardened. "A real marriage, Belle. A real home. Isn't that what you want? Isn't that what our baby deserves from us?"

She looked away and whispered, "I don't know."

Rising to his feet, he pulled her close and growled, "I think you do."

Her dark gaze seared his. "I want to marry someone I can love and respect. And you're not that man, Santiago, you know you're not."

The words caused a stab in his solar plexus. He hadn't known he could still be hurt by rejection. He'd thought he'd buried his heart long ago. To be hurt now, when he was trying his best to please her, when he was trying his best to be honest, stung him to the core.

He took a deep breath. "Love—perhaps not. But we both love our daughter. And if you give me a chance," he said in a low voice, "I will earn your respect. I swear it."

She looked at the fairy lights and the flowers on the stone table, at the diamond ring still in his hand.

"I'm not your toy," she said in a small voice. "Just because we slept together once and conceived this child, you can't just have me whenever you want amusement. You don't have any permanent claim over me."

"You're wrong." He lifted his gaze to hers. "I do have a permanent claim. Just as you've had a claim over me, from the moment you came to my bed."

"What are you talking about?"

"You," he whispered, cupping her cheek. "And how you've bewitched me."

Her eyes were big as she looked up at him. "You can find someone else—"

"*No.*"

"Yes you can! You've been with dozens of women since that night. Supermodels, actresses, socialites…" Her voice cut off as their eyes met. She choked out, "Haven't you?"

Never looking away, he shook his head, his jaw tight. "There's been no one. Because I don't want any other woman. I haven't, since our night together. I've only hungered for you." He narrowed his eyes as he looked down at her. His voice was a growl. "You will belong to me, Belle. You have no choice. I already belong to you."

I already belong to you.

It wasn't romantic. At all. He said it, Belle thought, as if he felt trapped. Oppressed, even. His dark eyes glittered.

"Are you telling me," she breathed, "you've been celibate all these months?"

"Yes." His voice was a low growl.

"But—but why?"

His eyes were dark. "You've ensorcelled me."

Ensorcelled. Such a strange, old-fashioned word. Such a gleam in his dark eyes and his powerful body towering over her with all his strength. She suddenly felt like she'd gone back hundreds of years, to a simpler time.

Belle shivered, struggling not to feel so aware of his body close to hers. His eyes were dark beneath the softly swaying lights. She saw the arrogant curve of his dangerously seductive mouth.

He was right, she realized. She did belong to him. From the moment he'd kissed her that cold January night.

No. She couldn't pretend it had been just that. It had been more.

She'd been able to be honest with him that night in a way she hadn't been since her mother died. She never had to pretend with Santiago. She didn't have to act cheerful and happy all the time. She could actually be herself.

She did want him. His warmth. His strength. She wanted the man who'd seduced her that cold winter's night, not just with his body, but with his words.

The only thing that kept her from falling into his arms now was remembering how she'd felt waking up alone that gray January morning, and all the mornings after, when he ignored message after frantic message.

"But I can't trust you," she said in a small voice. "Not anymore. If I give myself to you, how do I know I won't be left broken-hearted and alone?"

"Your heart will be safe. I'll never ask for it." Reaching out, he stroked her shoulder. His soft touch over the fabric of her red dress felt like fire. "And you'll never be alone again." He lifted her hand to his mouth. She felt the warmth of his breath as he kissed her palm, then the back of her hand. "Never," he whispered.

She couldn't hide her shiver beneath his seductive caress. Looking up at his darkly handsome face beneath the moonlight, at his powerful body towering over hers in the tuxedo, she wondered wildly if he could hear the pounding of her heart. "I can't..."

"Are you sure?" he whispered. Brushing back her hair, he kissed her forehead. Her cheeks. She trembled in his arms, hovering on the edge of surrender.

"Please don't do this." Pressing her palms against the lapels of his tuxedo jacket, she lifted her tearful gaze to his. "You don't know what you're asking me."

"So tell me."

Her hands tightened.

"To give up all hope of being loved," she choked out. "Now and forever."

"That kind of love is an illusion." He drew back. "I know. My mother was a maid working in my father's palace when she got pregnant with me. He was already married, and his duchess was heavily pregnant. He must not have found his wife sexually appealing, because one afternoon he pushed my mother into a closet and kissed her." His lips twisted. "She was barely nineteen, and so wrapped up in fairy-tale dreams she convinced herself the duke loved her. That only lasted until she got pregnant, too, and he threw her out of the palace. She was suddenly poor, a single mother, and dreams don't pay the bills. She thought only love could save her. So she married. Five times."

Santiago had never told her anything about his childhood before. Not one word. She sucked in her breath. "Five marriages?"

"And each husband worse than the last. Each time, her heart was broken. She didn't want to raise me alone," he said lightly. "She couldn't relax at night. Couldn't sleep. So she took sleeping pills. One night she took too many and died."

"How old were you?" she said, aghast.

"Fourteen. I called an ambulance when I found her. The authorities dragged me from the house and I was sent to an orphanage."

"Why didn't you go to your father?"

He snorted. "My father already had a son and heir. He did not care to recognize the bastard result of his affair with a maid. When I tried to see him at his palace in Madrid, he set the dogs on me."

"How could he?" Belle breathed.

Santiago turned away, blankly staring toward the pearlescent moonlight trailing across the lake. He finally looked at her.

"The man did me a favor," he said flatly. "And I'm doing you one now by telling you this. The fairy-tale dream doesn't exist. Only when you give it up will you have any possibility of happiness."

Belle could understand why he might think that, after everything he'd gone through. And yet… She bit her lip. "You never tried to speak to your father again? Or your half brother?"

"They had their chance." His eyes were hard. "I might have Zoya blood, but they mean nothing to me now."

Santiago looked down at her. "So now do you understand? I never intended this to happen. I never meant to marry, or have a child. What do I know of being a husband, or a father?" His eyes narrowed. "But I will not allow my child to have the lonely existence I had. She will not be rejected, raised in poverty by a delusional mother and a succession of uncaring stepfathers. She will have my name." He looked at her evenly. "You will marry me."

Belle licked her lips as she tried desperately, "But there are other ways besides marriage…"

Reaching out, he cupped her cheek.

"You will agree to marry me, Belle, or I will keep you here until the baby is born, and take the child from you. Do you understand?"

His tone was so gentle, it took her a moment to understand the meaning. Then her eyes went wide as she drew away sharply.

"You wouldn't."

"You are mistaken if you believe I am as soft-hearted as you. I am not."

She shivered, not doubting it. "So you're threatening me?"

"I am telling you how it will be. I won't let you put your own foolish dreams above the needs of our baby. Either you leave here with this ring on your finger, or you don't leave at all."

"You can't want to be married… To be loyal and faithful to one woman for the rest of your life? You don't even love me!"

"I will keep my vows," he said impatiently. "I expect you to keep them as well."

She blinked fast. "It's easy for you to give up all dreams of love. You've never loved anyone."

Her harsh words echoed in the silent evening. He stared at her for a long moment, his jaw clenching. When he finally spoke, his voice held no expression.

"So you agree?"

"Fine," she choked out.

"You accept my proposal?"

"You've left me no choice."

"As you've left me none." He slid the enormous platinum-set diamond over her finger. "This ring symbolizes how we are bound. For life."

The precious metal felt cold and heavy, both on her hand and on her heart. "Now what, a shotgun wedding at the nearest justice of the peace?"

He snorted, then sobered. "We will be married in New York."

Back to New York, the city that had chewed her up and spat her out, with a man who would never love her, and who for all his fine words, was practically blackmailing her into marriage? "This gets better and better."

"Our wedding will be a society event. As my wife, you will take your rightful place in New York society."

Belle looked at him incredulously. "Have you lost your mind? Me? A leader in New York society?"

"You will be."

Belle lifted her chin. "I told you. You don't own me."

Santiago looked down at her, his black eyes glittering. "You're wrong," he said softly. Taking her hand in his own, he looked down at the sharp shine of the ring in the moonlight. "From this moment on, I do."

She felt his hand enfolding hers, his palm rough and warm against her skin, and a skitter of electricity went up her spine. Her lips parted.

He pulled her into his arms, cupping her face in his hands. Deliberately, slowly, he lowered his mouth to hers.

The smooth caress of his hot satin lips seared her, making her weak. Ruthlessly, he deepened the kiss, tilting back her head, tangling his hands in her hair. Need raced through her, quickening her heartbeat, making her lose her breath.

Pressing her against the thick white column of the pergola, amid the bloom of pink flowers beneath the fairy lights, he slowly kissed down her throat. Her head fell back, her dark hair tumbling down, as her eyes closed against the sweet pleasure of sensation.

He ran his hands down her arms, over the soft red knit fabric of her low-cut dress. She felt his touch like a whisper over her full breasts, over her belly, over her hips. He lowered his head to kiss her naked collarbone, then the bare cleavage between her breasts.

"I want you," he whispered. Leaning forward, he whispered against the sensitive flesh of her earlobe, making her shiver, "Come to my bed tonight."

Belle opened her eyes. Frosted by moonlight and the silvery lake behind him, Santiago's face was in shadow as he towered over her like a dark angel. That had been the Spanish playboy's nickname in New York, she remembered. Ángel. Now she understood why.

And she could no longer resist. She could only surrender.

Santiago looked at her, then scooped her wordlessly into his arms. He carried her into the sprawling ranch house, down the silent hallway, into the enormous master bedroom, dark with shadows except for the shaft of moonlight pooling through the large windows.

He set her down almost reverently, and she stood in front of him, unsteady on her feet. Kneeling in front of her, he pulled off her shoes, one by one. Rising, he stood in front of her and kissed her again, deeply. When the kiss ended, as she tried to catch her breath, he circled her, his fingertips lingering against her body, and slowly unzipped her dress in the back. Gently, he drew the dress down her body, slipping it off her full breasts, down her arms. He tugged it slowly over her belly, to her hips, until the dress finally fell like a soft whisper to the floor.

She stood nearly naked in front of him, wearing only a silk bra and panties. Still fully dressed in his tuxedo, Santiago looked down at her in the moonlight.

"So beautiful," he whispered, reaching out to touch her shoulder. His hand traced down to cup a full breast over the sensuous silk bra. She nearly gasped as she felt the warmth of his hand pressing the smooth fabric against her heavy breast and aching nipple, which hardened beneath his touch.

He drew closer. His palms explored the full curve of her belly, down to her hips, stroking the naked skin along the edge of her silk panties. Reaching around her, he put his hands over her backside, taking her firmly in his grasp, pulling her hard against his body.

When he lowered his mouth to hers, his kiss was hungry, as he reached beneath the flimsy silk to cup her naked breasts. His thumb stroked her aching nipple. As she gasped with pleasure, he unclasped the sliver of silk and dropped it entirely to the floor.

He cupped both her breasts with his hands, as if marveling at their weight, then lowered his mouth to gently suckle her.

The sensation was so intense she jolted beneath his hot mouth, gripping his shoulders. Pleasure was rising so hard and fast inside her, she wondered if she could climax like this, with only his lips against her breast, his tongue swirling around her nipple, sucking her deeply into his hot, wet mouth.

She gasped, her fingernails digging into his shoulders. She realized with shock that he was still wearing his jacket. Reaching down, she undid his tuxedo tie, then roughly yanked his jacket down from his shoulders.

Rising, he looked down at her intently. Gaze locked with hers, he undid the buttons of his shirt and trousers then dropped them to the floor, along with his silk boxers. He stood naked, his body hard and jutting toward her. She looked down at him in amazement. Reaching out, she took his hard shaft fully in her hands—it took both her hands—and relished the soft, velvety feel of him, so thick and hard as steel.

Now he was the one to gasp.

With a low growl, he pulled her toward the king-sized bed bathed in moonlight, and drew her on top of him. She was shy and uncertain at first, until he pulled her head down into a kiss. Her dark hair tumbled down like a veil, blocking the moonlight, leaving their faces in darkness.

She felt his hands on her hips, moving her until her legs spread wide over his. She felt the hardness of him, insistent between her thighs, demanding entry. That single movement, feeling him pressing against the wet, aching center of her desire, was enough to make her hold her breath. Involuntarily, she swayed against him. With an intake of breath, he tightened his hands on her hips, lifting her off his body, positioning her. Then, with agonizing slowness, he lowered her again, filling her, inch by delicious inch.

She gasped from the pleasure as he slid inside her. Just when she thought her body couldn't take any more of him, he somehow went even deeper, all the way to the hilt, all the way to the heart.

He was hard and thick inside her as his large hands

gripped her backside, spreading her wide. She gasped, tossing back her head.

Then slowly, instinctively, she began to move her body against his, feeling the deliciously exquisite tension rise and build inside her as she slid against his flat, muscular belly. She felt his rough fingertips gripping into her hips as she began to ride him, harder, faster. Her breasts bounced against the swell of her belly as she rode him, soft and slow, then hard and deep. She rode him until her whole body started to tremble and shake.

As she cried out, she heard his low roar join hers, rising to a shout as he filled her so deep she exploded with joyful ecstasy. Her cry became a scream she didn't even try to contain, and he screamed with her, his body jerking and pulsing as he spilled himself inside her.

Exhausted, she collapsed beside him, and he held her. He cuddled her close, gently kissing her sweaty temple. But as she closed her eyes, she heard his dark whisper, so soft she wondered if she'd imagined it, like a whisper of her heart's deepest fear.

"You're mine now."

CHAPTER FIVE

THE LIGHTS OF New York City were dazzling and bright, but in the deep canyon between skyscrapers, Belle could no longer see the sky.

Sitting beside Santiago in the chauffeured black Escalade, with bodyguards following in another SUV, she'd felt numb as they traveled from the airport in New Jersey through Midtown, passing within blocks of the Broadway and Off-Broadway theaters that had rejected her so thoroughly.

As the saying went, if you could make it in New York, you could make it anywhere. But Belle hadn't made it here. She'd thought if she could be an actress, if she could earn a living by pretending to be someone else every day, she could be happy. Instead, the city had laughed in her face.

And Santiago expected her, a small-town girl who'd never gone to college, to know how to be a socialite in this wealthy, ruthless city?

All she'd ever done was work as a waitress and raise her brothers. If Santiago had needed her to remember six different dinner orders with special instructions and sauce on the side, and serve it all at once balanced on her arms, no problem. If he'd wanted her to rustle up a double platter of brownies for ten hungry teenage basketball players in no time flat, Belle could have handled it.

But knowing how to blend into high society? Knowing how to swan around being chic while making small talk to the highly educated and fashionable glitterati he mingled with?

It was all Belle could do not to hyperventilate.

She glanced mutinously at Santiago sitting beside her in the SUV. "I'm not going to do it."

He didn't even bother to look up from his phone. They'd been having this same argument since before they'd left his Texas ranch that afternoon. "You will."

"I'd only embarrass you. I don't know how to talk to rich people!"

This time, Santiago did look up. His dark eyes flashed with amusement. "You talk to them like people."

She sat back sulkily against the soft black calfskin leather of the luxury SUV. "You know what I mean."

"They're not people?"

"Not *normal* people. They all have advanced degrees from places like Oxford and Princeton. They're billionaire entrepreneurs and ambassadors and famous artists. They all grew up in castles with a full staff of servants…"

"You really are a romantic, aren't you?"

"The point is, we have nothing in common."

"You do." His dark eyes gleamed. "Me."

She stared at him, stricken. Then she turned away, looking out silently at the dark, sparkling city.

Last night, Santiago had brought her to the heights of ecstasy in bed. But he'd also proven how thoroughly he commanded her body, even when her heart tried to resist.

He'd given her deep pleasure, made her feel things—*do* things—she'd never imagined. But that morning, she'd once again woken up alone. Only now, she had a big diamond ring on her left hand.

She'd surrendered to his marriage demand, both for their child's sake and because he'd left her no choice. She'd given up any hope of love. She looked at her engagement ring, glinting beneath the city lights. So hard. So cold.

Like the man who'd given it to her.

Alone in the ranch's master bedroom that morning, she'd gotten dressed in an old stretchy T-shirt from high school, the faded words *Bluebell Bears* emblazoned over the picture of a bear that stretched over her big belly, and a pair of loose khaki shorts and flip-flops. She'd found him sitting at the breakfast table drinking coffee, wearing a sleek black button-up shirt and black pants, more sophisticated than she'd ever be. She'd trembled in the doorway, still feeling last night's kisses, wondering how he would greet her now they were engaged to be married for the rest of their lives.

"Good morning," he'd said, barely looking at her. "I trust you slept well. We will be returning to New York today."

That had been it. No warmth. No friendliness. No acknowledgement of the night they'd spent in each other's arms. No matter how exhilarating, amazing, explosive the lovemaking, it was empty, with no love to fuel the fire.

And now he'd dragged her back to the fairy-tale city that had broken her heart.

Belle whispered in the back of the SUV, "I can't possibly be your hostess in New York society."

"What are you afraid of?"

"They'll laugh in my face. Society people are even meaner than casting directors. I saw what they did to Letty, ripping her apart just because her father went to jail…"

"That was different."

"They're meaner than rattlesnakes." Belle looked down, feeling a lump in her throat as she stared down at the gorgeous, obscenely huge diamond engagement ring. "And they'll all think the same as you did. That I'm a gold digger who tricked you into marrying me, by deliberately getting knocked up."

"No one will think that," he said firmly, and his arrogant expression made her roll her eyes. Santiago really thought he could control everything, even the thoughts of strangers. She shook her head.

"You're just not the kind of man who marries a girl like me. And this ring…"

"What about it?" he said shortly. He sounded on edge. She wondered if she'd offended him.

"It's beautiful, but it looks weird on my hand. I've spent my life working. This ring should belong to a princess who's never had to lift a finger." She looked down at her casual shorts and high school T-shirt over her baby bump. "Your trophy wife should be an heiress or supermodel or movie star or something. Not a short, dumpy waitress."

"Don't talk about yourself like that." His jaw tightened, and his dark eyes turned hard in a way she didn't understand. "And movie stars are highly overrated."

Belle frowned, looking up at his handsome face. "Did you ever date one?"

He blinked, then abruptly turned away, looking at the bright city lights sliding past their chauffeured SUV.

"Romantic love is a dream of lust and lies," he said in a low voice. "It all turns to ash in the end." He turned to her. "Be grateful it's not part of our relationship."

Belle started to protest, then remembered how she'd felt when Justin dumped her right before their wedding. How she'd felt when she'd found out he was not only getting back with his ex-wife, but they were also expecting the baby she could no longer conceive. Love hadn't felt so great back then.

"It's not always like that," she tried.

His cruel, sensual lips twisted. "Give me an example of a romance working out."

"Um…" She tried to think, then said triumphantly, "Letty and Darius."

"That just proves my point. They didn't marry for love.

They got lucky. Or else they decided to make the best of things."

She bit her lip and said in a small voice, "Maybe we can do that, too."

He rewarded her with a smile. "My executive assistant has already planned a meeting with the most exclusive wedding planner in the city."

"You will meet with this planner?"

"No, you will. You're the bride. I have a company to run."

"I didn't realize you were so old-fashioned, with the gender roles."

He flashed a grin. "I know my place. The wedding day always belongs to the bride."

The dread in Belle's stomach only intensified. "I don't need a big wedding. We could just go to City Hall…"

"Like Letty and Darius?"

That shut her up. Though Letty and Darius were happy now, their wedding had been awful, no matter how Belle had tried to put a positive spin on it. "Fine," she said in a small voice. "Have it your way."

Reaching out, he touched her shoulder. "At least we know what we're getting into. Our marriage will last. No delusions of hearts and flowers. You won't expect me to fulfill your every girlish fantasy."

Pulling away, she tossed her head. "You couldn't, even if you tried."

Santiago gave her a sideways glance, his eyes suddenly dark as he murmured, "I could fulfill a few." As she shivered at the huskiness of his voice, the SUV stopped.

"We're here, sir."

"Thank you, Ivan. Come." He turned to Belle. "The staff is waiting to meet you."

"By staff, do you mean that butler I met?" she said nervously.

"Yes, but Jones isn't the only one. We have three live-in staff members. Four others live out."

"Just for you?" she said in dismay. He smiled.

"For us."

The door was opened by their driver, Ivan. As he and Kip, a bodyguard who had tattoos on his neck and a mean stare, brought in their luggage, Santiago helped Belle out of the SUV. Looking up at his brownstone mansion, she gulped.

When she'd first come here a few days ago to tell Santiago she was pregnant, she never could have imagined she'd return as his fiancée and mistress of the house!

Inside the front door, seven uniformed members of staff stood waiting in the enormous foyer beneath the skylight. At the head of the line was the butler who'd been so cold to her when she'd last visited the house. Looking at her, the man narrowed his eyes in a scowl.

Nervously, she tried to draw back, but Santiago held her hand securely.

"Good evening to you all," he said gravely. "Thank you for waiting for our arrival." He glanced at Belle. "I'm pleased to introduce you to my future bride, Miss Belle Langtry."

"Hello, miss."

"Welcome."

"Lovely to meet you, miss."

As each staff member introduced themselves to Belle in turn, she felt embarrassed. She felt like a fraud. Like she belonged in the staff line herself. What did she know about being the lady of the manor? Her friend Letty had been born to it, but Belle didn't have a clue, and she was sure it showed. She ducked her head bashfully.

"As my wife," Santiago continued, "Belle will be in charge of the house, so please teach her everything she needs to know." He glanced at the butler. "I'm relying on you, Jones."

"Of course, sir," the butler intoned, but the sideways glance he threw Belle was far from friendly. *I'm sure we'll be friends in no time*, she told herself, but she felt more ill at ease than ever.

"That's all for now. You may go," Santiago said. After the staff departed, he looked down at her and said softly, "I'll show you around your new home."

He drew her down the hallway of the mansion. The ceilings were high, with molded plaster and chandeliers. Their footsteps echoed on the hardwood and marble floors, walking past walls with oak paneling and stone fireplaces. "How old is this house?"

"Not very. It was built in 1899."

"That's older than my whole hometown," she replied in awe. "And three employees actually live here? Doesn't that feel weird, having your butler around when you're slacking on the sofa in sweatpants, eating chips and watching football on TV?"

He gave a brief smile. "The staff have their own quarters in the evenings. On the fifth floor."

"The *fifth*? How many floors are there?"

"Seven, if you include the basement."

"This isn't a house, it's a skyscraper!"

His smile spread to a grin. "Come on."

Belle's eyes got bigger as he showed her the rest of the house, from the wine cellar and home theater in the basement, to the ballroom—"but it's small, for a ballroom"—on the main floor, through five guest bedrooms and nine bathrooms.

"Why so many bathrooms?" she said curiously. "Is it so when one gets dirty, you don't need to bother cleaning it, but can just move on to the next one?"

He gave her a crooked half grin. "That's not necessary.

The staff takes good care of us. Let me show you my second favorite place in this house."

He led her onto the elevator, causing Belle to exclaim in wonder, "You have your own elevator?", and pressed the button for the roof. As she walked out into the warm, humid July night, she gasped.

A rooftop pool was illuminated bright blue, with lounge chairs and cabanas surrounded by flowers and plants. But the real star was the view. As they stood on the rooftop, fifty-floor skyscrapers surrounded them, shining brightly.

Going to the edge of the railing, Belle saw, far below, the noise and traffic of the street. There was only one dark spot, directly to the left: Central Park.

"Wow," she breathed, then looked at Santiago. "If this is only your second favorite part of the house, what's your first?"

His eyes were dark, his voice low. "I'll show you."

He led her back to the elevator, and pressed the button for the third floor, which she realized she hadn't seen at all yet. The elevator door opened on a small foyer. Beyond that was a single door.

"What's this?" she asked.

His hooded eyes looked at her. "Open the door."

Hesitantly, she obeyed. Behind her, he turned on the light.

She saw an enormous spartan bedroom, bigger than even the one in Texas. It had an enormous bed and a wall of windows covered with translucent curtains. There was a sitting area with a reading chair, a vanity table, a wet bar and a small library of books. Peeking into two side doors, she saw a large wood-paneled walk-in closet filled with dark suits, and an en suite bathroom in chrome and marble. The bathroom was so expensively minimalist that even the towels were tucked away.

Though this bedroom suite was huge and elegant, she

didn't see what could possibly make it more spectacular than the rooftop pool. Frowning, she turned back in puzzlement. "Your bedroom?"

He nodded.

"What do you love so much about it?"

Coming forward, he put his hands on her shoulders, his eyes alight. "That you'll be in it."

Belle shivered, remembering the heat and passion they'd shared at the Texas ranch. She wasn't hypocritical enough to pretend that the thought disgusted her. She bit her lip. "What would the staff think?"

He looked amused. "That I'd share my room with my pregnant fiancée? You think this will shock them?" He gave a low laugh. "Ah, *querida*, you are such an innocent. The servants think what I pay them to think."

She snorted, then paused. "Is that what you'll expect of me, too? That I'll just do what you tell me to do and think what you want me to think?"

His dark eyebrows lowered. "No." He pulled her into his arms, and ran his hand softly along her cheek. "You are not my servant, Belle. My expectations are different for you. I expect you to be yourself. And say what you actually think."

She looked at him skeptically. "You do?"

"Of course." His lips curved upward. "So I can convince you around to my way of thinking. The correct way."

She rolled her eyes. "Right."

"I have no interest in a silent doormat as a wife. I would rather have sparks between us, and yes, hatred at times, than be married to a ghost. I expect you to tell me when you are angry, rather than hide from me. You will be my wife and soon, the mother of my children…"

"Children?"

"Of course." He tilted his head. "You know how important siblings are. I was an only child. My life might have been very different if I'd had a sibling. Imagine how your younger brothers' lives might have turned out if they'd not had you to take care of them."

The thought gave her a chill. Her brothers would have been separated, sent to foster care. Or an orphanage, even, like Santiago. She bit her lip. "Of course it's important, but..."

"But?"

"This is all just so new to me. I feel like my life is already becoming unrecognizable. Planning a society wedding? Have more children? I don't know anything about running a mansion, or managing a staff."

"You will learn."

"I don't know about designer clothes, obviously—" she looked down at her stretchy *Bluebell Bears* T-shirt and shorts "—or elegant manners or..."

"I've arranged an appointment for you tomorrow at eleven with a personal stylist. Ivan will take you. Kip will go with you."

"Why would I need a bodyguard?"

"Consider him an accessory. You certainly won't be the only one with a bodyguard. Your stylist is..." He named a celebrity stylist so famous that even Belle had heard of her. "She'll provide you with clothes and everything else."

"Bodyguard. Stylist." She gave an incredulous, half-hysterical laugh. "I'm not some celebrity!"

"You are now, because of that ring on your finger." He gave her a slow, seductive smile. "As for the rest of what you'll need to learn, I'll teach as we go. It will get easier."

"How?" She was almost near tears. "How is this ever going to work?"

Reaching out, Santiago ran his hands down her arms, making her shiver with sudden awareness and desire as they stood in the shadowy bedroom.

"I'll show you," he whispered, drawing her to the enormous bed. "Starting with this."

And he kissed her.

Golden sunlight poured in through the high windows when Belle woke up the next morning. For a moment, she just stretched languorously in bed. She still felt him all over her body. Remembering last night curled her toes.

Then her smile faded as she realized she was waking up in New York just as she had in Texas: alone. His side of the bed was empty.

Last night, he'd made love to her so passionately he'd made all her fears disappear. She'd been lost in the sensuality of his body against hers. She'd felt need so hot and intense it burned everything else away.

But in the morning, reality felt as cold as his side of the bed.

Belle looked at the clock. It was ten in the morning. She sat up, eyes wide. She couldn't remember the last time she'd slept so late. Even in the earliest stages of pregnancy, when she'd been exhausted, she'd worked the early shift, forcing herself to get up at five on dark, cold winter mornings. She couldn't remember the last time she'd slept till ten. It felt sinful.

Rising from the bed, still naked as she'd slept, she stretched her arms and toes, and felt the baby kick inside her. She rubbed her belly, murmuring happily, "Good morning, baby."

Going to the en suite bathroom, she took a long, warm shower. Her meager belongings from her suitcases had already been unpacked. She wondered if it had been the butler or the maid who'd unpacked her clothes last night, when Santiago was giving her the house tour. She hoped it was the young maid. She felt uncomfortable at the thought of the supercilious butler looking down his nose at her simple clothing, all purchased from discount stores and washed many times.

"The servants think what I pay them to think," Santiago had told her grandly yesterday.

But Belle's own experience said otherwise. As a waitress, she'd been paid to serve breakfast and refill coffee; her opinion had always been her own. Her tart temper had gotten her in trouble more than once. Belle always believed in being polite, but that was different than letting a bully walk all over you.

"I have no interest in a silent doormat as a wife," he'd told her.

It was obviously true in bed. It was also true that in some ways, he made her feel stronger, braver and like she could really be herself, without pretending. But if Santiago thought Belle could ever be some kind of high society trophy wife, he'd soon realize his mistake. She was just afraid she'd humiliate all of them in the process.

After brushing out her wet hair, she pulled on a clean T-shirt and pair of shorts. They were getting too tight around her belly. Maybe a new wardrobe wasn't the worst idea, she thought. Brushing her teeth, she glanced at herself in the mirror. And heaven knew a stylist couldn't hurt. It would have to be a brave stylist, though, to want to take her on.

Ignoring the elevator—it seemed so pretentious—she went down the gleaming back stairs. She was just grateful Santiago had given her a house tour, or she'd have gotten totally lost. Approaching the kitchen, she heard a woman laugh.

"He can't be serious. We're really expected to follow her orders? That nobody? It's humiliating."

Sucking in her breath, Belle stopped outside the kitchen door, listening.

"Humiliating or not, we'll have to take her orders. At

least for now." The butler's voice was scornful. "However ridiculous they might be. Who knows what she might want?"

A different woman said, "A stripper pole?"

"Silver bowls full of pork rinds," the other suggested.

"But Mr. Velazquez has chosen her as his bride," the butler intoned, "so we must pretend to obey her for as long as the marriage lasts. But do not worry. Once the brat is born, she'll soon be kicked to the curb. Mr. Velazquez is seeing his lawyer today, hopefully drawing up an iron-clad prenup…"

Belle must have made some noise, because the butler's voice suddenly cut off. A second later, to her horror, his head peered around the door. Her own cheeks were aflame at being caught eavesdropping.

But Jones didn't look ashamed. If anything, his expression was smug, even as he said politely, "Ah, good morning, Miss Langtry. Would you care for some breakfast?"

Belle had no idea how to react. He knew she'd overheard, but wasn't remotely sorry. The butler was in charge here, not her, no matter what Santiago had said. Suddenly not the least bit hungry, she blurted out the first thing she thought of—the morning special she'd served at the diner. "Um…scrambled eggs and toast would be lovely… Maybe a little orange juice…"

"Of course, madam."

But as she walked forward with hunched shoulders, he blocked her from the kitchen, and gestured smoothly down the hall. "We will serve you in the dining room, Miss Langtry. There are newspapers and juice and coffee already set out. Please make yourself comfortable."

Comfortable was the last thing she felt as she ate alone at the end of a long table that would have seated twenty. Huge vases of fresh flowers made her nose itch, and she didn't find the *Financial Times* enough company to block out the memory of the staff's cruel words.

"Who knows what she might want?"

"A stripper's pole?"

"Silver bowls full of pork rinds?"

"She'll soon be kicked to the curb... Mr. Velazquez is seeing his lawyer today."

Santiago hadn't told her what his plans were today. He hadn't even said goodbye. He'd just made love to her hot and hard in the night, then disappeared before dawn. Like always.

Was he really with his lawyer right now, devising some kind of ironclad prenuptial agreement?

Of course he was, she thought bitterly. He wouldn't trust her, ever. That was what their marriage would be, in spite of all his fine words about friendship and partnership. It would be a business arrangement, based on a contract, where even the people running her own home despised her.

This mansion wasn't home, she thought with despair, looking up at the soaring chandeliers, the high ceilings of the dining room. She didn't belong here. She rubbed her belly. Neither did her baby.

She missed her brothers. She missed Letty, who was in Greece with her family. She missed her old friends back in Bluebell. Most of all, she missed having control over her life.

Why would any woman want to get pregnant by a billionaire, if it meant you'd always feel like an outsider? Would even her own child, raised in this environment, someday despise her?

Jones served her breakfast on a silver tray, then departed with a sweeping bow. But Belle saw his smirk. She managed to eat a few bites, but it all tasted like ash in her mouth. She was relieved when Kip, the muscular, tattooed bodyguard, appeared in the doorway.

"Ready to go, Miss Langtry? Ivan has already pulled around the car."

Belle had dreaded the thought of the appointment with that famous personal stylist, but at that moment hell itself sounded preferable to remaining in this enormous, empty house, filled with employees who scorned her. She got up from the breakfast table so quickly that Kip's eyes widened to see a pregnant woman move so fast.

But later that afternoon, when Belle finally returned to the house, she felt worse, not better. She'd been poked and prodded, manicured and, most of all, criticized. Her awful hair! Her awful clothes! Her ragged cuticles! The famous stylist had cried out in shock and agony, right in front of Belle, and sent her assistants scurrying. They seemed to think Belle was a rock, incapable of thinking or feeling, just the brute clay from which they, the long-suffering artists, would sculpt and construct their art.

Ten different assistants had worked on her at the stylist's private salon, which the stylist herself, the famous owner of the establishment, called her *atelier*.

Belle had never cared much about her appearance. She'd always had more important things to think about, like raising her little brothers and putting food on the table. So she'd tried to remain patient and silent as they picked out a wardrobe and hairstyle appropriate to her station as a rich man's wife.

Seven hours later, as Kip finally carried out her new wardrobe to the waiting car, the famous stylist had showed Belle a mirror. "What do you think?"

She'd sucked in her breath. Her dark hair was now perfectly straight, gleaming down her shoulders. Her face felt raw from the facials, shellacked with expensive lotions and makeup, including lipstick and mascara. Her pregnant shape was draped in a severely chic black shift dress, black capelet, her hips thrust forward by uncomfortably high heels.

Startled by the stranger in the mirror, Belle replied timidly, "I don't recognize myself."

To which the famously pretentious personal stylist responded with a laugh, "Then my job is done."

Now, Belle trudged into the brownstone mansion feeling ridiculous in the jaunty black capelet.

Tomorrow she was supposed to meet with the wedding planner. She could only imagine how that would go. Santiago had already mentioned an engagement party he meant to hold in two weeks, "after you've gotten a chance to get comfortable." Comfortable?

She felt sick with worry.

Belle saw the maid and the cook as she walked wearily into the house. The two women elbowed each other as they saw her new chic appearance.

"You look nice, ma'am," the maid said meekly. Belle wondered if she was mocking her.

"Thank you," she said flatly, and went up to the third floor bedroom suite to take a nap. The same maid knocked on the door a few hours later.

"Mr. Velazquez is home, miss. He's requesting that you join him downstairs for dinner."

Groggily, Belle smoothed down her dress and hair from her nap, then went down to the dining room.

Santiago's dark eyes widened when he saw her. Rising from the table, he came forward to kiss her.

"You look very elegant," he said, helping her into her chair. Sitting beside her, he smiled. "Who is queen of society now?"

He didn't seem to notice her lack of enthusiasm or her absence of appetite for dinner. But there was one thing he noticed fast enough. When he took her upstairs to bed and kissed her, she didn't respond. He frowned. "What is it?"

"It's this makeup," she improvised. "It feels like a Halloween mask over my face."

He stared at her, then gave her a slow-rising grin. "I can solve that."

He pulled her into the shower, turned on the water, and scrubbed the day off her until she felt almost like herself again. It was only then, when her skin was pink and warm with steam, as she stood in front of him with her baby bump and pregnancy-swollen breasts, that she felt like she could breathe again, and started returning his kisses.

"That's better," he whispered appreciatively and kissed her in the shower until her knees were weak. Turning off the water, he gently toweled her off and pulled her onto the bed, their bodies still hot and wet. Lying down, he lifted her over him and put his hand gently on her cheek.

"You're in charge," he whispered, and she was. It was ecstasy. It was glory. Their souls seemed to spark together into fire, as well as their bodies. When they were together in bed, she could forget all her fears. She felt nothing but pleasure. She was his. He was hers.

But when Belle woke up in the morning, she was alone.

CHAPTER SIX

TWO WEEKS LATER, Santiago came home from his forty-floor skyscraper in Midtown with a scowl on his face.

His company, Velazquez International, had spent two weeks in negotiations, trying and failing to nail down the acquisition of a Canadian hotel chain. He'd offered them an excellent price, but they continued to hold out—not for more money, but for his promise that he'd keep all their employees and stores intact. Santiago scowled, narrowing his eyes. What fool would promise such a thing? But now, because of their stubbornness, he was going to be late for his own engagement party. And no deal had been struck.

That was what was making him tense, he told himself. The business deal. Running late.

It had nothing to do with the thought of giving Belle the prenuptial agreement tucked into his briefcase.

Rushing up the stone steps of his brownstone, he ground his teeth. The wedding was planned for early September, just a month away, just a few weeks before her due date. Of course the agreement had to be signed. He was a billionaire. Belle had nothing. Without a prenuptial agreement, he'd be risking half his fortune from the moment he said "I do."

But his scowl deepened as he entered his Upper East Side mansion, lavish with flowers and additional hired serving staff, awaiting the first guest for their engagement party, when he would introduce his future bride to New

York society. He took the elevator to the third floor, then stopped when he saw Belle.

She was looking into a full-length mirror as she put on diamond earrings, wearing a sleek black dress, her dark hair pulled back into a tight chignon. Her face was perfectly made up, and the diamond earrings he'd given her yesterday sparkled as brightly as the ten-carat engagement ring on her finger. But as she turned to him, he saw that beneath the dramatic black sweep of her lashes and red ruby lips, her creamy caramel skin was pale.

"What's wrong?" he demanded.

She gave him a trembling smile. "I was starting to worry you might make me host this party alone."

"Of course not." Dropping his briefcase, he kissed her, stroking her soft cheek. He searched her gaze. "You look beautiful."

"I'm glad. So maybe the pain is worth it."

"Pain?" he said, surprised.

She held out her foot, shod in a sexy black stiletto heel. "And you should see my underwear," she said wryly.

"I'd like to."

She returned his grin, then sighed. "At least the baby is comfortable. All the clothes are loose around my waist." She glanced down at the briefcase. "So when are you going to spring it on me?"

His hand stilled. "What?"

"The prenuptial agreement."

He blinked. How had she known?

Of course she knew, he chided himself. Belle was intuitive and smart. "You know it's necessary."

"Yes. I know."

She didn't argue. Didn't complain. She just looked at him, her dark eyes like big pools in her wan, pale face. And he felt like a cad. That irritated him even more. Turning away, he changed his clothes, pulling on his tuxedo.

"Santiago, am I a trophy wife?" she asked suddenly.

"What are you talking about?"

"I met some other brides while waiting for my appointment with the wedding planner yesterday. They told me all about the life of a trophy wife. They made it sound like being an indentured servant." She looked at the closet. "I already have the uniform. Shift dresses in black and beige."

He felt irritated as he sat down on the bed to put on his Italian leather shoes. "I didn't tell you to only wear black and beige."

"No, but the stylist did. And she insisted I must always wear stilettos, to be taller. They're like torture devices…" She peered down at her feet, then looked up with a sigh. "I'll sorry. I'm doing my best. I'm just afraid I'll fail you," she said in a small voice. "That I can't be what you need, or ever fit into your world—"

"Fit in?" He looked up from tying his shoes. "I wasn't born in this world either, Belle. Growing up in Madrid, I had nothing. And I've learned the hard way there's only one way to fit into a world that doesn't want you. By force. You have to make it impossible for them to ignore you."

She stared at him for a moment, and he wished he hadn't brought up his own childhood. He was relieved when she shook her head. "Force? I can't even force our wedding planner to consider any of my ideas. Our wedding is going to be awful."

"Awful?"

Belle rolled her eyes. "She called it 'postmodern'. I'm to hold a cactus instead of a bouquet, and instead of a white wedding cake, we'll be serving our guests gold-dusted foam."

"Really."

"When I told her I didn't want to hold a cactus in my bare hands and just wanted a wildflower bouquet and a regular wedding cake, the woman laughed and patted me on the head. She *patted me on the head*," she repeated for emphasis.

Santiago gave a low laugh. "*Querida*, her weddings might be unconventional, but she is the best, and I told her I want you to have the most spectacular wedding of the season…"

"*Spectacular* means wasting millions of dollars on stupid stuff we don't want, to impress people we don't even like?"

"You said you want to fit in. A big wedding is a show of power."

"She won't even let me invite my brothers. She said it was because she didn't think a plumber and a fireman would be comfortable at such a formal event, but I think she was just afraid they wouldn't fit in with her décor!"

Not letting Belle invite her little brothers? He was willing to accept cactus and gold foam, but excluding beloved family members was unacceptable. Santiago frowned as he finished putting on his tie. "I'll talk to her." Rising to his feet, he held out his arm. "Shall we go downstairs?"

He felt her hands shake a little as they wrapped around the arm of his jacket, heard the sudden catch of her breath. "So many guests are coming tonight…"

"It will be fine," he said, but he understood why Belle was nervous. Their 'impromptu engagement party' had ballooned out of proportion. On August weekends, the city usually was so deserted he wouldn't have been half-surprised to see tumbleweeds going down Fifth Avenue. But to his surprise, everyone they'd invited had instantly accepted. Not only that, but more had asked to come, even coming in from Connecticut and the Hamptons.

Everyone, it seemed, was curious to see the pregnant Texas waitress who'd tamed the famous playboy Santiago Velazquez.

"Gossip has spread about me," Belle said glumly.

"Ignore it."

"The butler's right, I'm nobody."

"So was I, when I came to America at eighteen," Santiago pointed out.

"That just adds to your glory," she said grumpily. "Now you're a self-made billionaire. I bet you've never failed at anything."

That wasn't true. Just five years ago, Santiago had failed in spectacular fashion.

But he wasn't going to tell Belle about Nadia. Not now. Not ever.

Pushing the button for the elevator, he turned to her with a sudden frown. "What did you mean, the butler was right? Did he say something to you?"

Averting her eyes, she nodded. "I overheard the butler and cook and maid talking a couple weeks ago. They weren't happy about having me as their mistress. Mr. Jones told them I was a nobody, but they should pretend to obey me until the *brat* was born, when you'd get rid of me."

"What?"

"He knew I heard them talking, but wasn't even sorry." Lifting her gaze, she tried to smile. "It's no big deal. I'll get used to it."

But Santiago's jaw was tight with fury. That his own employees would dare to scorn his future wife, his unborn child, in his own house! His dark brows lowered like a thundercloud.

Once the elevator opened on the ground floor, he took Belle by the arm and led her down the hall, past all the extra hired staff who were setting out appetizers and flowers for the party.

In the kitchen, he found the butler busy with preparations for the meal, along with the two other live-in members of his staff—Mrs. Green, the cook, and Anna, the maid. The front doorbell rang, and the butler started to leave the kitchen.

"Jones, stay," Santiago ordered harshly, then turned to one of the temporary waiters walking past with a tray. "Tell Kip he's in charge of answering the door."

"Kip?"

"The one with a tattoo on his neck."

"Right."

Santiago turned back to face his employees.

"What is it, Mr. Velazquez?" Anna said anxiously.

"I should be answering the door for your party guests, Mr. Velazquez," Jones intoned.

Santiago looked at the three of them coldly.

"You are all fired."

They stared at him in shock, their mouths agape.

"Pack up your things," Santiago continued grimly. "I want you out of here in ten minutes."

"But—my food for the party—" Mrs. Green stammered.

"What did we do?" Anna gasped.

"You told him to fire us." The butler looked at Belle with venom in his eyes. "You just had to tattle, didn't you?"

"I never meant for this to happen…" Belle looked at Santiago. She put an urgent hand on his shoulder. "Please. You don't need to—"

But he moved his shoulder away. His fury was past listening as he stared at the three employees who'd dared to be rude to Belle. "This party is no longer your concern, and you now only have nine minutes left."

The butler drew himself up contemptuously. "I'll go. It would destroy my professional reputation to work for your wife, anyway. She doesn't belong here!"

"You think your reputation would be destroyed?" Santiago said coldly. "See what happens if you ever speak rudely about Belle again to anyone."

"Santiago," Belle said, tugging on his sleeve desperately. "I don't want anyone to lose their jobs. I just thought…"

"I should have known you'd rat us out, after you heard us talking that first day," Jones snarled.

The plump cook whirled to Belle with a gasp. "You heard us?"

But Belle was staring at the butler, and so was Santiago. So was the maid.

Jones's accent had slipped.

Suddenly Santiago knew why the butler had hated Belle on sight. She wasn't the only one who felt out of place.

"You're not even British," Santiago said accusingly.

"Nope." Jones yanked off the apron that had been over his suit and tie. "Born in New Jersey. I'm done with this butler stuff. No amount of money is worth this." He looked at Belle. "You might be stuck here till he dumps you. But I'm not. Forget this. I'm going to go start a band."

Throwing away his apron, he left.

Santiago looked at the two women. "Any last words?"

The young maid, Anna, turned to Belle, her cheeks red. "I'm sorry, Miss Langtry. I sneered at you about pork rinds because, well, I like them myself. But I eat them in secret. I didn't want Mr. Jones to know… "

The cook stepped forward, abashed. "And I taunted you about the stripper pole, because, well—" the plump middle-aged woman's cheeks reddened "—I was a stripper myself for a few months when I was young. It's not something I'm proud of, but my baby's father had abandoned us. I was desperate…" Turning to Santiago, she pulled off her cap. "That bit of employment wasn't listed on my résumé. I understand if you don't want me cooking for you no more. Especially after what I said. I'll go."

"Please don't fire me," Anna begged. "I need this job.

I'm working my way through law school and the hours are hard to find. The wages, too."

"It's not your choice." Santiago looked at Belle. "It's my fiancée's."

Belle glanced at the two women. The younger of them was looking at her with pleading eyes, as the older stared woodenly at the floor with slumped shoulders.

"Please stay." Her voice trembled slightly. "If you're not too embarrassed to work for me..."

"Oh, no!" Anna exclaimed fervently. "How could I be embarrassed of you? I'm only ashamed of myself."

"Me, too," the cook said softly. Looking up, her soft blue eyes filled with tears. "Thank you."

Belle gave them a wobbly smile. "I know what it feels like to be pregnant and alone. No one would judge you badly for doing whatever it took to take care of your baby." Glancing at Santiago out of the corner of her eye, she added, "In fact, you both get a raise."

"What?" the women said joyfully.

"Of thirty percent!"

"What?" Santiago said, not so joyfully.

"A raise," Belle repeated firmly, "as our household will be doing without a butler. Their extra responsibilities deserve it."

She made a good point. Santiago scowled at her. And he had to admit to himself that having a butler, especially a sniffy one like Jones, hadn't added much to the comfort of his home life.

"Fine," he said grudgingly, then turned to the others. "Don't give my bride reason to regret her generosity. There will be no second chance."

"Yes, sir!"

"Back to your duties."

"Right away!"

Mrs. Green scurried back to the enormous ovens, her plump face alarmed. "Oh, no—my salmon puffs!"

Taking Belle aside in the hallway, he growled, "Thirty percent?"

She lifted her chin. "They will be worth it."

"Right. And here I thought the most expensive thing would be getting you a new wardrobe."

"What about this?" She smiled, lifting up the huge diamond ring on her left hand. "I can't even imagine how much it cost."

Try free, he thought. He cleared his throat, then brightened. "And your earrings." Those, at least, had been specifically purchased for Belle.

She touched one of the diamonds dangling from her ears. "You could have bought me fake ones, you know. No one would have been able to tell the difference, least of all me. Big waste of money."

"You really are terrible at being a gold digger."

"I know," she agreed. She looked down at her ring. "It's beautiful, but it makes me feel guilty. This ring could have probably bought a car."

When he'd bought it five years before, the amount he'd spent could actually have bought a house. But of course he'd bought it for a different woman, so Belle had nothing to feel guilty about. He was tempted to tell her, but kept his mouth shut. Somehow he thought this was one situation when no woman on earth, even an ardent environmentalist, would think highly of recycling.

The doorbell rang again, and he saw the seven-foot-tall Kip head for the front door. Flinging it open, Kip glared at an ambassador, who looked startled, and his skinny, bejeweled wife, who looked terrified.

"Oh, dear," Belle sighed, following his gaze.

"I'm not sure Kip has the right skill set to be butler," Santiago said, hiding a smile.

"Let's go take over for him."

He frowned at her. "Answer the door ourselves?"

"What, don't you know how?" Giving him an impish smile, she took his hand. "Come on, Santiago. Let's give 'em a big Texas welcome."

Her hand was warm in his own, and as he looked down at the curve of her breasts revealed above the neckline of her gown, a flash of heat went through his body. "I thought you were afraid of society people."

"I am." She added with a rueful laugh, "But my mama always said there's only one way to get through something that scares you, and that's by doing it."

Looking at the resolve in Belle's beautiful face, at the gleam in her dark eyes and her half-parted ruby-red lips, Santiago was tempted to give her a counteroffer: that they throw all the guests out, lock the door, and make love right here, on the table between the flowers and the cream puffs.

Instead, as the doorbell rang again, Belle pulled him toward the door.

"I just fired Jones," Santiago told Kip. "Make sure he doesn't make off with the silver."

"Yes, sir," Kip said, looking relieved, and he fled.

Santiago stood beside Belle as they answered the door, welcoming all their illustrious, powerful guests. The people were all strangers to Belle, and yet she gave each of them a warm smile, as if she were truly glad to see them. Some of the guests seemed pleased, others slightly startled.

Santiago was enchanted.

Over the next few hours, as he watched Belle mingle at the party, he felt a mixture of pride and desire. He couldn't take his eyes off her. She was breathtaking.

In that dress and those high heels, with her makeup and hair so glossy and sophisticated, she might have fit in perfectly, except for one thing.

She stood out.

Belle was the most beautiful woman there.

Only he knew the fear and insecurity she'd hidden inside. That somehow made him even prouder of her. Tonight he admired her courage and grace even more than he admired her beauty.

The house had been filled with bright-colored flowers, and the hors d'oeuvres, overseen by Mrs. Green, were exquisite. But not half as exquisite as Belle, feverishly bright-eyed and lovely. The party was a huge success.

Because of Belle, he thought. She was the star.

Later that evening, he watched her across the crowded ballroom, now smiling at three of the board members of the Canadian hotel chain. He'd invited them to the party in an offhand way, but he hadn't really expected them to come. He watched as Belle smiled and said something that made all three men laugh uproariously.

Belle was as good at this as Nadia, he thought in astonishment. Maybe even better.

He'd met Nadia his first night at the orphanage in Madrid, when he was fourteen. She was blonde, beautiful, a year older, with hard violet eyes and a raspy laugh. He'd been immediately infatuated. When he told her he was breaking out to go live with his father, the Duke of Sangovia, she'd been awed. "Take me with you," she'd begged, and he'd agreed.

Nadia had watched from the bushes as the palace guards tried phoning his father, then at the duke's answer, turned on Santiago scornfully, setting the dogs on him. He'd run away from the snarling jaws and snapping teeth, staggering past the safety of the gate, to fall at her feet.

"No luck, huh?" Nadia had said, looking down at him coolly. She'd looked past the wrought-iron walls, ten feet tall, over the palm trees, toward the rooftops of the palace, barely visible from the gate. "Someday, I'll live in a place like this."

"I won't." Wiping blood from his face, Santiago had looked back at it with hatred, then slowly risen to his feet, ignoring the blood on his knees, the rips in his pants. "My house will be a million times better than this." He'd looked at the beautiful blonde girl. "And you'll be my wife."

"Marry you?" She'd looked at him coolly. "I'm going to be a movie star. There's no reason I'd marry you or anyone. Not unless you could give me something I can't get for myself." Her lovely face was thoughtful as she looked back toward the palace. "If you could make me a duchess…"

That was one thing Santiago could never do. He wasn't the legitimate heir. He was just a bastard by-blow, whose father couldn't be bothered to give him a home, a name, or even a single minute of his time. A sliver of pain went through him, overwhelmed by a wave of rage.

He would be better than his father. Better than his half brother. Better than all of them.

Lifting his chin, he'd said boldly, "Someday, I'll be a billionaire. Then I'll ask you. And you'll say yes."

Nadia had given a low, patronizing laugh. "A billionaire?" she'd said, putting out her cigarette. "Sure. Ask me then."

He'd officially made his first billion by the time he was thirty. But too late. The day his company went public, he flew his private jet to Barcelona, where Nadia was filming her latest movie. He'd fallen to one knee and held out the ring, just as he'd imagined for half his life. And then he'd waited.

One never knew where one stood with Nadia. She knew how to charm with a glance, how to cut out someone's heart with a smile. Sitting on her film set, looking beautiful as a queen, she'd fluttered her eyelashes mournfully.

"Oh, dear. I'm sorry. You're too late. I just agreed to marry your brother." She'd held out her left hand, showing off an exquisite antique ring. "I'm going to live in the

Palacio de las Palmas and be a duchess someday. I can only do that if I marry the Duque de Sangovia's legitimate heir. And that's not you. Sorry."

Strange to think that Nadia was living with his father and brother, Santiago thought, while he himself had never met either of them. Nadia had been married to his brother for five years now, and as she waited to be duchess she comforted herself with the title of *marquesa*, along with the other title given her by the European tabloids—"the Most Beautiful Woman in the World."

"Hell of a girl you've got there."

Coming out of his reverie, Santiago abruptly focused on the man speaking to him. It was Rob McVoy, the CEO of the Canadian family firm. "Thank you."

"Any man who could make a woman like Belle love him must be trustworthy. So I changed my mind. We'll take the chance." He gave a brusque nod. "We agree to the deal."

Santiago blinked in shock. "You do?"

The man clapped him on the shoulder. "Our lawyers will be in touch."

Santiago stared after him in amazement. After weeks of stalled negotiations, accusations of double-dealing and an almost total lack of trust, the Canadians were suddenly willing to sell him their family company, just after spending twenty minutes talking to Belle?

He was still in shock hours later, when the appetizers and champagne were almost gone, the flowers starting to wilt and the last guests straggling out. Belle had already gone upstairs. As a pregnant woman, no one thought less of her for being tired, and they'd all said goodbye to her with fond, indulgent smiles. Santiago was amazed. How had she become so popular with so many, so fast?

Not with everyone, of course. Some of the trophy wives and girlfriends, some of the more shallow hedge fund billionaires, had indeed looked askance, and whispered behind their hands, smirking.

Everyone else had loved her.

Going to the third floor, Santiago found her in their bedroom, sitting on their bed, her shoes kicked off. His gaze swept over the curves of her breasts as she leaned over to rub her bare feet, wincing. "These shoes. Murder!"

Dropping his tuxedo jacket and tie to the floor, he sat beside her on the enormous bed. Pulling her feet into his lap, he started massaging them.

"That feels fantastic," she murmured. Her eyes closed in pleasure as she leaned back against the pillows.

"Did you enjoy the party?" It took several moments for her to answer.

"Um. It was great."

He stopped rubbing her feet. "How was it really?"

With a sigh, she opened her eyes.

"Fine?" she tried, and it was even less believable. He snorted.

"You really are the worst actress I've ever seen," he observed. He started rubbing the arches of her feet, and she exhaled in pleasure.

"All right, it wasn't easy. Those shoes are like instruments of death. And people kept talking about things I didn't understand—effective altruism as related to overnight borrowing rates, for example…"

"Those aren't at all related."

She glared at him in irritation. "That's exactly my point. I don't know, and don't care." She yawned. "Then others started discussing the gallery show of an artist I never heard of. When I confessed as much, they were horrified and said you owned one of his paintings. Then they made me go take a look at it."

"Which painting?"

"The—um… Mira?"

"Joan Miró?"

"Yeah. They said you'd gotten it at a steal for ten million dollars. I barely restrained myself from yelping, 'That squiggle? I've seen better art done by preschoolers!'" Shaking her head, she added defensively, "And I have."

"Very diplomatic to restrain yourself from saying so."

"Took a lot of willpower, I'll tell you."

He smiled. "You were amazing tonight. Every time I glanced over at you, whomever you were talking to looked enthralled."

She blushed shyly. "Really? You're just being kind."

"Excuse me, have we met?"

She smiled. "Well, I tried my best. Any time I felt nervous, I forced myself to smile and say something nice, like my mama taught me. You know, 'Beautiful dress!' 'What a lovely necklace!'"

"What about the men? Did you compliment their neckties?"

She fluttered her dark eyelashes coyly. "I brought up football, or if that didn't work, horses. You apparently know a lot of polo players. As a last resort, politics."

"Do you follow politics?" he said, surprised.

"Not at all. But generally if you just start the ball rolling, the other person's happy to take it and run. At that point, all you have to do is make sympathetic noises." She rubbed the back of her neck and yawned again. "I'm exhausted. This must be what it's like to act in a play all night. The role of trophy wife."

"You closed a multi-million-dollar deal, Belle."

She frowned. "What?"

"The McVoys…"

She brightened. "Oh, the guys from Calgary? They were hilarious. They were talking about this action movie they saw last night, with that Spanish movie star, you know, the famous one…" She rolled her eyes. "I think they have a crush on her. She's married to some kind of prince already, but I told the guys it never hurts to dream." She gave a sudden grin. "Movie stars get married and divorced dozens of times, don't they? And you never know. She might decide what she really wants next is a middle-aged Canadian with hockey skills."

Santiago's body felt like ice. He cleared his throat. "I've been negotiating with the McVoys for weeks, trying to buy their company." His voice was still a little hoarse. He forced his lips into a smile. "They just agreed to the deal only because of you."

"Me?" she said, astonished.

"They said any man you love couldn't be all bad."

"Oh." Her cheeks went red as she said quickly, "I never told them I loved you."

"I guess they just assumed, since we're getting married and all," he said dryly. "Turn around." Reaching out, he started massaging the back of her neck, her shoulders, brushing back the dark tendrils of her hair. As she leaned against his hands, he breathed in the scent of her, like vanilla and orange blossoms.

She leaned back, looking at him over her shoulder. "Can I ask you something?"

"You'll ask it, whether I say yes or no."

"You're right." She flashed him a sudden grin, then grew serious. "What turned you against the idea of love?"

His hands stilled on her shoulders.

"I told you about my parents."

"That wasn't all, was it? There was something else. Someone else." She took a deep breath, and raised her eyes pleadingly to his. "You know about my sad romantic history, but I know nothing about yours...."

"You're right," he said slowly. "There was a woman."

Belle sat up straight. He saw that he had her full attention. He wasn't sure why he was telling her this. He'd never spoken about it to anyone.

"When I was a teenager, I met a girl in the orphanage. She was blonde, beautiful, with violet eyes…" He tensed, remembering how he'd felt about her as a boy. "She was older than me. Street-smart. Brave. We both had such big dreams about the future. We were both going to conquer the world." He gave a humorless smile. "At fourteen, I asked her to marry me. She told me to ask her again after I proved myself. So I did."

"How?"

"I earned a billion-dollar fortune. For her."

Her eyes went wide. "What?"

Santiago turned away, his jaw tight. "It took me sixteen years, but when my company went public five years ago, I went to Spain with a huge diamond ring."

His eyes fell unwillingly to Belle's left hand, but fortunately she didn't notice. Sitting across from him on the bed, she was staring at him with wide eyes.

"What happened?" she breathed.

His lips twisted at the edges. "I came too late. She wanted more than I could give her. She'd just gotten engaged to my brother."

Her expression changed to horror. "Your *brother*?"

He gave a crooked half grin. "She told me that she'd been attracted to Otilio in part because he reminded her of me. An upgraded version of me." His voice held no emotion. He'd had a lot of practice at showing none. Feeling none. "I couldn't even begrudge her choice. Marrying into the official Zoya family meant she would not be merely rich, but famous and powerful across Europe, and someday, after my father is dead, a duchess."

"Of all men on earth—your brother!"

"Their marriage was a huge social event in Madrid, I heard later."

"What a horrible woman!" she cried indignantly. Her lovely heart-shaped face was stricken as she faced him across the shadowy bed. "No wonder you think so little of love. And marriage, too. What did you do, after she told you she was marrying your brother?"

He shrugged. "I came back to New York. I worked harder. My fortune is bigger than theirs now. The Zoya family owns an *estancia* in Argentina, so I bought a bigger ranch in Texas. They have an art collection. Now mine is better. I don't need them now. They're nothing to me."

"They're your family," she said forlornly.

"They chose not to be."

Reaching out, Belle put her arms around him, hugging him close to her on the bed, offering comfort. For a moment, he accepted the warmth of her smaller body cradled against his. He exhaled deeply. He hadn't even realized his jaw had been tense, until now, as the tension melted away. Drawing back, he looked down at her, and gently tucked a dark tendril of hair back into her loose chignon.

She'd offered him comfort tonight, and loyalty, and her charm had even helped him close a business deal. She'd given it all without asking for anything in return.

He wanted to show his appreciation. Give her a present. But she wouldn't care about jewelry or clothes or art. *Especially* not art, he thought with amusement. So what?

Then he knew.

"I'll cancel the wedding planner, Belle. We can have any kind of wedding you want."

Her eyes lit up. It was worth it for that alone. She breathed, "Really?"

"I know you'll want your brothers to attend. I'll send my private jet to collect them. We don't have to hold the ceremony at the cathedral. I don't care about the details." He looked at her. "As long as we are husband and wife before our child comes into this world."

She tilted her head thoughtfully. "What about having the wedding here?"

"Here?"

She nodded eagerly. "I can have a flower bouquet, instead of holding a cactus. A real cake, instead of foam." She was beaming. "We can have good food that people might actually want to eat!"

"Ah, Belle." With a low laugh, he drew her closer on the bed, cupping her face. "Forget what I said about fitting in. You will never fit in." She looked hurt. Still smiling, he reached out and gently lifted her chin. "Because you were born to stand out, *querida*. You were the most beautiful woman at our engagement party. No one could even compare. I couldn't take my eyes off you."

Her cheeks flushed with shy pleasure. "Really?"

"Just one thing is wrong. That dress." He ran his hand along the black fabric. "It's driving me crazy."

Belle checked the back zipper self-consciously. "What's wrong with it?"

Sitting next to her on the bed, he pulled her into his arms.

"That you're still wearing it," he whispered, and lowered his mouth to hers.

CHAPTER SEVEN

For Santiago, sex had always been simple. Easy. A quick release. A brief pleasure, swiftly forgotten.

Sex with Belle was different than he'd ever experienced before. It was fire. A conflagration. A drug he could not get enough of.

But as with any drug, he was soon hit by unwanted, bewildering side effects.

Having Belle in his Upper East Side mansion, in his bed every night, he was shocked by the way their night-time pleasures started to bleed into his days. He could not refuse her anything.

First, he'd agreed to change their wedding, even though the celebration the famous wedding planner had proposed would have been the social event of the year. The wedding Belle wanted, small and private, without pomp or press coverage, would do nothing for the prestige of his name.

But he let Belle have her way. And it didn't stop there.

He found himself thinking about her during the daylight hours, when his focus was supposed to be on running his company. The Canadian deal had gone through, but other deals began to fall apart. He was distracted, and it was affecting his business. He found himself impatient, even bored, at meetings—even when he himself was the one who'd called them.

He'd spent almost twenty years focused on building Velazquez International to be a huge multinational conglomerate, owning a host of brands of everything from food and soft drinks to running shoes and five-star resorts. He'd spent the last five years at an almost obsessive expansion, buying up small companies with an eye to a future where he owned the world.

But now, as he signed documents to purchase his latest company, a valuable nutritional supplement firm based in Copenhagen, instead of triumph he felt only irritation.

He didn't give a damn about vitamins or protein powders. He wanted to be home with Belle. In her arms. In her bed.

And it was getting worse. At night, when he was in her arms, lost in her deep, expressive brown eyes, kissing her sensual mouth, he'd started to feel something he'd sworn he never would again. Something more than desire.

He found himself caring about her opinion.

He found himself…caring.

In daylight, the thought chilled Santiago to the bone. He couldn't let himself be vulnerable. He'd be marrying her in a matter of weeks, and soon afterward, they'd be raising a child together.

Marriage he could justify, as a mere piece of paper to secure his child's name.

But actually caring about Belle…

Needing her happiness…

Needing *her*…

That was something else.

He could never risk the devastation of loving someone again. He couldn't be that stupid. He couldn't.

But as the weeks passed and their wedding date approached, Santiago grew increasingly tense. Every day he was with Belle, every night, he felt intimacy building between them. The wedding he'd once insisted upon now started to feel like a ticking time bomb. Waiting to explode. To destroy.

It made him want to run.

I made a promise, he told himself desperately. *To Belle. To our child. I'm not going anywhere.*

But as their wedding grew closer, his fears intensified. No matter how much he tried to shove down his feelings. No matter how he tried to deny them.

I have to marry her. For my child's sake. It's just a piece of paper. Not my soul!

But the closer their wedding date became, the more edgy he felt.

Belle woke before dawn on her wedding day, and when she opened her eyes in the gray September light, she looked across the bed. A smile burst across her face brighter than the sun.

It was an omen. Today was their wedding day. And it was the first time she hadn't woken alone.

Santiago was sleeping in bed beside her.

With a rush of gratitude, Belle smiled to herself happily, listening to his deep breathing beside her in the shadows of their bedroom.

After all her fears and plans, she would marry him tonight. And just in time, since at three weeks from her due date, her belly had gotten so huge that she barely fit into her simple, pretty wedding dress. Tonight, in a candlelight ceremony on their rooftop garden, she would officially become Mrs. Santiago Velazquez.

The past month in New York had been filled with unexpected joys, like fixing up this house. It hadn't been a makeover, but a make-*under*. Seven stories, elevator, rooftop garden, wine cellar and all, it had become a real home as she believed a home should be: comfy and cozy. She'd softened the cold, stark modern design, replacing the angular furniture with plump sofas that you could cuddle in.

The master closet, sadly, was now full of fashionable,

scratchy black dresses and stiletto heels, but on the plus side, if she still hated going out into society, at least she loved coming home.

This house had somehow become her home.

After their rocky start, she'd become friends with the live-in staff—Dinah Green, the cook, and Anna Phelps, the maid. Belle often helped them with their tasks, just for the company, and because she liked taking care of her own home. She'd helped Anna study for tests for law school. Dinah had taught her some delicious new recipes, and Belle had already volunteered to cook on every holiday so the older woman could have the time off to visit her grown-up son in Philadelphia.

Together, the three women had worked together to plan everything for the wedding tonight.

It would be a simple affair, a short ceremony attended by family and friends, followed by a late dinner. A judge friend of Santiago's was going to officiate. They already had the marriage license. Afterward, there would be a sit-down dinner of roast beef and grilled asparagus on the rooftop desk, then dancing to music provided by a jazz trio, cake and champagne toasts, and all done by midnight.

Planning the event hadn't been too hard. Belle wasn't that picky, and besides, she'd discovered that living on the Upper East Side, with a driver and unlimited money, was an entirely different New York experience from when she'd shared a walk-up apartment and struggled to make the bills in Brooklyn.

Here, she had a concierge obstetrician who made house calls. Here, she had time. Here, she had space. Her heart fluttered when Santiago came home each night, and they ate dinner together at the long table. He was very busy with his company and often worked long days. But on weekends he would take her out to little cafés—which she enjoyed—and trendy restaurants—which she didn't.

He'd taken her to see a certain famous musical sold out on Broadway, with front-row tickets that the whole world knew were impossible to get. Sitting next to him in the audience that night, Belle realized that she wasn't wishing she could trade places with the actress on stage. She liked where she was, at Santiago's side, with his hand resting protectively on her baby bump. She'd looked at him in the darkened theater. Feeling her look, he'd squeezed her hand.

Then, a minute later, he'd abruptly dropped it.

It was strange. One minute she felt so close to him, as their eyes met in mutual understanding, or a shared joke. But the next minute, he would suddenly seem distant, or literally leave the room. She didn't know which was worse.

Maybe he was having annoyances at work. Maybe he was nervous about their baby's upcoming due date, in just three weeks. She could hardly wait to meet their baby and hold her in their arms.

She intended to have their baby sleep in a bassinet next to their bed at first, but she'd already decorated the nursery to be ready. It was a sweet room, with pale pink walls, a crystal chandelier, a pretty white crib, changing table and rocking chair. And a huge stuffed white polar bear in the corner.

That stuffed bear, twelve feet tall, had been brought home yesterday by Santiago, carried into the nursery with the assistance of Kip.

Belle had laughed. "And you say you have no idea how to be a father. Didn't they have a bigger one?"

"I'm glad they didn't. I would have had to bring it in with a crane through the window. It barely fit in the elevator."

"You're a genius," she'd proclaimed, kissing him happily. "And to think all I've done today for the baby is look through the baby name book."

"Find anything?"

"Well, maybe," she said shyly. He seemed in such a good mood, she'd ventured, "What would you think about naming her Emma Valeria, after both our mothers?"

Santiago's expression immediately turned cold.

"Name her after your mother, if you like. Keep mine out of it."

And he'd abruptly left the nursery.

She shivered. He was always going from hot to cold. It was bewildering. You never knew what might set him off. Even during their happiest moments, he could suddenly become remote. He could be passionate, demanding, infuriating; he could be generous and occasionally, even kind. But aside from the night after their engagement party, when he'd told her about that horrible woman who'd broken his heart, Santiago had never again let her close. Never let her in.

Thinking about it now, Belle shook her head firmly. There was no point in worrying. Today was her wedding day. She should just relish her joy that Santiago had actually woken up beside her.

Careful not to wake him, she rose quietly from the bed. Going to the bedroom's tall windows, she brushed aside the translucent curtains and looked down at the New York street, which was already starting to stir into life with taxi cabs and pedestrians, in a pale haze of pink and gray.

Tonight after dusk, she and Santiago would be bound together in lifetime vows, surrounded by family and friends. Letty and Darius had come back from Greece with their fat, adorable baby, specifically to attend. Letty would even be coming to the house a few hours early, to help Belle do her hair and makeup for the ceremony. And that wasn't all.

Two days ago, Santiago had sent his private jets to collect Belle's younger brothers: Ray from Atlanta, where he now owned his own plumbing business, and Joe from Denver, where he was training to be a fireman.

Belle had cried when her brothers arrived. It was the first time she'd seen them in two years. For a long time, the three siblings just hugged each other. Her brothers were excited to be uncles. They'd exclaimed both at the size of her belly and the luxurious brownstone mansion.

"You're in a new world now, Belle," Ray had said, pulling off his John Deere cap to survey the foyer in awe. Even their guest rooms had amazed them. Joe confided he was afraid to use the towels, until she'd tartly told him that this was her house and she wouldn't accept any more foolishness. Joe looked at her.

"You're happy, aren't you, Belle?" He shook his head. "I mean, I know this guy's got private jets and mansions and all that. But does he love you? Do you love him?"

And looking at her baby brother's hopeful, pleading face, Belle had done the only thing an older sister could do. She'd lied.

"Of course Santiago loves me." Then she'd realized something horrible. Something that wasn't a lie. She'd whispered, "And I love him."

Two days before her wedding, she'd been forced to face the truth. She was in love with Santiago.

When she'd first accepted his proposal—when he'd blackmailed her into it—Belle had told herself she shouldn't take it personally if Santiago didn't love her. He was just a hard-edged, ruthless tycoon who couldn't love anyone. Love wasn't in his character. She'd told herself she could live with it.

She was wrong.

"I earned a billion-dollar fortune. For her."

She could still hear the raw huskiness of Santiago's voice when he'd told her the story of the woman he'd once loved with all his heart. The night of their engagement party, all her rationalizations had fallen off a cliff.

Santiago did know how to love. Her stomach churned

now as she stared out the window at the waking city. He'd once loved a woman so much he'd spent literally years trying to win her, just like in the fairy tales Belle used to read her brothers when they were little. A peasant boy proves his worth by killing a dragon or vanquishing an army or sailing the seven seas to win the hand of the fair princess.

Only Santiago hadn't won his true love. Instead, the princess had just been one more privilege he was denied because he'd been born the bastard son of a maid. And everything he'd done to prove he didn't care about his father's rejection—from buying the historic ranch in Texas, to building a world-class art collection, to amassing a bigger fortune than him—only proved the opposite.

It doesn't matter, she told herself desperately. It all happened long ago. The woman had married his elder brother and they all lived in Spain, on the other side of the world.

But here in New York, the fairy tale was different. Belle was the peasant, and Santiago the handsome, distant king. She'd have given anything to win him. Slay any dragon, conquer any army. But how?

She might bear his child, but would she ever claim his heart?

Belle looked back at Santiago, still sprawled across their bed. The cool light of dawn was starting to add a soft pink glow through the windows. Her eyes traced the contours and outlines of his muscular, powerful body, with the white sheet twisted around his legs. She longed for him to be hers, really hers.

And in a way, he was. She would be his wife. His partner. His lover.

But never his love.

Going to the en-suite bathroom, she took a long, hot shower, trying to get the anxiety out of her body, and the growing fear of marrying a man she loved, but who would never love her back.

A man who, for all she knew, was still in love with that woman from long ago.

Maybe our baby will bring us together, she tried to tell herself, but she knew this was a delusion. Santiago would be a caring father, and he'd love their daughter. That didn't mean he'd feel anything more than respect for Belle as a partner. Anything more than desire for her in the night.

He would never let her in his heart. He would never slay dragons for her, sacrifice his life for her, as he had for that beautiful Spanish woman long ago.

Getting out of the shower, she wrapped herself in a white fluffy robe. Wiping the steam off the glass, Belle looked at herself in the bathroom mirror. Today was supposed to be the happiest day of her life, but her eyes were suddenly sad.

She looked down at the enormous diamond ring sparkling on her left hand. As ridiculously impractical as it was, as heavy and cold, it was beautiful and special. He'd picked it out just for her. Didn't that mean something, at least?

When she came out into their bedroom, Santiago was gone. He'd told her he would be at the office until shortly before their candlelight ceremony was due to begin, at seven, but she'd somehow hoped he would change his mind and be with her, today of all days. She was desperate for reassurance about their upcoming marriage. She was suddenly terrified she was about to make the biggest mistake of her life, and that she wouldn't be the only one to suffer for it.

Right or wrong, she told herself, the choice has already been made. *I'm marrying him today.*

But the day passed with agonizing slowness, with too much time for her to worry. She saw her brothers at breakfast, right before the two young men set out to see the Statue of Liberty and Empire State Building. She got one last checkup from her obstetrician, then finished last-minute wedding details.

In the late afternoon, it was finally time. She went to her closet and stroked the empire-waist wedding gown of cream-colored lace, tailored to fit her eight-months-plus pregnant belly. She'd found it at a vintage shop in Chinatown, and loved it.

She took a deep breath.

Smoothing rose-scented lotion over her skin, she put on her wedding lingerie, an expensive confection of white satin bralette, panties and white stockings with garter belt. Any moment now, Letty would be here to help with her hair and makeup. Belle would have to somehow pretend to be a blissfully happy bride, hiding how scared she really was that she was doing the wrong thing, permanently giving her life and heart to a man who would never love her back.

I'm marrying him for our daughter, Belle told herself desperately. But would her daughter grow up thinking it was normal for married parents not to love each other? That it was expected and right, to live without love?

Belle felt like she was hyperventilating as she went to the huge closet and took the beautiful wedding dress from the hanger. She heard a hard knock at the door.

Expecting Letty, she called, "Just a sec!"

But the door was flung open. Belle turned with a yelp of protest, trying to hide her half-naked body with the wedding dress. Then she gasped.

"Santiago! What are you doing here? Don't you know it's bad luck to see the bride in her wedding dr—?" Her voice cut off when she saw his face. "What's wrong?"

"My brother…"

"Your brother? Is he here?"

He gave a strangled laugh. "He's dead."

"What?"

His expression was pale and strange. "He died two days ago."

"I'm sorry," Belle whispered. Her wedding dress dropped unheeded to the floor as she went to him. Without thinking, she wrapped her arms around him, offering comfort, not caring that she was wearing only the bra and panties and that it was bad luck. "What happened?"

"Otilio had a heart attack and crashed his car. It's just lucky no one else was hurt."

"I'm so sorry," she repeated, her eyes filling with tears. "Even though you never met, and your relationship was complicated, he was still your brother and…"

"The funeral is tomorrow morning in Madrid."

Belle sucked in her breath. "You'll miss it. You…"

Then he met her eyes, and she suddenly knew.

"You're not going to miss it," she said slowly. "You're going to Madrid."

Santiago gave a single short nod. "I'm leaving immediately."

"But our wedding…" she whispered.

"I've already had my executive assistant start making calls. I'm sorry, Belle. Our wedding must be temporarily put off."

Belle had just been arguing that they were family, but now she said in a small voice, "But you don't even know them."

"My father needs me."

"He called you?"

His jaw tightened. "No. It was my brother's widow who called. She asked me to come, for my father's sake."

"Your brother's…" It took several seconds for this to sink in, and then Belle staggered back a step.

His brother's widow.

His *widow*.

The only woman Santiago had ever loved was free now.

Single.

What must the woman be like, since Santiago had spent years trying to win her love? Beautiful, chic, witty, powerful, sexy, glamorous? All of the above?

How could Belle compare with that?

She couldn't.

She felt sick inside.

"Belle?"

"Um." She tried to gather her thoughts. "It must have been…strange to talk to her again, after all these years."

"It was," he said in a low voice. "She said my father wants to see me. He has no one else now. His wife died years ago. Otilio and Nadia never had any children. I'm the last Zoya."

Belle's lips parted. "Are you saying…?"

"After thirty-five years, the Duque de Sangovia is willing to recognize me as his son."

And with that, Belle suddenly knew that her whole life, and her baby's too, had just changed, because a man she'd never met had had a heart attack in Spain.

"I'm sorry I have to postpone the wedding," he added, but something about his voice made her wonder how sorry he really was. Even as she had the thought, she reproached herself for it. How could she selfishly think about her own hurt, when Santiago's brother had just died, and his father was reaching out to him for the first time?

She put her hand on his arm urgently. "I'll come with you. To Madrid."

He shook his head. "It's across the Atlantic. You're getting too close to your due date to travel."

"I'll manage. I mean—" she gave an awkward laugh "—isn't that why you have a private jet? I just had a checkup this morning and I'm not anywhere close to labor. I'll be fine for a few days."

He looked at her, his jaw tight. "You would be willing

to go to so much trouble, to attend the funeral of a man you've never met? At your state of pregnancy? After I canceled our wedding like this?"

"Of course I would," she said over the lump in her throat. "I'm going to be your wife."

He set his jaw.

"Come, then."

She didn't get the sense that he was overjoyed.

"Unless you don't want me…"

"That's not it. I just don't want you to be uncomfortable."

"I'll be fine. I can't let you face it alone."

"That's very thoughtful." His eyes were unreadable as he looked down at her. "But then, I'd expect no less of you. Such a loving heart."

His words should have cheered her, and yet somehow, they didn't feel like a compliment. They felt like an accusation.

He looked her over in the white silk wedding lingerie, as if not even seeing her. "Change your clothes. Pack as quickly as possible. We leave in ten minutes."

She stared after him, her heart sick with fear.

When she'd woken up that morning, she'd been so scared of marrying Santiago and spending the rest of her life loving him, when he didn't love her back.

But now she realized there could be something even worse than that. Watching as Santiago fell back in love with the beautiful, aristocratic woman who'd once claimed his heart.

CHAPTER EIGHT

MADRID. ROYAL CITY of dreams.

The city was the third largest in Europe, built on a grand scale, from the classical grandeur of the Plaza Mayor to the world-class art of the Prado Museum and designer shops on the wide, graceful Gran Vía.

Santiago hadn't been back to this city since he'd fled at eighteen to make his fortune. Now he was back, no longer a desperate, penniless teenager, but a powerful tycoon, a self-made billionaire.

At fourteen, he'd begged his father to see him. Now the Duque de Sangovia was doing the begging, not him.

Actually, it had been Nadia who'd begged on his father's behalf. It had been strange, unpleasant, to hear her voice on the phone, like resurrecting a long-dead ghost. He'd felt nothing, not even hatred.

Perhaps he should thank her, he thought. She was the one who'd spurred him to become the man he was today. Powerful. Rich.

Heartless.

He stared out the car window as the Duque de Sangovia's chauffeur drove the limousine through the city's clogged morning traffic, carrying Santiago and Belle and their two bodyguards from the private airport. Madrid had once been a medieval dusty village, until King Phillip had moved the royal court here during the Spanish Golden Age. And even back then, the Zoya family had served their king, fighting his battles to build an empire of their own.

Each generation had become more powerful, with a better title to pass on to their heirs. His elder half brother Otilio had been born with the title of *marqués*, raised to be the next duke. But now his brother was dead.

Brother. Such a meaningful word for what had been, in their case, such a nonexistent relationship. Second only to *father.*

Today, at Otilio's funeral, he would finally meet his father in person. All Santiago knew of him came from the news and from his mother's scant stories, when he was very young. And he would see Nadia, the woman he'd once loved, whom he'd thought a kindred spirit. They'd both achieved the dreams they'd had at the orphanage, some twenty years before. He was a billionaire. She was a world-famous actress.

But not a duchess, he thought. That dream, at least, had been lost to her, from the moment her husband died.

He looked out at the weak morning light of Madrid. The September weather was chilly, the sky drizzling rain. He couldn't imagine a more perfect setting for a funeral.

Belle was sitting beside him in the back of the vintage Rolls-Royce limousine, wearing an elegant black shift dress with a long black jacket. It should have been chic, but was somehow ill-fitting and uncomfortable-looking on Belle's pregnant, curvaceous body. She wouldn't meet his eyes.

She'd barely spoken two words to him on the overnight flight across the Atlantic, leaving him alone with his own dark thoughts. She hadn't reproached him about canceling their wedding. Not a single word.

Not one woman in a million would have been so understanding, he thought. But of course Belle was always so kind. So loving.

Emotions were bubbling up inside him, hot as lava. He'd pushed his feelings down for most of his life. He wasn't sure how much longer he could keep it up.

He hadn't gone to his mother's funeral, twenty years before, because there hadn't been one. She'd had no money, the husbands she'd divorced were long gone, and in her frustration and bitterness, she'd alienated most of her friends. Her son was the only one left, and she'd done her best to make him hate her as well, knowing he couldn't leave.

As a young boy, he'd noticed other boys getting hugs and kisses from their mothers, and wondered why Mamá never treated him with such devotion. "Because you're bad all the time," she told him angrily. "You make your stepfathers angry when you don't put away your toys. You make them leave." It had hurt him when he was young. But by the time he was fourteen, he'd realized the real reason she never loved him. She blamed him for all the fairy tales gone wrong. Starting with his father, the duke.

Living in the orphanage, at least he'd known where he stood. He was on his own.

He'd loved New York from the beginning. The city was heartless and cold? Well, so was he. They were perfect for each other.

"Oh, my word," Belle breathed next to him. "Is that the crowd for your brother's funeral?"

Santiago blinked as he saw huge crowds of well-wishers and gawkers standing on the sidewalk outside the cathedral, held back by police. The driver pulled up to the curb, then opened their door.

Santiago got out of the backseat, turning back to assist Belle, who glanced nervously at the crowds, then looked up at him with dark stricken eyes.

Reaching for her hand, he helped her from the limo toward the gothic stone cathedral. The driver held an umbrella over their heads as the rain continued to drizzle from the gray clouds, falling against the vivid yellows and reds of the trees in September.

"It's like all Madrid is here," she whispered. "How famous was he?"

"They're not here for him," he ground out.

Belle frowned. "What do you mean?"

"There's something you should know about his wife…"

But before he could finish, the oversized door of the cathedral opened, and they entered. The nave of the cathedral was crowded with people who'd come to pay their last respects to Otilio, Marqués de Flavilla, the only legitimate son and heir of the powerful Duque de Sangovia, and the husband of the Most Beautiful Woman in the World.

"He died so unexpectedly," he heard someone say sadly as they passed. "Of a heart attack, and at only thirty-six. Such a tragedy to die so young."

"His poor wife…"

"Oh, her. I heard they've been separated for years. She's probably already thinking this will make spectacular PR for her next movie."

Setting his jaw, Santiago walked heavily up the center aisle of the cathedral in his black suit, holding Belle's hand tightly. The crowds parted for them like magic, people whispering around them, their eyes popping out of their heads.

"The duke's secret son…"

"His bastard son…"

"A self-made billionaire from America…"

Everywhere, he saw admiring eyes, curious eyes. All of them, these aristocrats and royals and politicians from around the world, seemed to admire him as he'd once only dreamed of being admired.

Ironic. All it had taken was the death of his brother, and suddenly Santiago had become a Zoya.

His jaw was taut as he came down the aisle, Belle directly behind him. Then he froze.

At the altar, surrounded by flowers, he saw a closed casket covered with a blanket embroidered with the family's coat of arms. The brother he'd never met, the chosen one, the rightful heir. Surrounding the coffin were flowers, tall silver candlesticks and officiants, ponderous in their robes.

Santiago's attention fell on two people in the front row. An old man in a wheelchair. His father. He looked old, compared to the pictures he'd seen. His face looked querulous, and his skin so pale it was almost translucent.

Beside him, patting him on the shoulder, a woman stood in a sleek, short black dress and chic little black hat with netting. Nadia.

At thirty-six, she was tall and thin and blonde, delicate and fragile, like an angel, severely elegant in her dark mascara and red slash of lipstick. He felt the shock of her beauty like the metallic tang of a remembered poison that had once been tasted and nearly been fatal.

Looking up, Nadia's violet eyes pierced him. She lowered her head to whisper to the man in the wheelchair, and the Duque de Sangovia's rheumy eyes abruptly looked up to see Santiago, his thirty-five-year-old bastard son, for the very first time.

For a second, Santiago held his breath. Then he exhaled. What did he care what the man thought of him now?

Behind him, Belle gave a soft, breathy curse that made him turn and stare. She'd never used a curse word in front of him before. Her eyes were wide with horror.

"That's your ex?" she said in a strangled voice. "Nadia *Cruz*?"

"So?" he said shortly.

"So—she's famous! I've seen her movies! She's one of the biggest movie stars in the world!"

"I know," he said impatiently, and strode forward to the end of the aisle, Belle trailing behind him.

"Santiago! Thank the heavens you are here at last," Nadia greeted him in Spanish, anxiously holding out her hands. "Quickly, quickly, it's about to start. We saved you a place…" She drew back with an irritated look as she saw Belle behind him, still clinging to his hand. "Who is this?"

"My fiancée," he responded in the same language. "Belle Langtry."

Belle's hand tightened. She didn't understand Spanish, but she understood her own name.

Nadia gave a smile that didn't reach her eyes and switched to say in clear English, "We only saved one place in the front row. For family only. She'll have to go behind."

"She stays with me," Santiago said automatically, but he was distracted as his father wheeled himself forward.

The Duque de Sangovia was even older than he'd expected. He seemed to have shrunken since last photographed, in the days since his heir had died. He said imperiously to Santiago, "You will sit between Nadia and me." He didn't look at Belle. "Your companion must find another place."

Bereaved or not, Santiago wasn't going to let the old man boss him around. "No, she stays."

But he felt Belle's hand pull away.

"It's fine. I'll get a spot in the back," she said quickly, and disappeared into the crowd. As the choir started to sing, everyone took their seats and Santiago found himself sitting between his father, whose attention he'd once craved so desperately, and the woman he'd once loved so recklessly.

Twisting his head, Santiago saw Belle in her dark black dress and coat sitting three rows behind them. Her lovely face was pale, her dark eyes luminous and sad. Was she so affected by the death of a man she'd never known? But when she met his eyes, she gave him an encouraging smile.

Always so thoughtful. Such a loving heart.

Luring him to trust her. To love her. Luring him to his own destruction.

Santiago turned away, a storm raging inside him.

The priest began the ceremony and he sat numbly, hardly able to feel anything. He barely heard the words as one officiant after another praised his brother, who apparently had been a paragon, beloved by all.

His heart was pounding as he stared at the closed casket, covered with the embroidered Zoya coat of arms and surrounded by flowers, barely hearing the eulogies.

He'd never imagined he would someday be seated beside his father, the duke, in a place of honor, for all the world to see. The old man actually looked at him once or twice during the ceremony, his wizened expression a little bewildered, tears in his eyes.

After the ceremony, they were whisked into the waiting limousine, which had been altered for his father's wheelchair. They were to be taken to the funeral reception at the Zoya *palacio*, a mile away from the cathedral. But as he was led to the limousine behind his father and Nadia, Santiago paused, looking around with a frown.

"Where is Belle?"

"Family only," Nadia told him firmly. He ignored her.

Striding back into the cathedral, he found Belle. "Come with me."

"Where?" She looked uncertain, ill at ease.

"The palace." This time, he wasn't going to let her slip away. Holding her hand tightly, he pulled her into the back of the stretch limousine, where Nadia and his father were already seated.

Belle sat beside him in silence, looking awkward and

uncomfortable and very pregnant, as they faced Nadia and his father, seated opposite. He saw Nadia and the duke both look at the swell of Belle's pregnancy, then look away, as if her condition were a personal affront.

Deafening silence filled the limousine as the driver took them from the cathedral to the Calle de la Princesa. In the middle of Madrid, surrounded by high-rise buildings, was the duke's city residence, the Palacio de las Palmas, with acres of lush greenery behind tall wrought-iron walls and a guarded gate. The same gate from which Santiago had been bloodily barred as an orphaned fourteen-year-old.

They drove past the wide open gate and past the luxurious gardens with the exotic palms for which the neoclassical palace was named. The limo stopped. Santiago's eyes were wide as he saw the nineteenth-century palace for the first time.

But as Santiago started to get out, the duke reached out a shaking claw to his shoulder.

"I thank God you've come to me, boy," he rasped in Spanish. "You are all I have left." He looked at him intently with his hooded gaze. "Truth be told, *mi hijo*, you are the only one who can save this family now."

It had been a very long day, Belle thought wearily. One thing after another. Her interrupted wedding. A private flight across the Atlantic. An elaborate funeral. A palace in Madrid. And oh, yeah, discovering that Santiago's ex was *Nadia Cruz*.

Now this.

Belle felt exhausted and overwhelmed as she looked up at the five-hundred-year-old castle. After the funeral reception had ended in Madrid, they'd traveled ninety minutes to the village of Sangovia, nestled in a valley beneath the castle on the crag, heart of Zoya history and power.

She nearly stumbled over the cobblestones, still slippery with rain in the darkness. Santiago grabbed her arm, steadying her.

He frowned, looking at her. "Are you all right?"

Belle tried to smile encouragingly. "I'm fine."

But she wasn't fine. Not at all. She hadn't been fine since Santiago had canceled their wedding yesterday.

She'd slept fitfully on the private jet over the Atlantic, tossing and turning. Then at the funeral she'd discovered it was even worse than she'd feared.

Santiago's ex, the widowed marquesa, was a famous movie star—famous, beautiful, powerful…everything that she, Belle, was not. And his father, the elderly Duque de Sangovia, had yet to acknowledge Belle's existence, even when he'd been sitting inches away, facing her in the limousine.

After the funeral, at the reception in the Palacio de las Palmas in the center of Madrid, she'd watched as Santiago stood beside his father and Nadia to gravely thank each of the illustrious, powerful guests—prime ministers, presidents, royalty—for coming to honor the late marqués.

Belle stood back, near the tables of food, feeling awkward and alone. The reception lasted for hours, until her belly felt heavy and tight and her feet throbbed with pain. She did not belong here, surrounded by all these wealthy, powerful people, in the gilded palace.

How could she compete with this—any of it?

She'd been intimidated by Santiago's mansion in Manhattan, but the Palacio de las Palmas, with its classical architecture and Greek columns, was an actual palace. There were layers of wealth on every wall, paintings and frescoes on the ceiling and sweeping staircases that led to more gilded rooms with yet more paintings of more illustrious Zoya ancestors.

When the reception finally ended, Belle had breathed a sigh of relief, hoping against hope that Santiago would shake hands with his father and Nadia—or better yet, just wave to the woman from a distance—and he and Belle could get back on a plane for New York.

Instead, Santiago had informed her that he would be remaining in Spain, staying at the castle of Sangovia with his father and Nadia.

"Just until Otilio's will is dealt with."

"Do we have to?"

"You don't. You can go back to New York tonight."

She'd looked up sharply. "No!"

"You are three weeks from your due date," he replied coolly. "You should be home."

He seemed as if he could hardly wait to get rid of her. Once, it would have been a dream come true for her to be sent away. But now, she could hardly bear the thought of it. She'd glared at him. "I'm staying with you."

He ground his teeth. "Belle—"

"We just got to Spain." Her voice trembled, but she lifted her chin. "I'm not going to turn around and fly back to New York. I'm exhausted. I'm staying."

He'd stared at her for a long moment.

"Fine. Stay. Just for a day or two. Then you're going back."

And he hadn't spoken to her again, the whole ninety minutes it took to drive with the duke and the movie star and their bodyguards to the medieval village of Sangovia, tucked in a green valley, beneath the looming castle at the top of the crag.

The castle had looked beautiful from a distance, but as Belle walked through the enormous door, she thought it felt impersonal and cold inside, far worse than the palace in Madrid. The castle of Sangovia wasn't gilded or gleaming like the neoclassical Palacio de las Palmas. The windows were small and far between, and the walls were cold stone. This castle came from an earlier, more brutal time of battles and blood.

The duke said something in Spanish to Santiago, and he replied with a nod. His father disappeared down the cold hallway, past a suit of armor, into a room she couldn't see.

Nadia then said something lightly in the same language, before she too disappeared. For a brief moment, Belle and Santiago were alone in the dark stone hallway. She was suddenly tempted to throw herself in his arms, to ask why he'd been so distant, to try to feel close to him again.

Then they heard a cough, and turning, they saw a uniformed maid. She said in English, "I'm here to take you to your rooms."

"Of course," Santiago said smoothly. "Thank you."

The maid led them through the castle, and up the stairs. A less homey or cozy domicile could scarcely be imagined. It was cold, drafty and damp. The stiff chairs they passed in the hallway all looked hundreds of years old and Belle feared might break if she actually tried to sit on one. Why would anyone choose to live here? she wondered.

The maid led Santiago and Belle to the east wing of the second floor. "All the family's bedrooms are down here," she said shyly, and pushed open a door.

The bedroom was formal and old-fashioned, filled with antiques, including a curtained four-poster bed. Belle glanced out the window at the view of the valley in the twilight.

"What do you think?" Santiago asked in an expressionless voice.

"It's very nice," Belle said politely.

"Thank you," the maid said. She turned to Belle. "I will take you to your room now, *señorita*."

Santiago suddenly scowled. "What are you talking about? My fiancée is staying with me."

"I am sorry, *señor*," the maid replied uncomfortably,

"but His Excellency does not approve of unmarried persons sharing sleeping quarters."

"Oh, really?" Santiago ground out. "Is that why he always used to seduce his maids in closets?"

The woman looked scared. *"Señor—?"*

"Forget it." He gritted his teeth. "You can just tell His Excellency—"

"No, Santiago. It's fine. Really." Belle put her hand on his arm anxiously. "This is his home. He just lost his son. I can sleep in a separate room for a night or two." She gave him a wan smile. "I'm tired. I just want to go to bed."

He started to argue, then scowled at the maid. "Fine. Take us to her room, then."

Rather than looking relieved, the maid looked even more nervous. "His Excellency asked that you come back down immediately to the salon, *señor.* I can take Miss Langtry the rest of the way upstairs."

"Upstairs? How far is it?"

"Um…"

"It doesn't matter," Belle interjected. "Your father needs you. Go to him."

He turned to Belle. "Are you sure?"

"I'm sure."

"I'll check on you later." His expression seemed distant. "And kiss you good night."

Maybe then, she thought hopefully, when they were alone, they could actually talk and try to work out whatever was making him so distant. "All right."

He kissed her gently on the forehead, his lips cool. "Until then."

"This way, *señorita.*"

Belle followed the maid down the hall. They went up a sweeping staircase, then a tightly winding flight of steps, then another. Belle's legs started to ache, and once or twice she leaned against the stone wall to catch her breath. The maid seemed to have no trouble whatsoever.

"How many people are on staff here?" Belle asked, to fill the silence as the maid waited.

"Thirty, *señorita*."

"Thirty people work here? To take care of how many?"

"Two."

Reaching a tower, they went up another tightly twisting flight of stairs, this one of rickety wood. Ducking her head, the maid pushed open a door at the back. She sounded embarrassed as she said, "Here is the room assigned to you, *señorita*."

Belle realized they'd put her in the attic, as if she were a mad relative, four floors above Santiago's room in the family wing.

"There's the bathroom," the woman added reluctantly.

Belle peeked past the door to a tiny bathroom, smaller than a closet, with a toilet, bare sink and shower so small she was afraid her belly wouldn't fit. A bare light bulb hung from the ceiling.

The family's opinion of her, and intention for her future, couldn't have been more clear.

"I'm sorry, *señorita*."

Belle forced herself to turn with a bright smile. "No, it's fine."

"You are too kind." The maid added under her breath, "If the marquesa had been assigned to such a room, we would have heard her screaming for miles."

Which was why, Belle reflected, beautiful women like Nadia Cruz ended up with everything they wanted, while girls like Belle ended up in rooms in the attic.

Soon after the maid left, Belle's overnight bag arrived, held by a huffing and puffing porter who glared at her, as if it were her fault he'd been forced to climb so many tightly twisting stone steps. "I'm sorry," she apologized, feeling guilty even though it hadn't been her idea.

Getting on her pajamas, she brushed her teeth and climbed into the tiny single bed, with the sagging mattress and squeaky metal frame, to wait for Santiago.

She looked out through the curtainless small round window. Sweeping moonlight showed all of the tiny village of Sangovia in the valley below the castle. With a shiver, she pulled up the thin blankets around her baby bump, and stared out into the starlit night.

Cuddling her belly, she leaned back against the lumpy pillow, yawning as she tried to stay awake until Santiago came to kiss her good night as he'd promised. She waited. And waited.

But he never came.

CHAPTER NINE

SANTIAGO STARED ACROSS the chilly salon, over a glass of even chillier Scotch, and looked down into his father's eyes, the chilliest of all.

"What are you saying?" His voice sounded strained, even to his own ears.

The old man's reply was a harsh rasp from the bowels of his wheelchair. "You will stay in Spain. As my heir."

Santiago paced a step in the oversized salon, which was filled with Renaissance art and leather-bound books that he'd wager no one had touched in years, except perhaps by the maids dusting them. The two men were alone.

When he'd come downstairs to see his father, the man had wheeled over to the liquor cabinet, poured him a drink, and then spoken his demand without preamble.

Once he would have killed to hear his father say those words. But now...

Santiago took a gulp of Scotch, then said coldly, "You've ignored me for my whole life. Why would I want to be your heir?"

"It is your birthright."

"It wasn't my birthright for the last thirty-five years."

"Everything changed with the death of my son." Suddenly, the old man sounded weary. He ran a hand over his wispy head. "I am dying, Santiago. You are all that is left of the Zoyas now. If you do not take over this family, there will never be another Duque de Sangovia."

Santiago's jaw tightened. "Why should I care? You abandoned my mother. You abandoned me before I was born. What is the dukedom to me? I have my own company. My own empire. My life is not in Spain."

"It could be."

"I came to Otilio's funeral to show my respect, nothing more. And because I was curious to meet the man who never wanted to recognize me as his son."

The elderly Duke said slyly, "And to see Nadia?"

That brought Santiago up short.

The man continued, "She has been a good daughter-in-law to me. She is beautiful, elegant, powerful, famous. The perfect consort." He paused. "Except for her inability to conceive the Zoya heir, but as for that, perhaps it is not too late."

Santiago's eyes narrowed. "What do you mean?"

"I know you and Nadia have a history. Perhaps this is fate. She could still bear the Zoya heir. To you."

Santiago stared down at him, unable to believe what he was hearing. "Have you lost your mind, old man? You've met my fiancée. Belle is upstairs right now. Our baby is due in weeks—"

"You must give that woman up," the Duque de Sangovia said harshly. "She will never be accepted, this country girl, not in Madrid nor in the elite circles of international aristocracy where you belong. It would be cruel to force her into a place where she would always be awkward, rejected, based on her unfortunate background."

"Oh, so you're just looking out for her—is that it?" Santiago said acidly. "You forget I was raised a bastard, without money or formal education—"

"You are different. You are my son, with Zoya blood. You have single-handedly built a business empire that must inspire respect."

In spite of himself, Santiago felt a strange zing of pride

at hearing his father speak those words. Then he caught himself. "So you expect me to abandon her," he ground out, "as you did my mother?"

"*Sí*, and for the same reasons," the duke said calmly. "I could not divorce my wife, the duchess, to run off with a maid. I would have lost all the fortune that came with her, and damaged my family honor and my name."

"Seducing an eighteen-year-old maid and then abandoning your own son is what you call honorable?"

"Sometimes difficult choices must be made. This girl, this Belle, has nothing. She is nothing. Toy with her if you must, even have a child with her, but do not marry her. If you wish to be my heir, you must marry as befits the future Duke of Sangovia."

"I will marry as I choose, and you and Sangovia and Nadia can all go to hell."

"Do not marry this American girl." The old man's rheumy eyes turned hard. "Do you really think she could ever be happy here, in this world? It would be cruel to her. And the child. Let her go."

Santiago opened his mouth to argue. Then he snapped it shut, thinking of the sad, haunted look in Belle's eyes ever since they'd arrived in Madrid.

"Excuse me, Your Excellency." A male nurse appeared at the door. "It is time for your medicine."

The duke nodded grimly. He started to push his wheelchair out of the room, but as he passed Santiago, the duke gripped his arm with a shaking hand.

"You have the power to choose, *mi hijo*. Let the girl go. Accept your birthright as my son. Become my heir, and the future duke, to continue a legacy that has endured for hundreds of years. The dukedom, combined with your vast business empire, plus a marriage to Nadia, would make you one of the most powerful men in the entire world." His beady eyes burned brightly in the shadowy salon. "Think about it."

Santiago was left alone in the salon, with nothing but the glass of Scotch and his own bleak thoughts for company.

His father was offering him everything he'd ever dreamed of as a boy.

A vindication of his worth.

Everything he'd hungered for as a young man.

But that wasn't the only reason he was suddenly tempted. He clawed back his hair.

For the last few months, he'd found himself growing closer to Belle in a way that he'd enjoyed at first, but now terrified him. As their marriage approached, he'd become increasingly on edge. In bed with her, he'd experienced physical joy beyond anything he'd ever imagined. But he'd started to have feelings for her, beyond partnership or even friendship. Against his will, Belle had become too important to him. Her beauty. Her kindness. Her wit. The deep luminosity of her brown eyes.

He found himself drawn to her. *Needing* her.

Like today. Even after he'd made the decision to send her back to New York so he wouldn't worry about her going into labor so far from home, all she'd had to do was raise her poignant gaze to his and ask to stay, and he'd immediately given in. Because he couldn't bear to see her unhappy, not even for a moment.

He didn't like it.

Santiago didn't want to need anyone. He didn't want to be dependent on their happiness for his own peace of mind. Because if you depended on someone—if you cared for them—it left you weak and vulnerable, to be crushed at will by their inevitable betrayal. He'd learned that from childhood. From Nadia.

I know you and Nadia have a history. Perhaps this is fate. She could still bear the Zoya heir. To you.

The thought repelled him. Nadia, for all her angelic beauty, had the soul of a snake. A mercenary, gold-digging snake. The thought of touching her disgusted him.

But at least Nadia would never again tempt him into risking his heart. Not like Belle.

If he was honest with himself, when he'd gotten the call about his brother's death, and realized it gave him the perfect excuse to cancel the wedding—the same wedding he himself had insisted on, demanded, blackmailed Belle into—part of him had been relieved.

Something inside him was afraid of marrying her now. He, who'd never been afraid of anything, was afraid of what would happen if he spoke those vows to Belle, the one woman on earth who held power over him.

Wearily, Santiago left the salon and went up the sweeping stairs toward the second floor. He stopped in front of his own door, suddenly remembering how he'd promised Belle he'd come up and kiss her good night.

He pictured her beautiful face. Her wide, haunting brown eyes, fringed with black lashes. Her full ruby-red lips. Her softness. Her sweetness.

She'd hated him when they'd first met, with good cause. Santiago had pushed people away for most of his life. It wasn't just a game to him; it was necessary for survival. But he'd known from the night he first seduced Belle that she, idealistic and romantic and good-hearted as she was, could be dangerous to his peace of mind. So he'd pushed her away.

That had all changed when he'd found out she was pregnant. He'd forced her into an engagement in Texas. She'd hated him for that.

But Belle didn't hate him anymore. Something had changed in her during their time living in New York. She'd been his hostess. She'd redecorated his home. She'd even traveled with him to Spain when, by rights, she should have

slapped his face for canceling their wedding to attend the
funeral of a virtual stranger half a world away.

Santiago wanted her. So much. Even picturing Belle
now, stretched out on a bed somewhere upstairs, he
yearned to see her, hold her, touch her. He'd meant to ask
the housekeeper for directions to her bedroom, which he
assumed to be even larger and more comfortable than his
own, as any pregnant woman deserved. But now...

Hesitating at his own bedroom door, he looked down
the dark hallway toward the stairs. His body yearned for
the electricity and comfort of her touch. He longed to feel
her sweet, hot, lush body naked against his own.

But the cost to his soul was suddenly too high.

Setting his jaw, he turned back to his own bedroom,
going inside, closing the door firmly behind him.

He would sleep alone.

Belle woke up alone in the shabby little attic room of the
castle, and sat up in a rush. He'd never come up to kiss
her last night.

Trying to ignore the hurt, she stretched her muscles,
aching from the lumpy mattress. She took a quick, awkward shower in the tiny beat-up bathroom with peeling
linoleum, then freshened up, putting on a new dress that,
with her full pregnancy, made her look as lumpy as that
bed.

Going downstairs, she went to Santiago's bedroom, only
to discover it was empty. So were the other bedrooms in
the wing. She wandered downstairs, feeling lost, until she
found an English-speaking maid who directed her to the
breakfast room.

"You should hurry, miss. I'm afraid you're late," she
said anxiously.

Late? How could she be late? No one had told Belle anything about breakfast being at any certain time.

She found the formal breakfast room, with its long elegant table, with food spread out on a side table and big arrangements of flowers that made her want to sneeze. When she arrived, Santiago set down his newspaper, his breakfast plate already empty. His dark eyes were cool as, rising from the table, he came forward.

"I missed you last night," she said, staring up at him.

"Sorry. I was busy." He barely looked at her, and kissed her on the cheek as if she were a stranger.

"Did you enjoy sleeping in, Miss Langtry?" cooed Nadia, also rising from the table, looking sexy and chic in a perfectly cut black skirt suit, her light blond hair pulled back into a chignon, a jeweled brooch on her lapel.

"Sleeping in?" Belle stammered.

"We expected you an hour ago."

The duke muttered something darkly in Spanish, but didn't bother to look in Belle's direction, as his servant pushed his wheelchair from the room.

Belle bit her lip as she looked between Santiago and Nadia. "You expected me at a certain time?"

"Breakfast begins strictly at eight," Nadia said sweetly. "As the housekeeper mentioned in your wake-up call this morning."

"I didn't get any—"

"Don't worry." The blonde swept her arm in a generous gesture. "You are a guest, so of course you are free to ignore the rules of our household, no matter how much trouble it might cause everyone. The food has grown cold, so I've instructed the servants to prepare you a fresh breakfast, in addition to their other duties."

"I didn't mean..." Belle stopped when Santiago kissed her forehead. He was dressed in a dark suit. "Are you going somewhere?"

"The lawyer's office," he said. "And to Madrid, to discuss the possibility of donating art to the museum and creating a wing in my brother's name."

"Otilio was an art lover," Nadia purred. Her stiletto heels clicked against the marble floor as she looked up at Santiago with a smile. "Shall we go?"

Oh, *hell* to the no. Belle looked between them. "I'll come with you."

"That's not necessary," Santiago said.

"But I want to."

"It will be very boring for you."

"Please," she implored, holding out her hand.

With visible reluctance, he took it. "As you wish."

She exhaled.

"It's really unnecessary, Miss Langtry," Nadia said. She looked seriously annoyed.

Belle was glad. The other woman might be in charge in this castle, arranging to exile her to the attic room and sabotaging her in front of Santiago and the household, but Belle wouldn't give up Santiago without a fight.

But, it seemed, neither would Nadia. Later that morning, as the duke and Santiago were in the adjoining office, speaking to the lawyers, the two women sat together in the posh waiting room.

Bright sunlight was pouring through the windows, and cushy chairs lined the walls. The sound of secretaries typing on keyboards came from the next room. Sitting across from Nadia, Belle felt nervous and awkward and tried to hide it by reading a magazine. In Spanish. Upside down.

"How charming," Nadia said suddenly.

Sheepishly, Belle turned around her magazine. But the other woman wasn't looking at her reading material. Reaching out, she touched the diamond on Belle's finger.

"Oh, the ring?" Belle smiled. "Yes, I love it. His proposal was very romantic, too." Maybe it was stretching the truth to call the way he'd blackmailed her into marriage in Texas romantic, but she hated the smirk on the movie star's face.

"Was it?" Nadia smiled back. "I mean, I know it's very *au courant* to recycle these days, but this is taking it a bit far, don't you think?"

"What do you mean?" Belle said stiffly. She guessed from the context that *au courant* meant trendy, though for all she knew it could have been a type of jam.

"Oh, didn't you know?" The blonde's smile widened. "That's the same ring Santiago once used to propose to me."

Belle's heart fell to the wooden parquet floor.

"No," she stammered. "You're mistaken. He picked it out just for me."

"Oh, didn't he tell you? That naughty creature." Nadia's smile turned wicked. "He tried to give it to me five years ago. Regrettably, he'd waited too long and I'd already been spoken for. But I know my diamonds."

Belle wrapped her hand around the ring, feeling completely betrayed. But she couldn't show it, couldn't let the other woman see how her barb had found its target. She tried to shrug. "Even if it's the same ring, we have a totally different situation. I never betrayed him."

"No, you just got pregnant."

Belle's eyes narrowed. "While you made him chase you all those years, then married his brother."

Nadia looked at her with a taunting smile on her red lips. "I'm not married to him anymore. Now I am free."

Belle stiffened, trying to hide her growing fear. "You think you can take him from me."

Nadia tilted her head, considering. "You're not so stupid after all."

Belle's cheeks flushed. "You don't deserve to be Santiago's wife."

"I'm more deserving than you."

"I love him."

"That I can easily believe." The movie star's famous violet eyes cut through her. "But does he love you?"

The burn on Belle's cheeks intensified.

Because that was the heart of it. Santiago didn't love her. He never had. He never would.

That was the truth she'd been fighting to deny, to hide, even from herself. Even though he'd once told her to her face that he would never love her, she'd dreamed he might change.

She mumbled, "He proposed to me…"

"He proposed to me first. With that exact ring." Nadia gave her a hard smile. "Curious, don't you think, that he kept it all these years?"

Belle tried to fight the emotions swirling inside her beneath the other woman's hard gaze. "He was the one who demanded marriage when he found out I was pregnant…"

"And he obviously felt strongly about it, since he couldn't even be bothered to get you your own ring." Nadia leaned forward in her chair, smiling pleasantly. "The ring was mine. As his love was mine. And both will be again."

Belle couldn't breathe. Her heart was pounding frantically. "You're wrong…he won't…"

"No?" Grabbing her arm, Nadia said, "I am Santiago's equal as you never were. We are meant to be together."

Each word hurt more than the last. "You gave him up," Belle choked out, struggling to pull her arm away.

"I had to be ruthless to get what I wanted. Santiago of all people will understand this, and respect it." Her red lips lifted in a smile. "He's loved me since we were teenagers. He's ached for me. Hungered for me. We belong together. My choice to marry his brother only made Santiago want me more." She looked Belle over contemptuously. "Do you really think he would ever choose you, now I'm free?"

No, she didn't. That was what hurt the most.

"There are two ways to do this," Nadia said sweetly. "Either give Santiago up gracefully. Or watch helplessly as I take him from you."

"You can't…"

"If you love him like you say you do, at least leave him thinking of you with some respect."

Pain ripped through Belle. She felt her baby kick inside her as if her daughter was angry, too. She put her hands over her belly. "He's the father of my child."

"After we are wed, I will give him another baby. He will forget yours." Nadia smiled. "Santiago is an honorable man. He will always provide for you and your child, as a matter of duty. You will never have to work again. Consider yourself lucky. Leave Spain. Go seek the love that Santiago will never give you."

Belle swallowed, her heart pounding.

As the door to the lawyer's office opened and the men came out, Nadia whispered, "End it quickly, and it will be better for everyone. Especially you."

With a final friendly pat to Belle's shoulder, Nadia rose to her feet with a beaming smile to greet the duke and Santiago, who was pushing his father's wheelchair.

"Are you boys finally done? Because we are due at the museum." She added teasingly, with her violet-blue eyes flashing between the duke and Santiago, "You men always like to talk and talk…"

Numbly, Belle pushed herself up from the chair. No one was paying attention to her. The three others were talking in Spanish as they walked ahead of her out of the lawyer's office.

In the limo, she sat silently beside Santiago as they traveled through the sun-drenched streets of Madrid. He gave her a curious glance.

But this time, she was the one avoiding his gaze.

"He's loved me since we were teenagers. He's ached for me. Hungered for me. We belong together."

Belle swallowed over the ache in her throat as she watched the passing city through the car window. She'd only met Santiago a year ago. He'd never loved her. And what did they even have in common, when she barely knew the name of her great-grandparents, compared with Santiago, who had an aristocratic bloodline that went back to the Middle Ages?

"After we are wed I will give him another baby. He will forget yours."

Belle knew Santiago's determination to uphold his honor and give their unborn daughter a better childhood than he himself had had. He would not abandon his promise to marry Belle.

She shivered as they traveled in luxury, in a limousine through the streets of Madrid.

The real question was, could she actually let him keep his word, and marry her, trapping them both forever in a cold marriage without love?

CHAPTER TEN

SANTIAGO GLANCED AT the duke as they drove through Madrid. His father had actually thanked him for helping deal with some legal business at the lawyer's office, some contracts that Otilio hadn't signed properly.

His father. It was strange thinking of the old man that way. For the first time, he had a real, flesh-and-blood father.

The old man wasn't affectionate, or even kind. He was arrogant and controlling, and seemed to think that he could boss Santiago around, using his inheritance as bait. Just look at his ridiculous demand that Santiago betray his promise to wed Belle…

He glanced at her now, sitting quietly beside him in the backseat, biting her lip as she stared out at the city streets. She'd been strangely quiet since they'd left the lawyer's office. It wasn't like her to be so quiet. Usually she couldn't wait to tell him exactly what she was thinking, particularly when it insulted him.

No, Santiago suddenly realized. That wasn't true anymore. She didn't insult him anymore, not like she used to. Now, she treated him with encouragement. With…love?

The limo bounced over a bump in the road, and his shoe hit the stiletto across from him. He looked up at Nadia, who was sitting across from him, beside his father. She lifted her dark lashes and smiled.

His father obviously wasn't the only one who believed he could get power over Santiago.

It made him incredulous. How could Nadia not realize he had nothing but contempt for her?

Both she and his father were trying to buy him. They offered him a dukedom like a prize, and thought they could use words like honor and fate, and welcome him into the castle, and Santiago would be grateful. They thought he'd never grown up from the childhood dream he'd had as a lonely, fatherless boy. They thought that all they had to do was offer and Santiago, a self-made independent billionaire, would instantly become an obedient son to the father who'd abandoned him, a grateful husband to the woman who'd betrayed him.

But Santiago Velazquez was no man's pawn—or woman's. His jaw tightened as he looked from Nadia to Belle, who was still staring out the window as if her life depended on it. He was just grateful that she had no idea what his father had proposed. He didn't want her hurt. Especially since…

As his gaze traced over her full rosy lips and the plump curves of her body, something twisted in his heart.

Belle was a woman like no other. Her loyalty and courage and honesty didn't just inspire respect, but reverence. She drew him in. He wanted to let her love him.

He wanted to love her back.

His heart was suddenly pounding.

No.

He couldn't be that stupid.

No one could be as honest, or loyal, or good as he thought Belle was. However she might seem. If he let her inside his heart, he would regret it.

When they reached the famous art museum in the heart of Madrid, he got out quickly, opening his passenger door before the driver could. Belle, too, stepped out quickly, as if she were afraid he might offer his hand to help her out.

At least they were in agreement on one thing right now, he thought grimly. Avoiding each other.

They were parked on the quiet side of the museum, far from the long queues of tourists. He pushed his father's wheelchair toward the side door, which led to the museum's administrative offices. Nadia walked beside the duke, chattering to him charmingly in Spanish. Belle walked silently behind, with the bodyguards and his father's nurse, as if she preferred to be with the staff, rather than with the aristocrats.

She probably did, Santiago thought.

Castilian-accented Spanish whirled around him as they were escorted into the lobby and whisked into the director's office, where they were offered champagne or coffee. Through it all, Belle held herself back from the others, looking miserable and wan and as if her feet hurt.

Becoming a duchess in Spain, traveling with the jet-set, would require more rules that Belle wouldn't like, Santiago thought. He would have to live by new rules as well, but at least he spoke Spanish. At least he was of Spanish blood. Belle wasn't.

Plus, she'd have to temper her honest, enthusiastic, joyful nature to be cool and calm, to know how to smile pleasantly while speaking cutting words, to maneuver the hard merciless edges of the highest of European high society—a world of not just mere money, but hundreds of years of history and breeding, of jostling for position.

Santiago knew he could win in that world, if he chose, because of both his heritage and his personal ruthlessness. He'd spent twenty years fighting in business, tearing other men's companies apart. He knew how to battle. He wasn't afraid of war. He had a thick skin and sharp weapons.

Belle was different. She wasn't a gold digger; she wasn't

a social climber. She'd barely seemed to tolerate New York City. He suspected she'd be happier just tending flowers in their garden, baking for their children, volunteering at their school and caring for her neighbors. She would be happy to be with a man who appreciated her every day when he hugged his family in a warm, loving home. A man who would fix things around the house. Who'd sit on the floor with their young daughter and patiently have a tea party with her dolls.

Belle didn't want to marry a powerful billionaire, or a sexy playboy, or a famous duke. What she really wanted— what she *needed*—was a good man who would love her.

His father's hoarse words came back to haunt him.

"Do you really think she could ever be happy here, in this world? It would be cruel to her. And the child. Let her go."

Belle climbed wearily up the last flight of stairs to her bedroom in the top tower of the castle, then fell exhausted into her small bed.

After the day she'd had, watching Santiago and Nadia and the Duque de Sangovia be fêted and honored in Spanish while she was shunted and ignored, she felt weary to the bone. To the heart.

They'd finally arrived back at the castle, and the others had gone for a drink in the salon. She'd come upstairs for a nap. She barely felt the late afternoon sunlight from the tiny round window warm her skin, and she fell asleep.

When she woke, the room was shadowy and gray, and she saw Santiago's handsome face above her, his jaw tight, his eyes hard.

"This is your bedroom? This—closet?"

She was startled, still half lost in the sensual, heart-breaking dream she'd been having about him. "What are you doing up here? What's wrong?"

"I came to get you for dinner. Nadia never sends anyone to tell you, does she?"

"No," she said frankly. "She wants you for herself."

His startled eyes met hers. "You know?"

"Of course I know. But she can't have you." Belle put her hand on his sculpted cheek, rough with a five-o'clock shadow. Something suddenly gave her courage. Maybe it was this moment of intimacy, of honesty. Maybe it was because, just a moment ago, she'd been dreaming of him making love to her. But looking him straight in the eye, she whispered, "Because I love you, Santiago..."

For a moment, she trembled with terror that she'd admitted it. She couldn't meet his eyes, so leaning up, she kissed him, full on the mouth. It was the first time she'd ever initiated a kiss, and she embraced him with all her pent-up hunger and desperate love.

And in the tiny single bed, tucked by the attic window, a miracle happened—Santiago gripped her shoulders tightly and kissed her back even more desperately than she'd kissed him. He held her as if he were drowning, and Belle was his only chance of saving himself. Exhilaration flooded through her body. She pulled away.

"I love you," she repeated joyfully, searching his dark gaze. "Could you ever love me?"

But when he looked down at her, his handsome face was suddenly cold.

"I never asked for your love, Belle. I never wanted it."

She sucked in her breath, annihilated by pain. How could he kiss her so desperately one moment, then push her away so coldly the next?

Then suddenly it all made sense.

The coldness. The distance. It had all started weeks ago.

He wasn't a fool. He must have realized she was falling in love with him, probably before she even realized it herself. So he'd started pulling away, acting cold. He must have started regretting his decision to propose. When he'd first heard the news of his brother's death—that was why he'd seemed almost relieved to have the excuse to cancel their wedding.

He didn't want her love.

Her shoulders fell. "You told me from the beginning that you'd never love me." Her voice was low. "But I fell for you anyway. For the man you are and the man you could be. I couldn't stop myself from loving you…"

Santiago gripped her shoulders. "Stop saying that." Taking her hand, he pulled her from the bed. "We'll discuss this later. We should go down to dinner. They're waiting for us."

He didn't look at her as they went down the twisting wooden staircase, and all the stairs after that, to the great hall.

Belle's throat ached with unshed tears as they reached the enormous room, two stories high, with paintings that looked hundreds of years old. At the center of the room was a long table that could have easily fit thirty people, but tonight had only two at the end: the elderly duke, who as usual didn't acknowledge Belle's existence, and Nadia, who as usual looked wickedly sexy and beautiful.

Behind her on the wall was an old portrait of a beautiful woman in a black mantilla and elaborate gown, with expressive eyes and a hard smile. Just like Nadia's.

Who was the obviously correct consort for Santiago now? Belle, with her average looks and former job as a waitress, a regular girl from small-town Texas? Or Nadia, an international movie star, the most beautiful woman in the world, who knew how to smile sweetly as she cut you to the heart—the woman Santiago had once loved so much that he'd literally earned a billion dollars to try to win her?

The duke muttered something in Spanish beneath his breath.

Looking up, Nadia said to Belle, "Late again? Honestly, you don't look like the kind of girl who's always late to meals."

Belle growled under her breath, but to her surprise, Santiago answered for her. "Thanks to you."

Nadia tilted her head innocently. "I don't know what you mean."

"You know perfectly well. Sticking Belle up in the tower. You've been doing your best to sabotage her. Stop it," he said sharply, then his voice turned gentle as he said to Belle, "Sit here. Beside me."

A moment later, Belle was eating dinner without much appetite, and drinking water as the others drank red wine and spoke in Spanish. She'd just told her future husband she loved him, and nothing had happened. Wasn't courage supposed to be rewarded in life?

But she didn't think it would be.

She ate numbly, then rose to her feet to escape the dreary, formal table. Santiago stopped her with a glance and four quiet words.

"We need to talk."

And looking at him, Belle was suddenly afraid.

He led her outside, to the Moorish garden behind the castle courtyard. She could see the lights of the castle above and the village below. A few lampposts dotted through the palm trees and fountains of the dark-shadowed garden. Moonlight silvered the dark valley.

Folding his arms, Santiago stood over her, handsome as a fierce medieval king. "Take back your words."

"I can't." She felt like she was going to faint. It was one thing for her to think of leaving him, but something different if he told her to go. Much more final.

His forehead furrowed as he came closer. He was

dressed in a sleek suit, his dark hair cut short. She missed the rougher man she remembered in New York. The one who could laugh, whose hair was a little more wild, especially when he raked it impatiently with his hands. "You don't even like it here."

"Because I don't belong here," she said quietly. "But neither do you."

For a long moment, he looked at her. She saw the clench of his jaw in the moonlight. When he spoke, his voice was hard.

"I'm sending you back to New York."

"You're staying?"

"Yes."

"And you're glad." She choked out a laugh, wiping tears that burned her. "Right. I get it. Let's face it, I was always your second-choice bride. You never really wanted to marry me. You just wanted to do the right thing for our baby."

"I still do," he said quietly. "But as I told you from the beginning, love was never supposed to be part of it."

Her honesty had ruined any chance they had, she realized. When she'd told him she loved him—that had been the thing that had made him finally decide to end this.

"I'm sorry," he said quietly.

She tried to smile, but couldn't. Her cheeks wouldn't lift. She turned away.

Suddenly, she just wanted this to be over as soon as possible. She pulled off her diamond ring, tugging it hard to get it off her pregnancy-swollen finger. Afraid to touch him—afraid if she did, she would cling to him, sob, slide down his body to the ground and grip his leg as she begged him never to let her go—she held it out. "Here."

He stared at the ring without moving to take it. Why was he trying to make her suffer? Why wouldn't he just take it? She slid it into his jacket pocket. She again tried to smile, and again failed. "The ring was never really mine, anyway. You bought it for her."

Santiago stared at her. "She told you?"

"At the lawyer's office." With a choked laugh, Belle looked up at the castle towers overhead. "You know, every time I hear the tap-tap-tap of her stiletto heels, I've started to feel like a swimmer seeing a shark fin in the water." Lifting her gaze to his, she took a deep breath and forced herself to say simply, "But she's like you. You've known her half your life. I can see why you love her."

"Love her?" He sounded shocked. "Don't be ridiculous. She's my brother's widow. He's not even cold in his grave."

Why was he trying to deny what was so plain, even to her? "And now she's free. The only woman you ever loved. The woman you spent years trying to deserve, like a knight on a charger, determined to slay dragons for her. Just like in a fairy tale." She looked up. "And now you'll be duke and duchess. You'll live in a castle in Spain." She looked up at the moonlit castle in wonder, then down at herself as she stood in the garden, heavily pregnant and with ill-fitting, wrinkled clothes, and whispered, "I'm no man's prize."

Reaching out, he cupped her cheek. "It's better for you, Belle," he said quietly. "I can't give you the love you deserve. Now, you'll have a chance at real happiness."

She felt frozen, heartsick. "And our baby?"

"We will do as you suggested in Texas, and share custody. Neither you nor our daughter will ever want for anything. You will always have more money than you can spend. I will buy you a house in New York. Any house you desire."

A lump rose in her throat. "There's only one house I want," she whispered. "*Our* house. The one I decorated, with our baby's first nursery. With Anna and Dinah. Our house, Santiago."

He looked down at her. "I'm sorry."

She looked down at her bare left hand. Once she left him, she thought, all his childhood dreams could come true. He would be a true Zoya. He'd have his father. His position as heir. The woman he'd once loved.

Life was short. Love was all that mattered.

She had to accept it. To set him free, and herself free as well.

Weak with grief, Belle looked up at him. And with a deep breath, she forced herself to say the words that betrayed her very soul. "I'll leave you, then. Tomorrow."

"Tonight would be better. I'll call my pilot and order the plane ready."

Santiago's voice was so matter-of-fact, so cold. As if he didn't care at all. While her own heart was in agony. She wanted to cry. Her voice trembled. "You're in such a rush to get rid of me?"

His jaw set. "Once the decision is made, it's best to get it over with. You deserve better than me. A good man who can actually love you back."

"You could be that man," she whispered. She struggled to smile, to find a trace of her old spirit, even as her eyes were wet with tears. "I know you could."

Emotion flashed across his handsome face, but before she could identify it, it was gone. He looked away.

"I am doing the best I can," he said in a low voice. "By letting you go."

It was a civilized ending to their engagement. They could both go forward as partners raising their baby, telling friends that the breakup had been "mutual" and their engagement had ended "amicably."

But Belle couldn't end it like that.

She couldn't just leave quietly, with dignity. Her heart

rebelled. She couldn't hold back her real feelings. Not anymore.

"I know I can't compete with Nadia," she choked out, "not in a million years. I'm not beautiful like her. I can't offer you the dukedom you've craved all your life. There's only one thing I can give you better than anyone else. My love. Love that will last for the rest of my life." She looked up at him through her tears. "Choose me, Santiago," she whispered. "Love me."

For a moment, blood rushed in her ears. She felt like she was going to faint in the moonlit garden. The image of the looming castle swirled above her. She swayed on her feet, holding her breath.

Then she saw his answer, by the grim tightening of his jaw.

"That's why I'm ending this, Belle," he said in a low, rough voice. "I care for you too much to let you stay and waste your life—your light—on me."

The brief hope in her heart died. Her shoulders sagged. "All right," she said, feeling like she'd aged fifty years. "I'll go pack."

But as she started to turn, he grabbed her wrist. "Unless…"

"Unless?" she breathed.

"You tell me you don't love me after all. Tell me you were lying. We could still be married, like we planned. If you don't ask for more than I can give."

He was willing to still marry her?

For a moment, desperate hope pounded through her.

Then she went still.

Seven years ago, when Justin had first proposed to her, she'd known even then, deep down, that he didn't love her. When he'd demanded Belle have the medical procedure to permanently prevent pregnancy—a monstrous demand, when she'd been only a twenty-one-year-old virgin—barely more than a kid herself—Belle had deluded herself into thinking she had to accept any sacrifice as the price of her love for him.

No longer. She looked up at Santiago in the moonlit garden.

"No," she said quietly.

He looked incredulous. "No?"

Belle lifted her chin. "I might not be a movie star, I might not have a title or fortune, but I've realized I'm worth something too. Just as I am." She took a deep breath. "I want to be loved. And I will be, someday." She gave him a wistful smile. "I just wish it could have been by you."

"Belle…"

Her belly suddenly became taut. Her lower back was hurting. She was still weeks from her due date so she knew it couldn't be labor. It was her body reacting, she thought, to her heart breaking.

"I will always love you, Santiago," she whispered. Tears spilled down her cheeks as she reached up to cradle his rough chin with her hand one last time. "And think that we could have been happy together. Really happy."

Standing on her tiptoes, she kissed one cheek, then the other, then finally his lips. She kissed him truly, tenderly, with all her love, to try to keep this last memory of him locked forever in her heart.

Then, with desperate grief, she pulled away at last.

"Goodbye," she choked, and fled into the castle, blinded by tears. She went up to her room in the tower and packed quickly. It was easy, since she left all of the expensive, uncomfortable new clothes behind. When she came downstairs, she saw a limo in the courtyard waiting for her.

"I'll take your bag, miss," the driver said.

Belle climbed in to the limo, looking back at the castle one last time. She had a glimpse of Santiago in the library window, alone in the cold castle, the future Duke of Sangovia, the future husband of a *marquesa*, a self-made billionaire, sleek and handsome with cold, dead eyes staring after her.

Then, like a dream, he was gone.

CHAPTER ELEVEN

SANTIAGO STOOD AT the library window, watching Belle's limo disappear into the dark night. He felt sick at heart. It was the hardest thing he'd ever done, letting her go.

"Finally. She's gone."

Nadia's voice was a purr behind him. Furious, Santiago turned to face her with a glare. She smiled at him, with a hand on her tilted hip, in front of the dark wood paneling and wall of old leather-bound books. She looked like a spoiled Persian cat, he thought irritably. He bared his teeth into a smile.

"You did your part to get rid of her, didn't you? Sticking her in the tower, undercutting her with the staff, telling her the engagement ring had once been yours?"

"She didn't belong here," she said lazily. "Better for her to just go."

Yes, Santiago thought dully. It would be better. That was the only reason he'd let Belle go. He couldn't bear to be loved by her, and she refused to marry him without it.

Belle, of all women on earth, deserved to be happy. She deserved to be loved.

The truth was, he had no idea what she'd seen to love in him. He'd taken her from her Texas hometown against her will, and yet she hadn't just gone back with him to New York: she'd done her best to fit into his life and play the role of society wife. He remembered how scared she'd been, but she'd done it anyway. Because he'd asked her to.

She'd redecorated his Upper East Side mansion, turning it from a cold showplace to a warm, cozy home. She'd reorganized his staff, removing the arrogant butler, making the household happier.

Belle had been unbelievably understanding when he'd canceled their wedding hours before the ceremony. She'd even insisted on coming to Spain with him.

"I can't let you face it alone," she'd told him.

But now he was alone, in this cold place.

"It was unpleasant, having her always hovering around us. Such a pushy girl," Nadia said, then gave him a bright smile. "Your father sent me to find you. He wants to discuss how soon you might take over the family's business interests." She gave a hard laugh. "You'll do better than Otilio did, that's for sure."

Santiago turned to her abruptly. "Did you love my brother?"

She blinked. *"Love* him?"

"Did you?"

Nadia laughed mirthlessly. "Otilio spent most of his time getting drunk and chasing one-night stands. You heard he died from a heart attack?"

"Yes…"

She shook her head. "He was drunk, and crashed his car into the window of a children's charity shop. It was night and the shop was empty, or else he might have taken out a bunch of mothers and their babies, too. That would have been awful…for our family's reputation." She sighed. "But he wanted a beautiful, famous wife, and I wanted a title. We were partners, promoting the brand of our marriage." She shrugged. "We tried not to spend too much time together."

Partners, Santiago thought dully. Just like he'd suggested to Belle. As if it would be remotely appealing to anyone with a beating heart to accept marriage as a business arrangement, as a brand, as a cheap imitation for what was supposed to be the main relationship of one's life.

He could hardly blame her for refusing.

I love you, Belle had whispered in the shadowy light of that threadbare little attic room. *Could you ever love me?*

And he, who was afraid of nothing, had been afraid.

Santiago told himself that he was glad Belle was gone, so he didn't have to see her big eyes tugging at his heart, pulling him to...what?

"The duke wants you to be on a conference call regarding the Cebela merger."

"Right." He hadn't been listening. He followed Nadia out of the library toward his father's study, feeling numb. He liked feeling numb. It was easy. It was safe.

But late that night, he tossed and turned, imagining Belle on his private jet, flying alone across the dark ocean. What if the plane crashed? And she was so close to her due date. What if she went into labor on the plane? Why hadn't he sent a doctor with her?

Because he'd been so eager to get her away from him.

Not eager. Desperate.

"I love you. Could you ever love me?"

When Santiago finally rose at dawn, he felt bleary-eyed, more exhausted than he'd been the night before. It was the middle of the night in New York, but he didn't care. He phoned the pilot. The man politely let him know that they'd arrived safely in New York, and Miss Langtry had been picked up at the airport by his usual driver and the bodyguard.

"Is there a problem?" the pilot asked.

"No problem," Santiago said abruptly and hung up.

He pushed down his emotions, determined to stay numb. He went downstairs in the castle and ate breakfast, reading newspapers, just as Nadia and his father did. Three people silently reading newspapers at a long table in an elegant room filled with flowers, the only sound the rustle of paper and the metallic clank of silverware against china.

Santiago went numbly through the motions of the day, speaking to his father's lawyers, skipping lunch for a long conference call with a Tokyo firm in the process of being sold to Santiago's New York-based conglomerate.

He didn't contact Belle. He tried not to think about her. He was careful not to feel, or let himself think about anything deeper than business. He felt utterly alone. Correction: he didn't feel anything at all.

Exactly as he'd wanted.

At dinner that night in the great hall, both his father and his sister-in-law were lavish in their abuse of the woman who'd left them the previous night.

"Nothing but a gold digger," Nadia said with a smirk. "As soon as I told her you'd always support the baby she left, didn't she?"

Santiago stared at his crystal goblet with the red wine. Red, like blood, which he no longer could feel beating through his heart.

"You did the right thing, *mi hijo*," the old man cackled, then started talking about a potential business acquisition. "But these money-grubbing peasants refuse to sell. Do they not know their place? They refused my generous offer!" He drank more wine. "So we'll just take the company. Have our lawyers send a letter, say we already own the technology. Check the status of the patents. We can ruin him then take his company for almost nothing."

"Clever," Nadia said approvingly.

Santiago didn't say anything. He just stared down at his plate, at the elegant china edged with twenty-four-carat gold. At the solid silver knife beside it. He took a drink of the cool water, closing his eyes.

All he could think of was Belle, who'd tried to save him

from the cold reality of his world. From the cold reality of who he'd become, as dead as the steak on this plate.

Belle had tried to be his sunshine, his warmth, his light. She'd loved him. And for that, he'd sent her away forever. Both her and his unborn daughter.

"You are very quiet, *mi hijo*."

"I'm not very hungry. Excuse me," Santiago muttered and left the dinner table with a noisy scrape of his hard wooden chair. In the darkened hallway, he leaned back against the oak-paneled wall and took a deep breath, trying to contain the acid-like feeling in his chest. In his heart.

Tomorrow, his father intended to hold a press conference to announce that Santiago would be taking the Zoya name as rightfully his, along with the Zoya companies, eventually folding his own companies into the conglomerate. The duke also would start the process of getting Santiago recognized as the heir to his dukedom.

He was going to be the rightful heir, as he'd dreamed of all his life. He was about to have everything he'd ever wanted. Everything he'd ever dreamed of.

And he'd never felt so miserable.

If he closed his eyes in the hallway, he could almost imagine he could smell the light scent of Belle's fragrance, tangerine and soap and sunshine.

Suddenly, he had to know she was doing all right. It was early afternoon in New York. Reaching for his phone, he dialed the number of the kitchen in his Upper East Side mansion.

Mrs. Green answered. "Velazquez residence."

"Hello, Mrs. Green," Santiago said tightly. "I was just wondering if my wife—" Then he remembered Belle was not his wife, not even his fiancée, and never would be again. He cleared his throat. "Please don't disturb Belle. I just wanted to make sure she is doing well after her trip home."

There was a long pause. Her voice sounded half surprised, half sad. "Mr. Velazquez, I thought you knew."

"Knew what?"

"Miss Langtry is at the hospital... She's in labor."

He gripped the phone. "But it's too soon—"

"The doctors are concerned. Didn't she call you?"

No, of course Belle hadn't. Why would she now, when he'd made it so clear he wanted nothing to do with her? Or their baby girl?

"Thank you, Mrs. Green," he said quietly and hung up. He felt sick, dizzy.

"Something wrong?"

Nadia found him in the hallway. He didn't like having her so close, blocking the sunshine and soap with her heavy smell of exotic flowers and musk.

She frowned, looking at the phone still clasped tightly in his hand. "Bad news?"

"Belle's in the hospital."

"She was hurt?"

"She's gone into labor early."

Nadia shrugged. "Maybe things will go badly. Otherwise you're on the hook for the next eighteen years. If you're lucky, they'll both conveniently die and... Stop, you're hurting me!" she suddenly cried.

Looking down, Santiago saw he'd grabbed her by the shoulder in fury, and his fingers were digging into her skin. He abruptly let her go. The skin on his hand still crawled from touching her.

"You are a snake."

Rubbing her shoulder, she said, "We both are. That's why we're perfect for each other."

He ground his teeth. "My brother is barely in his grave."

"It was always you I wanted, Santiago."

"You had a funny way of showing it."

Nadia shrugged, smiling, still certain of her charm.

"I had to be practical, darling. I didn't know then that you would turn out to be worth so much." She tilted her head, fluttering her long eyelashes. "And what can I say? I wanted to be a duchess."

His lip curled. "You disgust me."

Nadia frowned in confusion. "Then why did you send that girl away? Wait. Oh, no." Her lips spread in a shark-like smile. "You *love* her," she taunted. "Sweet, true, *tender* love."

His voice was tight. "I don't."

"You do. And that baby as well. You wanted to kill me just now, for speaking as I did. You love them both."

Santiago stared down blindly at Nadia in the castle hallway.

Love Belle?

Love her?

He'd let her go because it was better for her. That was all. Because she deserved to be happy. And because his family needed him here in Spain.

But he suddenly realized that wasn't the *whole* reason.

For months now, he'd been fighting his feelings for Belle. Because since he was a boy, every time he'd loved someone, they'd stabbed him in the back. He'd vowed to never play the sucker again.

But with Belle, he'd been tempted more than he could resist. He'd come to care about her too much. He'd started feeling that her happiness was more important than his own.

He hadn't sent Belle away so he could be with his family, but because he was fleeing from them.

Belle was his real family. Belle and the baby.

And that fact terrified him.

Santiago's knees trembled beneath him. He felt a wave rip through his soul, cracking it open.

He'd let her go because he was afraid. Afraid of being

vulnerable. Afraid of getting hurt. Afraid of what would happen, who he would become, if he let her love him.

If he loved her back.

"So it's really true." Nadia looked stunned. Her violet eyes narrowed with rage. "You'd choose that little nobody over me?"

Santiago thought of Belle's many joys, her tart honesty, her silliness, her kindness. He thought of her luminous eyes and trembling pink lips as she'd whispered, *"There's only one thing I can give you better than anyone else. My love."*

For the first time, he saw the truth.

When he was a boy, he'd dreamed of being loved by his father, who was rich and powerful and able to command people from a palace. He'd thought if he could just get the duke to call him son, he'd be happy.

As a young man, he'd dreamed of being loved by Nadia, with all her cold beauty and utter lack of pity. He'd thought he'd be happy if he could just win her. Like a trophy.

But today, at thirty-five, he suddenly realized happiness had nothing to do with that kind of so-called love. Wealth and power, physical beauty, what did they have to do with love? Those things didn't last.

Real love did.

Love was having the loyalty and devotion of a kind-hearted, honest woman. A woman who could make you laugh. Who always had your back. Who would protect and adore you through good times and bad. Who cared for your child. A woman who was the heart of your home. The heart of your heart.

There was only one way to be happy: to give everything he had, just as she had done.

He had to be willing to die for her. And even more important: live for her.

Choose me. Love me.

This was what love meant. What family meant. It didn't mean requiring someone to jump through hoops. It didn't mean a lifetime of ignoring someone until you found a use for them, as his father had done. It didn't mean abandoning them when you had a better offer, as Nadia had.

Love meant acceptance. Protection. It meant a lifetime of loyalty through good times and bad.

Love that will last for the rest of my life.

It meant forever.

Santiago sucked in his breath. Belle was his true family. She was his love.

And right now, Belle was in New York. In labor with their baby. Utterly alone.

Turning sharply, he checked for his wallet. He had his passport. He said, "I have to go."

"But—where are you going?" Nadia sounded utterly bewildered. "What about your father's press conference tomorrow?"

"Tell him to forget it."

"You're leaving us?"

Santiago looked at Nadia one last time. "I'm sorry. I don't really care about you, or the old man, either. Be honest. Neither of you really care about me. You ignored me until you had a use for me."

"But you're supposed to be the heir," she wailed. "You're supposed to make me a duchess!"

He snorted, shaking his head. "Tell my father that if he wants an heir, I recommend he marry you himself."

Leaving her behind, Santiago left the castle of Sangovia for good.

He was done with his old childish dreams. There was only one dream he wanted now. One dream that was real, and for that, he would risk everything he had. Heart and soul.

* * *

"Just a little longer…" her friend Letty pleaded.

Belle panted for breath, choked with tears of pain as the contraction finally ended. Stretched out in bed in the private room in the hospital, her legs beneath a blanket, she'd wanted to be brave, so she'd told the doctors she didn't need an epidural. It was a choice she was now sorely regretting.

The labor had already lasted for hours and hours, and it still wasn't time to push. Her daughter, after demanding to be born early, was suddenly taking her time.

"You're doing fine," Letty said, letting go of her hand with a wince, to reach for a cup of ice chips.

Belle took the cup gratefully and sucked on an ice chip, thirsty and exhausted in this brief respite between contractions. She knew that soon, the pain would start again, and hurt so much throughout her body that if she'd had anything left in her stomach, she would have thrown up.

"Thanks for being here with me," she whispered. "I just hope I didn't break your hand."

"It's fine," her friend said, stretching her hand gingerly. Her eyes narrowed. "It's nothing compared to how my hand will hurt after the next time I see Santiago's face. After what he did to you… The bastard! The total bastard!"

"Don't talk about him that way," Belle said weakly as she started to feel the beginnings of the next contraction. "He tried his…best. He couldn't…love me. So he let me go…"

They both turned their heads as they heard some kind of commotion in the hospital hallway, outside the door. It was loud enough to be heard over the medical equipment monitoring her heartbeat and the baby's with beeps and lights.

"What on earth…?" With a frown, the nurse who'd been hovering by Belle's bed went out to check, closing the door behind her.

But the noise only increased. Clutching her belly, Belle panted, "Go see what's happening."

"I'm not leaving you," Letty said stoutly.

"Any…distraction…is better…"

With a reluctant nod, Letty went out into the hall.

And then the yelling really started. For a moment, Belle lost track of her labor pains in her sudden fear that World War III had just started in the hospital hallway.

The shouting abruptly stopped. The door exploded open to reveal the last person she'd expected to see. Standing in the doorway was Santiago, tall and broad-shouldered, his dark eyes bright.

Was she dreaming? Had she died?

As the pain started to crest, she stretched out her hand to him with a choked gasp, and in two seconds, he crossed to her side, putting his hand in hers. With him there, though the pain was worse than ever, suddenly she felt stronger and braver, and knew she could endure. With his hand in hers, she knew she could squeeze as hard as she wanted, and it wouldn't hurt him. She didn't have to hold back. So she didn't. Clutching his hand tight, she screamed through the pain.

When the contraction finally was over, he had tears in his eyes. She was shocked.

"Did I hurt your hand?" she said anxiously.

"My hand?" he looked down at it in bewilderment, then shook his head. "It's fine."

"Then why—"

"Forgive me," he choked out.

Then to her astonished eyes, Santiago fell to his knees beside the hospital bed, next to the blanket that covered her legs. He looked up, his dark eyes searing her soul.

"I was a coward," he whispered. "Afraid to admit what was in my heart. I thought I could send you away and stay safe and numb the rest of my life. I can't." He set his jaw. "I won't."

"What are you saying?" she croaked out.

"You are everything I was ever afraid to want. Everything good. Everything I thought I didn't deserve. I need you, Belle." He took a deep breath. "I love you."

She gaped down at him. "I thought you could only love Nadia…"

"Nadia?" He snorted. "She was a trophy. Like art on my wall or a million-acre ranch. You are no man's trophy, Belle."

Her heart fell. She bit her lip. "No. I'm not."

"You're no trophy," he said in a low, intense voice, "because you're far more. You are my woman. My equal partner. My better half. My love. And if you'll have me," he said humbly, "my wife."

She sucked in her breath. "Your—"

Then the new contraction hit, and she reached desperately for his hand. Rising to his feet, he took it immediately, holding it close, against his heart. The pain built sharply, leaving her gasping for breath.

For what seemed like hours, he held her hand unflinchingly, speaking to her in Spanish and English, calming her with his deep voice, giving her his strength, helping her through the pain. As the contraction finally subsided, the nurse checked her beneath the blanket, then gave a quick nod. "I'm going to get the doctor."

Belle and Santiago were alone. She took a deep breath. "Thank you," she whispered. "For being here. For our baby."

His expression turned sad. "Just for the baby?" he said slowly. "It's too late, isn't it? I've hurt you too badly to ever hope for forgiveness…"

She said in a trembling voice, "Do you really love me?"

Sudden, shocked hope lit his dark eyes.

"With everything I have. Everything I am. I love you." Leaning over the hospital bed, he kissed her sweaty forehead tenderly. "Love me," he whispered. "Forgive me. Marry me."

Belle wondered if she was dreaming. Then she decided she didn't care. "Yes."

He drew back, looking down at her with joy. "You'll marry me?"

Wordlessly, she nodded. Rushing to fling open the door, he called two people inside: a man dressed in a plain black suit and Letty, following behind, holding a bag from the hospital gift shop.

"This is John Alvarez, the hospital pastor," Santiago told her. "He's going to marry us."

Her jaw dropped. "Right now?"

"What, are you busy?" he teased.

She snorted, then grew serious. "But…what about the big wedding you wanted?"

"We already have a license. I don't want to live another moment without you as my wife." He cupped her cheek. "I love you, Belle."

A slow-rising smile lifted her lips.

"I love you too," she whispered, tears falling down her face unheeded. Pulling on his hand, she brought him closer to the hospital bed and kissed him, laughing her happiness. Then she groaned, as she felt the next contraction begin to rise. "But we'd better do this fast."

And so it was that, plain gold bands from the hospital gift shop were slipped within minutes on both their hands, and they were declared man and wife. And just in time.

"Anyone that's not family, get out!" the nurse said, shooing the pastor and Letty into the hallway. In that moment, the doctor hurried into the room.

"All right, Belle," the doctor said, smiling. "Are you ready to push?"

Forty-five minutes later, their daughter, named Emma Jamie Velazquez after the baby's grandmother and grandfather, was brought into this world. A short while later, as Belle watched her husband—her *husband!*—hold their daughter, who was a fat eight pounds ten ounces, tenderly in his arms, she was overwhelmed with happiness.

"Someone wants to meet you," Santiago said, smiling, and gently placed their newborn daughter in Belle's arms.

As she looked down at their precious baby, the miracle she'd once thought she could never have, tears fell from Belle's eyes that she didn't even try to hide. She whispered, "She's so beautiful."

"Like her mother," Santiago said. Leaning down, he kissed her forehead with infinite tenderness, then kissed their sleeping baby's. He looked down at Belle—his *wife*—in the hospital bed. "I love you, Mrs. Velazquez."

She caught her breath at hearing her name for the first time.

Letty peeked around the door into the room to make sure it was safe, then entered, beaming at the baby before she turned to Santiago. "Um, you forgive me for slapping you earlier, right? I feel kind of bad about it now."

"I had it coming," Santiago said, adjusting his jaw a little ruefully. "Thanks for helping with the rings."

Letty grinned. "No problem. It was easy. It was either gold bands or the candy ones. Hey, you two lovebirds, there was one part of the wedding the pastor had to cut when we got kicked out." Letty looked between them. "You may now kiss the bride."

Santiago looked down at Belle with a gleam in his black eyes. "The perfect end to a perfect day."

Belle smiled through her tears.

Once, she'd thought that all her chances for love and happiness had passed her by. She'd thought that her choice to take care of her brothers instead of herself, to sacrifice her own dreams for others, meant that she'd ended her own chance for a bright future.

Now she realized that life wasn't like that.

Every day could be a new start. Every day could be a fresh miracle. And today, the first day of their marriage, the first day of her daughter's life, she knew it wasn't the end of anything. As her husband lowered his head to kiss her in a private vow that would last the rest of their lives, she knew it was all just beginning.

Santiago got married in a quick hospital ceremony just minutes before his baby was born, and his two best friends never let him forget it.

"And you said you'd never get married in some tacky quick wedding," said Darius Kyrillos, who'd married at City Hall.

"You said you'd never get married at all," said his friend Kassius Black, who'd wed at an over-the-top grand ceremony in New Orleans.

Santiago grinned. "A man can change his mind, can't he?"

He was on his third helping of Texas-style barbecue, and the three men were sitting across a huge sofa in a corner of the ballroom of his Upper East Side mansion. Officially, it was a party to celebrate the christening of six-week-old Emma. Unofficially, it was also a wedding reception. The house was crowded, decidedly a family affair filled with friends and relatives, including Belle's two brothers who'd come up to New York for the event, and neighbors, employees and their families. For dinner, they'd had champagne, beer, barbecue, corn on the cob and homemade ice cream. It was November, the time of Thanksgiving. But Belle had definite ideas about how she wanted this party to be.

"Fun like home," she'd said with a grin.

So there was a bluegrass band playing, to the mild shock

of the foreign dignitaries that had been invited. But they seemed to like it, and even strangers had become friends, with people dancing and kids running around. And did he actually see someone's golden retriever running madly across the house…?

The only family not in attendance was his father, the Duke of Sangovia, who had recently, and rather shockingly, wed his former daughter-in-law, the famous movie star. Another marriage "partnership." Santiago shuddered thinking of it. And those were the people he might have spent his life with, like a prison sentence, if Belle hadn't saved him. If she hadn't taught him to be brave enough to risk his heart and soul.

If she hadn't taught him what love actually meant.

Now, as the three husbands sat together, drinking frosty mugs of beer and watching the crowd, Santiago looked down at his daughter, who'd fallen asleep in his arms. After six weeks, he was starting to feel like a pro as a dad.

Kassius and Darius, who'd also brought their wives and children to the party, looked down at the fat baby in Santiago's arms.

"Babies are adorable," Kassius said.

"Especially when they're sleeping," Darius said.

"That's what I meant," he said.

"To sleeping babies—" Santiago raised his beer mug "—and beautiful wives." They all clinked glasses. Softly, so as not to wake the baby.

Across the crowd, Santiago saw Belle, and as always, he lost his breath.

She was beautiful—the center of this house as she was the center of his world. Her long dark hair tumbled over her shoulders, over her curvaceous body in the soft red dress. As she felt his glance, their eyes locked across the crowd. Electricity raced through his body.

Santiago had spent his whole childhood dreaming of

having a place in the world. A home. A family. It had come true, just not in the way he'd expected.

He hadn't been born into this family. He'd created it. He and Belle together. From the moment they'd fallen into bed and accidentally conceived a child.

Had it been an accident? he suddenly wondered. Or was it possible he'd always known, from the moment he first met Belle, that she would be the one to break the spell?

Because that was what she'd done. It was funny. Belle had once compared him to a knight, saying he'd slain dragons for Nadia like something out of a fairy tale. But he hadn't. All he'd done was make a lot of money. He'd never risked anything. He'd never saved anyone.

Not like Belle.

She was the true knight. She was the one who'd slain the dragon. She was the one who'd saved his soul. He would always be grateful for that miracle.

Tomorrow, they would leave on a two-month honeymoon—bringing baby Emma, of course—on a trip around the world. Belle had planned this reception, so he'd insisted on organizing the honeymoon. "What are your top five dream travel destinations?"

"Paris," she'd said instantly, then "London." She'd bitten her lip. "The Christmas markets in Germany. The neon lights of Tokyo. Or maybe—" she'd tilted her head "—a beach vacation in Australia? The Great Barrier Reef?" With a sigh, she'd shaken her head. "I'm glad I'm not the one who has to decide!"

But as it turned out neither did he. Because they were going to see everything. Emma would be a very well-traveled baby before she even had her first bite of baby food.

Their family would see the world together, all of them for the first time. It would all be new to Santiago, too. Because this time, he'd be leading with his heart.

In the ballroom, Belle came up to the sofa, smiling. "You boys having fun?"

"Yes," they all said cheerily, and in Kassius's and Darius's case a little tipsily. Belle grinned at Santiago.

"Want to help cut the cake?"

"Absolutely." He rose to his feet, their sleeping baby still tucked securely against his chest. With his free hand, he suddenly pulled his wife close and kissed her. Not a little kiss, either. He kissed her long and hard, until they started getting catcalls and whistles and cheers from the guests, and he felt her tremble in his arms.

She drew back, her eyes big. "What was that for?"

"It's the start of a whole life loving you," he whispered, cupping her cheek. "I wanted to do it right."

Belle leaned her head against his shoulder, and for a moment, the three of them stood nestled together. Then they heard someone yell, "Come quick! The kids are coming at the cake with spoons, and there's a dog close behind!"

Laughing, Santiago and Belle, with their sleeping baby, went to cut the cake. And as they were toasted and cheered by their family and friends, he looked down tenderly at his wife, who smiled back at him, her eyes shining with love. And Santiago knew, for the first time in his life, that he was finally home.

* * * * *

HER LITTLE
SPANISH SECRET

LAURA IDING

This book is dedicated to the Milwaukee
WisRWA group, thanks to all of you for your
on-going support.

PROLOGUE

Four and a half years earlier...

KAT had never seen so much blood—it pooled on the floor and stained the walls of the O.R. suite. Dr. Miguel Vasquez, along with two other trauma surgeons, had worked as hard as they could to stop the bleeding but to no avail. Their young, pregnant patient and her unborn baby had died.

After the poor woman's body had been sent to the morgue, Kat was left alone to finish putting the supplies and equipment away while the housekeepers cleaned up the blood. Only once they were finished did she head over to the staff locker room. Thankfully, her shift was over, she was exhausted. Yet as tired as she was physically, she was emotionally keyed up, and couldn't get the horrific scene from the O.R. out of her mind. They hadn't had a case like that in a long time.

After she changed out of her scrubs into a pair of well-worn jeans and a short-sleeved sweater, she found Dr. Vasquez sitting in the staff lounge, holding his head in his hands. He looked so upset and dejected that she stopped—unable to simply walk away.

"Please don't torture yourself over this," she urged

softly, as she sank down beside him on the sofa close enough that their shoulders brushed. "Her death wasn't your fault."

Miguel slowly lifted and turned his head to look at her, his eyes full of agony. "I should have called the rest of the team in earlier."

"You called them as soon as you discovered her abdomen was full of blood and they came as soon as they could," she corrected. "No one knew she was pregnant, it was too early to tell."

"I should have examined her more closely down in the trauma bay," he muttered, more to himself than to her. "Then we would have known."

"Do you really think that would have made a difference?" she asked softly. "Even if the other two surgeons had been notified earlier, they wouldn't have been able to come right away. Dr. Baccus said they were resuscitating a patient in the I.C.U. All of us in the O.R. suite did the best we could."

He stared at her for a long moment, and then sighed. "I can't help thinking about what I should have done differently. I know we can't save every patient, but she was just so young. And pregnant. I can't help feeling I failed her."

She put her hand on his arm, trying to offer some reassurance. "If three of the best trauma surgeons in the whole hospital couldn't save her or her baby, then it wasn't meant to be."

A ghost of a smile played along the edges of his mouth, and she was glad she'd been able to make him feel a little better. Because what she'd said was true. Everyone talked about Miguel's skill in the O.R. He could have stayed here in the U.S. once his fellowship was finished, even though he'd made it clear that wasn't part of his plan.

She reluctantly slid her hand from his arm and rose to her feet. But she'd only taken two steps when he stopped her.

"Katerina?"

She hesitated and turned to look back at him, surprised and secretly pleased he'd remembered her first name. They'd operated on dozens of patients together, but while she'd always been keenly aware of Miguel, she had never been absolutely sure he'd noticed her the same way. "Yes?"

"Do you have plans for tonight? If not, would you join me? We could get a bite to eat or something."

She wasn't hungry, but could tell Miguel didn't want to be alone, and suddenly she didn't either. Word amongst the O.R. staff was that Miguel wasn't in the market for a relationship since his time in the U.S. was limited, but she ignored the tiny warning flickering in the back of her mind. "I don't have any plans for tonight, and I'd love to have dinner." *Or something.*

"Muy bien." He rose to his feet and held out his hand. She took it and suppressed a shiver when a tingle of awareness shot up her arm.

But she didn't pull away. Instead, she stayed close at his side while they left the hospital together.

CHAPTER ONE

"Down, Mama. *Down!*"

"Soon, Tommy. I promise." Katerina Richardson fought a wave of exhaustion and tightened her grip on her wriggly son. She couldn't imagine anything more torturous than being stuck in a plane for sixteen hours with an active soon-to-be four-year-old. She didn't even want to think of the longer flight time on the return trip.

Plenty of time to worry about that, later. For now they'd finally arrived in Seville, Spain. And she desperately needed to get to the hospital to see how her half sister was doing after being hit by a car. The information from Susan Horton, the coordinator for the study abroad program, had been sketchy at best.

"I can't believe the stupid airline lost my luggage," her best friend, Diana Baylor, moaned as they made their way out of the airport to the line of people waiting for taxis. "It's so hot here in April compared to Cambridge, Massachusetts. I'm already sweating—I can't imagine staying in these same clothes for very long."

Kat felt bad for her friend, who'd only come on this trip in the first place as a favor to her, but what could she do? Diana's lost luggage was the least of her concerns. "Don't worry, I'll share my stuff or we'll buy what you need."

"Down, Mama. Down!" Tommy's tone, accompanied by his wiggling, became more insistent.

"Okay, but you have to hold my hand," Kat warned her son, as she put him on his feet. She'd let him run around in the baggage claim area while they'd waited for their luggage, but even that hadn't put a dent in his energy level. She was grateful he'd slept on the plane, even though she hadn't. Kat grabbed hold of his hand before he could make a beeline for the road. "Stay next to me, Tommy."

He tugged on her hand, trying to go in the opposite direction from where they needed to wait for a taxi. Thank heavens the line was moving fast. Her son was as dark as she was blonde and if she had a nickel for every person who'd asked her if he was adopted, she'd be rich. Even here, she could feel curious eyes on them.

"No, Tommy. This way. Look, a car! We're going to go for a ride!"

His attention diverted, Tommy readily climbed into the cab after Diana. They all squished into the back seat for the short ride to their hotel. "Hesperia Hotel, please," she told the taxi driver.

"Hesperia? *No comprendo* Hesperia." Their cab driver shook his head as he pulled out into traffic, waving his hand rather impatiently. *"No comprendo."*

Kat refused to panic and quickly rummaged through her carry-on bag to pull out the hotel confirmation document. She handed it to him so he could read the name of the hotel for himself. He looked at the paper and made a sound of disgust. "Es-peer-ria," he said, emphasizing the Spanish pronunciation. "Esperia Hotel."

Properly chastised, she belatedly remembered from her two years of high-school Spanish that the H was silent. Being in Spain brought back bittersweet memories of Tommy's father, especially during their three-hour layover in Madrid. She'd briefly toyed with the thought of trying to find Miguel, but had then realized her idea was ludicrous. Madrid was a huge city and she had no idea where to even start, if he'd even be there, which she seriously doubted. He may have studied there but it was possible he'd moved on. "*Sí*. Hesperia Hotel, *gracias.*"

The taxi driver mumbled something unintelligible and probably uncomplimentary in Spanish, under his breath. Kat ignored him.

"Are you going to the hospital today?" Diana asked with a wide yawn. "I'm voting for a nap first."

"I doubt Tommy will sleep any time soon," she reminded her friend. "And, yes, I'm going to head to the hospital as soon as we get the hotel room secured. I'm sorry, but you'll have to watch Tommy for a while."

"I know," Diana said quickly. "I don't mind." Kat knew Diana wouldn't renege on her duties, seeing as Kat had been the one to pay for her friend's airfare, along with footing the hotel bill. Kat hadn't minded as she'd needed someone to help watch over her son. "Wow, Kat, take a look at the architecture of that building over there. Isn't it amazing?"

"Yeah, amazing." Kat forced a smile, because Diana was right—the view was spectacular. Yet the thrill of being in Europe for the first time in her life couldn't make her forget the reason they were there. The knot in her stomach tightened as she wondered what she'd discover when she went to the hospital. Susan Horton, the director of the study abroad program at Seville University, had called just thirty-six hours ago, to let her know that her younger half sister, Juliet, had a serious head injury and was too sick to be flown back to the U.S. for care.

Kat had immediately made arrangements to fly over to Seville in order to be there for her sister.

She and Juliet hadn't been particularly close. And not just because of the seven-year age gap. They had different fathers and for some reason Juliet had always seemed to resent Kat. Their respective fathers had both abandoned their mother, which should have given them something in common. After their mother had been diagnosed with pancreatic cancer, Kat had promised her mother she'd look after Juliet.

Juliet had gone a little wild after their mother's death, but had settled down somewhat after she'd finished her second year of college. At the ripe old age of twenty-one, Juliet had insisted on studying abroad for the spring semester of her junior year. Kat had been forced to pick up a lot of call weekends in order to pay for the program, but she'd managed. To be fair, Juliet had come up with a good portion of the money herself.

Kat felt guilty now about how she'd been secretly relieved to put her younger sister on a plane to Spain. But even if she'd tried to talk Juliet out of going, it wouldn't have worked. Juliet would only have resented her even more.

How had the accident happened? All she'd been told

was that Juliet had run out into the street and had been hit by a car, but she didn't know anything further.

Getting to the hotel didn't take long, although there was another hassle as she figured out the dollar to Euro exchange in order to pay the cranky cab driver. As soon as Diana and Tommy were settled in the hotel room, Kat asked the front-desk clerk for directions to the hospital. She managed to figure out how to get there on the metro, which wasn't very different than using the subway back home.

Seville's teaching hospital was larger than she'd expected and that gave her hope that Juliet was getting good medical and nursing care. Kat found her sister in their I.C.U and walked in, only to stop abruptly when she saw Juliet was connected to a ventilator. Her stomach clenched even harder when she noted several dark bruises and small lacerations marring her sister's pale skin.

"Dear heaven," she breathed, trailing her gaze from her sister up to the heart monitor. She'd done a year-long stint in the I.C.U before going to the O.R. so she'd known what to expect, but had hoped that Juliet might have improved during the time it had taken her to make the travel arrangements and actually arrive in Seville.

A nurse, dressed head to toe in white, complete with nurse's cap on her dark hair, came into the room behind her. Kat blinked back tears and turned to the nurse. "How is she? Has her condition improved? What is the extent of her injury? Can I speak to the doctor?"

The nurse stared at her blankly for a moment and then began talking in rapid Spanish, none of which Kat could understand.

Kat wanted to cry. She desperately paged through the English/Spanish dictionary she held, trying to look up words in Spanish to explain what she wanted to know. *"¿Donde esta el doctor? ¿Habla Ingles?"* she finally asked. Where is the doctor? Speak English?

The nurse spun around and left the room.

Kat sank into a chair next to Juliet's bed, gently clasping her half sister's hand in hers. Maybe the age difference, and completely opposite personalities, had kept them from being close, but Juliet was still her sister. With their mother gone, they only had each other.

She had to believe Juliet would pull through this. Her sister was young and strong, surely she'd be fine.

Kat put her head down on the edge of Juliet's bed, closing her eyes just for a moment, trying to combat the deep fatigue of jet lag and her fear regarding the seriousness of her sister's injuries.

She didn't think she'd fallen asleep, but couldn't be sure how much time had passed when she heard a deep male voice, thankfully speaking in English. She lifted her head and prised her heavy eyelids open.

"I understand you have questions regarding the condition of Juliet Campbell?"

"Yes, thank you." She quickly rose to her feet and blinked the grit from her eyes as she turned to face the doctor.

His familiar facial features made the room gyrate wildly, and she had to grasp the edge of her sister's side rail for support. "Miguel?" she whispered in shock, wondering if she was dreaming. Had thoughts of Tommy's father conjured up a mirage? Or was it just the doctor's Hispanic features, dark hair falling rakishly over his forehead, deep brown eyes gazing into hers, that were so achingly familiar?

"Katerina." His eyes widened in surprise, and she couldn't help feeling relieved to know she wasn't the only one knocked off balance at this chance meeting. For several long seconds they simply stared at each other across the room. Slowly, he smiled, relieving part of the awkwardness. "What a pleasant surprise to see you again. How are you?"

She tightened her grip on the bed rail behind her because her knees threatened to give away. "I'm fine, thanks." She struggled to keep her tone friendly, even though for one beautiful night they'd been far more than just friends. Yet despite her fanciful thoughts during the Madrid layover, she hadn't really expected to see Miguel again.

He looked good. Better than good. Miguel was taller than most Latino men, with broad shoulders and a golden skin tone that showcased his bright smile. His dark eyes were mesmerizing. If not for his full name, Dr. Miguel Vasquez, embroidered on his white lab coat—she'd for sure think this was a dream.

She knew Juliet's condition needed to be her primary concern, but she had so many other questions she wanted to ask him. "I'm surprised to find you here in Seville. I thought you lived in Madrid?"

He didn't answer right away, and she thought she saw a flash of guilt shadow his dark eyes. She glanced away, embarrassed. She didn't want him feeling guilty for the night they'd shared together. Or for leaving so abruptly when notified of his father's illness. It wasn't as if they'd been dating or anything.

Neither was it his fault she'd let her feelings spin out of control that night.

When she'd discovered she was pregnant, she'd called his cell phone, the only number she'd had, but the number had already been out of service. She'd assumed he hadn't kept his old American phone once he'd returned to Spain. She'd looked for him on several social media sites, but hadn't found him. After about six months she'd stopped trying.

"I live here," he said simply. "My family's olive farm is just twenty minutes outside Seville."

"I see," she said, although she really didn't. Obviously, she hadn't known much about Miguel's family. She could hardly picture him growing up on an olive farm. She'd simply assumed because he was a Madrid exchange student that he'd lived there. She forced a smile, wishing they could recapture the easy camaraderie they'd once shared. "How's your father?"

"He passed away three and a half years ago." The shadows in Miguel's eyes betrayed his grief.

"I'm sorry," she murmured helplessly. She'd known that Miguel had needed to return to Spain when his father had been sick, but she was a little surprised that he'd stayed here, even after his father had passed away.

During the night they'd shared together he'd confided about how he dreamed of joining Doctors Without Borders. When she hadn't been able to get in touch with Miguel once she'd discovered she was pregnant, she'd imagined him working in some distant country.

Why hadn't he followed his dream? He'd told her about how he was only waiting to be finished with his family obligations. And his father had passed away three and a half years ago. He should have been long gone by now.

Not that Miguel's choices were any of her business.

Except, now that he was here, how was she going to tell him about their son?

Panic soared, squeezing the air from her lungs. She struggled to take a deep breath, trying to calm her jagged nerves. Right now she needed to focus on her sister. She pulled herself together with an effort. "Will you please tell me about Juliet's head injury? How bad is it? What exactly is her neuro status?"

"Your sister's condition is serious, but stable. She responds to pain now, which she wasn't doing at first. She does have a subarachnoid hemorrhage that we are monitoring very closely."

A subarachnoid hemorrhage wasn't good news, but she'd been prepared for that. "Is she following commands?" Kat asked.

"Not yet, but she's young, Katerina. She has a good chance of getting through this."

She gave a tight nod, wanting to believe him. "I know. I'm hopeful that she'll wake up soon."

"Katerina, I have to get to surgery as I have a patient waiting, but I would like to see you again. Would you please join me for dinner tonight? Say around eight-thirty or nine?"

She blinked in surprise and tried to think of a graceful way out of the invitation. She knew he was asking her out from some sense of obligation, because they'd spent one intense night together.

But she needed time to get the fog of fatigue out of her mind. Time to think about if and when to share the news about Tommy. Obviously Miguel deserved to know the truth, but what about Tommy? Did he deserve a father who didn't want him? A father who'd made it clear he wasn't looking for a family?

She didn't know what to do.

"I'm sorry, but I'm sure I'll be asleep by then," she murmured, averting her gaze to look at her sister. "I just flew in today and I'm a bit jet-lagged."

She steeled herself against the flash of disappointment in his eyes. Juliet's well-being came first. And Tommy's was a close second.

As far as she was concerned, Miguel Vasquez would just have to wait.

Miguel couldn't believe Katerina Richardson was actually here, in Seville.

He allowed his gaze to roam over her, branding her image on his mind. She wasn't beautiful in the classical sense, but he'd always found her attractive with her peaches and cream complexion and long golden blonde hair that she normally wore in a ponytail. Except for that one night, when he'd run his fingers through the silk tresses.

To this day he couldn't explain why he'd broken his cardinal rule by asking her out. Granted, he'd been devastated over losing their patient, but he'd been determined to avoid emotional entanglements, knowing he was leaving when the year was up. He knew better than to let down his guard, but he'd been very attracted to Katerina and had suspected the feeling was mutual. That night he'd given up his fight to stay away.

But then the news about his father's stroke had pulled

him from Katerina's bed the next morning. He'd rushed
home to Seville. His father's condition had been worse
than he'd imagined, and his father had ultimately died
twelve painful months later. His mother was already
gone, and during his father's illness his younger brother,
Luis, had started drinking. Miguel had been forced to
put his own dreams on hold to take over the olive farm,
which had been in the Vasquez family for generations,
until he could get Luis sobered up.

His visceral reaction to seeing Katerina again stunned
him. He hadn't allowed himself to miss her. Besides, he
only had three months left on his contract here at the
hospital and he'd be finally free to join Doctors Without
Borders.

And this time, nothing was going to stop him. Not
his brother Luis. And certainly not Katerina.

He shook off his thoughts with an effort. Logically
he knew he should accept her excuse, but he found himself pressing the issue. "Maybe a light meal after siesta,
then? Certainly you have to eat some time."

There was a wariness reflected in her green eyes
that hadn't been there in the past. He wondered what
had changed in the four and a half years they'd been
apart. He was relieved to note she wasn't wearing a
wedding ring even though her personal life wasn't any
of his business. He couldn't allow himself to succumb
to Katerina's spell—he refused to make the same mistakes his father had.

"You've described my sister's head injury, but is
there anything else? Other injuries I need to be aware
of?" she asked, changing the subject.

He dragged his attention to his patient. "Juliet was

hit on the right side. Her right leg is broken in two places and we had to operate to get the bones aligned properly. She has several rib fractures and some internal bleeding that appears to be resolving. Her head injury is the greatest of our concerns. Up until late yesterday she wasn't responding at all, even to pain. The fact that there is some response now gives us hope she may recover."

Katerina's pale skin blanched even more, and his gut clenched when he noted the tears shimmering in her bright green eyes. They reminded him, too much, about the night they'd shared. An intense, intimate, magical night that had ended abruptly with his brother's phone call about their father. She'd cried for him when he'd been unable to cry for himself.

"When can she be transported back to the United States?" she asked.

The instinctive protest at the thought of her leaving surprised him. What was wrong with him? He wrestled his emotions under control. "Not until I'm convinced her neurological status has truly stabilized," he reluctantly admitted.

Katerina nodded, as if she'd expected that response. "Are you my sister's doctor? Or just one of the doctors here who happen to speak English?" she asked. Her gaze avoided his, staying at the level of his chest.

"Yes, I'm your sister's doctor. As you know, I'm a surgeon who does both general and trauma surgery cases."

"Do any of the nurses speak English?"

Seville didn't have the same tourist draw as Madrid or Barcelona, which meant not as many of the locals spoke English. Miguel had originally learned English from his American mother, who'd taught him before she'd died. He'd learned even more English during his time at the University of Madrid. In fact, he'd earned the opportunity to live and study medicine in the U.S. at Harvard University.

There he'd ultimately become a doctor. And met Katerina. He dragged his thoughts out of the past. "No, the nurses don't speak much English, I'm afraid."

She closed her eyes and rubbed her temples, as if she had a pounding headache. Once again he found himself on the verge of offering comfort. But he didn't dare, no matter how much he wanted to.

"I would appreciate periodic updates on my sister's condition whenever you have time to spare from the rest of your patients," she said finally.

The way she turned her back on him, as if to dismiss him, made him scowl. He wanted to demand she look at him, talk to him, but of course there wasn't time. Glancing at his watch only confirmed he was already late for his scheduled surgery. "I'd be happy to give you an update later today, if you have time at, say, four o'clock?" He purposefully gave her the same time he normally ate a late lunch, right after siesta.

She spun around to face him. "But—" She stopped herself and then abruptly nodded. "Of course. Four o'clock would be fine."

He understood she'd only agreed to see him so that she could get updates on her sister, but that didn't stop him from being glad he'd gotten his way on this. "I look forward to seeing you later, then, Katerina," he said softly.

He could barely hide the thrill of anticipation racing through him, knowing he'd see her again soon, as he hurried down to the operating room.

CHAPTER TWO

"So WHAT do you think? Do I really need to tell Miguel about Tommy?" Kat asked, after she'd caught up with Diana and Tommy at the park located right across the street from their hotel. The park was next to a school and seeing all the kids in their navy blue and white uniforms playing on the playground wasn't so different from the preschool Tommy attended back in the U.S.

"I don't think you should do anything yet," Diana advised. "I mean, what do we know about the custody laws in Spain? What if Miguel has the right to take Tommy away from you?"

The very thought made her feel sick to her stomach. "Tommy is a U.S. citizen," she pointed out, striving for logic. "That has to count for something."

"Maybe, maybe not. I don't think you should say anything until we know what we're dealing with. Miguel is a big important doctor at the largest hospital here. Maybe he has connections, friends in high places? I think you need to understand exactly what you're dealing with if you tell him."

Kat sighed, and rubbed her temples, trying to ease the ache. Lack of sleep, worry over Juliet and now seeing Miguel again had all combined into one giant, pounding headache. "And how are we going to find out the child custody laws here? Neither one of us can speak Spanish, so it's not like we can just look up the information on the internet."

"We could check with the American Embassy," Diana said stubbornly.

"I suppose. Except that seems like a lot of work when I'm not even sure Miguel will bother to fight me for Tommy. During our night together he told me his dream was to join Doctors Without Borders. He made it clear he wanted the freedom to travel, not settling down in one place."

"Except here he is in Seville four and a half years later," Diana pointed out reasonably. "Maybe he's changed his mind about his dream?"

"Maybe." She couldn't argue Diana's point. She still found it hard to wrap her mind around the fact that Miguel was here, in Seville. She'd stayed with her sister for another hour or so after he'd left, slightly reassured that Juliet's condition was indeed stable, before she'd come back to the hotel to unpack her things. Seeing Miguel had made her suddenly anxious to find her son.

Tommy was having a great time running around in the park, chasing butterflies. As she watched him, the physical similarities seemed even more acute. She realized the minute Miguel saw Tommy, he'd know the truth without even needing to be told.

Although Miguel wouldn't have to see him, a tiny voice in the back of her mind reminded her. Tommy could stay here with Diana and in a couple of days hopefully Juliet would be stable enough to be sent back to the U.S. Miguel didn't need to know anything about their son.

As soon as the thought formed, she felt a sense of shame. Keeping Tommy's presence a secret would be taking the coward's way out. Diana was worried about the Spanish custody laws, but Kat had other reasons for not wanting to tell Miguel about Tommy. Being intimate with Miguel had touched her in a way she hadn't expected. When she'd discovered she was pregnant, she'd been torn between feeling worried at how she'd manage all alone to secretly thrilled to have a part of Miguel growing inside her.

She knew he hadn't felt the same way about her. Men had sex with women all the time, and lust certainly wasn't love. She knew better than to get emotionally involved. In her experience men didn't remain faithful or stick around for the long haul. Especially when there was the responsibility of raising children. Her father and Juliet's father had proven that fact.

She gave Miguel credit for being upfront and honest about his inability to stay. He hadn't lied to her, hadn't told her what he'd thought she'd wanted to hear. It was her fault for not doing a better job of protecting her heart.

Telling Miguel about Tommy opened up the possibility that she'd have to see Miguel on a regular basis. If they were raising a child together, there would be no way to avoid him. She would have to hide her true feelings every time they were together.

Unless Miguel still didn't want the responsibility of a son? There was a part of her that really hoped so, because then he wouldn't insist on joint custody.

Now she was getting way ahead of herself. Maybe she could tell Miguel about Tommy and reassure him that she didn't need help, financially or otherwise, to raise her son. She and Tommy would be fine on their own. The way they had been for nearly four years.

"Don't agonize over this, Kat. You don't have to tell him this minute, we just got here. Give me a little time to do some research first, okay?"

"I guess," she agreed doubtfully. Diana was clearly concerned, but she was confident that Tommy had rights as an American citizen. "I won't do anything right away, although I really think I'm going to have to tell him eventually. I tried to call him when I discovered I was pregnant, even tried to find him on all the popular social media websites. Now that I know he's here, I need to be honest with him."

"Then why do you look like you're about to cry?" Diana asked.

"Because I'm scared," she murmured, trying to sniffle back her tears. "I couldn't bear it if Miguel tried to fight for custody."

"Okay, let's just say that the Spanish law is the same as the U.S. regarding joint custody. You mentioned he wasn't wearing a wedding ring, but we both know that doesn't always mean much. Miguel might be married or seriously involved in a relationship. Could be the last thing on earth that he wants is to fight for joint custody."

"You're right," she agreed, even though the thought of Miguel being married or involved with someone didn't make her feel any better. "Okay, I need to get a grip. Maybe I'll try talking to Miguel first, try to find out about his personal life before springing the news on him."

Diana nodded eagerly. "Good idea. Meanwhile, I'll see if I can call the U.S. embassy to get more information."

Kat nodded, even though deep down she knew she'd have to tell him. Because Miguel deserved to know. Besides at some point Tommy was going to ask about his father. She refused to lie to her son.

The spear in her heart twisted painfully and tears pricked her eyes. As difficult as it was to be a single mother, she couldn't bear the thought of sending Tommy off to be with his father in a far-away country. Although she knew she could come with Tommy, no matter how difficult it would be to see Miguel again.

If Miguel was truly planning to join Doctors Without Borders, maybe all of this worry would be for nothing. She and Tommy would go back home and continue living their lives.

Tommy tripped and fell, and she leaped off the park bench and rushed over, picking him up and lavishing him with kisses before he could wail too loudly. "There, now, you're okay, big guy."

"Hurts," he sniffed, rubbing his hands over his eyes and smearing dirt all over his face.

"I know, but Mommy will kiss it all better." Holding her son close, nuzzling his neck, she desperately hoped Miguel would be honorable enough to do what was best for Tommy.

Kat returned to the hotel room to change her clothes and freshen up a bit before going back to the hospital to see

Juliet and Miguel. She'd left Diana and Tommy at the local drugstore, picking out a few necessities for Diana to hold her over until her luggage arrived. They'd also picked up two prepaid disposable phones, so they could keep in touch with each other. After fifteen minutes, and with the help of one shopkeeper who did speak a bit of English, they had the phones activated and working.

The metro was far more crowded towards the end of the workday, forcing her to stand, clinging to the overhead pole.

At her stop, she got off the cramped carriage and walked the short distance to the hospital. The temperature had to be pushing eighty and by the time she arrived, she was hot and sweaty again.

So much for her attempt to look nice for Miguel.

Ridiculous to care one way or the other how she looked. Men weren't exactly knocking down her door, especially once they realized she had a son. Not that she was interested in dating.

She hadn't been with anyone since spending the night with Miguel. At first because she'd been pregnant and then because being a single mother was all-consuming. But she didn't regret a single minute of having Tommy.

In the hospital, she went up to the I.C.U. and paused outside Juliet's doorway, relieved to discover Miguel wasn't there, waiting for her. Her sister had been turned so that she was lying on her right side facing the doorway, but otherwise her condition appeared unchanged.

She crossed over and took Juliet's hand in hers. "Hi, Jules, I'm back. Can you hear me? Squeeze my hand if you can hear me."

Juliet's hand didn't move within hers.

"Wiggle your toes. Can you wiggle your toes for me?"

Juliet's non-broken leg moved, but Kat couldn't figure out if the movement had been made on purpose or not. When she asked a second time, the leg didn't move, so she assumed the latter.

She pulled up a chair and sat down beside her sister, glancing curiously at the chart hanging off the end of the bed. She didn't bother trying to read it, as it would all be in Spanish, but she wished she could read the medical information for herself, to see how Juliet was progressing.

She kept up her one-sided conversation with her sister for the next fifteen minutes or so. Until she ran out of things to say.

"Katerina?"

The way Miguel said her name brought back a fresh wave of erotic memories of their night together and she tried hard to paste a *friendly* smile on her face, before rising to her feet and facing him. "Hello, Miguel. How did your surgery go this morning?"

"Very well, thanks. Would you mind going across the street to the restaurant to talk?" he asked. "I've missed lunch."

She instinctively wanted to say no, but that seemed foolish and petty so she nodded. She glanced back at her sister, leaning over the side rail to talk to her. "I love you, sis. See you soon," she said, before moving away to meet Miguel in the doorway.

As they walked down the stairs to the main level of the hospital, he handed her a stack of papers. "I spent some time translating bits of Juliet's chart for you, so that you can get a sense as to how she's doing."

Her jaw dropped in surprise and for a moment she couldn't speak, deeply touched by his kind consideration. "Thank you," she finally murmured, taking the paperwork he offered. Miguel had often been thoughtful of others and she was glad he hadn't changed during the time they's spent apart. She couldn't imagine where he'd found the time to translate her sister's chart for her between seeing patients and doing surgery, but she was extremely grateful for his efforts.

He put his hand on the small of her back, guiding her towards the restaurant across the street from the hospital. The warmth of his hand seemed to burn through her thin cotton blouse, branding her skin. She was keenly aware of him, his scent wreaking havoc with her concentration, as they made their way across the street. There was outdoor seating beneath cheerful red and white umbrellas and she gratefully sat in the shade, putting the table between them.

The waiter came over and the two men conversed in rapid-fire Spanish. She caught maybe one familiar word out of a dozen.

"What would you like to drink, Katerina?" Miguel asked. "Beer? Wine? Soft drink?"

"You ordered a soft drink, didn't you?" she asked.

He flashed a bright smile and nodded. "You remember some Spanish, no?" he asked with clear approval.

"Yes, *muy poco*, very little," she agreed. "I'll have the same, please."

Miguel ordered several *tapas*, the Spanish form of appetizers, along with their soft drinks. When the food arrived, she had no idea what she was eating, but whatever it was it tasted delicious.

"Do you want to review Juliet's chart now?" he asked. "I can wait and answer your questions."

"I'll read it later, just tell me what you know." She wanted to hear from him first. Besides, there was no way she'd be able to concentrate on her sister's chart with him sitting directly across from her.

He took his time, sipping his drink, before answering. "Juliet has begun moving around more, which is a good sign. She will likely start to intermittently follow commands soon. We have done a CT scan of her brain earlier this morning and the area of bleeding appears to be resolving slowly."

She nodded, eating another of the delicious *tapas* on the plate between them. There were olives too, and she wondered if they were from Miguel's family farm. "I'm glad. I guess all we can do right now is wait and see."

"True," he agreed. He helped himself to more food as well. "Katerina, how is your mother doing? Wasn't she scheduled to have surgery right before I left the States?"

She nodded, her appetite fading. "Yes. The result of her surgery showed stage-four pancreatic cancer. She died a couple months later." Despite the fear of being a single mother, at the time of her mother's passing, her pregnancy had been one of the few bright spots in her life. Things had been difficult until Juliet had gone off to college. Thankfully, her friend Diana had been there for her, even offering to be her labor coach.

"I'm sorry," he murmured, reaching across the table to capture her hand in his. "We both lost our parents about the same time, didn't we?"

"Yes. We did." His fingers were warm and strong around hers, but she gently tugged her hand away and reached for her glass. She tried to think of a way to ask him if he was married or seeing someone, without sounding too interested.

"I have thought of you often these past few years," Miguel murmured, not seeming to notice how she was struggling with her secret. He took her left hand and brushed his thumb across her bare ring finger. "You haven't married?"

She slowly shook her head. There was only one man who'd asked her out after Tommy had been born. He was another nurse in the operating room, one of the few male nurses who worked there. She'd been tempted to date him because he was a single parent, too, and would have been a great father figure for Tommy, but in the end she hadn't been able to bring herself to accept his offer.

She hadn't felt anything for Wayne other than friendship. And as much as she wanted a father for Tommy, she couldn't pretend to feel something she didn't.

Too bad she couldn't say the same about her feelings toward Miguel. Seeing him again made her realize that she still felt that same spark of attraction, the same awareness that had been there when they'd worked together in the U.S. Feelings that apparently hadn't faded over time.

"What about you, Miguel?" she asked, taking the opening he'd offered, as she gently pulled her hand away. "Have you found a woman to marry?"

"No, you know my dream is to join Doctors Without Borders. But I can't leave until I'm certain my brother has the Vasquez olive farm back on its feet. Luis has a few—ah—problems. Things were not going well here at home during the time I was in the U.S." A shadow of guilt flashed in his eyes, and she found herself wishing she could offer him comfort.

"Not your fault, Miguel," she reminded him, secretly glad to discover he hadn't fallen in love and married a beautiful Spanish woman. "How old is Luis?"

"Twenty-six now," he said. "But too young back then to take on the responsibility of running the farm. I think the stress of trying to hold everything together was too much for my father." He stared at his glass for a long moment. "Maybe if I had been here, things would have been different."

She shrugged, not nearly as reassured as she should be at knowing his dream of joining Doctors Without Borders hadn't changed. She should be thrilled with the news. Maybe this would be best for all of them. He'd go do his mission work, leaving her alone to raise Tommy. Miguel could come back in a few years, when Tommy was older, to get to know his son.

All she had to do was to tell him the truth.

Diana wanted her to wait, but she knew she had to tell him or the secret would continue to eat at her. She'd never been any good at lying and didn't want to start now. She swallowed hard and braced herself. "Miguel, there's something important I need to tell you," she began.

"Miguel!" A shout from across the street interrupted them. She frowned and turned in time to see a handsome young man, unsteady on his feet, waving wildly at Miguel.

"Luis." He muttered his brother's name like a curse

half under his breath. "Excuse me for a moment," he said as he rose to his feet.

She didn't protest, but watched as Miguel crossed over towards his brother, his expression stern. The two of them were quickly engrossed in a heated conversation that didn't seem it would end any time soon.

Kat sat back, sipping her soft drink and thinking how wrong it was for her to be grateful for the reprieve.

"Luis, you shouldn't be drinking!" Miguel shouted in Spanish, barely holding his temper in check.

"Relax, it's Friday night. I've been slaving out at the farm all week—don't I get time to have fun too? Hey, who's the pretty Americana?" he asked with slurred speech, as he looked around Miguel towards where Katerina waited.

"She's a friend from the U.S.," he answered sharply. "But that's not the point. I thought we had an agreement? You promised to stay away from the taverns until Saturday night. It's barely five o'clock on Friday, and you're already drunk." Which meant his brother must have started drinking at least a couple of hours ago.

"I sent the last olive shipment out at noon. I think you should introduce me to your lady friend," Luis said with a sloppy smile, his gaze locked on Katerina. "She's pretty. I'd love to show her a good time."

The last thing he wanted to do was to introduce Katerina to his brother, especially when he was intoxicated. Luis had been doing fairly well recently, so finding him like this was more than a little annoying.

What was Luis thinking? If he lost the olive farm, what would he do for work? Or was this just another way to ruin Miguel's chance to follow his dream? He was tired of trying to save the olive farm for his brother while taking care of his patients. He was working non-stop from early morning to sundown every week. It was past time for Luis to grow up and take some responsibility.

"Go home, Luis," he advised. "Before you make a complete fool of yourself."

"Not until I meet your lady friend," Luis said stubbornly. "She reminds me a little of our mother, except that she has blonde hair instead of red. Are you going to change your mind about going to Africa? She may not wait for you."

Miguel ground his teeth together in frustration. "No, I'm not going to change my mind," he snapped. He didn't want to think about Katerina waiting for him. No matter how much he was still attracted to her, having a relationship with an American woman would be nothing but a disaster. His mother had hated every minute of living out on the farm, away from the city. And far away from her homeland. He was certain Katerina wouldn't be willing to leave her home either. "Katerina's sister is in the hospital, recovering from a serious head injury. She's not interested in having a good time. Leave her alone, understand?"

"Okay, fine, then." Luis shook off his hand and began walking toward the bar, his gait unsteady. "I'll just sit by myself."

"Oh, no, you won't." Miguel captured his brother's arm and caught sight of his old friend, Rafael, who happened to be a police officer. "Rafael," he called, flagging down his friend.

"Trouble, amigo?" Rafael asked, getting out of his police car.

"Would you mind taking my brother home?" He grabbed Luis's arm, steering him toward the police car, but his brother tried to resist. Luis almost fell, but Miguel managed to haul him upright. "I would take him myself, but I'm on call at the hospital."

"All right," Rafael said with a heavy sigh. "You'll owe me, my friend. Luckily for you, I'm finished with my shift."

"Thanks, Rafael. I will return the favor," he promised.

"I'll hold you to that," Rafael muttered with a wry grimace.

Miguel watched them drive away, before he raked a hand through his hair and turned back towards Katerina. As if the fates were against him, his pager went off, bringing a premature end to their time together.

"My apologies for the interruption," he murmured as he returned to the table. "I'm afraid I must cut our meal short. There is a young boy with symptoms of appendicitis. I need to return to the hospital to assess whether or not he needs surgery."

"I understand," Katerina said, as he paid the tab. She gathered up the papers he'd given to her. "Thanks again for translating Juliet's chart for me. I'm sure I'll see you tomorrow."

"Of course." When she stood, she was so close he could have easily leaned down to kiss her. He curled his fingers into fists and forced himself to take a step backwards in order to resist the sweet temptation. "I will make rounds between nine and ten in the morning, if you want an update on your sister's condition."

"Sounds good. Goodbye, Miguel." She waved and then headed for the metro station, located just a few blocks down the street.

Back at the hospital it was clear the thirteen-year-old had a classic case of appendicitis and Miguel quickly took the child to the operating room. Unfortunately, his appendix had burst, forcing Miguel to spend extra time washing out the abdominal cavity in order to minimize the chance that infection would set in. Afterwards, he made sure the boy had the correct antibiotics ordered and the first dose administered before he headed home to his three-bedroom apartment located within walking distance of the hospital.

It wasn't until he was eating cold leftover pizza for dinner that Miguel had a chance to think about Katerina, and wonder just what she'd thought was so important to tell him.

CHAPTER THREE

"Look, it's a shopping mall!" Diana exclaimed. Then she frowned. "I almost wish my luggage hadn't shown up this morning, or I'd have a good excuse to go buy new clothes."

Kat nodded ruefully. She was surprised to find Seville was a city of contrasts, from the modern shopping mall to the mosques and bronze statues straight out of the sixteenth century. "A little disappointing in a way, isn't it?" she murmured.

"Hey, not for me," Diana pointed out. "I mean, the history here is nice and everything, but I'm all in favor of modernization. Especially when it comes to shopping."

They'd walked to a small café for breakfast, and found the shopping mall on the way back to the hotel. "Maybe you can explore the mall with Tommy this morning while I'm at the hospital, visiting Juliet."

"Sounds good. Although don't forget we plan on taking the boat tour later this afternoon," Diana reminded her.

"I won't forget," Kat murmured. Sightseeing wasn't top of her list, but it was the least she could do for Diana as her friend spent a good portion of every day watching her son. Besides, sitting for hours at the hospital wasn't going to help Juliet recover any quicker.

"Here's the metro station," Kat said. "Call me if you need anything, okay? I'll see you later, Tommy." Kat swept him into her arms for a hug, which he tolerated for barely a minute before he wiggled out of her grasp.

"We'll be fine," Diana assured her, taking Tommy's hand in a firm grip.

"I know." She watched them walk away towards the mall, before taking the steps down to the metro station to wait for the next train. Despite the fact that she still needed to break the news about Tommy to Miguel, she found she was looking forward to seeing him again. Last night, before she'd fallen asleep, Miguel's words had echoed in her mind, giving her a secret thrill.

I've thought of you often over these past few years.

She doubted that he'd thought of her as often as she'd thought of him, though. Mostly because of Tommy since he was the mirror image of his father. Yet also because Miguel had taken a small piece of her heart when he'd left.

Not that she ever planned on telling him that.

She needed to let go of the past and move on with her life. Whatever her conflicting feelings for Miguel, she couldn't afford to fall for him. They wanted different things out of life. She wanted a home, family, stability. Miguel wanted adventure. He wanted Doctors Without Borders. He wanted to travel. The only time they were in sync was when they had worked as colleagues in the O.R..

And, of course, during the night they spent together.

Walking into the hospital was familiar now, and she

greeted the clerk behind the desk in Spanish. *"Buenos dias."*

"Buenos dias," the clerk replied with a wide grin. One thing about Spain, most people seemed to be in a good mood. Maybe because they had a more laid-back lifestyle here. She found it amazing that the shops actually closed down for three hours between noon and three for siesta. She couldn't imagine anyone in the U.S. doing something like that.

Yet if the people were happier, maybe it was worth it?

Kat took the stairs to the third-floor I.C.U., entered her sister's room and crossed over to the bedside, taking her sister's small hand in hers. "Hi, Jules, I'm back. How are you feeling, hmm?"

She knew her sister wasn't going to open her eyes and start talking, which would be impossible with a breathing tube in anyway, but Kat was convinced patients even in her sister's condition could hear what was going on around them, so she decided she'd keep up her one-sided conversation with her sister.

"Seville is a beautiful city, Jules, I can understand why you wanted to study here. I wish I knew exactly what happened to you. No one here seems to know anything more than the fact that you ran into the road and were struck by a car. Can you hear me, Jules? If you can hear me, squeeze my hand."

When Juliet's fingers squeezed hers, Kat's knees nearly buckled in relief. "That's great, Juliet. Now wiggle your toes for me. Can you wiggle your toes?"

This time Juliet's non-casted left leg moved again. It wasn't wiggling her toes, exactly, but Kat was still thrilled at the small movement. Her sister was truly doing better. Juliet would probably only follow commands intermittently, but each day she'd improve and do better.

Exactly the way Miguel had assured her she would.

"Good job, Jules. I'm so glad you can hear me. You're still in the hospital in Seville, but as soon as you're better, you're going to be sent to an American hospital back home. Can you understand what I'm saying? If you can understand me, squeeze my hand."

Juliet squeezed her hand again, and relieved tears blurred her vision. Her sister was going to make it. Juliet might have a long road to recovery ahead of her, but she was going to make it.

"Katerina?"

At the sound of Miguel's voice she whirled around and quickly crossed over to him. "She's following commands, Miguel!" she exclaimed. "She's starting to wake up!"

He caught her close in a warm hug. "I'm glad," he murmured, his mouth dangerously close to her ear.

She wanted to wrap her arms around his waist and lean on his strength, but she forced herself to step away, putting badly needed distance between them. What was wrong with her? It wasn't as if she'd come to Seville in order to rejuvenate her feelings for Miguel. Better for her if she kept him firmly in the friendship category. As if their one night together had been an aberration.

One that had produced a son.

There was no reason to feel as if being around Miguel was like coming home. Truthfully, she'd never been farther from home.

"I'm sorry," she said, wiping her tears on the back

of her hand while searching for a tissue. "I didn't mean to get all emotional on you."

"Here." He grabbed the box of tissues from the bedside table and handed them to her. "Don't apologize, I know how worried you've been."

She blew her nose and pulled herself together, forcing a smile. "I hope this doesn't mean you're going to send Juliet home right away, are you?"

"Not yet. I would like your sister to be completely off the ventilator and more awake before she's transported back to the U.S."

"Sounds good." She was relieved to know they wouldn't have to leave Seville just yet. Especially as she hadn't told Miguel about Tommy. A wave of guilt hit hard. Should she tell him now? No, this wasn't exactly the time or the place for a heavy conversation. Besides, Miguel was working, making rounds. No doubt he had many patients to see.

She was about to ask him what time he got off work when he reached over to take her hand in his. "Katerina, will you have dinner with me tonight?"

She hesitated just a moment before nodding her assent. Wasn't this what she'd wanted all along? A good time and place to tell him about his son? A quiet dinner with just the two of them would be the perfect time to give him the news. "Yes, Miguel. Dinner would be wonderful."

"Excellent," he murmured. His gaze was warm and she had to remind herself this wasn't a date. Her son's future was what mattered here, not her roller-coaster feelings for his father.

"What time?" she asked.

"We'll go early as I know you're not used to our customs yet. Shall we say eight o'clock?"

A wry grin tugged at the corner of her mouth because eight o'clock wasn't at all early back home. "All right. Where should I meet you?"

"I will pick you up at your hotel. Which one are you staying at?"

"We— I'm at the Hesperia hotel," she said, using the correct Spanish pronunciation while hoping he didn't catch her slip.

"Excellent. There is a wonderful restaurant just a few blocks away." He glanced at his watch. "I'm sorry, but I need to finish making rounds. Did you have any questions about the chart copies I gave you?"

She'd read through his entire stack of notes early that morning, before Tommy had woken up. "I noticed her electrolytes keep going out of whack—do you think that's because of her head injury?"

"Yes, brain injuries cause sodium levels to drop, but try not to worry as we are replacing what she's lost."

She'd noticed the IV solution running through Juliet's IV was similar to what they'd use in the U.S. Except for the equipment being a little different, the basics of medical and nursing care were very much the same.

"Thanks again, Miguel, for everything," she said in a low voice, trying to put the depth of her feelings into words. "I'm so relieved to know my sister is in such good hands."

"You're very welcome, Katerina. I'll see you tonight, yes?"

"Yes," she confirmed. After he left, she walked back and sat down at her sister's bedside.

She was lucky that Miguel was here. Not just because he spoke English, which was a huge help, but because she knew he was an excellent surgeon.

Ironic how fate had brought her face to face with Tommy's father after all these years. Her previously suppressed feelings for Miguel threatened to surface and she took a long, deep breath, ruthlessly shoving them back down.

She needed to protect her heart from Miguel's charm. And even more importantly, she needed to preserve the life she'd built with her son.

Miguel finished his rounds and then took a break to call his brother. Unfortunately, Luis didn't answer the phone so he left his brother a message, requesting a return phone call.

He rubbed the back of his neck, debating whether he should go out to see his brother after work or not. He should have time before dinner as he wasn't on call this evening. But at the same time, going all the way out to the farm and back would take at least two and a half hours, and he didn't want to be late for his dinner date with Katerina.

Miguel was pleased Katerina had agreed to see him again tonight. He felt the need to make it up to her for leaving so abruptly after finding out about his father's stroke. The night they'd spent together had been incredible. There had always been the hint of awareness between them while working together in the operating room. At times it had seemed as if Katerina could practically read his mind, instinctively knowing what he'd needed before he'd had to ask.

He'd been tempted to pursue a relationship, but had told himself it wouldn't be fair since he wasn't planning on staying. Maybe if things had been different...

No, he'd made his decision. He'd already given notice at the hospital that he was leaving at the end of the academic year, which was just three months away. He'd first heard about Doctors Without Borders in Madrid from one of his colleagues. He'd quickly decided that he wanted to join as well once he'd finished his training. He'd known early on he didn't want to stay on his family's olive farm. He'd wanted to travel. To learn about other cultures. He'd jumped at the opportunity to study in the U.S. and now couldn't wait to join Doctors Without Borders.

So why was he torturing himself by seeing Katerina again? If he had a functioning brain cell in his head, he'd stay far away from her until her sister was stable enough for transport back home.

Katerina wasn't the woman for him. He knew he shouldn't measure all women against his American mother, but after living in both cultures he understood a little better why his mother had reacted the way she had. The two lifestyles were very different. Maybe if the olive farm hadn't suffered two bad years in a row, there would have been money for vacations back in the U.S. Would that have been enough for his mother? Or would that have only emphasized her loss?

Truthfully, he couldn't understand why his mother just hadn't purchased a one-way ticket to New York and returned home if she'd been so desperately unhappy here. Instead, she'd stayed to become a bitter woman who'd made all their lives miserable. Until she'd unex-

pectedly died of an overdose, which had been determined to be accidental rather than a suicide attempt.

Miguel shook off his dark thoughts and concen-
trated on his patients. He loved everything about being
a surgeon. There wasn't nearly as much trauma here in
Seville as in Cambridge, Massachusetts, but he didn't
mind. One thing he never got used to was losing patients.

Especially young patients. Like the twenty-five-year-
old pregnant mother they'd lost during his last shift in
the U.S.

After finishing his rounds on the adults in his case
load, he made his way over to the children's wing, which
happened to be in the oldest part of the hospital. He
wanted to visit Pedro, his young appendectomy patient.
The young boy would need to stay a few days for IV
antibiotics before he could be discharged.

This was the other part he loved about being a doctor
in Spain. There weren't large children's hospitals here,
the way there were in the U.S. He was glad to have the
opportunity to take care of both children and adults,
rather than being forced to decide between them.

"*Hola,* Dr. Vasquez," Pedro greeted him when he
entered the room.

"*Hola, Pedro. ¿Como estas?*"

"*¿English, por favor*? I'm fine."

Miguel grinned and switched to English for Pedro's
sake. The youngster was part of a group of teenagers in
Seville who were committed to learning English. Many
of them didn't bother, but even when Pedro had been in
pain in the emergency department yesterday, the boy
had informed him he was going to America one day.

"May I examine your incision?" Miguel asked politely.

Pedro frowned, probably having trouble with the word "incision", but lifted his hospital gown anyway. "It's healing well, no?"

"Very much so," Miguel said, pleased to see there were no signs of infection. Although the bigger problem Pedro faced was an infection in the bloodstream from the burst appendix. "Where is your mother? I think you'll need to stay for a couple more days yet."

Pedro smiled broadly as he drew his hospital gown back down. "She's caring for my younger brothers and sisters. She'll be here soon. And I'm glad to stay, Dr. Vasquez, because you will have more time for me to practice my English with you, yes?"

Miguel couldn't help but grin at the awkwardly worded sentence. "Yes, Pedro. We will practice while you are here, but even after you go home, we can practice when you return to clinic to see me, okay?"

"Okay. Thanks, Dr. Vasquez."

Miguel went on to see his second patient, a young girl who'd sustained a compound fracture of her left arm. They had orthopedic specialists, but since the fracture wasn't complicated he'd simply set it himself and casted it.

Marissa's room was empty so Miguel went to find the nurse, only to discover that the young girl was getting another X-ray of her arm.

He decided to return to the I.C.U., vowing to come back to check on Marissa later, but as he reached the third floor, the entire building shook and the lights flickered and went out. It took him a moment to realize what had happened, even though he'd been through this scenario once before.

Earthquake!

Kat was about to leave the I.C.U., intending to head back to the hotel, when she felt the building shake with enough force to make her fall against the wall.

The lights flickered and then went out. She froze, waiting for them to come back on.

Juliet's ventilator!

Instinctively, she ran back down the hall to her sister's room, able to see somewhat from the daylight shining through the windows. She saw Miguel going into another room but didn't veer from her path. After rushing over to Juliet's bedside, she reached for the ambu-bag hanging from the oxygen regulator. She turned the dial up, providing high-flow oxygen as she quickly disconnected the ventilator and began assisting her sister's breathing.

She forced herself to calm down so she wouldn't hyperventilate Juliet, hardly able to believe that the power was still out. Didn't they have back-up generators here? What had caused the shaking? Did they have earthquakes here? And where was everyone? She'd hadn't seen anyone other than the glimpse of Miguel going into another patient's room.

After what seemed like forever, the lights flickered back on, but only part way, as if conserving energy. At least Juliet's ventilator and heart monitor came back on.

She connected the ventilator back up to Juliet's breathing tube, but before she could go out and find the rest of the hospital staff, Miguel showed up in the doorway.

"What happened?" she asked.

"Earthquake. Nothing too serious, probably about a five or six on the Richter scale. We've had one similar to this before. But I need your help."

Earthquake? She was a little shocked, but strove to remain calm. "Me? What for?"

"I've just been told that a very old tree fell against the corner of the building and we need to evacuate the patients. They are all pediatric patients in the children's wing located on the fourth floor. As it is a weekend, we do not have full staffing. We could use an extra pair of hands if you're willing to stay?"

"Of course," she said, knowing she couldn't simply walk away, even though she needed to know her son was safe. She was tempted to call Diana right away, except that she didn't want Miguel to ask questions. So she promised herself she'd wait until she could steal a few minutes alone to call her friend.

"Let's go," Miguel said, and she followed him out of the I.C.U. and down the hall, trying to make sense of what was happening. Clearly, the earthquake must have caused the tree to fall on the hospital building. What other damage had occurred? And what about the hotel? Was everything all right there?

As they walked down the hall, she peered through the windows to look out over the city. She was relieved when she didn't see any evidence of mass destruction. As she followed Miguel, she hoped and prayed Tommy and Diana were someplace safe from harm.

CHAPTER FOUR

KAT was horrified to see the amount of damage the building had sustained when they arrived in the children's ward. Many of the younger kids were crying, but one older boy had already stepped up to take charge. He'd obviously gathered all the children on several beds located as far away as possible from the crumbled corner of the building.

"Good job, Pedro," Miguel said as they rushed in. "Where's your nurse, Elouisa?"

"I'm not sure, but I think she went to get medication," Pedro answered. Kat was impressed that the boy spoke English and seemed to accept the responsibility of staying here with the children alone.

Miguel's mouth tightened, but he didn't say anything else. "Okay, then, we'll need to transport the sickest patients down to the I.C.U. first."

"DiCarlo is the worst, I think," Pedro said, pointing to a boy who was lying listlessly in bed. Kat estimated there were at least a dozen kids gathered on three beds surrounding the obviously very sick boy. "Elouisa said something about how he needed more antibiotics."

"She should have stayed here with all of you. He can get his antibiotics in the I.C.U.," Miguel said firmly.

"I'll take him down, but do you think it's safe to use the elevators?" she asked warily. She didn't mind transporting the sick child downstairs but the thought of being stuck in an elevator alone with him was scary.

Just then Elouisa returned, hurrying in with an IV bag in her hand. She came straight over to DiCarlo's IV pump to prepare the medication.

Miguel said something to her in Spanish, which she assumed was something related to the care of the children. She responded in Spanish as well, even while she hung the IV antibiotic. When they finished their conversation, Miguel turned to her.

"Okay, you and I together will take DiCarlo in his bed down to the I.C.U. Elouisa has promised to stay with the children." He turned to Pedro. "I am counting on you to stay here and to help Elouisa until I can return, okay? Once we have DiCarlo safe in the I.C.U., we can find other beds for the rest of you."

Pedro nodded. "I understand Dr. Vasquez. You should have trust that I will wait here for you."

"Good, Pedro. Thank you."

"Give me a quick rundown on DiCarlo's condition," she said to Miguel as Elouisa used an old-fashioned crank to lift the bed higher off the floor so it would be easier for them to push him. "I need to understand what to watch for."

Miguel set a small bin of emergency supplies on DiCarlo's bed, and again she was struck by the similarities between medical care here in Seville and in the U.S. When she worked in the I.C.U., they would always take a small pack of emergency supplies on what they called road trips, when patients needed to leave the I.C.U. to go down for certain X-rays or CT scans. Miguel started pushing the boy's bed towards the elevator as he gave a brief report.

"What started as pneumonia has turned into full-blown sepsis. He's been fighting the infection as best he can, but he's had heart trouble since he was born so he's not as strong as most children his age."

She digested that bit of information as they left the children's ward through a long, empty hallway. As they waited for the elevator, which seemed to take a very long time, she looked down at DiCarlo's wan features, hoping and praying he'd survive the infection.

Miguel's impatience was obvious when he stabbed the elevator button a second time.

"Where is everyone?" she asked. Miguel's features tightened. "We were short-staffed to begin with, but some left, wanting to check on their loved ones. I honestly didn't think we would lose this many staff members."

She could understand why some staff had felt compelled to leave, and worry over the safety of her son gnawed at her. She pushed her fears aside. For one thing, Diana would have called her if something bad had happened. Their hotel was new and sturdy. Surely they'd be safe. The elevator arrived and she helped Miguel push DiCarlo's bed inside. The doors closed and she pushed the button for the second floor when suddenly the boy began coughing so hard his face turned bright red.

"Miguel, he's having trouble breathing," she said urgently, reaching for the dial on the oxygen tank and turning the knob to give him more oxygen. "Do we have a pediatric ambu bag?"

"Yes, along with intubation supplies." Miguel opened the small bag of emergency supplies and pulled out the ambu bag. "We can intubate if we have to."

She hadn't assisted with an intubation since the time she'd worked in the I.C.U., but she nodded anyway. She gently placed the small face mask over DiCarlo's mouth and nose, and used the ambu bag to give him a couple of breaths.

DiCarlo squirmed beneath the ambu bag, fighting her at first, but then abruptly went limp, and she quickly reached over to feel for a pulse. "Miguel? His pulse is fading fast."

"I'll have to intubate him now, rather than waiting until we reach the I.C.U." He took the laryngoscope in his left hand and then gently slid the endotracheal tube into DiCarlo's throat. She took Miguel's stethoscope from around his neck and listened to the boy's lungs to verify the tube was in the correct place. Thankfully, it was. She quickly connected the ambu bag tubing to the end of the endotracheal tube so she could give DiCarlo several breaths.

Miguel secured the tube with tape and then gestured behind her. "Check his pulse and then push the button again. The doors have already closed."

She'd never heard the elevator ding. She made sure DiCarlo's pulse was stable before she turned around to hit the button for the third floor. This time it only took a couple of minutes for the doors to open.

She was very happy to see the critical care area. "Which bed?" she asked, as she walked backwards, pulling the bed as Miguel pushed, keeping one hand on the child's endotracheal tube.

"Twelve," he directed.

She knew the basic layout of the unit from visiting her sister and quickly pulled the bed towards the vacant room number twelve. Nurses came over and assisted her with getting DiCarlo connected to the heart monitor overheard.

"Gracias," she murmured, smiling weakly. She glanced up and was reassured to note that DiCarlo's pulse had stabilized. Miguel spoke to them in Spanish, and they quickly brought over a ventilator. She stepped back, allowing the staff room to work.

Crisis averted, at least for the moment.

She hesitated, not sure if she should go back down to the children's wing alone or wait for Miguel. He was still examining DiCarlo, and the grave concern in his gaze as he listened to the boy's lungs wrenched her heart.

Would he look at Tommy like that?

Just then he glanced up and caught her staring at him. She swallowed the lump in her throat, holding his gaze for a long moment. Watching him, the way he was so gentle with DiCarlo, gave her hope and reassurance that he would never do anything to hurt their son. Including taking him away from her.

"He's fine for now," Miguel said, putting his stethoscope away. "Give me a few minutes here while I make sure his orders are up to date."

"Of course," she murmured, turning away, her hand on her phone. Outside DiCarlo's room, she made sure she was out of Miguel's hearing distance before she quickly pressed the number for Diana, holding her breath while she waited for an answer. Diana's voice brought instant relief. "Kat? Are you okay?"

"Yes. Are you and Tommy safe? Was there damage to the hotel?"

"We lost power for a while, and there seems to be a lot of confusion, but we're fine. No damage to the hotel that we know of."

Kat closed her eyes with relief. "I'm so glad. Listen, I have to stay here for a bit yet—will you be okay for a while?"

"Sure. We'll be fine."

"Thanks, I'll check in with you later." She closed her phone just as Miguel came around the corner of the nurses' station. She quickly tucked the phone back into her pocket.

"Ready to go?" Miguel asked.

"Of course." She felt bad for deceiving him, but obviously this wasn't the time or place for a conversation about his son. As they walked together toward the stairwell, their hands brushed lightly. A tingle of awareness shot up her arm.

"So, maybe I should apply to be a nurse here, huh?" she said jokingly, in a feeble attempt to break the closeness that seemed to grow deeper between them every moment they spent together.

"Are you planning to stay?" he asked, in shocked surprise. The brief flash of horror in his eyes pierced the tiny balloon of hope that had begun to grow in her heart.

"No! Of course not. That was a joke, Miguel." Ridiculous to be hurt that he didn't want her to stay. She preceded him down the stairwell, wondering if he'd change his opinion once she told him about Tommy.

She had to tell him about his son. The sooner, the better.

* * *

Miguel mentally smacked himself on the side of the head, understanding from the stiffness in her shoulders and the sharpness of her tone that he'd inadvertently hurt her.

He hadn't meant to make it sound like he didn't want her to stay. He'd just been taken aback by her statement, especially after they'd worked together to save DiCarlo. He couldn't help making comparisons with his mother. Maybe if his mother had been able to work in a career, other than helping his father run the olive farm, she would have been happier.

Could Katerina really be happy in Seville? And why did it matter as he himself wasn't planning to stay?

He hadn't slept well last night because all he'd been able to think about had been Katerina. And even now, in the aftermath of a small earthquake, he still wanted her.

But their situation was no different than it had been back when he'd met her in Cambridge. He'd already committed to Doctors Without Borders. He was finally going to live his dream. He couldn't start something with Katerina that he wasn't willing to finish.

A tiny voice in the back of his mind wondered if she'd be willing to go with him. But then he remembered Juliet. No, the Katerina he knew wouldn't pack up and leave her sister. Especially not when Juliet had a potentially long road of recovery ahead of her. Several months of rehab at least.

He pushed thoughts of Katerina possibly going with him to Africa aside to concentrate on the situation down in the children's ward.

Thankfully, Elouisa had kept her word, staying with

the rest of the children. He was glad to see an additional staff nurse had come up to help.

"Which wing can we use as the children's ward?" he asked, joining the group. "I'd like to keep them together if possible."

"We can use the east wing of the third floor," Elouisa informed him. "I too would like to keep them together if possible. How is DiCarlo?"

"Very ill. We had to intubate him in the elevator," Miguel said. "You were right to make sure he received his antibiotic," he said by way of apology. He'd been upset to find the children alone, but he understood she'd prioritized the best she could.

"I was hoping to get him to the I.C.U.," Elouisa admitted. "But you were right, I shouldn't have left the children alone."

"Difficult decision either way, so don't worry about it." He noticed Pedro was listening to their conversation. He was impressed with how the boy had taken charge in Elouisa's absence. "Pedro, are you able to walk or would you like us to get you a wheelchair?"

Pedro practically puffed out his chest. "I can walk. I'm fine, Dr. Vasquez."

He could tell Pedro had some pain, but the boy wasn't about to admit it. He vowed to make sure Pedro took some pain medication as soon as they were all relocated in their new rooms.

Elouisa gathered up several wheelchairs and between the three of them they assisted getting all the children ready for transport. Pedro helped, as if he were a hospital staff member rather than one of the patients needing to be relocated.

The elevator was too small for everyone to go at once, so Elouisa and Pedro took three children first, while the second nurse, Maria, took two patients with her. Miguel and Katerina waited for the next elevator with their three patients. They were lucky there hadn't been more patients in the children's wing.

"Pedro's English is amazing," Katerina said while they waited for the elevator. "I'm impressed at how he seems to understand everything we're saying."

"He takes learning English very seriously as he is determined to go to America one day," he admitted. "You'd never know he had a burst appendix last evening, would you?"

Katerina's eyes widened. "No, I certainly wouldn't. He's doing remarkably well."

"Yes, but as his appendix ruptured, I want him to get a good twenty-four to forty-eight hours of IV antibiotics before he's discharged."

The elevator arrived and as they quickly maneuvered the three remaining patients into the elevator, Miguel found himself watching Katerina with awe. He'd always known she was an excellent O.R. nurse but seeing her interact with the young patients, managing to overcome the language barrier with smiles, simple words and hand gestures, he thought her skills would be better utilized in a position where she could care for awake and alert patients on the ward or in the I.C.U.

Or in the Doctors Without Borders program. They needed nurses to work with them, too.

Not that her career choices were any of his business.

It didn't take long to get the children settled on the east wing of the third floor. The entire layout of the area was very similar to the one where the building had collapsed. Even Pedro reluctantly took to his bed, and Miguel made sure he took a dose of pain medication that was long overdue.

Afterwards, he glanced at his watch, thinking he should go up and check on DiCarlo. But he was hesitant to leave Elouisa here alone as Maria had been called away to help elsewhere. He walked up to the nurses' desk where Elouisa was busy organizing the charts. "Have you requested additional nursing support?" he asked.

"*Sí,* but so far Maria has not returned," she told him. "Thankfully, most of the children are very stable, especially now that DiCarlo is in the I.C.U."

"True, but I still think you should have someone with you. What if you have to leave the unit for some reason?"

Katerina stepped forward. "I can stay for a while," she volunteered. "I would just like a few minutes to check on my sister first."

He nodded, filled with gratitude. Even though Katerina wasn't licensed to practice nursing here in Seville, she could stay on the unit as a volunteer, offering a second pair of hands as needed. And her knowledge of nursing would be invaluable. He would feel much better knowing Elouisa wasn't here on the children's wing alone.

"Why don't you run over to see your sister, and I will wait here until you return?" he offered.

"*Gracias,*" she murmured. "I promise to be quick."

He couldn't begrudge her the chance to make sure Juliet's condition hadn't changed since they'd been up there. "I will need to check on her too, but I will wait for you to return."

"¿Que?" Elouisa asked, indicating she hadn't understood his conversation, so he quickly translated for her. "Both of you go and check on her sister," Elouisa said firmly. "I will be fine alone here for five minutes until Katerina returns. Pedro has been a huge help. He will get help in an emergency."

Miguel reluctantly agreed and led the way down to the I.C.U., using the stairwell as the elevator was so slow.

"You're going to have to make Pedro an honorary nurse, soon," Katerina teased as they walked towards Juliet's room. "Maybe after all this he'll decide to pursue a career in medicine?"

He chuckled. "There are not nearly as many male nurses here in Seville as there are back in America."

They entered Juliet's room and Katerina immediately crossed over to take her sister's hand. "I'm here, Jules," she said in a gentle tone. "Don't worry, you're still doing fine."

Juliet was moving restlessly on the bed, as if she was uncomfortable. Katerina tried to comfort her, talking to her in a soothing voice as Miguel took the clipboard off the foot of the bed and scanned the latest laboratory results and vital signs that had been recorded.

"Miguel?" He glanced up at Katerina's urgent tone. "Look! I think she's having a seizure!"

CHAPTER FIVE

"DISCONNECT the ventilator and use the ambu bag to assist her breathing," he directed quickly. He leaned over to hit the emergency call light and in less than thirty seconds two nurses came running in. He gave them orders in Spanish for a loading dose of IV dilantin followed by a continuous infusion. Also five milligrams of Versed to calm the effects of the seizure and for new IV fluids to correct Juliet's electrolyte imbalance.

His heart twisted when he saw the sheen of tears in Katerina's eyes. Thankfully, the seizure didn't last long, and within ten minutes he was able to put Juliet back on the ventilator. The medications he'd ordered worked beautifully, and Kat looked relieved when Juliet was resting quietly in her bed.

"She's going to be okay," he murmured to Katerina as they moved back, allowing the nurses to complete the dilantin infusion along with the new IV fluids he'd ordered. "This isn't a sign that her head injury is worse, but more likely as a result of her electrolyte imbalance."

Katerina rubbed her hands over her arms, as if she was cold, and he couldn't stop himself from putting a strong arm around her shoulders and drawing her close. "Are you going to do a CT scan of her head, just to be sure this isn't related to her intracranial hemorrhage?" she asked.

He hesitated because normally he wouldn't order such a test for that purpose. But he found himself wanting to reassure her in any way possible. "Let's wait to see how she does after the electrolytes are in, okay? If there is any change in her neuro status, I will order the scan immediately."

Katerina pulled away from him, turning to look at her sister, and he sensed she wasn't happy with his decision.

He wasn't used to explaining himself—especially not to a family member of a patient. "Listen to me, the earthquake has caused some chaos here in the hospital. I see now that your sister didn't get the new IV fluids I'd ordered during rounds. I truly believe, Katerina, her seizure is the result of an electrolyte imbalance."

She swiped a hand over her eyes, sniffed loudly and nodded. "All right, Miguel, we can wait to see how she does once the electrolytes are corrected."

He reached out to put a hand on her shoulder, wanting nothing more than to offer comfort, easing her fears. "I promise you, I'll take good care of your sister, Katerina."

For a moment he didn't think she'd respond, but then she suddenly turned and threw herself into his arms. Surprised and pleased, he hugged her close.

"I can't lose her, Miguel. I just can't," she said in a muffled voice. "I promised my mother I'd take care of her. She has to be okay, she just has to!"

Her despair tore at his heart. "I know, Katerina," he whispered, brushing his cheek against her silky hair, ignoring the shocked stares from the two nurses. "I know."

As soon as the IV medications were flowing according to his prescribed rate, the two nurses left them alone in the room. He continued to hold Katerina close, smoothing a hand down her back, giving her the emotional support she needed while trying to ignore the sexual awareness zinging through his bloodstream. He was stunned to realize how much he wanted her, even after all this time. And the feeling was impossibly stronger than it had been during the night they'd shared together four and a half years ago.

He hadn't left her by choice, returning home because of his father's stroke, but he hadn't sought her out afterwards, either. Had he made a mistake? Was he wrong not to have gone back to be with her again?

He pressed a kiss along her temple and the slight caress must have been too much for her because she pulled away abruptly, straightening her spine and swiping at the wetness on her face. "I'm sorry, Miguel. I don't know what's wrong with me. I'm usually not this much of a mess."

"Give yourself a break, Katerina. It's understandable that you're worried about your sister. And this has been incredibly stressful for all of us. Despite what you may think, we don't have earthquakes here often." He lifted a hand to wipe a strand of hair from her cheek. "You don't have to stay to help if you don't want to. Maybe you should go back to the hotel for some rest."

She bit her lower lip and he could sense her inner struggle, knowing she was tempted to take him up on his offer. But then she sighed and shook her head. "I can't leave Elouisa all alone with those sick children. I will stay, but only for an hour or so. Hopefully by then, some of the staff will have returned."

He nodded, admiring her strength and determination. "I would like to think so, too."

For a moment she simply stared at him, and then she totally shocked him by putting her hand on his chest and going up on tiptoe to kiss his cheek. It was everything he could do not to pull her into his arms for a real kiss. The feather-light touch was too brief and before he could blink, she drew away. "I'll see you later, Miguel," she whispered, before leaving to return to the children's ward.

His throat was so tight, he couldn't speak. He spent several long minutes wrestling his warring emotions under control. Part of him knew he was playing with fire, yet he couldn't stay away from Katerina. Couldn't keep himself at arm's distance. He longed to kiss her. To make love to her.

Taking a deep breath, he tried to relax his tense muscles. He hadn't forgotten their dinner plans for later this evening, but with the earthquake there was a possibility the restaurants would be closed.

But he refused to consider breaking their date. No, he could always cook for her at his place, if necessary.

The idea grew on him as he continued to make rounds on his patients. He would be happy to prepare Katerina a meal she would never forget. And maybe they could explore the attraction that simmered between them.

Kat tried to concentrate on distracting the children, but she couldn't stop worrying about her sister and her son.

Even though she'd spoken to Diana just a little over an hour ago, she wanted to talk to her again.

Tommy was pretty young to talk on the phone, but she needed to hear his voice, just for a moment.

She ducked into a bathroom, seeking a moment of privacy. She called Diana again, and her friend answered right away. "Hi, Kat."

"Diana, I'm sorry, but I'm still here at the hospital. Some of the staff left and I'm volunteering on the children's ward. How's Tommy?"

"He misses you, but we've been playing video games since the power has come back on. Truly, he's fine."

"Can I talk to him? Just for a minute?"

"Sure, just a sec. Tommy, say hi to your mama, okay? Say hi," she urged.

"Hi, Mama." Tears pricked her eyelids when she heard her son's voice.

"Hi, Tommy. I love you very much. Be good for Aunt Diana, okay?"

There was a moment of silence and then Diana came back on the line. "I know you can't see him, but he's nodding in agreement to whatever you said, Kat."

Knowing that made her smile. "I'm glad. I told him to be good for you. Diana, I'm sorry we can't go on the boat ride," she murmured. "Maybe things will be back to normal tomorrow."

"Sure. Just come back as soon as you can, okay?"

"I will. Take good care of Tommy for me." Kat had to force herself to hang up, or she'd be bawling again.

Okay, she needed to get a grip here. She was becoming an emotional basket case. She quickly used the facilities and then splashed cold water on her face, pulling herself together.

As she returned to the children's ward, she found herself looking for Miguel. Ridiculous, as he was obviously spending time with the sicker patients. She hoped DiCarlo was doing better as she made rounds on the sick children, pleased to note they were doing fairly well.

She saved Pedro for last, knowing he'd want time to talk. "How are you, Pedro?"

"Very good, miss," he said, although his smile was strained, betraying his pain.

"Please, call me Kat," she instructed, coming over to stand beside his bed. "When was the last time you took a dose of pain medication?"

He shrugged one thin shoulder and angled his chin. "I'm fine. I'm not sick like these other children."

"Pedro, you had surgery less than twenty-four hours ago," she reminded him gently. "Taking pain medicine is not a sign of weakness. You need to conserve your strength so your body can heal."

She watched as he seemed to consider her words. "Maybe it is time for a pill," he agreed reluctantly.

"I will ask Elouisa to come," she said, turning toward the door.

"Miss Kat?" His voice stopped her.

"Yes, Pedro, what is it?"

"Are you and Dr. Vasquez…" He paused and frowned, as if searching for the right word. "Boyfriend and girlfriend?" he asked finally.

She couldn't hide her shock. "No! Why would you ask something like that, Pedro?"

His dark eyes crinkled with humor. "Because to me

it seems that you like each other very much," he said reasonably.

"Of course we like each other, we're friends, Pedro. We're friends, nothing more," she said firmly, trying not to blush. The boy was too observant by far. She really needed to keep her emotions under strict control. "I will go and get your pain medicine, which you will take, okay?"

She didn't wait for his response, but went out to find Elouisa. So far, she and the nurse had managed to communicate with facial expressions and hand gestures, intermixed with brief phrases.

"Pedro—medication *para dolor*," she said, using the Spanish word for pain. She found it amazing how the occasional word from her two years of high-school Spanish flashed in her memory.

"*Sí,* okay." Elouisa seemed to know right away what she meant. As the nurse went to get the pain medication, she couldn't help glancing at her watch. She'd been here almost an hour, and as much as she wanted to stay and help, she also longed to return to the hotel to see her son.

Surprisingly, it was only two o'clock in the afternoon, although it seemed as if she'd been here at the hospital for ever. She vowed to stay just another thirty minutes and no longer. For one thing, she was very hungry. And for another, she wanted to hold her son close, kiss his cheek and reassure herself that he was truly okay.

Elouisa returned, holding out a small paper medication cup, very similar to the ones they used in the hospital back home. Kat and Elouisa went back to Pedro's room to give him his medicine.

They found him standing in the doorway, a frightened expression on his face. "Pedro? What's wrong?"

He brought his hand away from his abdomen, revealing a bright crimson stain spreading across his hospital gown. "I'm bleeding," he said, as if he could hardly believe it.

"Elouisa, call Dr. Vasquez, Hurry! ¡Rapidamente!" The nurse rushed for the phone while she quickly crossed over to put her arm around Pedro's shoulders. "You've broken open your stitches," she told him calmly. "Come, now, you need to get back to bed."

Pedro murmured something in Spanish, and the fact that he was too stunned to practice his English worried her more than the blood staining his gown. She should have inspected his incision. "Stay still, Pedro, Dr. Vasquez will be here soon."

True to her word, Miguel strode in just moments later. "What happened?"

"I'm not sure," she was forced to admit. "I knew he was having pain, but I didn't realize he'd broken open his stitches."

"Everything he did today was too much for him." Miguel's compassionate gaze did not hold any blame.

"I should have examined his incision," she admitted softly. "I'm sorry, Miguel."

He shook his head as he turned toward Pedro. "Do not take this on yourself, Katerina. Will you please get me some gauze dressings? I need to see how bad the wound looks."

She knew he was trying to offer Pedro some privacy and quickly left the room, searching for the supply cart. She found the gauze without too much trouble and then returned to Pedro's room, hovering outside the door-way until she knew the boy was adequately covered.

"Do you have the gauze?" Miguel called, indicating it was safe to enter.

"Yes." The sheets were arranged so that his body was covered except for his belly. The small gaping hole in Pedro's abdomen worried her, although she tried not to let it show. "Will he need to go back to surgery?" she asked as she opened the gauze packet for him, keeping the contents sterile.

He took the gauze with his gloved fingers and turned back to Pedro. "I'm afraid so. Pedro, I will need to fix this open incision right away, understand?" He spoke in Spanish too, likely repeating what he'd said.

"I understand," Pedro murmured.

"You'll need to talk to his mother. I'll ask Elouisa to get hold of her."

"Thanks."

She left the room, and made sure Elouisa understood she needed to call Pedro's *madre* before she returned. Miguel had just finished dressing the wound, stepping back and stripping off his soiled gloves. "I will call down to surgery to make sure they have a room available and staff to assist."

She chewed her lower lip nervously. "And what if they don't have staff to assist?" she asked.

Miguel hesitated. "I'm afraid I will have to ask for your assistance, Katerina. You are a skilled O.R. nurse and we have worked together many times."

She opened her mouth to protest but stopped herself, realizing Pedro was listening to the interaction between them. She didn't want to say anything to upset the boy. "I can certainly help as needed," she agreed.

Miguel hurried away, apparently to make the necessary phone calls. She forced a reassuring smile on her face as she crossed over to Pedro's bedside, taking his hand in hers. "You're going to be fine, Pedro. Dr. Vasquez is a very talented surgeon. He will fix you up in no time."

"Will you assist him, Miss Kat?" Pedro asked, his eyes betraying a flicker of fear. "If there is no one else?"

"Of course I will do whatever is needed, Pedro. Don't you worry about a thing, okay? You're going to be fine."

"Gracias," he murmured, tightening his grip on her hand.

When Miguel returned, the tense expression on his face told her without words that her help would be needed. "There is a theater available, but the staff nurses who have stayed and the surgeon on call are busy with a trauma patient. Either Pedro waits until they are finished or you come down to assist me. It's your choice, Katerina. I know I have asked a lot from you today."

She didn't hesitate, knowing she could never let Pedro down. "I will be happy to help," she said firmly.

Miguel flashed a grateful smile. "Thank you, Katerina. This is a small surgery and shouldn't take too long."

She glanced down at Pedro's small brown hand clasped tightly in hers. She couldn't have left him any more than she could have left her own son. "I know. Remember, Pedro, Dr. Vasquez and I have worked together often in America. We made a good team."

"Yes, we did." Miguel's soft tone reminded her of

the night he'd made love to her. She needed to protect her heart from his lethal charm.

"Dr. Vasquez?" Elouisa poked her head into the room and said something about Pedro's mother. Miguel excused himself and went out to take the call.

Within minutes he'd returned. "Your mother will try to be here soon, but I'd rather not wait if that's okay. I need to repair the incision to protect against infection."

"I know. It's okay, she has my younger brothers and sisters to care for. I will be fine."

Kat's heart went out to Pedro, bravely facing surgery without his mother being here to hold his hand, to kiss him and to wish him well. She could tell Miguel felt the same way, from the way his gaze softened as he looked down at Pedro.

"You are very brave, Pedro," Miguel murmured. "I am extremely proud of you."

The simple words brightened Pedro's face and he beamed up at Miguel as if he were some sort of miracle worker. She couldn't help wondering about Pedro's father, why he wasn't here if his mother was home with the other children.

Miguel oozed confidence and kindness at the same time. Obviously, he cared very much for children. First DiCarlo and now Pedro. Both were patients under his care, but she knew that was only part of it.

Miguel would be the same way with his own child. With Tommy. The truth was staring her in the face.

As they wheeled Pedro's bed down to the elevator to go to the surgical suite, she knew that she couldn't put off telling Miguel about his son for much longer. She didn't know if he still planned on keeping their dinner date, so much had happened since then.

But even if their dinner plans had to be cancelled, she would have to tell him. Tonight.

No more excuses.

CHAPTER SIX

Miguel worked as quickly as he dared, first exploring the open wound in Pedro's abdomen and then irrigating with antibiotic solution. He believed the wound might have opened from a combination of an infection starting to take hold internally along with Pedro's physical exertions during the earthquake disaster.

He was lucky to have found an anesthesiology resident willing to stay after his shift. And Katerina was doing a phenomenal job of being his assistant. They settled into the old familiar routine as if the four and a half years hadn't gone by.

"Three-O silk," he said, but before he finished his statement Katerina was already handing him the pickups prepared with the suture. He grinned, even though she couldn't see behind the face mask, and gave his head a wry shake. "You always did have a way of reading my mind, Katerina."

She went still for a moment and he wondered if he'd somehow offended her. When she remained silent, he couldn't help trying to make amends.

"My apologies. I truly meant that as a compliment."

She lifted her head and looked at him, her beautiful green eyes probing as if she could indeed read his internal thoughts. "No apology necessary, Miguel," she finally said lightly. "I was thinking that I was glad that our roles weren't reversed and you were the one trying to read my mind."

"Really?" Closing the small incision didn't take long and he turned to face her as he set the pick-ups back down on the surgical tray. "Now you have piqued my interest. What is it you don't want me to read in your mind, I wonder?"

"Surely you don't expect me to answer that, do you?" Her green eyes crinkled at the corners, making him believe she was smiling. He relaxed, realizing he didn't like the thought of her being angry with him. "Pedro will be all right, won't he?"

"Yes, certainly. He must rest, though, and take care of himself. No more playing hero."

She nodded and there was a hint of relief in her gaze. "Good. That's very good."

She backed away from the surgical field and he had to bite back a protest, even though he knew her volunteer shift was over. Truly, she'd gone well above and beyond the call of duty. When she stripped off her face mask, he followed suit. "Katerina, I hope you will still allow me to take you to dinner this evening?"

She hesitated, and he sensed she wanted to refuse, but she surprised him by turning back to face him. "Of course, Miguel. But I need to return to my hotel for a bit. I'm still feeling the effects of jet-lag."

He couldn't blame her. The hour was still early, just three-thirty in the afternoon, and as much as he wanted to take her straight to his home, he couldn't begrudge her some down time. Especially not after everything she'd done for them today. "I will see you in a few hours, then?"

"Yes. I'll be ready." She glanced once more back at Pedro, where the anesthesiology resident was reversing the effects of his anesthesia, before she turned and disappeared through the doorway in the direction of the women's locker room.

He instantly felt isolated and alone after Katerina left, which was completely ridiculous. He stepped back, allowing the anesthesiologist to wheel Pedro's cart over to the recovery area.

As he washed up and changed his clothes, he spent time considering what meal he would prepare for her tonight. He wasn't a stranger to the kitchen. Living on his own, he'd been forced to learn how to cook, but he wanted to be sure the meal was to Katerina's liking.

For some odd reason he couldn't help feeling that tonight was incredibly important, a turning point in their renewed relationship.

And he was determined to make their evening together special.

"Mama!" Kat braced herself as her son launched himself at her, his chubby arms wrapping tightly around her neck.

"Oh, Tommy, I missed you so much!" She held him close, nuzzling his neck, filling her head with his scent, eternally grateful to have him in her life. The more difficult times of being a single mother were easily forgotten during joyous moments like this.

"We were just going to try and find something to

eat," Diana said with a tired smile. "I'm glad you came home before we left."

"I'm so hungry I could eat a bear," Kat murmured, still holding Tommy close. For once her active son seemed content to stay in her arms. "I'm surprised you didn't order room service."

"Can't read the room-service menu, it's in Spanish," Diana muttered with a heavy sigh. "Besides, we've been cooped up in here long enough. Believe it or not, there is a small café that's open just a few blocks away. We should be able to get something to eat. I have to tell you, the earthquake was a bit scary. There's one person behind the desk downstairs who speaks English and told us to stay in our rooms for a while. But I've been looking outside and haven't seen much damage."

Kat hadn't seen much evidence of damage either, and wondered if the tree outside the hospital had been partially dead already to have fallen on the building. "I'm so glad you're both safe."

"We're fine. We took a walk and found a couple of broken windows and a couple of uprooted trees. Nothing too awful."

"All right, let's go eat." She knew she had to tell Diana her plans for later that evening. But first she desperately needed something to eat. The gnawing in her stomach was almost painful.

While they ate, she explained how she'd helped out at the hospital in the children's ward, including doing surgery on a thirteen-year-old boy. As much as she didn't like being away from Tommy, she couldn't deny the satisfaction she'd felt by helping out.

"Hmm." Diana sat back in her seat, eyeing Kat over

the rim of her soft drink. "So basically you spent the entire day with Miguel, huh?"

Kat finished the *tapas* they'd ordered, not exactly sure what she was eating but enjoying the spicy food just the same, before answering. "Yes. And you may as well know I'm having dinner with him later tonight."

Her friend's eyes widened in horror. "No! You're going to tell him?"

"Don't," Kat said in warning, glancing at Tommy slurping his soft drink loudly through a straw. "Not now."

"But..." Diana sighed heavily, understanding that Kat didn't want to have this conversation with Tommy sitting right there. "I haven't had time to call the embassy," she complained in a low voice. "You agreed to wait."

"Doesn't matter." Kat was pleased to note how Tommy enjoyed the Spanish food. Must be part of his natural heritage, a trait passed down to him from Miguel. "Trust me when I tell you I know what I'm doing."

But Diana was shaking her head. "You don't know Miguel well enough yet," she protested.

"We worked together all day, moving the sick pediatric patients out of the children's wing. I helped him intubate a small child in the elevator and operate on a young boy. I know enough, Diana. You have to trust me on this."

Diana didn't say anything more, although the disapproval in her expression was clear. Even though Kat knew she was doing the right thing, she understood why her friend was worried. Seeing Miguel at the hospital today, there was no denying the powerful standing he had within the community, not to mention being on friendly terms with a police officer. A minor detail she hadn't dared tell Diana about. She hadn't understood exactly what they'd been saying, but when the police officer had taken Miguel's brother away, she'd had the impression he'd acted out of friendship.

But deep down those reasons weren't enough to hold her tongue. She knew Miguel was incapable of hurting a child, especially his own son. And he'd been so incredibly nice and supportive of her. Right from the very beginning, when he'd translated Juliet's chart for her. Spending time together today had only made her admire him more. No matter what Diana said, she would not back down from her decision.

Telling Miguel was the right thing to do.

"I hope you're not making a big mistake," Diana said.

"I'm not. Are you finished eating? We could take a little walk, maybe check out the church over there." Kat was determined to change the subject. She had a good hour yet before she needed to return to the hotel room to shower and change.

Better she keep her mind occupied with sightseeing rather than dwelling on the sweet anticipation of seeing Miguel again.

Kat pulled on the only dressy outfit she'd packed, a long gauzy skirt with a white tank top that molded to her figure. She left her long blonde hair straight and loose, rather than pulled back in the usual ponytail, knowing Miguel preferred it that way.

"You're dressing up for him as if this is some sort of hot date," Diana observed mildly.

She couldn't deny it. "Wanting to look nice isn't a crime." She needed some semblance of being in control. And maybe a part of her wanted to remind Miguel of the night they'd shared. A night of passion. A night that had produced a son.

Tommy was already falling asleep, and Kat couldn't help feeling guilty that she was leaving, forcing Diana to stay in the hotel room again. "I promise we'll do more sightseeing tomorrow," she said by way of apology.

"It's okay." Diana shrugged, even though Kat could sense her friend's keen disappointment. "This is why you paid my way to come here, right? There's no way we could have predicted the added complication of Miguel."

Truer words were never spoken. She went over to give her best friend a quick hug. "Thanks for being here, Diana."

Diana hugged her back, her good humor seeming to return. "You're welcome. Now, you'd better go downstairs, Miguel might just decide to come up here."

"He can't. They would make him call up here first," she protested. Still, she quickly crossed over to her half-asleep son, brushed a kiss on his brow and murmured how much she loved him before taking the room key Diana held out for her and letting herself out of the hotel room.

The elevators seemed to take for ever, but since she didn't know where the stairwells were, she forced herself to be patient. When the doors opened to reveal

Miguel standing there, she nearly screamed, her pulse leaping into triple digits.

"You scared me!" she accused, putting hand over her wildly beating heart. "What are you doing here?"

His teeth flashed in a bright smile, but he stood back, allowing her room to enter the elevator. "I'm sorry to have frightened you, but it's already five minutes past eight. I was worried you'd forgotten about our dinner date and had fallen asleep."

She struggled to breathe normally, but being in the small elevator so close to him was extremely nerve-racking. He was impeccably dressed in a crisp white shirt and black slacks, and his scent made her knees week. "How did you know what room I'm in? They're not supposed to tell you that. What if I didn't want to see you?" She was outraged that her privacy had been so easily violated.

"Hush, now, don't be so upset. The clerk at the front desk is one of my patients from the hospital. She knows I wouldn't hurt you."

As he spoke, the doubts Diana had voiced seeped into the back of her mind. Miguel knew everyone, had connections everywhere. He'd gotten her room number without any effort at all. What if he really did plan to take Tommy away from her?

She had to believe he wouldn't. But she wasn't willing to let him or the clerk off so lightly. "It's not right, Miguel. Just because she happens to know you, it doesn't mean she has the right to give you my room number. I intend to file a complaint."

He seemed taken aback by her biting anger. "I'm

sorry, Katerina. The fault is mine. Please don't get her in trouble for my mistake."

She knew she was overreacting, but the near miss had rattled her. What if he'd gotten a glimpse of Tommy? She didn't want him finding out about his son by accident. Back in the hotel room she'd been confident they could work something out, but now she wasn't so sure.

It was tempting to beg off their plans, but keeping Tommy a secret was already eating at her. She couldn't hold off another twenty-four hours, so she did her best to relax and smile. "Okay, fine, Miguel. I won't file a complaint, although you know I have a right to be upset. You forget I'm a single woman in a strange country where few speak my native language. I have a right to be concerned about strange men being allowed up to my room."

He lightly skimmed a hand down her back in a caress so light she thought she might have imagined it. "You are right, Katerina," he murmured contritely, although with a hint of steel. "I would not be at all happy if any other man was allowed access to your room."

The macho tone put her teeth on edge, but when the elevator doors opened she quickly escaped, putting badly needed distance between them.

She needed to stay in control. This wasn't a date, and she realized she'd made a grave mistake by dressing up for him as if it were. She was on an important mission, one that would have a great impact on her son's life, his future. Her future.

This was not a date!

* * *

Miguel cursed himself for being so stupid. If he'd been patient, they wouldn't be starting the night off on the wrong foot with an argument.

Katerina was breathtakingly beautiful. He'd never seen her in a dress and it was taking all his will-power to keep his hands to himself. He'd wanted to sweep her into his arms, to kiss her the way he had over four years ago.

His car was waiting, and he gently cupped her elbow, steering her towards the vehicle. Of course she dug in her heels. "I thought the restaurant was close by?"

"Please, get in the car. The restaurant nearby is closed due to the earthquake." After a brief pause she did as he asked, sliding into the back seat. "I'm afraid I have another sin to confess," he murmured, once they were settled and the driver had pulled away from the curb.

Her brows pulled together in a frown. "Really? And what sin is that?"

He subtly wiped his damp palms on his pants, more nervous than he'd ever been in his life. He was used to women coming on to him, many made it no secret they wanted to be the one to help end his bachelor ways. But he suddenly cared what Katerina thought of him. It was telling that she hugged the door as if she might escape at any moment. He flashed his most charming smile. "I have made dinner for us tonight."

"You?" her eyebrows shot upwards in surprise. And then the full meaning sank in. "We're going to your home?"

She acted as if he intended to take advantage of her. Had he read her wrong? Was it possible that she didn't feel the same sexual awareness that he did? Or had his stupid stunt in going up to her room broken her trust? "If you'd rather not, we can wait until tomorrow to dine. Hopefully the restaurants will reopen by then. I'm more than willing to ask my driver to return to your hotel." He tried not to let his hurt feelings show.

There was a long pause before she let out a small sigh. "No need to go back, Miguel," she said softly. She lifted her gaze and he saw the faint glint of amusement there. "I must say, I'm stunned to learn you know how to cook."

He relaxed and lifted her hand to his mouth, pressing his mouth to her soft skin. "There are many things you don't know about me, Katerina."

She gasped and tugged on her hand, which he reluctantly released. "And maybe, Miguel, there are a few things you don't know about me."

He couldn't deny the burning need to get to know all her secrets. The driver pulled up to his home and she glanced out the window. "You live right by the hospital," she said, recognizing the landmarks.

"Yes, very convenient for those nights I'm on call," he agreed.

His home was on the top floor, and they rode the elevator up in silence. He unlocked the door and then stepped back, allowing Katerina to enter first.

"Wow, very nice," she murmured, and he was ridiculously pleased she liked his home. "Bigger than I expected for a man living alone."

She didn't sit, but wandered around looking at his things with interest. When she approached the hallway farthest from the kitchen, he said, "Feel free to explore.

There are three bedrooms, although our rooms tend to be smaller than you're used to back in the U.S."

He turned to check on the food, which was being kept warm in the oven, and when he turned around he was startled to find her standing right behind him.

She was so beautiful, he ached. "Katerina, please don't be angry with me." He stepped closer, reaching up to thread his fingers through the silky golden strands of her hair. "I wanted tonight to be special."

A strange expression, something akin to guilt, flashed in her eyes, but then she smiled and he knew he was forgiven. "I'm not angry," she murmured.

"I don't think I've thanked you properly for your help today," he murmured, moving closer still. She stared up at him, standing her ground, and he couldn't resist the soft invitation of her mouth for another minute. Without giving her a chance to say anything more, he gently cupped her face in his hands and kissed her.

CHAPTER SEVEN

KAT didn't know how she allowed it to happen but the instant Miguel kissed her, memories of the night they'd shared came rushing back to her, flooding her mind, making her melt against him. Instinctively, she opened her mouth, wordlessly inviting him to deepen the kiss.

One moment his mouth was gentle, the next it was demanding, needy, stirring up flames of desire she'd tried to forget, vowed to live without.

She'd missed this. Missed him. Missed the way he made her feel, alive, vibrant, attractive. She wrapped her arms tightly around his neck, hanging on for dear life as a storm of desire washed over her, nearly drowning her with its intensity.

"Katerina," he whispered, as he pressed soft, moist kisses down the side of her neck. "You are so beautiful to me. I've never forgotten you. Never."

For one long moment she almost gave in to his sinful temptation. His hand came up to gently cup her breast, his thumb stroking her nipple through the thin layer of cotton, and her body reacted, arching into his, desperately needing to feel his hands on her bare skin.

She wanted nothing more than to close her eyes and give in to the whisper of pure pleasure, but she wasn't that younger, carefree person any more. She was a single mother with responsibilities.

Appalled with herself, she quickly broke off the embrace, forcing herself to let Miguel go, stumbling in her haste to put the width of the kitchen table between them. She grasped the back of a chair so tightly her knuckles were white. "I'm sorry, but I can't do this. I didn't come here to—to pick up where we left off, Miguel."

She couldn't allow the flash of hurt in his eyes to get to her. Too bad if his macho pride had taken a low blow. He would survive. She had to think about Tommy now. She watched him struggle to pull himself under control and she was a little ashamed of herself for being glad he'd been as aroused as she had been. At least she knew for sure the attraction wasn't one-sided.

"Of course you didn't," he said slowly, as if articulating each word helped him to maintain control. "I promised you dinner and I always follow through on my promises."

Dinner? Food? He had to be joking. She couldn't have eaten a bite to save her life. She shook her head and took a long deep breath, before letting it out slowly. "Miguel, listen to me. I came here because I have something to tell you. Something very important." She forced herself to meet his gaze.

He seemed truly baffled and took a step towards her, and she instinctively took a quick step back. "What is it, Katerina? Are you all right? It's not…your health, is it?"

She couldn't help being touched that he cared enough to worry about her health. And if she was sick, would he stand by her? Or would he look for an excuse to leave?

She didn't want to consider the answer to that question, so she ruthlessly shoved the thought aside.

Obviously, he wasn't going to be able to figure this out on his own. She'd have to come right out to say it. "I'm fine, Miguel. But there is something you should know." She took a deep breath and bravely faced him. "I have a son. *We* have a son. He will be four years old in a little less than three months."

He gaped at her in shock, and for several long seconds the silence was heavy between them. She wished she could read his mind to know what he was thinking. "A son?" he echoed, almost in disbelief.

"His name is Tomas. I named him after you." During the night they'd shared, Miguel had confided that Tomas was his middle name. And his father's name.

Miguel dragged a hand down his face, as if still hardly able to comprehend what she was saying. "I don't understand. How did this happen? We used protection."

She batted down the flicker of anger—hadn't she asked herself the same question while staring down at the positive pregnancy test? But having him think, even for a moment, that she might have done this on purpose made her grind her teeth in frustration. "Protection can fail, Miguel. I'm sorry to spring this on you so suddenly. You need to know I tried to find you after you left. I called your cellphone and searched for you on all the popular social media websites. When I couldn't find you, I assumed you were working somewhere remote with Doctors Without Borders, following your dream." She spread her hands wide. "I didn't know Seville was your home. Had no way of knowing you were here all this time."

Miguel looked in shock and he lowered himself slowly onto a kitchen chair. "A son. Tomas. I can barely comprehend what you are telling me."

Relieved to have the secret out in the open, she sank into a chair across from him and reached for her purse. "I have a picture. Would you like to see?" Without waiting for his reply, she slid Tommy's picture across the table. "He looks very much like you, Miguel."

He stared at the glossy photograph for several long moments before he dragged his gaze up to meet hers. "This is such a shock. I don't know what to say, other than that he's amazing. Thank you for bearing him."

There had really been no choice, not for her. The way Miguel stared at the picture, as if awestruck, made her a bit nervous. Was he already thinking of taking their son away from her? Beneath the table she linked her fingers together, tightly. "Miguel, I only told you about Tommy because you had a right to know. Please be assured, I'm more than capable of raising him. I don't expect anything from you."

For the first time since arriving in Spain she saw his gaze darken with anger directed at her. "I will not avoid my responsibility, Katerina," he murmured in a low tone. For just a brief moment she thought he looked upset, but then the fleeting expression was gone. In its place was grim resolution. "Of course I will provide for my son. And I would like to make arrangements to meet him. As soon as possible. I know Juliet will be here for a few more days, but I can make arrangements for the two of us to return immediately to the U.S."

She stared at him, realizing in some portion of her brain that Miguel didn't know Tommy was here in

Seville with her. Was, in fact, sleeping soundly back in her hotel room. If she told Miguel he was there, she had no doubt he'd swoop in and wake him up, scaring the poor child to death. She strove to keep her tone level. "Miguel, be reasonable. He's a young boy, not yet four. He won't understand or recognize you. You will be a stranger to him. We need some time to think this through, to figure out what we're going to do. Besides, I don't want to leave Juliet yet."

Miguel slowly rose to his feet, staring down at her arrogantly. "If you think I will let you raise my son without me, you are sorely mistaken. I will be a part of his life, and nothing you do or say will change my mind."

The sick feeling in her stomach intensified as she stared up at him helplessly, knowing he meant every single word. And while she knew she'd have to share custody of Tommy with Miguel, she wasn't at all sure what that exactly meant regarding their future.

Would Miguel play at being a father at first but then lose interest in them? Would he decide to up and leave, just like her father had? The way Juliet's father had?

Seeing him with Pedro earlier, she'd thought Miguel would be a good father to her son. But now she couldn't prevent the doubts from seeping in. And she desperately needed time. Needed to understand exactly what the future truly held for them.

How much would she have to sacrifice for her son?

Miguel inwardly winced when Katerina eyes filled with wounded shock. He knew he'd crossed the line, had put her on the defensive by practically threatening her, but he couldn't seem to stop.

She'd borne his son. Had been raising him alone for years. Deep down he was outraged that he had been cheated of precious memories, yet logically he knew the situation wasn't her fault. He'd left to return home after his father's stroke, leaving Katerina to fend for herself. He'd simply assumed she'd be fine. Bitter guilt for not talking to her again after he'd left coated his tongue. She'd had every right to believe he was working in some distant country—after all, he'd told her about his dream. And truthfully, if not for his brother's drinking problem, he would have already been in Africa, working with those in need. He wouldn't be here now, hearing the truth about having a son. And she'd searched for him, too.

For a moment his resolve wavered. For so long he'd dreamed of joining Doctors Without Borders. Now his dream would have to be put on hold once again. Indefinitely. Maybe for ever.

He squelched the feeling of despair and refused to allow himself to think about that now. Instead, he glanced once more at the glossy photograph of a young boy with light brown skin, dark hair, and big dark eyes. His bright smile was the only facial feature that resembled Katerina. He trailed his fingertips over the photo and had the strongest urge to hop onto the first plane to the U.S. to see Tomas in person.

"Miguel? I smell something burning," Katerina said in a tight voice.

He whirled around in surprise, having totally forgotten about the meal he'd prepared. He went over to pull the chicken dish from the oven, waving the smoke away. "I don't think it's too badly burned," he said, even though the chicken looked a bit on the overdone side.

"I'm not hungry," Katerina murmured. She pushed away from the table and rose to her feet. "I think it's best that I go back to the hotel now. We can discuss this more tomorrow."

He swung around to face her, unwilling to call an abrupt end to their evening. "Don't leave," he said, his voice sharply commanding rather than pleading with her, the way he should. He forced himself to soften his tone. "If you could spare a few minutes, I would like to hear more about Tomas."

She stood indecisively, wringing her hands together, and he silently cursed himself for being so stupid. He'd frightened her, instead of reassuring her that he intended to be there for her and for Tomas. Maybe a part of him mourned the loss of his dream, but he refused, absolutely refused, to ignore his responsibilities.

He'd been selfish once, following his dream to study abroad, and his brother Luis had suffered for it. His father had suffered too. He would always regret not being there when his father had sustained his stroke. The fact that he'd saved countless patients' lives wasn't enough to make up for his failures regarding his family.

He couldn't bear to fail his son.

"There isn't much to tell," she protested. "He's hardly more than a baby."

Katerina avoided his direct gaze and he wished he could cross over and take her once again into his arms. Kissing her had felt like heaven and he'd nearly lost all control when she'd wantonly kissed him back.

"He's not stubborn, like his mother?" he asked, trying to lighten the mood by gently teasing her. "I find that difficult to believe."

She narrowed her gaze and flipped her long golden hair over her shoulder. "Believe me, Tommy gets his stubborn streak from his father."

He tried not to wince at the shortened version of his son's name. He didn't understand this American tendency to give nicknames rather than using given names. "I bet he's smart, then, too. Just like me."

Katerina rolled her eyes. "Of course he's smart. I read to him before he goes to bed at night and he has memorized every story. He attends preschool and already knows his letters and numbers."

Hearing about his son's life, bedtime stories and preschool caused helpless anger to wash over him. He'd missed so much. Too much.

She was right, his son didn't know him. He couldn't bear the thought of being a stranger to his own son. "I can't wait to see him, Katerina. I want to see him, to hold him in my arms. I feel like I've missed too much already."

Her expression went from tolerant amusement to frank alarm. "Miguel, you can't just barge into his life like a steamroller. You'll be a stranger to him. You have to give him time to get to know you. And what exactly are you suggesting? That we'll just move here to Seville to be near you? Neither one of us speaks the language here and, besides, Tommy is an American citizen. We have a life back home." As she spoke, Katerina edged closer to the door, her eyes wide with panic.

"I'm sorry, but this is too much stress for me to handle right now, Miguel. I came to Seville because of

Juliet's injuries, remember? And after working all day, I can barely think straight. We'll talk tomorrow."

"Katerina…" he protested, but too late. She already had her hand on the front door. He knew he was pushing her too hard, too fast. "All right. We can talk more tomorrow. I'll be happy to take you back to the hotel."

"I'll ride the metro," she said, lifting her chin in the stubborn gesture he secretly found amusing. Except that her eagerness to get away from him wasn't at all comical.

"Katerina, please allow me to take you." When she still looked like a rabbit ready to bolt, he added, "If you insist on taking the metro, I will have no choice but to follow you. We will ride together."

Her mouth tightened, but after a moment she gave a small, jerky nod. "Fine. We'll take your car. But I'd like to go now, Miguel."

He couldn't think of a way to talk her out of it, so he simply nodded and reached for his cellphone. He called his driver, Fernando, and requested him to return right away. Fernando sounded surprised, but readily agreed. "My driver will be here in five minutes," he assured her.

Katerina didn't move away from the door, but simply looked at him from across the room, a long awkward silence stretching between them. He glanced over at the photograph of Tomas, still sitting on the kitchen table. "May I keep the picture of my son?" he asked in a low voice.

For a moment he thought Katerina was going to burst into tears, but she bit her lip and nodded. "Of course," she murmured in a husky voice. "I have others at home."

The way she said the word home, as if he wasn't included, made his temper flare, but he managed to hold his tongue. Thankfully, Fernando arrived quicker than expected.

Katerina didn't say more than a couple brief sentences on the way back to her hotel. He couldn't think of anything to say to put her mind at ease. Because even though he didn't want to upset her, there was no way on earth he was going to give his son up easily.

"Thank you for the ride," she said politely, when Fernando pulled up in front of her hotel. "I'm sure I'll see you some time tomorrow."

He caught her hand before she escaped from the car. "Katerina, wait. How about if we agree to meet at eleven o'clock tomorrow morning? I will have finished making rounds by then. We'll meet in your sister's room and then we can go somewhere for a cup of coffee, okay?"

"Fine. I'll see you at eleven." She looked pointedly down at where his hand was locked around her wrist and he forced himself to let her go. "Goodnight," she said, and didn't wait for him to respond before slamming the door shut and practically sprinting into the lobby.

He watched her hurry away, trying not to panic at the realization that she could easily catch a flight home tonight, making it extremely difficult for him to find her. And his son.

"Ready, sir?" Fernando asked from the front seat.

He hesitated, fighting the urge to follow her upstairs to her hotel room before she could slip away, maybe for ever. He wanted to talk to her about how they would deal with this situation, to insist they finish their conversation right this minute.

He took several deep breaths, fighting to stay calm.

Logically, he knew Katerina wasn't going to run away. She wouldn't leave Juliet, not when her sister had suffered seizures earlier that afternoon. Besides, no one had forced her to tell him about his son. Truthfully, Katerina could have kept Tomas a secret, simply returning home without telling him a thing. The fact that she had told him indicated she wanted their son to have a father. The thought calmed him.

"Yes, I'm ready, Fernando," he said, giving his driver the signal to leave. As they pulled away from the curb and headed home, Miguel sat back in his seat, his mind whirling.

He had until tomorrow morning at eleven to come up with a new plan. He needed some way to convince Katerina that Tommy would benefit from having them all be together as a family, rather than living apart. Surely she wanted such a thing as well, or she wouldn't have told him her secret.

Granted, the obstacle of living in different countries was no small thing. They both had family members to take into consideration as well. He had his brother Luis, who still needed support, and she had Juliet, who might need ongoing medical care.

The entire situation seemed impossible, but he was determined there would be a way to make things work out to everyone's satisfaction.

Grimly, he stared out through the night, knowing he would fight anyone and anything that stood in the way of establishing a relationship with his son.

CHAPTER EIGHT

KAT barely made it up to her hotel room where she collapsed in the chair beside the bed and buried her face in her hands, trying not to give in to mounting hysteria.

Miguel wanted to meet his son, and it sounded pretty certain that he would want custody. All this time she'd figured he wouldn't want the responsibility of having a family, yet he'd made it clear that he intended to follow her back to the U.S. in order to claim Tommy as his own.

"Kat?" Diana whispered from the bed. "Are you all right?"

She lifted her head and struggled to swallow her tears. Thankfully, Tommy was sleeping in the small roll-away bed as he would only be upset to see her crying. The room was dark, but they always left the bathroom light on in case Tommy needed to get up. "Fine," she whispered back, subtly swiping her hands over her wet cheeks. "We'll talk in the morning."

She wished Diana was asleep already too, because her emotions were too raw, too fragile to talk now.

Maybe Diana had been right to encourage her to wait before telling Miguel about Tommy. She wished she'd listened to her friend's advice. But it was too late now.

There was nothing to do except to move forward from here. Telling Miguel about his son was the right thing to do, but while she thought she'd prepared herself for the conversation, Miguel's reaction had overwhelmed her.

He'd assumed she'd left her son back home, and she hadn't possessed the courage to tell him otherwise. She could rationalize the reason was because Miguel would have come right up here to the room, demanding to see Tommy regardless of the fact that he was already asleep. Regardless of the fact that seeing a stranger might upset him.

But deep down she knew her reasons for keeping silent were far more selfish. She'd needed a little time to come to grips with how her life would change from this point on. Miguel's demand to return immediately to the U.S. had frightened her. The fantasy she'd harbored, where Miguel would allow her to continue to raise his son while he joined Doctors Without Borders, had exploded in her face.

She crept over to the side of the roll-away bed where Tommy was sleeping to gaze down at his sweet, innocent face. He was clutching his favorite stuffed animal, Terry the tiger, to his chest. She lightly brushed her fingers over his silky dark hair, being careful not to wake him up. She wanted to gather him close into her arms, as if to reassure herself that she wasn't going to lose him.

She pressed a soft kiss to the top of his head, before heading into the bathroom to wash her face and change into her nightgown. She crawled into her bed and stared blindly up at the ceiling, knowing she'd never relax enough to fall asleep.

Going back over the events of the evening, she

couldn't help remembering, in vivid detail, the way Miguel had kissed her. Before he'd known about Tommy. He'd clearly wanted her, his body's reaction had been no secret. Had he assumed that since they'd made love four and a half years ago she wouldn't think twice about doing so again?

It had been tempting, far more tempting that she wanted to admit, to give in to the passion that shimmered between them. Truthfully, Tommy was the main reason she'd pulled back. If not for her son, she knew that she and Miguel would have continued where they'd left off all those years ago.

Because she cared about Miguel. More than she should. And while they might be able to get along enough to share custody of their son, she wasn't sure how to get past her personal feelings for him.

"Mama, wake up!" Tommy said, climbing up on her bed. "I'm hungry."

Kat forced her gritty eyelids open, inwardly groaning. She'd been awake half the night, worrying herself sick about the future, and could easily have slept for several more hours. But as a parent she was used to putting her needs aside for her son. "I'm awake," she murmured, trying to focus on the clock across the room and wincing when she realized it was seven a.m.

"Do you want me to take Tommy down to the café for breakfast?" Diana asked as she came out of the bathroom. "You can probably catch another hour or so of sleep."

"No, that's fine. I want to come with you." Kat sat up, running her fingers through her hair. "I was thinking maybe we should go on the boat tour this morning, instead of waiting until later."

Diana's eyes lit up. "That would be great."

Kat didn't have the heart to tell her friend that by early afternoon she'd likely be arranging a meeting between Miguel and Tommy. Better to put that conversation off for a little while yet. "Give me fifteen minutes to get ready, okay?"

"Sure."

Kat freshened up in the bathroom, forgoing a shower to pull her hair back into its usual ponytail. During the long night, when she'd tossed and turned for hours, she'd decided Tommy needed his father, so she planned to present Miguel with her joint custody proposal. As much as it pained her, she thought that having Tommy spend summers here with Miguel, along with a few holidays, would probably be the least disruptive to their lives. And she could travel with Tommy to make sure things went well, at least for the first few years. She could only hope that Miguel would find parenting too much work. Although remembering the way he cared for the pediatric patients in the hospital, like Pedro and DiCarlo, she knew he wouldn't.

Tommy ran into the bathroom and grabbed her hand. "Mama, let's go."

"All right, all right. Slow down. Diana, do you have your room key?"

"Right here." Diana held it up.

"All right, here's mine. After we go on the boat ride, I'm going to head over to the hospital to see Juliet." And Miguel, although she didn't voice that last part.

"Do you want to stop on the way?" Diana offered.

She did, very much, but at the same time she was too afraid they'd run into Miguel. And since she'd promised Diana and Tommy a boat ride, she was determined to follow through on her promise. If she was back in the U.S., she could simply call the hospital to see how her sister was doing, but with the language barrier she had no choice but to actually go in to see Juliet for herself. And it didn't help that Miguel's eleven o'clock time frame hung over her head like a time bomb. "No, that's okay. Let's do the boat tour first."

As they left the hotel and walked down the street to their favorite breakfast café, she was determined to have this short time to play tourist with Diana and Tommy. A few hours alone, before their lives changed, for ever.

"Look at these bikes, Kat—isn't this the coolest idea?" Diana said as she gestured toward the bike rack located a few feet from the café. "I found out that this is a type of public transportation offered in Seville. For a small annual fee you can take one of these bikes, ride it to your destination, park it in another bike rack and then use it again to go home. No need to buy a bike of your own. These bike racks and bikes are located all over the city."

Kat smiled when she saw an elderly gentleman ride away on one of the red and white bikes, his front basket full of groceries. "Very cool idea."

"Have you notice the people walk or bike everywhere? No wonder they're healthier than Americans." Diana was starting to sound like a TV commercial sprouting the benefits of living in Seville.

"Remember, this is southern Spain where the weather

is mild and we live in the northeast of the U.S. Biking in snow and ice isn't an easy task."

"Maybe," Diana murmured. "But I have to say, this trip has really opened my eyes to how other cultures thrive."

Kat couldn't disagree. They finished their breakfast and took the metro to the heart of the city, where the sidewalk vendors sold tickets for the boat tours. Tommy was happy to be on the move, running from one location to the other. She gave him room to run, knowing that his boundless energy had to be let loose some time.

They had to wait almost thirty minutes for the next tour, and Kat kept an eye on the time, knowing she needed to head back to the hospital in order to meet Miguel by eleven o'clock. As much as she wanted to enjoy the tour, her stomach was knotted with nerves.

The boat tour wasn't crowded this early in the morning and they had almost the entire upper deck of the boat to themselves. Tommy was thrilled when she lifted him up so that he could see over the railing.

The tour lasted almost an hour, and by the time they disembarked from the boat Kat knew they needed to head back toward the hotel. "No, we need to go this way, Tommy," she called, when he took off down the sidewalk.

Her son ignored her instruction and Diana glanced at her. "I'll get him," she offered.

"No, I'll go." Kat took off after Tommy, who was running and laughing as if they were playing a game of chase. She wanted to be mad at him, but just listening to him laugh made her smile. She gained on him and tried to get his attention. "Tommy, come on, now. We have to go for a ride on the metro."

A woman walking a dog was heading towards them and Tommy suddenly swerved right in front of them. The dog was on a leash but reacted instinctively by jumping up and nipping at him at the same time both Kat and the dog's owner shouted, "No!"

Tommy let out a wail as the dog's owner yanked the dog back and Kat rushed over, picking Tommy up and carrying him out of harm's way. "Shh, it's okay. You're okay, Tommy," she crooned as she tried to examine him for injuries.

Her heart sank when she found puncture marks in the fleshy part of Tommy's arm a few inches above the wrist. The wounds were bleeding, and she glanced up as Diana joined them, feeling like the worst mother on the planet. "The dog bit him."

Diana was a nurse too, and she looked at the wounds with a grimace. "We need to get that cleaned up right away."

"Yeah, but I think he'll need antibiotics too. Do they have clinics here? Or should we go straight to the hospital?" She hated knowing this was all her fault. She shouldn't have let Tommy run around. She should have anticipated something like this.

The dog owner was talking in rapid Spanish, clearly upset about what happened. Kat tried to smile, shaking her head. *"No comprendo Espanol,"* she said.

"They must have clinics," Diana was saying with a frown. But Kat had already made up her mind.

"We'll go to the hospital where Juliet is being cared for. I saw an emergency department there."

"Are you sure that's a good idea?" Diana asked. "We could run into Miguel."

"It's a risk, but Tommy needs good medical care. Miguel is a surgeon—chances are good that we'll be in and out of there without him knowing." And even if they weren't, she wasn't going to worry about Miguel's reaction at seeing them. Tommy's health was far more important.

Diana reluctantly agreed. Kat made sure they stopped in a restroom to wash the dog bite with soap and water, before taking the metro back to the hospital. As they walked into the small emergency room, Kat couldn't help glancing around for any sign of Miguel.

Tommy was, of course, her first concern. Miguel already knew about their son, but she didn't really want him to find out like this that Tommy was here in Seville. She would much rather tell him herself.

The woman at the desk in the emergency room didn't speak any English, and she showed her the dog bite on Tommy's arm, pulling out her Spanish dictionary to find the word for dog. *"Perro,"* she said, demonstrating the action of biting.

"Sí, un momento." The woman spoke to someone else in Spanish, and then took them back to a small exam room. Kat was glad to see the nurse bring in a wash basin.

She relaxed, feeling better now that they were actually getting medical care for Tommy. She glanced at her watch, realizing she was going to be late for her meeting with Miguel.

"I can stay with Tommy if you need me to," Diana offered, sensing her distress.

She slowly shook her head. "No, I can't just leave. Not until I know the wound is clean and that he'll get the antibiotics he needs."

If she had a way to call Miguel, she would. But as she didn't, she could only hope Miguel would have patience and wait for her.

Miguel arrived at the hospital early, unable to contain his excitement. He'd found a flight to Cambridge that was scheduled to leave early the next morning and he'd been tempted to go ahead and book it, except that he wasn't sure when Katerina's return flight was scheduled for. It wouldn't help him to get there before she arrived. Yet he was thrilled that he was closer than ever to meeting his son.

He went up to see how Juliet was doing, hoping that she would soon be stable enough to transfer home. He was pleased to discover that she was following instructions again and hadn't had any more seizures. Her electrolytes were back to normal, which was also a very good sign. He left orders to begin weaning her from the ventilator.

She wasn't quite ready for transfer back home but would be soon.

Since he was early, he decided to check on his other patients. First he checked on DiCarlo, who remained in the I.C.U. The boy was still critical, but his vitals were stable. From there, he headed over to the temporary children's ward to visit with Pedro.

"Hi, Dr. Vasquez," Pedro greeted him. The boy looked a little better, although still a little too pale and drawn. He didn't like seeing the dark circles beneath Pedro's eyes.

"Pedro, how are you feeling?" He crossed the room and checked the nursing notes on the clipboard. "Why aren't you taking pain medication?"

Pedro grimaced. "I don't like the way they make me feel."

"Maybe not, but I don't think you're getting enough rest. Sleep is very important. You will heal much faster if you take some pain medication at nighttime."

The boy flashed a wan smile. "You sound like Miss Kat. That same thing she explained to me yesterday."

Miguel nodded, sensing a bit of puppy love for Katerina in Pedro's gaze. "Katerina is a very smart lady. You would do well to follow her advice."

Pedro was quiet for a moment. "I thought she might come to visit me today."

He saw the stab of disappointment in the boy's eyes. "She is planning to come later, and I'm sure she will visit. I'll need to talk to your mother about keeping you here another day, Pedro."

"She won't care. She is too busy at home with my brothers and sisters."

Miguel wished there was something he could say to make the boy feel better. "That may be true, but you also help her, don't you? I'm sure she misses you."

"Of course." Pedro winced as he shifted in the bed. He put a tentative hand over his incision. "But I don't think carrying my brothers and sisters is a good idea right now."

"No, that would not be good," Miguel agreed. He lifted Pedro's hospital gown and gently peeled back the gauze dressing to examine his wound. The skin around the incision was a little red and he gently palpated the area to make sure there was no pus beneath the skin. There wasn't, but he decided to add yet another anti-biotic just to be on the safe side. The risk of infection was high. "Looks good, but you have to take your pain medications. I need you to get up and walk the hallways. Staying in bed all day isn't healthy."

Pedro nodded. "Okay, I will do that."

Miguel called for the nurse and waited until Pedro had taken the ordered pain medication before he moved on to the next patient. He took his time making rounds, wanting to be sure to have everything finished before he spent time with Katerina.

He returned to Juliet's room at exactly eleven o'clock, frowning when he discovered Katerina hadn't arrived yet. He went back out to the nurses' station. "Has Juliet's sister been here to visit?" he asked in Spanish.

"No, Dr. Vasquez, she has not been here yet."

He gave a brief nod, hiding his impatience. He went back to DiCarlo's room, reviewing the chart to make sure his orders had been carried out, secretly watching for Katerina to arrive.

At eleven-thirty his temper began to simmer. Was it possible his worst fears had been realized? That she'd actually taken an earlier flight home in an attempt to hide Tomas from him? He didn't want to believe she would do such a thing, but as the minutes passed with agonizing slowness, he couldn't help believing the worst.

At noon he muttered an oath and left the hospital, calling his driver to take him to Katerina's hotel. He had to know she was still here in Seville. And if she was simply trying to avoid him, he would make certain she never did such a thing ever again.

His driver pulled up in front of the hotel and Fernando had barely put the car in park before Miguel shot out of the back seat, striding purposefully up to the front desk. "I need to speak with Katerina Richardson in room 212," he said.

"I will ring the room," the clerk said. After a few minutes he shrugged and hung up. "I'm afraid there is no answer."

"But she's still a guest here, right?" Miguel persisted. The time was almost twelve-thirty and most of the flights back to the U.S. left early in the morning, but there had been one early-afternoon flight.

"*Sí, señor,* she is still a guest. If you would like to wait, I suggest you have a seat in the lobby."

Miguel was too keyed up to sit in the lobby so he went back outside to let Fernando know he'd be staying for a while. He paced back and forth for several minutes, before taking a seat in the outside café adjacent to the hotel. He ordered a soft drink, although he was in the mood for something far stronger.

Within minutes a familiar voice reached his ears. "Walk, Tommy, don't run. Here, take my hand."

He went still, hardly able to believe his ears. Tommy? Slowly he turned in his seat in time to see Katerina walking up the sidewalk toward the hotel, holding the hand of a young boy.

The same boy in the photograph she'd given him.

Their son!

CHAPTER NINE

MIGUEL slowly rose to his feet, his anger towards Katerina fading as he drank in the sight of his son. Seeing Tomas in person was so much better than a photograph. The boy was so animated, Miguel could barely breathe.

Katerina abruptly stopped in her tracks, going pale when her gaze locked on his. But then she took a deep breath and said something in a low voice to her companion, a woman with dark hair who looked vaguely familiar, as she resumed walking.

He wanted to rush over and sweep his son into his arms, but remembering what Katerina had said yesterday about how he was a stranger to Tomas, it gave him the strength to stay right where he was. It wasn't until Katerina and Tomas came closer that he noticed the white gauze dressing on his son's left forearm.

"Hi, Miguel," she greeted him. "I'm sorry I missed you at the hospital. This is my son, Tommy, who had a small accident. And you remember my friend, Diana Baylor?"

He cleared his throat, striving to play along as if seeing his son in person hadn't completely knocked him off balance. "Of course I remember. Diana, it's good to see you again. And this is your son, Tommy?" He purposefully used Katerina's dreadful nickname and crouched down so he was at eye level with the child and wouldn't seem so intimidating. "Hi, Tommy, my name is Miguel Vasquez. I'm very happy to meet you."

Tomas stared at him with his large brown eyes and shrank back toward his mother, as if suddenly shy. Miguel didn't want to frighten the boy, but at the same time he couldn't help being frustrated that his son didn't know him.

He had to remind himself that the situation was his own fault. Not Katerina's. And certainly not the child's.

"It's okay, Tommy," Katerina said, brushing a hand over his dark hair. "Miguel is a good friend of mine. Show him where the dog bit you on the arm."

Tomas held out his arm, the one covered in gauze. "Bad doggy bit me," he said solemnly.

"Tommy, remember how you ran straight at the doggy? He only nipped at you because he was scared," Katerina said, filling in the gaps of what had happened for Miguel. "And the emergency-room nurse gave you a lollipop, didn't she?"

There was a hint of red staining the child's fingers and teeth as he nodded vigorously. "I'm a good boy."

"I'm sure you were a very good boy," Miguel said with a smile, relieved to know that his son had received appropriate medical care for the dog bite. Obviously, this was the reason Katerina hadn't met him in her sister's room. A very good excuse, except that it didn't at all explain why she'd let him believe Tomas was back in the U.S.

Although he'd assumed that, hadn't he? Katerina hadn't lied to him, but she had withheld the truth.

He would grant her a pass on this one, but now that she was here, with Tomas, he was determined to spend as much time with his son as possible.

And Katerina had better not try to stand in his way.

Kat had been shocked to find Miguel waiting for her outside their hotel, but by the time she noticed him it was too late as he'd already recognized Tommy. At least now there were no more secrets. She could see Miguel wasn't happy with her, but there wasn't much she could do. This had already been a rough day, and it was barely one o'clock in the afternoon.

"Katerina, do you think the three of us could take a walk?" Miguel asked, as he rose to his feet. "No offense, Diana, but I'd like some time alone with Katerina and Tomas."

Diana crossed her arms over her chest and shrugged, glancing over at her. "Kat? What would you like to do?"

Kat knew her friend would stand by her, if asked, but she'd known that Miguel would want to spend time with his son and there was no good reason to delay. "We'll be fine, Diana. You deserve some down time anyway. Should we meet back here at the hotel in an hour or so? Tommy will be more than ready for his nap by then."

"Sure thing." Diana's gaze was full of suspicion as she glanced over at Miguel. "Nice meeting you again, Dr. Vasquez," she said politely, before turning to walk away.

"I'm getting the sense she doesn't like me very

much," Miguel murmured after Diana was out of earshot.

"Diana has always been there for me when I needed her. She was my labor coach and has helped me out more times than I could count, especially on days when I needed child care when Tommy was sick." Her temper flared. She was unwilling to allow him to put down her friend.

Miguel winced as her barb hit home. "In other words, she blames me for not being there with you."

Kat glanced down at Tommy and decided this wasn't the time or the place to argue about the past. "You wanted to take a walk, so let's walk. There's a park not far from here, down the block and across the street."

Miguel nodded and fell into step beside her, keeping Tommy between them. "Yes, I played at that park often as a young boy. See that school there?" He gestured toward the white building across the street. "That's where both my brother and I attended school."

She remembered seeing the young kids all wearing their navy blue and white plaid uniforms running outside at recess. Today was Sunday, so there weren't any children playing now, but she couldn't help wondering if Miguel was insinuating that he wanted Tommy to attend the same school he had. She struggled to remain calm. "Yes, I saw the students playing outside in their uniforms the other day. I was struck by how similar the school was to ours back home."

"Tommy, do you like school?" Miguel asked, turning his attention to their son.

"Yeah." Tommy seemed to be slowly warming up to Miguel. "School is fun."

"Do you play games at school?" Miguel persisted.

"Yep. I play with my friends."

Kat couldn't help smiling as Miguel tried to have a conversation with their son. Too bad that having a rational conversation with an almost four-year-old wasn't easy. Miguel was lucky to get anything more than one- or two-word answers to his questions.

When they reached the park Tommy tugged on her hand so she let him go, allowing him to run over to the water fountain. He looked over the cement edge, peering into the water.

"I can't believe you didn't tell me he was here," Miguel said in a low tone. "Do you realize I almost booked a flight to Cambridge this morning?"

"I'm sorry, Miguel. But Tommy was already asleep and I couldn't risk you marching into the room and waking him up. Besides, I honestly planned on bringing him with me to see you today. Unfortunately Tommy's dog bite prevented me from meeting you at the hospital, as we'd planned."

He sensed the truth in her words and forced himself to relax.

"But why would you book a flight without discussing your plans with me?" she continued. "You can't bulldoze your way into Tommy's life, Miguel. What we want doesn't matter here. The only thing that matters is what's best for Tommy." She turned to face him. "I told you about our son, first because you deserved to know, and second because Tommy deserves a father. I would like to think we could work something out together."

"Joint custody?" Miguel's nose wrinkled in distaste.

"Impossible with both of us living in two different countries."

"Not impossible," she countered. "Tommy could visit you in the summer and maybe over the holiday."

"While he lives the rest of the time with you?" Miguel asked. "I hardly think that arrangement is fair."

"Fair? Do you think it was fair to leave me pregnant and alone? I tried to find you, Miguel, but you certainly didn't try to find me. So don't stand there and try to tell me what is or isn't *fair*."

There was a charged silence between them as Kat tried to rein in her temper. She'd long ago accepted that the night she'd spent with Miguel meant nothing to him. Yet deep down she had to admit there was still a small kernel of resentment.

"You're right, Katerina. I must accept responsibility for my actions."

Miguel's acquiescence shocked her. So much that she didn't have any idea how to respond.

"I can only ask that you give me some time now to get to know my son. And, of course, we will need to agree to some financial arrangements."

"I don't want your money, Miguel," she protested. "We're not rich, but we're not poor either."

"I insist," he said. And she could tell by the edge to his tone that there was no point in arguing.

She let out her pent-up breath in a silent sigh. "Fine. We can discuss that more later." She should be thrilled that he hadn't put up much of a fight. But as Miguel left her side to cross over to where Tommy was digging in the dirt with a stick, she couldn't help feeling a sharp

stab of disappointment that apparently they wouldn't
be raising their son together.

As a family.

Miguel wanted to protest when Katerina insisted it was
time to head back to the hotel, but even he could see that
Tomas was getting cranky. He didn't doubt her wisdom
regarding the fact that their son needed a nap.

He cared for pediatric patients in the hospital, but
obviously he didn't know the first thing about raising a
child. How was he to know that almost four-year-olds
still took naps?

"Up, Mama, up," Tomas whined.

"Is your arm hurting you?" she asked, swinging the
boy into her arms and cuddling him close.

Miguel wanted, very badly, to be the one to carry his
son, but suspected his offer of assistance wouldn't be
welcomed by Tomas. He'd started to make friends with
his son, but the boy still clung to his mother for comfort.

"Yeah," Tomas said, burying his face against her
neck.

"I'll give you something to make your pain go away
when we get back to the hotel room, all right?"

"They gave you pain medication?" he asked in surprise.

"No, but I have children's ibuprofen at the hotel, although I suspect he'll practically be asleep by then,
anyway."

Katerina was correct. Tomas had closed his eyes and
fully relaxed against his mother by the time they approached the hotel lobby.

"Wait for me here," Katerina told him, as she stabbed

the button to summon the elevator. "I'll only be a few minutes."

He stepped back, resisting the urge to follow her up to their room. He was surprised she'd asked him to wait, figuring she'd want nothing more than to put distance between them. Although it was possible she simply wanted updated information on Juliet.

True to her word, Katerina returned a few minutes later. "Thanks for waiting, Miguel. I'm planning to head over to the hospital, and figured we could ride the metro together."

"I'm happy to ask Fernando to drive us there," he offered.

A grimace flashed over her features, but then she nodded. "I can't get used to the idea of having someone drive me around, but that's fine."

He called Fernando, and then gestured towards a small park bench sitting beneath the trees. "Have a seat. Fernando will be here in a few minutes."

"Why haven't you learned to drive?" she asked.

"I do know how to drive," he said testily, even though, truthfully, it had been a long time since he'd sat behind the wheel. "Fernando is a former patient of mine. He has a wife and three children. He lost his job after his accident and subsequent surgery, so I hired him."

She didn't say anything until Fernando drove up in Miguel's sleek black car. "That was very kind of you, Miguel."

He shrugged and strode forward, opening the back passenger door for her. Once she was seated inside, he closed the door, went around to the other side and slid in.

"Take us to the hospital, please, Fernando," he said in Spanish.

"Sí, señor," Fernando said, his gaze resting curiously on Katerina.

"Juliet is doing better today," he said, as Fernando pulled away from the curb. "Her electrolytes are all within normal range and she's following instructions again. I left orders this morning to begin weaning her off the ventilator."

Katerina smiled and relaxed against the seat. "I'm so happy to hear that. I feel bad I haven't been in there to see her yet today. Sounds as if she'll be ready to return home soon."

Now that he knew Tomas was here in Seville, he wasn't so anxious to pronounce Juliet stable enough for transport back to the U.S., but obviously he couldn't keep Juliet, or Katerina for that matter, hostage here. Maybe he'd be booking that plane ticket to Cambridge after all. "Perhaps," he responded slowly. "But I would like to make sure she's off the ventilator first."

She raised a brow, as if she was able to read his mind. But instead of pushing the issue, she changed the subject. "Tell me, how are DiCarlo and Pedro doing?"

"DiCarlo is still in the I.C.U., but his condition is stable," he admitted. "Pedro is doing well, too. He asked about you this morning. I think he was hurt that you didn't come to visit him."

"I'll visit him this afternoon," she promised. "He's a good kid, Miguel. I know his mother has several other children at home, but it breaks my heart to see him lying in that hospital bed all alone."

"Mine, too, Katerina," he murmured. There was no

denying the soft spot in his heart he had for the boy. "His father is off for weeks at a time as a truck driver, so she isn't ignoring him on purpose. Regardless, I know he'll be thrilled to see you."

The ride to the hospital didn't take long. He put on his lab coat and then gave Fernando some well-deserved time off, seeing as he was close enough to walk home from the hospital.

"I'd like to see Juliet first," Katerina said as they entered the elevator.

"Of course." Several of the staff greeted him as they walked down the hallway of the I.C.U., and if they were surprised to see him once again with Katerina, they didn't say anything to his face. No doubt, there was plenty of gossip going on behind his back and he was glad no one else knew about Tomas.

"Hey, sis, I'm back," Katerina said, as she crossed over to Juliet's bedside. "I'm sorry I couldn't be here earlier, but Tommy was bitten by a dog and I had to bring him to the emergency room."

Miguel was pleasantly surprised when Juliet opened her eyes and turned her face to look at Katerina.

"Juliet! You're awake!" Katerina took her sister's hand and leaned over to press a kiss on her forehead. "I was so worried about you."

Juliet looked as if she wanted to talk, but the breathing tube prevented her from making a sound. Before Miguel could step forward, Katerina took control.

"Don't try to talk—you still have that breathing tube in. But don't worry, Dr. Vasquez is trying to get that removed very soon. Which means you have to cooperate with him. You have to show us that you can breathe okay on your own. Can you understand what I'm saying?"

Juliet nodded and pointed to the tube, demonstrating with hand gestures that she wanted it out.

He crossed over to pick up the clipboard hanging off the end of the bed. "Good afternoon, Juliet. I can see here that your weaning parameters look very good."

Katerina glanced at him, her eyes full of hope. "Does that mean we can get the tube out now?"

He hesitated. Juliet had suffered a seizure just twenty-four hours ago, but he'd been convinced all along that she'd be fine once he got her electrolytes under control. "Let me listen to her lungs first," he said, replacing the clipboard and pulling his stethoscope from the pocket of his lab coat. Katerina went down to crank the head of the bed up so that Juliet was sitting upright. He helped her lean forward so that he could listen to her lung sounds.

"Well?" Katerina demanded when he'd finished.

Even though he knew that this meant Juliet would be discharged back to the U.S. soon, he nodded. "Yes, her lungs sound clear. I will get the nurse to come in and assist."

Katerina looked relieved and stood back as he and Maria, Juliet's nurse, took out her endotracheal tube.

"Water," Juliet croaked.

Katerina quickly came over to hold the small plastic cup and straw up so that Juliet could take a sip.

"Hurts," Juliet whispered hoarsely, putting her hand up to her throat.

"I know. Try to rest," Katerina said, putting a hand

on her arm. "Breathe slow and easy. You're going to be just fine, Jules."

"Where's Mom?" Juliet asked.

Katerina tossed him a worried look. "Mom's gone, Juliet. She passed away three years ago."

"Remember, she's still recovering from her head injury," he murmured.

"Don't talk, Jules. Just relax."

"I thought you were a dream," Juliet said, rubbing her obviously sore throat.

"I'm not a dream. I came as soon as I heard. I love you, Jules. Very much." Bright tears filled Katerina's eyes.

Miguel slipped out of the room, giving the two sisters time to be alone. He was pleased with Juliet's progress, even though he knew she still needed time to recover fully. Yet his heart was heavy as he went back to the nurses' station to write new orders. Obviously, if Juliet continued doing this well, she'd be stable enough to move to a regular room in the morning.

That would give him no choice but to deem her stable enough for transportation back to the U.S. as soon as arrangements could be made.

As he wrote instructions for breathing treatments and another chest X-ray in the morning, he vowed to let his boss know he needed a leave of absence as soon as possible. He couldn't bear the thought of Katerina and Tomas leaving so soon. He'd barely spent an hour with his son. And even though he would consider Katerina's proposed custody arrangements, he wasn't going to give up that easily.

There was no way he was going to settle for some long-distance relationship with Tomas. He was going to need that plane ticket after all.

CHAPTER TEN

KAT spent several hours with her sister, enormously relieved that she seemed to be doing so much better. But Juliet was also still very confused, not understanding that she was in Spain or that their mother was gone.

When Kat finally left, she was surprised to find Miguel sitting out at the nurses' station, clearly waiting for her. He rose to his feet when he saw her approach.

"Do you have time to visit Pedro?" he asked, meeting her halfway.

She nodded, ashamed to realize she'd completely forgotten about the young teen. "Of course. But you didn't have to stay, Miguel."

"I wanted to," he said simply.

She was touched by his dedication, even though logically she knew that he was glued to her side because of Tommy more than anything. Still, when he put his hand in the small of her back, her traitorous body reacted by shivering with awareness.

When the elevator doors closed, locking the two of them inside, the tension skyrocketed, his familiar scent filling her head. For a moment she couldn't think of anything except the heated kiss they'd shared.

She sneaked a glance at him from beneath her lashes,

wondering if she was losing her mind. Why did she have this strange attraction to him? She'd avoided personal entanglements with men because she didn't want to be left alone, like her mother had been.

Yet here she was, wishing for another chance with Miguel.

The doors opened and she stepped forward quickly, anxious to put space between them.

Thankfully, Pedro was a good distraction, greeting her enthusiastically. "Miss Kat! I'm so glad you came to visit."

"Hi, Pedro," she said, going over to take his hand in hers. She gave him a mock frown. "I hear you're not taking your pain medication as Dr. Vasquez ordered."

"Yes, I am," he corrected. "I took some earlier today when you were here, Dr. Vasquez. Don't you remember?"

Miguel sighed. "Pedro, that was almost eight hours ago. Do you mean to tell me you haven't taken anything since?"

He ducked his head sheepishly. "I wanted to wait until it was nighttime. You said that sleep was important."

Kat put her hands on her hips. "Pedro, you promised me you would take the pain medication."

"I'm sorry. I will take more tonight. Why are you so late here at the hospital?"

"Well, it was quite a busy morning," she said, as Miguel went out into the hall, probably to flag down Pedro's nurse. "I have a four-year-old son named Tommy and he was bitten by a dog so I had to take him to the emergency department to get antibiotics."

"I didn't know you have a son," Pedro said in surprise, and she belatedly realized she hadn't mentioned Tommy earlier. For a moment Pedro seemed almost disappointed by the news, but then he recovered. "Having a dog bite is very scary. Is he okay?"

"He's fine." She refused to look at her watch, not wanting Pedro to think she was in a hurry. Even though she knew Tommy would be up from his nap and ready to eat dinner soon. "But tell me how you're doing, other than not taking your pain medication."

"I walked today, the way Dr. Vasquez told me to. I went up to visit DiCarlo." Pedro grimaced and shrugged. "But I'm bored here with nothing to do all day. One of the nurses did play a word game with me, but she would only use Spanish words. How am I to learn English without practice?"

She'd noticed the game next to his bed. "How about we play a game before I leave? But our rule will be that we only use English words. Okay?"

"Really? You would do that for me?" He looked so happy that she wished she'd thought of it earlier.

"Of course." She pulled out the game and then sat next to his bed. She couldn't just leave, no matter how much she wanted to see Tommy.

"May I join you?" Miguel asked.

"Yes, more players will be more fun," Pedro said excitedly.

As Miguel pulled up a second chair, she realized Miguel would make a wonderful father.

But even as she acknowledged that truth, she knew there was no way to know for sure if he would be just as good a husband.

* * *

At the end of the second game Kat threw up her hands in defeat. "I give up. It's embarrassing to lose to both of you when I'm the one who speaks English."

Miguel flashed a conspiratorial grin at Pedro. "What do you think, amigo? Maybe we should have let her win one."

Pedro nodded. "I think we should have. It's only polite to allow a woman to win."

She rolled her eyes and stood. "I don't need either of you to do me any favors. You each won fair and square. But I'm afraid I need to go. Pedro, I'll visit again tomorrow, okay?"

"Okay. Thank you for staying," Pedro said. "I had much fun."

Miguel also stood. "I'll take you back to the hotel. And, Pedro, take your pain medication, please."

"I will." Pedro looked sad to see them go, but she'd already stayed far longer than she'd planned. She gave him a quick embrace before heading down the hall, anxious to get back to the hotel.

She glanced at Miguel as they waited for the elevator. "I can ride the metro back, there's no reason for you to go out of your way."

He didn't answer until they were inside the elevator. "I would like to see Tommy again, if you wouldn't mind. I thought I would take you all out for dinner."

She wanted to refuse, because being around Miguel was wearying. She was constantly on edge, trying not to let her true feelings show. But glancing up at him and seeing the hope in his eyes, she found she couldn't say no. "Tommy can't wait that late to eat. We usually have dinner at six or six-thirty."

"That's fine with me." When the elevator doors opened on the lobby level, he once again put his hand in the small of her back, gently guiding her. "I will take every moment possible to see my son."

She nodded, realizing with a sense of dread that they would have to make more specific plans for the future, especially now that her sister was doing better. How much longer would Juliet be allowed to stay in Seville? Probably not long. She swallowed hard and tried not to panic.

She wasn't surprised to see that Fernando was waiting outside for them. Now that she knew the reason Miguel had hired him, she found she was happy to have him drive them around. "*Buenos noches,* Fernando," she greeted him.

He flashed a wide smile. "*Buenos noches, señorita.*"

"And that's pretty much the extent of my Spanish," she muttered wryly, as she slid into the back seat.

"I'd be happy to teach you," Miguel murmured after he climbed in beside her. "Tomas should learn both languages too."

She bit back a harsh retort, turning to gaze out the window instead. Her anger wasn't entirely rational, yet the last thing she needed was Miguel telling her how to raise her son.

Their son.

Her lack of sleep the night before caught up with her and tears pricked her eyelids. Telling Miguel about Tommy had been the right thing to do so there was no reason to be upset.

"Katerina, what is it? What's wrong?" Miguel asked. He reached over to take her hand and she had to struggle not to yank it away. "Becoming bilingual is a good thing. If my mother hadn't taught me English, I would not have been given the opportunity to study abroad. We never would have met."

And if they hadn't met, Tommy wouldn't exist.

She momentarily closed her eyes, struggling for control. "Miguel, can't you understand how difficult this is for me? Tommy has been my responsibility for almost four years. I was pregnant and alone. I did the best I could. Now it seems like you're planning to barge in and do whatever you want. Without bothering to consult with me."

His hand tightened around her. "Katerina, I am more sorry than you'll ever know about how I left you alone. I will always regret not keeping in touch with you after leaving the U.S. And not just because of the time I missed getting to know my son. But because I realize now how much I missed you."

She sniffed and swiped her free hand over her eyes. "You don't need to flatter me, Miguel. If I hadn't shown up here to visit my sister, we wouldn't have met again. You never would have tried to find me."

There was another long pause. "Katerina, do you believe in fate? Believe that some things just happen for a reason?" His husky voice was low and compelling. "It's true that my dream was to join Doctors Without Borders, and if not for the difficulties with my brother, I probably would not have been here when your sister required emergency care. But I was here. And you arrived with our son. What else could this be if not fate?"

"Coincidence." Even as she said the word, she knew it wasn't entirely true. Was there really some cosmic force at play here? Drawing the two of them together after all this time? She generally believed that hard work and taking responsibility for your choices was the way to get ahead, but she couldn't totally renounce Miguel's beliefs.

"Fate, Katerina," Miguel whispered. "I believe we were meant to be together."

Together? As in as a family? She didn't know what to say to that, and luckily Fernando pulled up in front of her hotel. She gratefully tugged her hand from Miguel's grasp and reached for the doorhandle. "*Gracias, Fernando*," she said, before climbing hastily from the car.

But as quick as she was, Miguel was that much faster. He caught her before she could bolt and gently clasped her shoulders in his large hands. "Katerina, please talk to me. Tell me what has caused you to be so upset?"

She tipped her head back and forced herself to meet his gaze. "I'm more overwhelmed than upset, Miguel. And I'm not sure how you can stand there and claim we were meant to be together. We're not a couple. We're simply two adults who happen to share a child."

One of his hands slid up from her shoulder to cup her cheek. "You can't deny what is between us, *querida*."

She was about to tell him not to call her darling, but he quickly covered her mouth with his, silencing her with a toe-curling kiss.

She told herself to pull away, even lifted her hands to his chest to push him, but instead her fingers curled in his shirt, yanking him closer as she opened for him, allowing him to deepen the kiss.

All the pent-up emotions she'd tried so hard to ig-nore came tumbling out in a flash of pure desire. She forgot they were standing on the sidewalk in front of the hotel. Forgot that Fernando was still there, watching them with a huge, satisfied grin.

Forgot that she wasn't going to open herself up to being hurt again.

Everything fell away except this brief moment. A stolen fragment of time when they were able to communicate perfectly without words.

"*Querida,* Katerina, I need you so much," he murmured between steaming-hot kisses. "I can't understand how I lived all this time without you."

She pulled back, gasping for breath, bracing her forehead on his chest, wishing she could believe him. Wishing he'd felt a tenth of what she'd felt for him back then.

"Kat?" the sound of Diana's shocked voice had her jumping away from Miguel.

"Good evening, Diana. Hello, Tommy." Miguel smoothly covered the awkward pause. "Katerina and I were just about to ask you both to join us for dinner."

Kat avoided Diana's accusing gaze as she went over and gathered her son close. "Hi, Tommy, I'm sorry to be gone so long. Are you hungry?"

Tommy nodded. "I'm starving."

"Well, then, let's get going," Miguel said. "I understand there is an American restaurant nearby that serves great food, including hamburgers."

As much as she enjoyed the tangy bite of Spanish food, the thought of a simple American meal was tempting. "We can go somewhere else," she offered.

"Actually, other than smaller places that serve only

tapas, the main restaurants don't open this early," Miguel said with a note of apology.

"I'm all in favor of having good old-fashioned hamburgers," Diana said. "But let's hurry, okay? Tommy's bound to get cranky if he doesn't eat soon."

Kat couldn't help feeling guilty all over again. She shouldn't have stayed at the hospital so long. And she really, really shouldn't have kissed Miguel again.

The American restaurant was within walking distance, so Miguel sent Fernando away for a couple of hours. Diana's sour mood evaporated as they enjoyed their meal. When they were finished, Miguel took Tommy over to play a video game, leaving the two women alone.

"Kat, do you think it's smart to get emotionally involved with Miguel?" Diana asked in a low voice.

"I'm already emotionally involved with him, Diana," she responded wearily. "He's Tommy's father, remember? It's not like I can avoid him."

"Avoiding him is very different from having sex with him."

"It was a kiss, Diana." Although she suspected that if they'd been somewhere private, without the added responsibility of caring for Tommy, nothing would have stopped them from making love. "Besides, we'll be going home pretty soon. Juliet woke up and is off the breathing machine. She's still confused, but she's doing a lot better. I'm certain she'll be stable enough to be transferred home very soon."

"Already?" Diana looked disappointed with the news. "But we've hardly had time to sightsee."

"I know. I'm sorry." She did feel bad that Diana had

been stuck babysitting Tommy. "Maybe tomorrow I can take Tommy to the hospital to visit Juliet, giving you time to go see the cathedral. I hear it's spectacular."

"All right. But what about Miguel? What's he going to do?"

Good question. "I'm not sure, but I suspect he'll come visit me and Tommy in Cambridge. After that, I just don't know."

Diana was silent for a moment. "Are you going to move to Seville?"

"No!" Kat stared at her friend in shock. "Of course not. What on earth gave you that idea?"

Before Diana could respond, Miguel and Tommy returned to the table. "We blowed things up," Tommy said excitedly. "Bang, bang, bang!"

Kat grimaced and glanced at Miguel, who didn't look the least bit repentant. "Tommy has very good hand-eye coordination," he said proudly. "We scored many points."

They left the restaurant a little while later so that Miguel could enjoy this time with his son. They went for a long walk, enjoying the warm night air.

When they returned to the hotel, Tommy was definitely looking tired. "I'll take him upstairs, he'll need a bath before bed," Diana said.

Kat enjoyed giving Tommy his bath, but before she could utter a protest, Miguel spoke up. "Thank you, Diana. I have a few things to discuss with Katerina."

"No problem," Diana said with false brightness. "Say goodnight to your mom, Tommy."

"G'night." Tommy held out his chubby arms for a

hug and a kiss. And then he shocked her by reaching over to give Miguel a hug and a kiss too.

"Goodnight, Tomas," Miguel murmured, as he finally set Tommy down on the sidewalk.

They stood for several moments until Diana and Tommy had gone into the elevator of the hotel. Kat rubbed her hands over her arms, suddenly chilled in her short-sleeved blouse and Capri pants, uncertain what exactly Miguel wanted to talk about.

"Katerina, would you join me for a drink?" Miguel asked, as Fernando pulled up.

A drink? Or something more? The kiss they'd shared simmered between them and suddenly she knew he planned to pick up where they'd left off before Diana had interrupted them.

"Please?" He reached over to take her hand in his.

She hesitated, feeling much like she had four and a half years ago when Miguel had asked her out after losing their young patient. But she was older now, and wiser. She shouldn't be a victim to her hormones.

When he lifted her hand and pressed a kiss to the center of her palm, her good intentions flew away.

"Yes, Miguel," she murmured. "I'd love to."

CHAPTER ELEVEN

MIGUEL could barely hide the surge of satisfaction when Katerina agreed to have a drink with him. He took her hand and turned to head outside where Fernando was waiting inside the car parked out at the curb.

"Where are we going?" she asked, when they stepped outside into the warm night air.

"My place will provide us with the most privacy," he murmured, gently steering her towards the car. When she stiffened against him, disappointment stabbed deep. "Unless you'd rather go somewhere else?"

He practically held his breath as she hesitated. Finally she shook her head and prepared to climb into the back seat of the car. "No, that's okay. Your place is fine," she agreed.

His relief was nearly overwhelming, and as he rounded the car to climb in beside her, it took every ounce of willpower he possessed not to instruct Fernando to break the speed limit to get to his apartment as soon as possible. Once he was seated beside her, he reached over and took her hand. "I want you to know, Katerina, I think you have done an amazing job with raising our son."

She glanced at him in surprise. "For some reason, I keep expecting you to be angry with me."

No, he was only angry with himself. "After tonight it is easier for me to understand your desire to protect Tomas from being hurt." He'd been surprised at the strong surge of protectiveness he'd felt when he'd spent time with his son this evening. "But I hope you can also trust me enough to know I would never willingly do anything to upset him."

"I do trust you, Miguel." Her soft admission caused the tension to seep from his shoulders, allowing him to relax against the buttery-soft leather seats. "Somehow we'll find a way to work this out."

He wanted to do more than to just work things out, but he refrained from saying anything that might cause an argument, unwilling to risk ruining their fragile truce. He wanted this time they had together to be special. So he kept her hand in his, brushing his thumb across the silky smoothness of her skin.

Katerina was always beautiful to him, no matter what she wore. Even dressed casually, in a short-sleeved green blouse that matched her eyes and a pair of black knee-length leggings that displayed her shapely legs, she was breathtaking.

Fernando pulled up in front of his apartment and he reluctantly let her go in order to open the door to climb out. She didn't say anything as they made their way up to his apartment. Once inside, he crossed over to the small kitchen. "What would you like to drink?" he asked.

"Um, a glass of red wine would be nice," she said, clutching her hands together as if nervous.

"Excellent choice." He pulled out a bottle of his favorite Argentinean wine from the rack and quickly removed the cork before pouring them two glasses. She stood awkwardly in the center of the living room as he approached and handed her the glass.

"I feel like I should make a toast," he murmured as he handed her one glass and tipped his so that the rims touched. "To the most beautiful mother in the world."

She blushed and rolled her eyes, taking a step backwards. "Exaggerate much?" she asked, her tone carrying an edge.

He wasn't exaggerating at all, but he could see she was struggling to hold him at arm's length, as if uncomfortable with drawing attention to herself. Or believing in herself.

That thought brought him up short, and he paused, wondering if his leaving so abruptly after their magical night together had caused her to lose some of her self-confidence.

If so, he'd wronged her in more ways than one.

"Katerina, why do you doubt my feelings?" he asked softly. "Surely my attraction to you is no secret by now. Four and a half years ago I succumbed to the keen awareness between us. And obviously that same attraction hasn't faded over time."

"But you still left," she pointed out.

"Yes, but if my father hadn't suffered his stroke, I'm sure that we would have continued to see each other." He knew that he wouldn't have possessed the strength to stay away. Even for her sake.

She eyed him over the rim of her wineglass. "You don't know that, Miguel. Rumor amongst the O.R. staff was that you didn't want any emotional attachments because you weren't planning to stay in the U.S. I doubt that you would have changed your mind about that, even for me."

He shouldn't have been surprised to know his plans had been fodder for gossip, but he was. There had been many women who'd expressed interest in him, and he'd often used that line to avoid entanglements. "I can't deny that I wasn't planning to stay. I didn't keep my dream of joining Doctors Without Borders a secret. And even then I was hesitant to start a relationship with an American."

She looked shocked by his revelation. "Why?"

He wished he hadn't gone down this path. "My mother was American and she wasn't happy living here in Spain. But that part isn't important now. Suffice it to say that had I stayed three more months to finish my trauma surgery fellowship, I would have been there when you discovered you were pregnant. If not for my father's stroke, we could have handled things very differently." He wasn't sure exactly how, but at least he would have known about his son.

She stared at him for several long moments. "Maybe. But playing the what-if game isn't going to help. We can't go back and change the past."

"I don't want to change the past, Katerina," he countered. "I wouldn't give up Tomas for anything. Yet this evening isn't about our son. It is about you and me."

Her lips parted in shock, making a small O, and she carefully set down her wineglass as if afraid she might drop it. "I don't understand."

Obviously he wasn't being very articulate. "Perhaps you would allow me to show you what I mean instead."

When she didn't voice an objection, he stepped closer and drew her deliberately into his arms. He didn't pounce but stared deep into her eyes so that she could read his intent and see the desire he felt for her. When she still didn't utter a protest, he lowered his mouth to capture hers.

She held herself stiffly in his arms, and just when he thought she would push him away, she softened against him and opened her mouth, welcoming his kiss.

Desire thundered in his chest and he gathered her closer still, pulling her softness firmly against his hard muscles and tipping her head back so that he could explore her mouth more fully.

He forced himself to take his time, savoring the exotic taste, when all he really wanted to do was to rip their clothing out of the way so that he could explore every inch of her skin.

"Miguel," she gasped, when he finally freed her mouth in order to explore the sexy curve of her jaw, the hollow behind her ear.

"Say yes, Katerina," he murmured between kisses. He wanted to make love to her, right here, right now. "Say yes."

He continued his leisurely exploration, kissing his way down her neck, dipping further to the enticing valley between her breasts, as if waiting for her answer wasn't killing him.

"Yes, Miguel," she whispered in a ragged voice, arching her back to give him better access to her breasts. "Yes!"

He didn't trust his voice so he swept Katerina up into his arms and strode down the hall to his bedroom, hoping and praying that she wouldn't change her mind.

Kat didn't allow herself to second-guess her decision, every nerve-ending was on fire for Miguel. She hadn't felt this way since their one and only night together. No other man made her feel as beautiful and desirable as Miguel did.

When he swept her into his arms, she pressed her mouth against the hollow in his neck, nipping and licking, savoring his scent and enjoying the way his arms tightened around her in response.

In his bedroom he flipped on a single lamp and then paused near the bed. He gently slid her body down the front of his so that she could feel the full extent of his desire. She shivered, but not with cold, when he unbuttoned her blouse and shoved the cotton fabric aside, revealing her sheer green bra and then ultimately the matching sheer green panties.

She was grateful she'd worn decent underwear, even though it didn't stay on long. She should have felt self-conscious to be naked before him, but she wasn't. His gaze devoured her as he quickly stripped off his own clothes.

"Katerina, *mi amore*," he muttered as he gently placed her on his bed, before covering her body with his. "I don't deserve you."

She was pretty sure he had that backwards, but then she wasn't thinking at all because he'd lowered his mouth to the tip of her breast. She writhed impatiently beneath him but he took his time, giving equal attention to both breasts before trailing kisses down her abdomen to her belly button. And then lower still.

There was a brief moment when she worried about the faint stretch marks along her lower abdomen, but when he swept long kisses over every single one, the last vestiges of doubt vanished. She was practically sobbing with need when he finally spread her legs and probed deep, making sure she was ready.

"Now, Miguel," she rasped.

His dark eyes glittered with desire but he simply shook his head and dipped his head again, this time replacing his fingers with his tongue. Something he'd done that first time they'd made love.

Her orgasm hit fast and hard, deep shudders racking her body. He quickly rose up, rolled a condom on with one hand before he thrust deep, causing yet another orgasm to roll over her.

She was sure she couldn't take much more, but he whispered to her in Spanish, lifting her hips so they fit more snugly together, gently encouraging her to match his rhythm. Slow and deep at first, and then faster and faster, until they simultaneously soared up and over the peak of pleasure.

Kat couldn't move and not just because of Miguel's body sprawled across hers. Every muscle in her body had the consistency of jelly, making it impossible to move even if she wanted to.

Which she didn't.

After several long moments Miguel lifted himself up and rolled over, bringing her along with him, so that she was now lying fully against him. She rested her head against his chest, listening to the rapid beat of his heart.

The chirping sound of a cellphone broke the silence and she froze, trying to remember if that was how her small disposable cellphone sounded. Was Diana calling because Tommy needed her? Maybe the dog bite on his arm was getting infected?

When Miguel muttered something in Spanish beneath his breath, she realized the call wasn't for her. It was for him. There was a strong sense of déjà vu as she remembered the phone call he'd received the morning after the night they'd spent together. She forced herself to lift her head, to look at him. "Do you need to get that? Is that the hospital?"

"I'm not on call tonight," he said with a dark scowl. "Whoever it is can wait."

After several rings the phone went silent and she relaxed against him. When she shivered, he pulled up the sheet and blanket to cover her. She would have been happy to stay like this with him for the rest of the night, but she knew she should go back to the hotel in case Tommy needed her.

She couldn't help thinking about what he'd revealed earlier about his mother being American and not liking it here in Spain. She'd known his mother had spoken fluent English, which had been how he'd picked up the language so quickly.

But what did this all mean about the future?

A loud buzzer sounded, echoing loudly across the apartment, startling her. Miguel muttered something rude before pulling away from her.

He fumbled for his clothing, pulling on his pants before heading out to answer the door. She was grateful he closed the bedroom door, giving her privacy.

She didn't hesitate but quickly found her clothes and got dressed, hardly able to contain her curiosity about who'd come to Miguel's home at ten o'clock at night. She crossed the room, trying to listen, unsure if she should go out there or not. When she heard a female voice speaking in rapid Spanish she froze, the blood draining from her face.

Was it possible that Miguel was actually involved with a woman after all?

Miguel wasn't the least bit happy to see the woman his brother used to date standing on the other side of the door. He tried to rein in his temper. "What do you want, Corrina?"

"Luis is missing, Miguel. I need you to help me find him."

Corrina was a pretty girl with dark wavy hair, who for some unknown, self-destructive reason was still hung up on his brother, despite the fact that Luis had broken her heart more than once.

"Come in," he said rather ungraciously, stepping back to give her room to enter. "How do you know he's missing?"

"He spent last night at my place but this morning he was gone. I've looked everywhere for him, Miguel. He's not at home or working on the olive farm or at any of his usual hang-outs." Corrina's eyes filled with tears. "I'm afraid something has happened to him."

He suppressed a sigh. His brother wasn't exactly known for his tact and could very easily have been looking for an excuse to avoid Corrina. "Did you no-tify the police?"

"Yes, but they said there's nothing they can do." Corrina stared up at him defiantly. "I know everyone thinks he's avoiding me, but I don't think so. Something is wrong, Miguel. I feel it here," she said, dramatically putting her hand over her heart.

The concern in her eyes was real enough, but he didn't share her fears. Besides, he didn't want to end things so abruptly with Katerina. Not again. Not when their time here in Seville was so limited.

But then his bedroom door opened and Katerina emerged, fully dressed, and with a sinking heart he knew their evening had already come to an end. "Excuse me, I was just leaving," she said, avoiding his gaze as she swung her purse over her shoulder and headed for the door.

"Katerina, wait. This is Corrina Flores, my broth-er's girlfriend. It seems she believes Luis is missing."

There was a flash of surprise on Katerina's face and she paused, glancing back with concern. He realized she'd assumed the worst, believing Corrina was one of his former lovers. He was frustrated by her lack of trust yet at the same time grimly pleased that she cared enough to be jealous.

"Missing since when?" Katerina asked.

"Just since this morning. I'm sure he's fine, there's no need to rush off." Selfishly, he wanted her to stay, needed her support as he looked for his brother.

She grimaced and toyed with the strap of her purse. "Actually, I really should go, Miguel. I want to be there in case Tommy wakes up. The dog bite may cause him some pain."

He understood, even though he didn't want to let her go. There was so much yet that they needed to discuss before he released Juliet to return home. He'd used the short time they'd had together to make love, rather than planning their future.

Something he couldn't quite bring himself to regret.

"All right, let me call Fernando, he'll drive you back to the hotel. Why don't we plan to get together first thing in the morning? I'll take you and Tommy out for breakfast and then we'll visit your sister."

"Ah, sure. But don't bother Fernando this late," she protested. "I'll take the metro."

"It's no bother. He's probably just finishing dinner and I'll need his assistance myself, anyway." He certainly wouldn't allow her to go back to the hotel alone. And as much as he wanted to spend more time with Katerina, he couldn't bring himself to ignore Corrina's concerns about Luis.

"I hope you find your brother," Katerina murmured.

"I'm sure we will. And it's about time he learns to take responsibility for his actions. Luis can't expect me to keep bailing him out." He didn't bother to hide his annoyance.

Corrina wisely kept silent as he called Fernando and then walked Katerina outside.

"Thank you, Katerina, for an evening I'll never forget," he whispered, hugging her close and giving her another heated kiss.

"Goodnight, Miguel," she murmured, breaking away from his embrace and climbing into the back seat of the car. He couldn't help feeling as if he'd said something wrong when she ignored him to chat with Fernando.

Grinding his teeth together, he had little choice but to shut the car door and step back, allowing Fernando to drive Katerina away. He stared after the red tail-lights, fighting the urge to demand Fernando return at once so he could figure out what had caused Katerina to be upset.

Annoyed with himself, and his brother, he reluctantly turned and went back upstairs to where Corrina waited. All he could think was that he'd better not find out that his brother was simply trying to avoid his old girlfriend or he wouldn't hesitate to box Luis's ears.

This was the second time his family problems had pulled him away from Katerina. And he was determined that it would also be the last.

CHAPTER TWELVE

THE following morning, Kat was surprised when Miguel didn't show up as promised. As Tommy was hungry, she and Diana took him out for breakfast. As they enjoyed fresh pastries, she couldn't help wondering if Miguel had found his brother or if he'd stayed up the entire night, searching for him.

"I'll take Tommy with me to see Juliet now that she's doing better," she offered. "That way you can go and see the cathedral before we have to leave."

"If you're sure you don't mind," Diana said, before shoving the last bit of pastry in her mouth.

"I don't mind at all." In truth she would have loved to see the cathedral too, but coming to Seville hadn't been a vacation for her. She'd only come because her sister had been injured.

And there was a strong possibility she'd be back in the not-too-distant future if Tommy was going to be spending time with his father. She glanced around, silently admitting that, as beautiful as Seville was, she couldn't really imagine living here.

Once again she found herself thinking about Miguel's mother. Clearly he'd avoided dating anyone back in the

U.S. because he didn't plan to relocate to the U.S. on a permanent basis.

And considering the problems he'd had with his brother, she couldn't imagine him changing his mind. Which left them where? Back to a joint custody but separate countries type of arrangement?

She would have been satisfied with that before, but not any more. Not since making love with Miguel. She wanted it all.

She wanted a true family.

"Mama, go. Now," Tommy said insistently.

"Okay, I'm ready." She paid the bill and then used a wet napkin to clean up Tommy's sticky fingers. "We're going to go visit Aunt Juliet. Won't that be fun?"

He nodded vigorously and dropped from the chair, making her grin at the amount of energy radiating off his tiny frame. Had Miguel been the same way as a child? She suspected he had been.

She started walking toward the nearest metro stop, holding Tommy's hand as they took the stairs down to the lower level. There was a strong possibility that if Miguel had gotten home late, he'd decided to simply meet her at the hospital.

Suspecting that her sister might have already been moved out of the I.C.U., she stopped at the front desk. *"¿Donde esta mi hermana*, Juliet Campbell?" Where is my sister?

There was a flood of Spanish that she didn't understand. When she looked blankly at the woman, she wrote down the room number and handed it to Kat.

"Gracias," she murmured, looking down at Juliet's

new room number, 202. "This way, Tommy," she said, steering him toward the elevator.

Juliet was sitting up at the side of the bed, finishing her breakfast, when they entered. Kat was very relieved to find her sister looking much better. She crossed the room to give Juliet a hug. "Hey, sis, how are you feeling today?"

"Kat! You brought Tommy, too?"

"Yes. Tommy, you remember Aunt Juliet, right? Can you say hi to her?"

"Hi," Tommy said, and then ducked his head, refusing to relinquish Kat's hand.

"Hi, Tommy. It's good to see you. Wanna see my cast?" Juliet said, moving the blankets off her right leg.

Ever curious, the cast was enough to draw Tommy forward. He knelt beside Juliet's right leg, lifting his fist to knock on the fiberglass cast.

"Don't worry, that's the one part of my body that doesn't hurt," Juliet muttered dryly.

"Are you in pain, Jules?" she asked, moving closer. "Dr. Vasquez told me that you had some cracked ribs, too."

"Everything hurts," her sister admitted. "And don't bother asking me what happened, I honestly can't remember."

"Don't worry, I'm sure your memory will return in time." Although there was certainly no guarantee. The numerous bruises and lacerations were already starting to fade, but Kat could well imagine that her sister's muscles were also still sore.

She wanted to ask her sister more questions, to make

sure Juliet wasn't as confused as she had been yesterday, but they were interrupted by a knock at the door.

"Good morning, Juliet," a plump woman greeted her sister. "And you must be Katerina Richardson. Nice to meet you in person."

Kat stared at the woman, certain she hadn't met her before. She would have remembered someone speaking English, for one thing. The familiarity of the stranger's greeting was unnerving.

"My name is Susan Horton and I'm the study abroad program coordinator. I'm the one who contacted you about Juliet's accident, remember?"

Of course she remembered now. So much had happened since the first day she'd arrived, she'd completely forgotten about the woman. "Yes."

"I'm glad you're both here," Susan said, "because we need to make immediate arrangements for Juliet's transfer back to the United States."

Kat tried to hide her shock. "So soon? Don't we need Dr. Vasquez to sign off on Juliet's case first?"

"There's another doctor covering for Dr. Vasquez today, and he's already given his approval. So, if you'd come with me, we'll begin making the necessary arrangements."

"Right now?" Kat cast a helpless glance toward her sister, before following Susan out of the room. She could only hope Miguel would show up soon or they might have to leave without saying goodbye.

Miguel shouldn't have been surprised to find Luis in jail. His friend, Rafael Hernandez, had finally called him to let him know Luis had been driving under the influence. He'd called Corrina to make sure she knew, but then he debated with himself over whether or not to post Luis's bond. It wasn't the money but the principle of bailing his brother out of trouble again.

In the end they wouldn't let him post bail until the morning. Which ruined his plans to meet Katerina and Tomas for breakfast.

"Thanks for picking me up," Luis said, wincing at the bright light.

"Luis, you're either going to kill yourself or someone else if you don't stop this," Miguel said with a heavy sigh. "You'd better figure out what you want to do with the rest of your life, and quick."

"Don't worry about me, just go on your stupid mission trip," his brother muttered, scrubbing his hand over his jaw.

"I'm not going to Africa, I'm going back to the U.S., at least temporarily." He glanced over to where Luis was slouched in the corner of the car. "I have a son, Luis. A son I didn't know about until just a few days ago. But he and his mother live in Cambridge, Massachusetts."

Luis lifted his head and peered at him with bloodshot eyes. "You're going to live there? With them?"

He hadn't realized until just now how much he wanted to be with Katerina and Tomas on a full-time basis, but he wasn't keen on living in the U.S. for ever. Yet he couldn't ask Katerina to move here, not when she had her sister to worry about. And even once Juliet was better, he didn't want to risk the same thing happening to Katerina that had happened to his mother. He couldn't wait to see Katerina and talk to her about his idea of moving to the U.S. temporarily.

"I'm not sure where I want to live, but I do want to be a part of my son's life," he said slowly. "But I can't leave you like this, Luis. You need help. Professional help."

His brother was silent for a long moment. "Will you let me sell the olive farm?" he asked.

Shocked by the question, Miguel nearly swerved into the other lane. "You want to sell the farm? Why? What will you do to support yourself?"

"I've always wanted to work in construction," Luis admitted. "I hate farming. I want to build things. Houses, buildings."

Build things? He turned to stare at his brother, stunned by his revelation. Granted, Luis had built a new warehouse on the farm last year, but all this time he'd had no clue that his brother hated farming.

"Are you sure about this, Luis?" he asked. "Once you sell the farm, there's no going back."

"I'm sure. Corrina's father wants me to help in his construction company. I've been trying to get up the nerve to ask you about selling the farm."

"Do you think working for her father is wise? You haven't treated Corrina very well these past few years."

"I know I've made a mess of my life," Luis said in a low voice. "But I really want to do this, Miguel. I know the farm has been in our family for generations, but I feel trapped there. It's too far from town, for one thing. I realized when I built the new warehouse that I gained more satisfaction from doing that than all the years I've spent picking olives. And I care about Corrina. I kept breaking things off because I couldn't imagine raising a family on the farm. I keep remembering how Mom died there."

He couldn't hide his surprise yet at the same time he understood how Luis felt. "Why didn't you say something sooner?" he asked.

"I was afraid you would be upset. You and Papa always talked about how the Vasquez farm had sustained families for generations. That it was a family tradition."

Miguel winced, knowing Luis was right. He hadn't stayed on the farm, choosing to go into medicine at the university as soon as he'd been able to. It shamed him to realize he hadn't ever asked Luis what he wanted to do. "I'm sorry, Luis. I never realized how badly you wanted to leave the farm, too."

"So you're not mad?" Luis asked, looking pathetically eager despite his rough night in a jail cell. "Because Señor Guadalupe once asked me about selling. I would like to call him to see if he's still interested. If he will buy the farm, I can start working for Corrina's father right away."

"I'm not mad, Luis," he said. "By all means, call Señor Guadalupe. If he's not interested, let me know. I'll see what I can do to help."

Fernando pulled into the driveway of the Vasquez olive farm, and for a moment Miguel simply sat there, staring out at the rows upon rows of olive trees.

It was a little sad to think of selling the farm to strangers, yet at the same time he was a doctor. A surgeon. Saving lives was important and satisfying. He'd never planned on working the farm himself, yet had he subconsciously forced Luis into the role because he hadn't wanted to let go of the past?

The idea was humbling.

"Thanks for the ride," Luis said as he climbed from the car.

"Let me know when you have a buyer lined up."

"I will." Luis looked positively happy and waved as Fernando backed out of the driveway. He then headed into the house.

"Are you really moving to the U.S.?" Fernando asked from the front seat.

He met the older man's gaze in the rear-view mirror. "Yes, for a while, Fernando."

Fernando nodded. "Señor Vasquez, I wonder if you would be so kind as to give me a reference before you go so that I can apply for a job."

Miguel mentally smacked himself in the forehead. Why hadn't he thought of this earlier? "Fernando, how do you feel about being an olive farmer?"

"I would be willing to learn."

He grinned and reached for his cellphone. Everything was going to work out just fine. Luis didn't need to bother Señor Guadalupe after all.

Fate had helped him out once again.

Kat could only sit in stunned silence as Susan Horton finalized her sister's travel arrangements. Everything was set. They would be leaving Seville by one-thirty that afternoon. It was the latest flight out, and they wouldn't arrive back in the U.S. until nearly ten o'clock at night, but when Kat had tried to protest, Susan had remained firm that Juliet would be on that flight, regardless of whether or not Kat wanted to go with her. Given that choice, she'd quickly arranged for additional seating for herself, Diana and Tommy.

She'd also called Diana right away, arranging to meet back at the hotel immediately. The airport was only thirty minutes away, but they would need to get there by eleven-thirty, two hours before departure time, and it was already almost ten now. They had just over an hour to get back to the hotel, pack and check out of the hotel.

She left the hospital, carrying Tommy to make better time. Luckily the metro ran often and it didn't take her long to get to the hotel. She didn't waste any time tossing stuff into their suitcases.

"I can't believe they're making us leave today," Diana said as she helped Kat pack Tommy's things. "Like letting your sister stay one more day would make such a big difference?"

"I know. Although I suspect if they had come to visit Juliet on Sunday, they would have made us leave on an earlier flight."

"I suppose. Okay, that's everything," Diana said. They'd worked like speed demons, and had managed to get everything together in twenty-minutes flat.

Kat made one more sweep of the room, making sure Tommy hadn't left anything behind. "All right, let's haul all this down to the lobby so we can check out."

"What about Miguel?" Diana asked, as they crowded into the elevator.

"As stupid as it sounds, I don't have his phone number." Miguel was on Kat's mind, especially after the night they'd shared, and because they still hadn't made plans for the future. Kat had hoped that Miguel would show up at the hospital before they left, but she hadn't seen him. And now they'd be leaving the hotel shortly. "I'm sure he'll figure out what happened once he discovers Juliet has been discharged." She wished she didn't have to leave without saying goodbye, though.

"Did you guys decide on some sort of joint custody arrangement?" Diana asked.

"I'm not sure if we really agreed on that or not," she said truthfully. She hadn't told Diana about the evening she'd spent making love with Miguel either. Had she done the right thing by saying yes to Miguel? If only she'd waited. Obviously, it would have been smarter of her to avoid getting emotionally involved. Again.

"Stay here with Tommy while I check out." Kat crossed over to the counter, asking for the bill and for a taxi to take them to the airport where they would meet up with Juliet.

They arrived at the small Seville airport with time to spare, so they stopped for something to eat. Kat could barely concentrate—she kept scanning the area, looking for any sign of Miguel.

Where was he? Surely once he'd gone to the hospital and realized Juliet had been discharged, he would know to come and find her at the airport. Something bad must have happened to Luis for him to not be here.

Unless he'd changed his mind about being a part of Tommy's life?

No, she couldn't believe that. Not after the way he'd made love to her. Not after everything they'd shared.

Although she couldn't help coming back to the fact that he'd never wanted to be with an American. Like her.

"Kat, look, there's your sister."

She looked over in time to see Susan Horton pushing Juliet in a wheelchair through the small terminal, followed by an airport employee wheeling Juliet's large suitcase. "Watch Tommy for a minute, okay?" Kat said, before hurrying over to her sister.

"Hey, Jules, how are you?" Kat tried not to be upset at the way they were being rushed out of there. "Are you in pain?"

"I have her pain medication right here," Susan said before Juliet could answer. The woman's brisk, impersonal attitude made Kat grind her teeth in frustration. "Now, is there anything else you need? If not, I'll be leaving Juliet in your hands."

Kat wrestled her temper under control. "We'll be fine," she said, taking over the task of pushing Juliet's wheelchair.

"Are you ready to go through security?" Diana asked, holding onto Tommy's hand. They needed the assistance of two airport employees to manage their luggage.

She sighed, glancing back over the crowd of people one more time, wishing more than anything that Miguel would come. But there was still no sign of him. As much as she wanted to wait, getting Juliet and Tommy through the airport security line would be difficult and time-consuming. She didn't dare wait much longer.

"Sure thing. Let's go."

Going through security took far longer than she could have imagined, especially with Juliet needing so much assistance. She tried not to think about the fact that they would have to change planes four times, before arriving at home. Once they were finished with security, they put their carry-on luggage back together and made their way down to their assigned gate.

Diana flopped into one of the hard plastic chairs with

a groan. "Somehow, going home isn't nearly as much fun," she muttered.

Kat pasted a smile on her face, unwilling to let on how much she was hurting inside, as she made sure Juliet was comfortable.

She'd really, really, expected Miguel to show up here at the airport. And now that he hadn't—she wasn't sure what to think.

Had he changed his mind about wanting to be a father to Tommy? Did he regret making love to her? She wished she knew more about Miguel's mother. He'd mentioned she'd died several years ago, when he'd still been in high school. Whatever had happened had made him determined not to become emotionally involved with an American.

With her.

Her heart squeezed with pain and tears pricked her eyes as she realized she'd foolishly fallen in love with Miguel.

CHAPTER THIRTEEN

MIGUEL strode into the hospital, knowing he was beyond late. He wasn't due to work today but he knew Katerina would come to visit her sister.

He walked into room 202 and stopped abruptly when he saw an elderly man lying in the bed. He frowned and glanced at the room number, making sure he had the correct one.

After murmuring a quick apology, he spun around and went back to the nurses' station. They must have moved Juliet to a different room for some unknown reason.

But, no, her name wasn't on the board at all. With a frown he picked up the phone, intending to call down to the front desk, when he saw his colleague, Felipe. "Felipe, where's my patient, Juliet Campbell?" he asked.

Felipe turned around. "Miguel, what are you doing here? I thought I was to cover your patients today?"

"You are, but I was actually looking for Juliet's sister, Katerina. What room did Juliet get moved to?"

Felipe looked puzzled. "I discharged her, Miguel. Señora Horton from the study abroad program wanted her to be sent back to the U.S., so I went ahead and gave the discharge order."

"What?" A knot of dread formed in his gut and he grew angry with himself for not anticipating that something like this might happen. He'd known the minute he'd given the orders to have Juliet transferred to a regular room that her time here was limited. "When? How long ago?"

Felipe shrugged. "I'm not sure, maybe two or three hours?"

Three hours? No! He struggled to remain calm as he glanced at the clock. It was almost eleven-thirty already. "Was that when you wrote the order? Or when she actually left?"

"I didn't pay attention," Felipe admitted. "Miguel, what's the problem? Clearly, she was stable enough to travel."

He forced a smile, knowing none of this was Felipe's fault. "I trust your judgment. Excuse me but I need to catch up with them." Before Felipe could say anything more, he left, lengthening his stride to hurry as he called Fernando, instructing his driver to meet him outside.

"We need to stop at home, so I can get my passport. From there we're heading straight to the airport," he said, the moment he slid into the back seat. A few days ago, when he'd reviewed flights out of Seville heading to the U.S., he'd noticed the last flight was at one o'clock in the afternoon.

He grabbed his passport, and not much else. He'd have to buy what he needed once he arrived in the U.S. Back in the car, he called the airline in an attempt to book a seat as Fernando navigated the city streets.

"I'm sorry, but we can't book any more seats at this

time," the woman said. "We stop selling tickets two hours before the flight."

He resisted the urge to smack his fist on the counter. "I need to get on that flight. I'm sure you can make an exception."

There was a pause, and he held his breath. "I'll check with my supervisor," she finally said.

He tightened his grip on the phone, willing Fernando to hurry. But the traffic was heavy today, and they were moving at a snail's pace. The airport was normally a thirty-minute drive, and he could only hope and pray that the traffic would break soon. He had to get there in time. He had to!

"I'm sorry, Señor Vasquez. We are not able to sell you a ticket."

He closed his eyes and swallowed a curse. He forced himself to be polite. "Thank you for checking."

"Problems?" Fernando asked, catching his gaze in the rear-view mirror.

He shook his head. "Just get to the airport as soon as possible. I want to see Katerina before she leaves."

He'd have to buy a ticket in order to get past security, but at this point he was willing to do anything to see Katerina, talk to her one more time before she and Tommy boarded that plane. The panic that gripped him by the throat surprised him. He hadn't realized until she was gone just how much he cared about Katerina.

It wasn't just that he missed his son. Katerina would agree to share custody, he knew. But at this moment he didn't care about custody arrangements.

He cared about Katerina.

* * *

When the airline attendant asked for all passengers needing help to board, Katerina stood up. "I think that means us. Are you ready to go, Juliet?"

"Sure." Her sister already looked exhausted and they hadn't even started their long flight. Kat couldn't suppress a flash of anger toward Susan Horton for rushing Juliet out so fast. As Diana had said earlier, what was one more day?

Maybe she should have put up more of a fight, even though Susan Horton hadn't been interested in listening to reason. Besides, it was too late now. She bent over to release the locks on the wheelchair and then pushed her sister forward, leaving Diana and Tommy to follow.

Getting Juliet safely transferred into an aisle seat was no easy task. The only good thing was that they were given a spot in the front row of a section, leaving plenty of room for her leg that was still in a cast. Juliet groaned under her breath as she used the crutches, favoring her right side where she had her cracked ribs.

They were both sweating by the time they were finally settled. Diana and Tommy were immediately behind them, which was a mixed blessing.

"Tommy, stop kicking the seat," she said for the third time, trying not to snap at him. "It feels like you're kicking me in the back."

"Sorry, Mama."

"Do you want me to switch places with him?" Diana asked, leaning forward anxiously as if sensing her frayed nerves.

"No, he'll only end up kicking Juliet." She was tense and crabby but did her best not to let it show as her bad mood certainly wasn't Tommy's fault. Or Diana's. Or Juliet's.

She was upset because she'd really expected Miguel to come to the airport to find her. But for all she knew, he was still looking for his brother. She tried to tell herself that this way was for the better. Things had moved pretty fast between she and Miguel so a little time and distance would likely be good for both of them.

Yet regret at leaving Seville so abruptly filled her chest, squeezing her lungs. There hadn't been time to say goodbye to Pedro. As the plane slowly filled up with passengers, she wondered how Miguel would manage to find her in Cambridge.

If he decided to come at all.

Miguel purchased a ticket to Madrid and managed to get through security in time to find Katerina's plane had just started to board. He rushed over to the gate and swept his gaze over the group of passengers. After several long moments he was forced to admit they must have already boarded. Which made sense, as Juliet had a broken leg and had probably needed help to get into her seat.

He went up to the desk. "Excuse me, but I need to speak to passenger, Katerina Richardson. I think she may already be on the plane."

"I'm sorry, but there's nothing I can do. You're not allowed on the plane without a boarding pass," the attendant said with a false smile.

So close. He was so close! "Just five minutes. You could ask her to come back out here and I promise she'll be back on the plane in five minutes."

"I'm sorry, Señor, I can't help you." The woman's false smile faded and he could see a security guard making his way over. She glanced past him as if he weren't there. "May I help you?" she asked the next person in line.

Miguel quickly left the counter, preferring to avoid the security guard. He still had a ticket to Madrid, and from there he was sure there would be a better selection of flights to the U.S. But considering his flight didn't leave for two more hours, he knew there was no chance in the world of arriving in time to see Katerina or Tomas.

He called his police friend, Rafael, asking for help in finding Katerina's address back in Cambridge. Rafael called him back within twenty minutes with the address. At least that was one problem solved.

With a heavy sigh he crossed over to his own gate and settled into one of the uncomfortable plastic chairs. He wished more than ever that he'd spent more time talking to Katerina last night, rather than making love. Not that he regretted that part. He just wished they would have talked first.

He could only hope she would be willing to listen, to give him another chance, once he arrived in the U.S.

Nineteen and a half hours later Kat, Tommy and Juliet finally arrived home. Diana had gone to her own apartment and Kat couldn't blame her friend for wanting to sleep in her own bed.

Kat was exhausted, but she was far more worried about her sister. Juliet's pain had gotten worse the more they'd moved, and changing planes and then taking a train back to Cambridge had obviously been too much for her.

She was tempted to take Juliet straight to the hospital, but since the time was close to midnight, she decided against it. Rest would be the best thing for her sister, so she helped Juliet get into bed before giving her more pain medication. She'd have to arrange for follow-up doctor's appointments in the morning.

Unfortunately, Tommy wasn't nearly as tired. Just like on the way over to Spain, he'd slept on the plane and she wanted to burst into tears when he started bouncing on his bed.

After several minutes of fighting she gave up. "Okay, fine, let's go downstairs and watch a movie."

She put in a DVD and stretched out on the couch, holding her son in front of her, determined to get in at least a short nap. With any luck, Tommy would be tired enough to sleep after the movie was over.

Between Tommy's messed-up sleep cycle and her sister's pain, Kat only managed to get about four hours of sleep. Not nearly enough, but she would just have to make do. After making breakfast and encouraging Juliet to eat, she spent a good hour on the phone, making arrangements for Juliet to be seen by a doctor who specialized in head injuries.

Her sister was still slightly confused, but she was certainly better than she'd been when the breathing tube had been removed. At least she wasn't asking about their mother any more.

There was a loud knock at her front door at ten-thirty in the morning, and Kat fully expected to see her friend Diana had returned.

When she saw Miguel standing there, she stared in shock, wondering if her eyes were playing tricks on her. She blinked, but he didn't vanish. As she stared at him, she realized he looked as disheveled as she felt, indicating he must have been traveling all night. On one level she was glad to see him, but at the same time his timing couldn't have been worse.

"Miguel? How did you find me?" She didn't mean to sound ungracious, but lack of sleep made it difficult to think clearly. She was shocked to see him, but she couldn't deny she felt a warm glow at the knowledge that he'd come all this way to find her.

"I just missed you at Seville airport. I'm sorry we didn't get a chance to talk before you had to leave." He stared at her for a long moment as if trying to gauge her reaction. "May I come in?"

She smiled, although her eyes were gritty with lack of sleep. "Sure, but unfortunately, we're just getting ready to leave. Juliet has a doctor's appointment with a neurologist at Cambridge University Hospital." She stepped back, allowing him to come into her home. She frowned when she realized he didn't have so much as a suitcase with him.

For a moment her tired brain cells couldn't make sense of it all. Was Miguel planning to stay here with her? No, it made more sense that he must have left his luggage back in his hotel room.

"I think that is a good idea," Miguel was saying. "The doctors there will make sure she's really okay. Is she still confused?"

"A little. Not as bad as before, though."

"She probably just needs a little time." Miguel fell

silent and she wondered what he was thinking as he glanced around her small home. After her mother had died, she had taken over the house payments and promised Juliet her half when she graduated from college.

"Maybe we can get together later on?" she suggested, glancing at the clock. If they didn't leave soon, they'd be late.

"I could stay here with Tomas, if you think that would help," Miguel offered.

She opened her mouth to refuse, even though going to the doctor's appointment would be much easier without dragging Tommy along. Tommy had only met Miguel twice and she couldn't bear to leave him with someone he probably still considered a stranger. "I don't know if that's such a good idea," she said slowly.

Glancing over her shoulder, she noticed Tommy hovering in the kitchen doorway, staring at Miguel with wide eyes. He wasn't crying, but he wasn't rushing over to greet Miguel either.

"Please?" Miguel asked. "I think he'll be fine. He doesn't seem afraid of me."

"Tommy, do you remember Mr. Vasquez?" she asked.

Tommy nodded, sticking his thumb in his mouth, something he only did when he was really tired. And suddenly, knowing that Tommy would probably fall asleep sooner than later, she made up her mind to take Miguel up on his offer.

"All right, you can stay here with Tommy. I would suggest you put a movie on for him as he's probably going to fall asleep soon. His days and nights are a little mixed up from the flight home."

Miguel's smile warmed her down to her toes. "I think I can manage that."

She forced herself to look away, trying not to think about the fact that Miguel was here for his son first and foremost. Obviously, Miguel wanted more time to get to know his son. But she couldn't help feeling a pang of resentment that Miguel was acting as if the night they'd spent together hadn't happened. "All right, we'll be back in a couple of hours."

Miguel helped her get Juliet out to the car, before going back inside. Leaving him in her house felt weird, but she kept her attention focused on her sister.

She could only manage one crisis at a time.

Kat was thrilled when Dr. Sandlow announced that Juliet's head injury seemed to be resolving without a problem. After a long exam, blood work and a follow-up CT scan of her head, he'd decided Juliet was stable enough not to be admitted. "I'd like to see her back in a week," he said. "And she also needs to start attending physical therapy three days a week."

She tried not to wince, wondering how in the world she'd be able to return to work while taking Juliet to therapy three days a week. She still had at least another week of vacation time saved up, but after that was gone, she'd need to apply for a leave of absence.

Time to worry more about that later.

The appointment had lasted longer than she'd anticipated, which was fine, except that they'd missed lunch. She stopped on the way home and picked up a bucket of fried chicken, mashed potatoes and coleslaw in case Miguel and Tommy were hungry too.

She parked her car in the driveway, rather than pulling into the garage, so that it was easier to maneuver Juliet out of the front passenger seat. She was somewhat surprised that Miguel didn't come out to help as she hooked her arms under Juliet's armpits to help her stand.

"Are you okay?" Kat asked, as she grabbed the crutches from where she'd propped them against the door.

"Fine," Juliet murmured, although her upper lip was beaded with sweat.

"Just a few more feet and you can rest, okay?" Moving around was obviously good for Juliet, but it was almost time for more pain medication. The way Juliet winced and groaned with every single swing of the crutches made Kat feel bad.

They managed to get into the house without incident and she immediately steered her sister towards the guest bedroom. Once Juliet was settled, she went back out to the main living area to look for Miguel and Tommy.

She found them on the sofa in the living room, both of them asleep. Miguel held Tommy close against his chest.

She stared at the two of them, father and son, feeling abruptly alone. The two had bonded while she'd been gone and Tommy clearly needed his father the same way Miguel needed him. She should be thrilled that they were together at last.

But she couldn't shake the sense of desolation. All this time she'd told herself she wanted a family. But she'd had a family, with Tommy and Juliet.

Now she was forced to realize what she really wanted was for Miguel to love her as much as she loved him.

But did Miguel have the capability of loving her the way she wanted him to? Would he stick by her and Tommy not just in the good times but through the bad times as well?

Or would he leave the minute things got rough, just like her father?

CHAPTER FOURTEEN

MIGUEL felt a soft weight being lifted off his chest, and his arms tightened, instinctively holding on. He forced his eyes open and found Katerina leaning over him, her exquisite green eyes snapping with fury.

Confused, he tried to comprehend what he'd done to upset her. For a moment he didn't even remember he was in the U.S., until he glanced down to see Tomas was fast asleep on his chest. Abruptly all the memories tumbled to the surface.

"Let him go, Miguel. I need to put him down in his bed," Katerina said curtly. Still foggy with exhaustion, he released his hold so that she could lift their son into her arms. He instantly missed the warmth radiating from Tomas' soft body.

She disappeared from the living room and he used the few moments alone to pull himself together. How long had he been asleep? He couldn't remember.

With a guilty glance at the clock, he knew he'd slept longer than he should have. A part of him was disgusted that he'd wasted a good hour sleeping when he could have been making up for lost time with his son.

Although they would have plenty of time to get to know each other. Wouldn't they? On the long flight to the U.S. he'd finally realized that where he and Katerina lived wasn't important. Being together was all that mattered.

He kept waiting for the reality of his decision to sink in, but he didn't have the itchy feeling of wanting to leave. Was it possible that joining Doctors Without Borders really wasn't his dream?

Had it just been a way to escape?

He frowned and stretched in an effort to shake off his deep thoughts. Lifting his head, the distinct scent of fried chicken made him realize how hungry he was. He followed his nose into the kitchen.

There were bags of food lying haphazardly on the table, as if they'd been set down in a hurry. Before he could reach for one, Katerina returned.

"Tommy will be down soon, he wouldn't go back to sleep." Her slightly accusing gaze made him wonder if she believed that was his fault. Maybe it was. "We'll have lunch and then you'll need to leave, Miguel. I can't deal with you right now. I have Tommy and Juliet to care for."

He wanted to argue, but the lines of fatigue on her face tugged at his heart. She looked so exhausted he wanted to sweep her up and take her to bed. But, of course, he couldn't.

Somehow he'd thought she'd be happy to see him. But so far she'd seemed more annoyed. Had he misunderstood her feelings towards him? His heart squeezed in his chest.

He told himself to have patience, even though it wasn't easy. Tomas came running into the room and he helped Katerina pull out the fried chicken, mashed potatoes and coleslaw. He noticed that she made sure Tomas had some food on his plate and that she made a plate for her sister, before worrying about eating anything herself.

"I'll be right back," she murmured, taking the food down the hall towards a small bedroom. He felt guilty all over again, knowing that Katerina had managed to get Juliet inside without his assistance.

He watched Tomas eat, determined to wait for Katerina. She returned quickly enough, dropping into a chair across from him.

"How is she?" he asked.

"Sleeping. Dr. Sandlow said she's fine, though. She needs to start physical therapy three times a week. I'll help her with her lunch later." She took a healthy bite of her chicken, and then seemed to notice he hadn't eaten. "Don't you like fried chicken?" she asked.

"Of course. Who doesn't?" He flashed a reassuring smile before turning his attention to his own plate. He wanted to help her, but sensed he was treading on thin ice. For some reason, she'd been angry with him for falling asleep. Either because she thought he'd put Tomas in danger, or because he'd slept when she couldn't. Or maybe because he'd made himself at home. Regardless, he knew he could help ease her burden by staying, if she'd let him.

"Lean over your plate, Tommy," she said gently when pieces of fried chicken dropped from his mouth and hit the floor. "Don't make a mess."

"No mess," Tomas said with his mouth full.

"Is the shopping mall still located a few miles from

the hospital?" he asked. "I need to purchase clothes and toiletries."

She frowned. "Did the airline lose your luggage?"

"No. I didn't bring anything except my passport. I was racing to catch up with you and Tomas. As you'd already boarded the plane, they wouldn't let me talk to you. I ended up going through London to get here."

She looked shocked to hear he'd followed her. After several long moments she finished her meal and sat back in her chair. "Yes," she murmured. "The shopping mall is still there."

"Katerina, we need to talk." He glanced at Tomas, who was starting to wiggle around in his booster chair. He was tempted to smile at how their son had smeared mashed potatoes and gravy all over himself.

"Not now. As I said, I have other things to worry about at the moment. Tommy needs a bath and then I need to care for my sister. I'm sorry, but I'm afraid you'll have to wait until I get things caught up around here." She stood and picked up Tommy. "Goodbye, Miguel."

She turned and left, no doubt intending to give Tomas a bath. He wanted nothing more than to help, but she'd made her wishes very clear.

With a sigh he pushed away from the table and began clearing the dirty dishes, storing the leftovers in the fridge. Maybe she wanted him gone, but he wasn't about to leave this mess for her. Not when she looked like she was dead on her feet.

He wanted to believe that Katerina was just tired and jet-lagged, that she didn't mean what she'd said.

But since he'd arrived, she hadn't given any indication of wanting to pick up their relationship where they'd left off. If not for his brother going missing, they would have had time to talk. To plan. Surely there was a way to make this work? Surely Katerina felt something for him?

So why was he feeling as if she wished he hadn't come to the U.S.?

As he washed and dried the dishes, he racked his brain for a way to bridge the gap that had somehow widened between them.

Because if she thought he was giving up that easily, she was dead wrong.

Kat ran warm water and bubble bath into the tub for Tommy, knowing she'd been unfair to Miguel. He'd come all this way, had actually followed her to the airport in Seville, flying all night, only to have her demand that he leave. She hadn't even asked about Luis.

She set Tommy into the tub, kneeling alongside to keep a close eye on him. Tommy played in the water, splashing bubbles everywhere. She was so exhausted, so emotionally drained that she didn't even notice bubbles had landed on her hair.

She'd been badly shaken by the sight of Miguel holding Tommy, both of them looking adorable as they'd slept. She was a terrible mother to be jealous, even for an instant, of her son's love for his father. And the sad truth was that Tommy didn't even know that Miguel was his father yet.

But he would, soon.

For a moment she rested her forehead on the smooth, cool porcelain of the tub. She should be glad Miguel wanted to be a part of Tommy's life. She should be glad that he'd come here to Cambridge, rather than asking her to consider moving to Seville.

Yet, she couldn't help wishing that they would have time alone, to explore the passion that simmered between them. She knew Miguel wanted her, but she didn't know if there was any way he'd ever come to love her. She felt confused and exhausted.

She had her sister to care for, and Tommy too. And soon she'd have to go back to work. There wouldn't be time for her and Miguel to renew their relationship. But there would be plenty of time for him to establish a relationship with his son.

She lifted her head, instantly ashamed of herself for being selfish. Her son was what mattered, not her own ridiculous feelings. Giving her head a shake to clear the troublesome thoughts, she quickly washed Tommy's hair and then pulled him out of the water, engulfing his slippery body in a thick, fluffy towel.

After getting Tommy dressed in clean clothes, and straightening out her own disheveled appearance, she went back out to the kitchen, half-afraid Miguel would still be there. He wasn't, but she was pleasantly surprised to find her kitchen was spotless, every bit of mess cleaned up, including the floor around Tommy's booster chair.

His kind thoughtfulness only made her feel more miserable for her earlier abruptness. Was it too late to catch up to him? She almost headed for the door when she heard thumping noises coming from Juliet's room. Juliet was up, trying to navigate with her crutches, leaving her no choice but to hurry down to help her sister.

Forcing her to push thoughts of Miguel firmly out of her mind.

An entire twenty-four hours went by without any word or visit from Miguel. Kat should have been relieved to have one less thing to deal with, but instead she was on edge. Had something happened to him? Had he decided she was too much of a witch to deal with? Had he decided to return to Spain after all?

She still didn't know his phone number, or if his cellphone from Spain would even work here in the U.S. She felt much better after getting a good night's sleep and was pleased to note that Juliet was also doing better every day.

Getting her sister to therapy wasn't too bad, especially as Juliet insisted on doing things for herself. There was a truce between them, a closeness that hadn't been there before Juliet had left to study abroad. Kat hoped that this terrible accident would bring them closer together.

"Where's that Spanish doctor?" Juliet asked, when they'd returned from therapy.

Kat shrugged. "I'm not sure. Why?"

"Come on, sis, you're not fooling me. He's obviously Tommy's father. And you love him, don't you?"

She wanted to protest, but really what was the point? "My feelings don't matter as he doesn't feel the same way."

Juliet stared at her for a long moment. "You never

asked me what happened. I mean, how I ended up getting hit by a car."

Kat pulled up a chair to sit beside her sister's bed. "Jules, you were in the I.C.U. on a ventilator when I came to visit. And by the time you'd recovered, you were confused and told me you couldn't remember. Has that changed? Do you remember what happened?"

Juliet took a deep breath and let it out slowly. "I fell in love with a guy named Enrique. He was much older and so mature. I never told him how I felt, but I thought we had this great connection. Until I found him with another woman."

Kat sucked in a harsh breath. After having both of their fathers leave their mother, she knew that would be the worst betrayal of all. "Oh, Jules…"

"I was so upset I started crying and ran into the road." Juliet shrugged. "Thankfully, I don't remember much after that."

"I'm so sorry." Kat reached out and took her sister's hand. "I'm sure that was really difficult for you to see him with someone else."

"Yes, it was. After the way my dad left, I spend half my time waiting for the guy I'm dating to show his true colors. But now I wonder if I just liked Enrique because he was safe. I think I've been avoiding relationships, Kat. Because of our fathers."

Kat tried to follow her sister's logic. "But you just said you fell for Enrique. Wasn't that a relationship?"

"Not really. He was older and friendly with me. But it wasn't like we even kissed or anything. There was another guy who liked me, who was closer to my age, but I avoided him. I told myself it was because I liked

Enrique, but the truth of the matter was that I was avoiding being hurt." Juliet tightened her grip around Kat's fingers. "Don't do that, Kat. Don't avoid Miguel because you don't want to get hurt."

Juliet's words struck a chord deep inside. For someone so much younger, Juliet had great insight. "It's more complicated than that, Jules. He's Tommy's father. We have to get along, for his sake."

"Tell him how you feel," Juliet insisted. "Don't let your pride or fear get in the way."

Was her sister right? Had she avoided talking on a personal level with Miguel because she was afraid of being hurt? They'd never really talked about their joint custody arrangement because she'd avoided the topic. The realization made her wince.

Maybe her sister was right. "Get some rest Jules, okay?" she said, changing the subject. "We'll eat around six o'clock. I have a pot roast in the slow cooker for dinner."

"Okay," Juliet murmured, closing her eyes.

Kat left her sister's room to head for the kitchen. She was surprised to hear the sound of voices.

"Meegl," Tommy shouted and it took her a minute to figure out that it was a mangled version of Miguel.

"Tomas!" Miguel responded, and she entered the kitchen in time to see her son launch himself at his father. Miguel laughed and clasped Tommy close, looking dangerously attractive wearing casual clothes, jeans and a long-sleeved denim shirt. "I've missed you," he said, nuzzling Tommy's neck.

"Me too," her son said, hugging him.

For a moment, seeing the two of them together, father

and son, made her want to cry. But then Miguel lifted his head and caught her gaze, with such intensity she could barely breathe. "Hi, Miguel," she said inanely.

"Katerina," he murmured, and for a moment she thought she saw frank desire in his gaze, before he bent over to set Tommy back on his feet. "Would you allow me to take you out for dinner this evening?"

"I'm sorry, I would but I don't have a babysitter," she said, tearing her gaze from his. She figured that he wanted to finalize their co-custody agreement and was determined not to continue avoiding the topic. Thankfully, she felt better prepared now after a good night's sleep. She forced a smile. "I have a pot roast in the slow cooker if you want to stay."

"Diana said she'd come over to babysit. And she's more than capable of watching over Juliet as well." He took a step toward her, holding out his hand. "Please?"

He'd called Diana? She could hardly hide her surprise. And now that he'd taken that excuse away, she couldn't think of a reason to refuse. "All right," she agreed. "But I need some time to change."

"I'll wait," he said.

The next few hours flew by as she showered, changed and then greeted Diana, who seemed glad to be back on American soil. As Miguel held the door of his rental car open for her, she felt a bit like a girl going out on her first date.

"Are you sure you know how to drive?" she asked, as he slid behind the wheel. "Maybe you should have brought Fernando here with you."

His teeth flashed in a broad smile. "Fernando is taking over the Vasquez olive farm. Believe it or not, my brother Luis has decided he wants to build things, instead of being a farmer."

"So he's okay, then?" she asked. "You found him all right?"

"He's fine. He was afraid to tell me how much he hated the farm." For a moment a dark shadow crossed his face, but then it was gone. "I'm convinced he's going to be fine now that he's following his dream."

Dread knotted her stomach, and she had the most insane feeling he was about to tell her he was going to follow his own dream. His dream of joining Doctors Without Borders. "I'm glad," she said in a choked tone.

He slanted a glance in her direction as he pulled into the driveway of a well-known hotel located mere blocks from her house. "I hope you don't mind if we have a quiet dinner here?"

"Of course not."

He led the way inside to the fancy restaurant located just off the hotel lobby. There weren't too many people dining, but it didn't matter as they were led to a small quiet table in the back.

Miguel treated her courteously, holding her chair for her and then asking what she'd like to drink. They started with a light appetizer and a bottle of Shiraz.

"Katerina," he said, reaching over to take her hand. "I have something very important to ask you."

She felt surprisingly calm, despite knowing they were about to settle their future joint custody arrangement once and for all. Her sister's advice echoed in her mind.

"Yes, Miguel?" She took a sip of her wine and carefully set it down.

In a flash he was out of his seat and kneeling in front of her chair. She stared at him in shock when he flipped open a small black velvet ring box, revealing a large diamond ring. "Katerina, will you marry me?"

For a moment her heart soared and she wanted to shout yes at the top of her lungs.

Except he hadn't said anything about love.

"Miguel, we don't have to get married," she said, tearing her gaze away and wishing she'd ordered something stronger than wine. "We'll work something out so that we'll both be actively involved in Tommy's life. I'll even consider moving to Seville, after Juliet is better, if that's what you want. You don't have to do this."

He never moved, still kneeling before her, his gaze steadily holding hers. "Katerina, I love you. I was foolish to leave you four and a half years ago. I let my mother's bitterness affect my outlook on life. It's true that I want to be a part of my son's life, but that's not why I'm asking you to marry me. I'm asking because I can't imagine my life without you."

She felt her jaw drop open in shocked surprise. She wanted so badly to believe him. Trusting men wasn't easy for her, but wasn't this what she'd secretly wanted? She couldn't allow her mother's tragic life to affect her ability to find happiness.

"Miguel, are you sure? Because there's no rush. Besides, I thought you always wanted to work with Doctors Without Borders? I don't want you resent us at some future point because you didn't get to follow your dream."

"My dream isn't to join Doctors Without Borders any more," he said. "It pains me to say this, but I realize now I've been partly using that dream to avoid getting close to anyone. Until I met you. I've fallen in love with you, Katerina. And I don't care where we live, here or Seville, it doesn't matter. Nothing matters except you and our son. And any other children we decide to have."

He loved her? She wanted so badly to believe him. Her small sliver of doubt faded when she saw the pure emotion shining from his dark eyes. And somehow she managed to find the courage to open her heart to him. "Yes, Miguel," she murmured huskily. "I will marry you. Because I love you, too. And I can't imagine my life without you either." She felt wonderful saying the words, knowing deep in her heart that they were true.

"*Te amo,* Katerina," he murmured, taking out the ring and slowly sliding the band over the fourth finger of her left hand. She barely had time to enjoy the sparkle when he stood and then drew her to her feet before pulling her gently into his arms. He kissed her, gently at first and then with such passion she almost forgot they weren't alone.

He gently pulled back, simply staring down at her for a long moment. "I love you, so much, Katerina," he whispered. "I promise to show you just how much I love you every day for the rest of our lives."

"I love you, too, Miguel." She lifted up on tiptoe to kiss him again, ignoring the waiters and waitresses clapping in the background. "And I want Tommy to have at least one brother and one sister."

He laughed. "Anything you say," he agreed huskily, before kissing her again.

As she clung to his shoulders, reveling in the kiss, she realized that with a little faith and love…dreams really could come true.

EPILOGUE

Miguel was pleased and humbled that Katerina had wanted to be married in Seville. He stood at the front of the church, amazed at how crowded it was. Apparently everyone in Seville wanted to be there to share in their wedding. Juliet was there too, standing as Katerina's maid of honor. She was fully recovered now from her accident and was determined to finish her semester abroad. His brother Luis hadn't touched a drop of alcohol since selling the farm, and he stood straight and tall next to Miguel as his best man.

There were many friends and family in the church, some even having come all the way from the U.S. to be there. And he couldn't help smiling when he saw Pedro sitting near the front, wearing his Sunday best, craning his neck to get a glimpse of the bride.

When the music began, the first one to walk down the aisle was Tomas. Miguel grinned when his son walked slowly as if afraid he might drop the small satin pillow holding their wedding bands. When Tomas reached the front of the church, Luis stepped forward and took the rings. Miguel put a hand on his son's shoulder, keeping him at his side.

"Hi, Daddy," Tomas said in a loud whisper. "I didn't drop them."

"Good boy," he whispered back.

Juliet was next, walking with only the slightest bit of a limp, hardly noticeable to anyone except him.

And then Katerina stepped forward, so beautiful his chest ached. The entire church went silent with awe, but when she caught his gaze and smiled, the love shining from her eyes made him catch his breath. He forced himself to stay right where he was when he wanted very badly to rush forward to greet her.

They had two priests, one who spoke English for Katerina, even though she was already broadening her knowledge of the Spanish language.

"Mama's beautiful, isn't she?" Tomas said again, in a loud whisper.

"Very beautiful," Miguel agreed. "Be quiet now, Tomas, okay?"

"Okay," he agreed, nodding vigorously. When Katerina reached his side, he took her hand in his and together they turned to face the two priests.

As anxious he was to have Katerina become his wife, he planned to enjoy every moment of this day, the first day of their new life, together.

* * * * *